RICHARD EDNEY

AND

THE GOVERNOR'S FAMILY.

A RUS-URBAN TALE,

SIMPLE AND POPULAR, YET CULTURED AND NOBLE,

OF

MORALS, SENTIMENT, AND LIFE,

PRACTICALLY TREATED AND PLEASANTLY ILLUSTRATED

CONTAINING, ALSO,

HINTS ON BEING GOOD AND DOING GOOD.

BY THE AUTHOR OF

"MARGARET," AND "PHILO."

"MARGARET, A TALE OF THE REAL AND THE IDEAL," AND "PHILO, AN EVANGELIAD."

By

Sylvester Judd.

BOSTON:

PHILLIPS, SAMPSON & COMPANY.

1850.

Stereotyped by
HOBART & ROBBINS;
New England Type and Stereotype Foundery,
BOSTON.

NOTE.

Just as we have sent the last sheet of the manuscript to the printer, our publishers write that an Introduction, a brief one, is desirable. We might yield to their judgment what we should be slow to extract from our own indifference. A Preface is an author's observation on his own writings. It might be presumed that a reader would be better prepared to understand, and more disposed to listen to what an author would say, at the end of a book than at the beginning. Acting upon this consideration, we have included in the last chapter certain paragraphs that may seem to possess a prefatory character. To these all persons interested are respectfully referred. We have endeavored, moreover, that, in the progress of the work, the curiosity of the reader should be duly satisfied on any points that might engage it. A Tale is not like a house, except in its door-plate, the title-page. It does not require an entry or a reception-room. It is rather like a rose, the sum of the qualities of which are visible at a glance; albeit it will repay a minute attention, and affords material for prolonged enjoyment. It is like a landscape, which appeals in like manner to a comprehensive eye, rather than to critical inquiry. We incline, then, to the rose and the landscape, notwithstanding there may be a defective leaf in the first, or a rude hut in the last. Not that we object to Prefaces; — we like them, we always read them, and frequently find them the best part of a book. But this book is written, and the author has put his best things into it; he cannot hope to improve it by anything he might here add, and he is indisposed to peril its fortunes on any uncertainties of speech or manner; and therefore prefers to submit it as it is.

CHAPTER I.

RICHARD COMES TO THE CITY.

It began to snow. What the almanac directed its readers to look out for about this time — what his mother told Richard of, as she tied the muffler on his neck in the morning — what the men in the bar-rooms, where he stopped to warm himself, seemed to be rubbing out of their hands into the fire — what the cattle, crouching on the windward side of barnyards, rapped to each other with their slim, white horns — what sleigh-bells, rapidly passing and repassing, jingled to the air — what the old snow, that lay crisp and hard on the ground, and the hushed atmosphere, seemed to be expecting — what a "snow-bank," a dense, bluish cloud in the south, gradually creeping along the horizon, and looming midheavens, unequivocally presaged, — a snow-storm, came good at last.

Richard had watched that cloud, as it slowly unfurled itself to the winds, and little by little let out its canvas, till it seemed to be the mainsail of the huge earth, and would bear everything movable and immovable along with it. He saw the first flakes that skurry forwards so gingerly and fool-happy through the valleys, as if they had nothing to do but dance and be merry, and were not threatened by a howling pack behind. He rejoiced in the feeling of these herald drops on his cheeks, and caught at them with his lips, refreshing himself in the dainty moisture; for he had walked a long distance, and, though it was mid winter, his blood was warm, and his throat dry. The regular brush commenced, — a right earnest one it was; and he had something else to do than dally with it; — he must brave the storm, and cleave his way through it. He had some miles to go yet, and night was at hand. The pack he bore grew heavier on his shoulders, his feet labored in the new-fallen snow, and what with frequent slips on the concealed ice, his endurance was sore taxed. But he was cheerful without, and strove to be quiet within; and made as if he were independent of circumstance, and free from anxiety. The storm had a good many plans and purposes of action. It riddled the apple-trees; it threw up its embankments against the fences; it fell soft and even upon shrubs and flowers in the woods, as if it were tenderly burying its dead; it brought out the farmer, to defend his herds against it; it stirred the pluck of the school-boys, who insulted it with their backs, and laughed at it with their faces; and, as if to spite this, it turned upon an unprotected female, a dress-maker, going home from her daily task, and twisted her hood and snatched off her shawl; but, failing in the attempt to rend her entire dress to pieces, it blinded her with its gusts, and pitched her into the gutter. This was too much for Richard. If his blood was hot before, it boiled now; and flinging down his bundle, he sprang to the rescue. He raised the woman, refitted her wardrobe, and sent her on her way with many thanks. The storm, maddened and unchecked, rallied, to stifle and subdue this new champion of woman's rights. It smote Richard violently in the face, snatched away his morsels of breath, and would have sunk him, by sheer weight, in the White Sea that surrounded him. When it could not do this, it flapped its enormous wings in his face, so he could not see his way. Anon it raised its sweep aloft, and left a little clear space, through which he beheld houses with bright hearth-fires, and tables savorily spread for the evening meal, and little children getting into their mothers' laps, as if to plague him in this fashion. The flakes, as if each one had an individual commission, flew in under the vizor of his cap, settled upon his eyelashes, clung to his muffler; some penetrated into his neck; others explored his nostrils. He tried to whistle; but the storm kept his lips so chilled he could not do that: he attempted to laugh; certain flakes that sat on his lips seized the moment to melt and run down his throat. When the storm could not arrest his course, it began to trick him for everybody to laugh at: it whitened his black suit, till he looked like a miller's apprentice; the flakes piled themselves in antic figures on his pack and shoulders, and strewed his buttons with flaunting wreaths; they danced up and down on his cap. But he pressed on, with a whistling heart, as if he thought it was mere facetiousness in the elements to do so. He knew there was love and gladness at the core of all things; and the feathery crystals that frolicked about him, and then laid themselves down so quietly to sleep for the dreary months of winter, were full of beauty, and there was a luminousness of Good Intent in all the haze and hurly-burly of the storm. Richard was deeply religious; and he knew God said to the snow, Be thou on the earth; and he felt that the Divine Providence cared for the lilies of the field as well in their decay as in their bloom; and that a ceaseless Benignity was covering the beds where they lay with the lovely raiment of the season, and cherishing in the cold ground the juices that should, after a brief interval, spring forth again, and create a gladsome resurrection of nature.

He had none but kindly feelings when there passed him a sleigh, with its occupants neck deep in buffalo-robes and coats, and comfortably intrenched behind a breastwork of muffs and tippets; and the horse, he knew, was merry, by the way he shook his bells. He even went one side, and stood knee-deep in the drifts, for a slow ox-sled to pass. "Ho! my good fellow!" he cried to the teamster, who sat on a strip of board, with his back bowed and braced against the storm, as if there was to *his* mind certainly something in the case suggestive of the knout; "you must bide your time."

"That is the first truth I have heard to-day," responded a gloomy voice, which, with the coarse shape in which it was wrapped, soon swept out of hearing.

"One truth to-day," said Richard to himself, "is something, though it is towards night."

He relapsed into musing and philosophizing on the world and life, the day and hour, and on himself and his objects, and on the City in which truth was so scarce. Of a sudden, the Factories burst upon him, or their windows did, — hundreds of bright windows, illuminated every night in honor of Toil, — and which neither the darkness of the night, nor the wildness of the storm, could obscure, and which never bent or blinked before the rage and violence around. The Factories, and factory life, — how it glowed at that moment to his eye! and even his own ideal notions thereof were more than transfigured before him, and he envied the girls, some of whom he knew, who, through that troubled winter night, were tending their looms as in the warmth, beauty, and quietness of a summer-day. The Factories appeared like an abode of enchantment; and the sight revived his heart, and gave him a pleasant impression of the City, as much as a splendid church, or a sunny park of trees, or fine gardens, would have done. He was too much occupied to notice a spread umbrella that approached him, moving slantwise abreast the storm, now criss-crossing, now plunging forward, as it were intoxicated. It struck him, and in his insecure footing, threw him.

"What is it?" said the umbrella, peering about on every side.

"It is nothing," replied Richard, who could hardly be distinguished from the snow in which he rolled.

The umbrella raised itself, as if it were one great eyelid, in astonishment, muttering, at the same time, "That 's it; I knew I should do it, and now I have!"

Beneath the umbrella was really a man, but apparently a cloak, a long and slim cloak, with a shawl about its head and ears; and it looked, also, as if this cloak was hung by some central loop to the handle of the umbrella, and as if the umbrella was the only live thing in the whole concern; and it kept bobbing up and down in the wind, wrenching and prying, as if it would draw the vitals from the cloak. The language of the thing favored the idea of evisceration. "I am almost dead!" it said.

"Let me help you," said Richard.

"I have only a little further to go," replied the other.

"How far have you come?" asked Richard, sympathetically, thinking of the many miles he had fared that day.

"Across the River," was the reply.

"Is it so far?" rejoined Richard, despairingly.

"A hundred rods or so. But one meets with so many accidents here; and nobody's ways are taken care of, and life is of no value whatever, in these times."

Richard, delighted at the near end of his journey, did not conceal his pleasure.

"You will not laugh, when you have experienced what I have," said the man.

"Is there nothing to do here?" asked Richard.

"Yes, everything," was the answer.

"Then I am secure," added Richard.

"Move carefully!" — such was the advice of the retreating shadow; "it is a slip, or a slump, all the way through. You will be running into somebody else, or somebody will run into you."

Richard grew thoughtful; but he repelled the phantom of discouragement, and clung closer to the good angel of common sense and rational hope, that ever attended him.

He was coming to Woodylin to find employment. The construction of mill-dams and railroads had sounded a general summons, throughout the country, for capital and labor to flow in thither. Business, which means the combined and harmonious activity of capital and labor, was reported to be good. The City was evidently growing, and there were those who hesitated to say how large they thought it would become, lest they should appear vain. Many young men were attracted thither, and among these was Richard Edney. He came from a farm, in a small interior village, and brought with him considerable mechanical expertness; and now, just turned of age, on the evening of the day in which he set out to seek his fortune, or, more strictly, to find a snug operative's berth, he appears before the reader. He had a married sister in town, whose house he would make his home.

He came to the covered bridge, and entering by the narrow turn-stile, found a breathing-place from the storm in that labyrinth of timbers. He stamped the snow from his feet, and, unbuttoning his over-coat, seized the lappels with his two hands, and shook them heartily, as if they were old friends whom he had not seen for a long time, and then folded them carefully to his breast.

One or two lamps suggested the idea of light, and that

was about all. Their chief effect was shadow; they made darkness visible, and very uncomfortably so. They worked it into uncouth shapes, which were put skulking among the arches, set astride of the braces, hung up like great spiders on the rafters, and multitudes of them lay in ambuscade under the feet of passengers. No; — if there were kind feelings in that Bridge, — if any pulse of philanthropy ran through those huge beams and iron-riveted joints, — if there were any heart of good-will in that long vault, well studded at the sides, close-pent above, and firmly braced under foot, it was an unfortunate bridge; unfortunate in its expression, unfortunate in its efforts to show kindness.

The readers of this story would like to know how Richard felt. To speak more in detail, there are two popular impressions anent the Bridge, one of which Richard avoided, and into the other he fell. The first is, that the Bridge is of no use, that it is a damage to the community; in other words, that it defeats the very object for which it was built, the facilitation of travel and increase of intercourse. For instance, you will hear men say they could afford to keep a horse, if it were not for the Bridge; some, that they should ride a great deal more, if it were not for the Bridge; one, that while his business is on one side of the water, he should like to live on the other, but cannot because of the Bridge; ladies, visiting on the opposite side of the river, are always in haste to return before sunset, on account of the Bridge. So business and pleasure, in innumerable forms, seem to be interrupted by this structure. This feeling, of course, Richard had not been long enough in the neighborhood to understand or to share. But the other popular impression, which indeed is connected with the first, he did, in some degree, though perhaps unconsciously, entertain; this, — that the Bridge is useful as a shelter from storms, from cold, and from the intense heat of summer. It has this credit with the people; a passive credit, a credit bestowed without the least idea of desert on its part; an accidental good, wholly aside from the original design of the thing, which it cannot help but bestow, and which it would not bestow, if it could help. It is as if, in this vale of winds and rain, the Bridge were a little arbor one side of the way, to which the weary pilgrim can betake himself. So, in summer, when the mercury is at ninety, or at any time in a storm, or when the roads are muddy, you will see people hastening to the Bridge; wagons are driven faster, and foot-people increase their momentum. "We shall soon be at the Bridge," they say; or, "Here is the Bridge; I do not care, now." Umbrellas are furled, cloaks are loosened, feet cleaned, and there is a smile of contentment and of home in all faces, as soon as they reach that pavilion.

How fine a refuge it was from the hurtling snow, how admirably it was adapted to protect one in this extremity of the season, how dry and warm it was, what a convenient place to take breath in; — this Richard felt. He had this feeling even deeper than most folk. Blinded as he was by the storm, tired by his long journey, lonely in feeling, knowing no one, harrowed a little by the dark intimations that had accosted him just as he got into the City, even the small lamp that glimmered aloft had a friendly eye; and he overflowed with gratitude to the little twinkler that worked so patiently and so hopefully in the deathlike, skeleton ribs of the edifice; and as he seated himself on a sill, since he did not know anybody in particular, and had not participated in those feelings to which we have referred, he thanked God for the Bridge. The tramping of horse-feet, grating of sleigh-runners, and buzz of lively voices, were heard in the darkness; and immediately there passed near him an empty sleigh, driven by a man on foot, and four or five men and women, likewise walking.

"Horrid!" exclaimed one. "What a place for robbers!" cried another. "I had rather face it out there," added a third, jerking his head towards the gate, "than have my shins barked here." "I think the lecturer might have spent a few evenings in a bridge like this," interposed a fourth; "it corresponds to his ideas of Gothic architecture. There is the dimness, awe, and faint religious light; and there is no place where one is so reverential, or walks so circumspectly, as here." These were young people, returning from the Athenæum, and among them were members of the Governor's Family, — a name that appears on our title-page; and these observations fell from them while they waited for the gate to be opened. "What is that by the post?" exclaimed one. "A drunken man!" echoed another. The ladies faintly screamed, and rushed towards the gate. "You are mistaken," said Richard, calmly, but a grain piqued. His tone and manner recalled the young folk to their senses, and not the least to a sense of injustice toward a stranger; and they all stopped and looked towards him. The light of the lamp revealed brotherly faces of young men, and gentle faces of young women, and Richard spoke freely. "I am very tired," he said; "I have walked forty miles since breakfast, and I was glad to sit here. But you alarm me. Is this such a horrid place?" "No, indeed," replied one of the girls; it was the Governor's daughter Melicent, that spoke. "We are addicted to scandalizing the Bridge, just as one finds fault with his best friends."

"I do not mean that," answered Richard, "but all through here — what is about you here — this neighborhood?"

"There are rum-shops hereabouts, and there is the foot of Knuckle Lane," said a young man.

"I did not see them," replied Richard.

"We live in St. Agnes-street," said one of the females, laughing very hard, "and you may have passed our houses, the minister's, the Governor's, and all. And we all belong here. I hope you don't think evil of us."

"I was warned of evil hereabouts," responded Richard. "But I am sure I have nothing to fear from you."

"Melicent! Barbara!" cried the laughing voice, "has he anything to fear from you?"

"I have been misunderstood," said Richard, laughing in turn. "But really I have had as pure religious feeling, while I have been resting myself on this bridge, as I ever enjoyed, notwithstanding your slight and caricature of the spot."

"Benjamin!" cried the same bright voice, "defend yourself; it is your ribaldry the young man has overheard."

"We have come from a lecture on Architecture," said Benjamin Dennington; "and the rest is obvious. Fantastic associations are awakened here."

"You will not say," answered Richard, "that religious sentiment is fantastic!" This was seriously said, and the company became silent when he spoke. "I mean," he added, "may not religious feeling be as pure in this place, at this hour, as in any place at any hour?"

"Certainly, certainly," said Melicent. "But who are you that says this?"

"I am Richard Edney," said our friend. "I am seeking employment; can turn my hand to almost anything; would like a chance in a saw-mill. Can you tell me where Asa Munk lives?"

"I cannot," said Benjamin; and none of them could. "I am shivering with the cold," said the laughing one, "and I would advise the young man to learn better manners than to sit here and scare folks in the night." "I should think he might find some place more suitable for his devotions," added one of the girls. "Perhaps a mill-log would be as agreeable for him to kneel upon as a hassock," continued the laughing one.

"I fear this *is* a bad place," said Richard. "Farewell to you all, gentle ladies," he added, and went on his way.

"May it fare well with you!" rejoined Melicent Dennington, sending her voice after him.

Richard crossed the Bridge, and by dint of information plucked from the few people abroad at that time, he made his way to a story-and-a-half white house, with doric pilasters, that stood near the bank of the River, just above the first dam.

He went in at the front door without ringing, traversed with a quiet step the narrow, dark entry, and let himself into the kitchen, where he knew he should find his friends. He was evidently looked for, and warmly welcomed; his sister embraced him affectionately, and his brother-in-law shook his hand very cordially. They were sitting in front of the stove, near a large table drawn to the centre of the room, on which burned two well-trimmed lamps. His sister was mending a child's garment; his brother was smoking, and reading a newspaper. These people were about thirty years of age; his sister had dark eyes and hair, and a face that had once been handsome, but it now wore a sallow and anxious expression; she was neatly dressed in dark-sprigged calico. The brother-in-law, or Munk, as everybody called him, had a freer look, and more sprightly bearing. He had a small, twinkling, blue eye, a long, good-humored chin, and slender, sorel whiskers. He wore a stout teamster's frock, girded at the waist. If a shadow of seriousness sometimes stole over him, it was instantly dissipated, or illumined, by a cheerful voice and a jocund laugh.

Richard laid off his pack and over-coat. "Do not shake off the snow here, brother," said his sister; "let Asa take the things into the shed."

Richard took off his boots, and sank into the rocking-chair his sister drew up for him, with his feet bolstered on the clean and bright stove-hearth. As he has now got out of the storm and his storm-gear, and looks like himself, our readers would like to know how he looks. He, like his sister, had dark eyes and hair; his features were comely, his forehead was fairly proportioned, his eyebrows were distinct and well placed, his mouth was small, and his teeth white. His predominant expression was cheerfulness, frankness, earnestness. He had what some would call an intellectual look; and, judging from the contour of his head, one would see that he possessed a modicum of moral qualities. His cheeks were browned by the weather, but his forehead preserved a belt of skin of remarkable whiteness. He was of medium height, and his body was strongly built, and in all its members very regularly disposed. He wore a red shirt, and a roundabout, sometimes called a monkey-jacket. His coat, vest and pantaloons, were of a dark, stout cloth, which his mother had evidently manufactured, as she possibly had been the tailoress of her son.

His sister hastened supper for him; she toasted the bread, cut fresh slices of corned beef, and prepared a cup of fragrant, hot tea. They all sat round the table, and each had many inquiries to make, and many to answer; and many details of home, and friends, and life, to dilate upon. The supper was abundant, and freely eaten, but it was not satisfying; an uneasiness remained—so much so, that, although Richard resumed his chair by the stove, he could not sit in it. He looked from side to side of the kitchen, and at last thrust his head into a partly-opened door, that led into the bed-room. "Not to-night," whispered his sister, earnestly. "I must," said Richard. "Let him, Roxy," said Munk. "I must see them," said Richard. "You will wake them," replied his sister. "I have made it a rule not to have them waked after they have once been put to sleep. It will get them into bad habits, and they have troubled me about going to bed." "I will not wake them," added Richard, pushing himself still further into the room. "Only let me see them; let me have a light, that I may look at them." "Not on any account!" exclaimed his sister. "I always said, if ever I had a child, it should not be waked up after it was put to sleep." But he seized a lamp, which his brother, despite the remonstrances of Roxy, handed him, and shading it with his fingers, went into the room. Munk followed, and leaned upon the door-post, with much fatherly fondness, and perhaps some brotherly pride. His sister went too, plainly with the expectation of beholding her predictions verified, and with the desire, also, of having displayed before the eyes of her husband the consequences she had so often denounced. What appeared? Two little children, snugly asleep in their truckle-bed; two girls they were, — one about four years old, the other of a year and a half. Two beautiful cherub heads were all that could be seen, and if they were not truly alive, they might have been taken for the best of sculpture. The hair of the oldest one had been treated with a cap, which had fallen off; and that of the youngest was free and loose, soft, silvery, and running every way in little shining curls, and half-formed natural ringlets. "I see," said the mother. "So do I," said the uncle, as, holding the lamp over his head, he stooped towards the sweet, tempting faces. "You mean to wake them!" cried the mother. "I mean to kiss them," responded Richard. "Let him," whispered the father. "It is impossible," said the mother; "it is contrary to all the rules I have laid down for the children, and what Mrs. Mellow said." "I will not do *that*," added Richard; and, making an effort, he did not; but hovered about the faces of the children, put his mouth towards one, and then the other, and kissed the air between, as if that was sweet enough; experimented with the light on this side and on that, to get every possible view of them; with his thumb and finger took hold of the little velvety hands, that lay over the quilt. "Did they not know I was coming?" he asked. "They have talked about nothing else all day," replied his brother; "Memmy asks about Uncle Richard; Bebby can't articulate, but she mows and winks, and knows all about it." "They have the promise of seeing you in the morning," said his sister, "and went quietly to sleep on that." The children slumbered on, undisturbed alike by the storm above the roof, and the deep anxieties and affections that were shaking beneath. "Mother sent them some cakes and apples; they are in my luggage. I should love to give them to them to-night."

"How foolish you are, brother!" said Roxy. "I would not have them eat such things, just before going to bed, for the world."

But Richard got the apples, large and rosy, which he held insinuatingly before the closed eyes of the children; pleased himself with imagining how they would like to eat them; put them close to their cheeks, as it were comparing colors; and, when he had finished this pantomime, laid them on the coverlid in front of their mouths; and they left the room.

This slight ripple of discord having spent itself, their hearts returned to their old and proper level of kindness and brotherly feeling. They resumed their seats by the fire, which burned briskly and noisily. Roxy took her sewing; Munk leaned back against the wall, with his feet on a round of his wife's chair, and continued to smoke; and Richard. by the warmth of his heart, as well as that of the fire, tried to subdue the chills with which a long walk in the open air had infused his system.

"I do not doubt," said Roxy, "that Richard loves the children, and that their father does; but you are very injudicious."

"Perhaps I was hasty," said Richard.

"I believe I shall go to California," said Munk. This last remark was evidently thrown in, not to aid conversation, or even to decoy it, but to quench it altogether, when it happened to take a disagreeable turn.

Richard went to bed. His chamber — such as a story-and-a-half house affords — was small and low, with sloped ceiling, but plastered, papered, and quite convenient. It contained a looking-glass, side-table, and fireplace. The single window of which it could boast looked out upon the River, and a beautiful landscape beyond. The bed was soft and warm; and, after offering his evening thanksgiving to the Giver of all good, exhausted and weary, our young friend sank into a sound sleep.

Early in the morning, he was aroused by the clamor of voices at his bed-side; there stood the disputed little ones, in their night-gowns, each with an apple in its hands, with which they were pummeling the face of their uncle, and at the same time making very awkward attempts to clamber into the bed. One of them, as the father said, could talk, and the other could make a noise; but neither lacked the power of rendering itself intelligible. Their uncle lifted them up, and had them on either side of him, where he kissed and embraced their tender bodies to his heart's content. But they were not for lying there. They mounted his neck and shoulders; they took all sorts of liberty with his nose and eyes, and ended with an endeavor to drag him from the bed. He yielded to the children what the storm could not accomplish, and came almost headlong to the floor. Presently, taking Bebby in his arms, and mounting Memmy on his back, he went below.

CHAPTER II.

THE GOVERNOR'S FAMILY.

LET us go back to the previous evening, and down St. Agnes-street, into the Governor's house, soon after the young people have returned from the lecture.

This house, of a fashion forty years old, was large, three-story, brick, surrounded by a portico, and pleasantly embayed in trees, some dozen or fourteen rods from the street.

On this boisterous winter night, the family are gathered in a spacious apartment, called the sitting-room. In the centre of the room is a large mahogany table, carefully covered with a damask counterpane, over which a solar lamp sheds its strong light. Around the table are seated the family, if we may except the Governor himself, who, in front of a blazing wood fire, reclines in a rocking-chair, with his feet on the jamb. The mother of the family, or as she is commonly known, Madam Dennington, controls one side of the table, with her sewing spread before her. She has also under her special control a spermaceti candle, and a pair of silver snuffers, with which, in moments of excitement, she makes energetic starts for the candle-wick. It was not her wish to have the solar lamp. Her father, Judge Weymouth, used candles, and she had used them for thirty years; and they answered their purpose, and she was indisposed to see their province invaded. She wore a turban, out of regard to her mother. She was short, erect, and retained that vigor of eye and dignity of manner for which her family were celebrated.

About the table were the children and relatives of the family. The governor had twelve children, of whom eleven survived. The name of the deceased one, Agnes, was preserved in the street on which they resided. Four were married from home. The others, in order, were Roscoe, Benjamin, Melicent, Barbara, Eunice, and two smaller ones, who at this hour were abed. Roscoe was about twenty-six, and the rest succeeded in due course of nature.

The relatives were Miss Rowena, a cousin of Madam's, and Mrs. Melbourne, a lady reared in the family of the Rev. Dr. Dennington, father of the Governor, and who, for many years, had been a member of the household of the latter.

Roscoe was addicted to bachelor habits, and bachelor moods; he had no fondness for society, and a good education he found scope for in the management of his father's farm. Benjamin was a lawyer.

Madam was nervous, and, above all things, dreaded a scene; and when the wind howled at the house, and shook the windows, she started, as if one was coming. She was religious, and seasoned her words with verses of Scripture. She was industrious, and plied the needle assiduously; yet not for herself, but for others; and not always for the work to be done, but for the example to be set.

If she relished the old régime, she was charitable to the new; and while she sought to preserve the times past, her good sense and strong faith inspired her with interest in those to come. She reverenced the clergy, and defended the reformer.

Her daughters were passing from the flower of youth into the beauty and richness of womanhood. Their dress honored the simple taste of their mother; it was plain, becoming, and neat without ornament. The two relatives were benevolent looking people, whose happiness seemed to consist in making the family happy.

Miss Rowena had a lively and jocose turn; while Mrs. Melbourne was subject to depression of spirits, in which moments her vision was hazy, and her feelings petulant.

We have said this was a large room; it had, also, an air of great amenity and comfort. The lamp wrought a quiet but deep illumination in all parts of it; the open fire was cheerful; nay, it was inspiring, at such times as these, when that well-meaning but stupid creature, with a cast-iron face, has undertaken to perform for us the office of warmth and sociability through the long months of winter, but which the Governor, with a luxurious or an antiquated feeling, summarily dismissed from his premises. Pictures garnished the walls, a sofa invited to repose, a piano suggested music, a stand in one corner was enriched with choice literature; under one of the windows was a table, stocked with flower-pots, and bearing geraniums and roses in bloom, and many plants whose living verdure was a shelter for the feelings from the storm; the mantel-piece constituted a general news office, and collected the papers, pamphlets, letters, for daily distribution; above it was suspended a shell card-rack, the more select depository of the lace-edged and enameled missives of fashion and polite society. A large mirror, on one wall, reproduced, in attractive vista, this pleasant scene, and prolonged the interest which the room afforded to contemplation.

The Governor left his rocking-chair, and paced to and fro on the back side of the room. He had always condemned rocking-chairs, and now, in his advancing years, he would not sit in one a great while at a time; thus keeping on good terms his age and his principles. His hands locked behind him under his dressing-gown, his head bent forwards, he seemed to be in a brown study; — it was a passive habit. He stopped against the window, and looked askance at the storm, as if he were suspicious of it, but said nothing. He had practised, all his life, the school-boy direction of not speaking until he was spoken to; and, on the whole, not without a certain advantage, since he acquired more than he gave out, and not being over-communicative, he was deemed very trustworthy; and since every one has some things to say which he does not wish to have said again, it follows that a silent man in society must gather up a vast deal of confidence, like a well-regulated institution, in which people like to vest their spare capital, knowing that it will not break; — sometimes awfully like the sea, into which malefactors hurl dead men's bodies, and even their frightful bags of gold, knowing they will not rise again.

In the kitchen, if any of our readers are disposed to make a further survey of the premises, is also what must now be called an old-fashioned fire; yet one, judging from the size of the sticks, destined to do good service yet, and of a sort of wood that, without fruit in its living state, when brought to the hearth, bears the richest flame-blossoms, and expires in a ruddy, glowing crop of coals, — rock-maple. Here were also a man-servant and a maid-servant; the one, in one corner of the hearth, engaged, as probably fifty thousand of our population are at this moment, reading a newspaper, lamp in hand. The woman, modestly retired to the other corner, at a small table, is turning an old silk dress into a mantilla.

A fresh gust of wind, like a wave of the sea, struck the house, and moaned piteously in every crevice of door and window.

"God remember the poor!" said Madam, in an under but earnest voice, without looking at anybody in particular; at the same time hurrying the snuffers into the candle, as if she would extinguish all the poverty in creation, and pressing the cloth she was sewing with her left hand tightly on the table, as if she were, in her own mind, stanching the sorrows of the race.

"They will need some additional help," added the Governor, in a quiet way.

"Yes, indeed!" replied his wife; and she recited that passage of Scripture which intimates how vain it is to bid the destitute be warmed, without giving them what is needful. Then she asked, "Has that wood gone to the O'Conners?"

"I heard the crackling of it in their stove, this afternoon," said Melicent, "and saw the joyous glow of it in the faces of the family."

Once more the storm thwacked the house, to keep stirring and active in its inmates the remembrance of humanity; and, at this time, to give additional pathos to its proceedings, it roared up and down the chimney, as it were mimicking, in condensed reverberations, the hollow, unheeded moan of universal wretchedness.

Madam acknowledged the force of this appeal; but she was not to be thrown from her balance, and she snuffed the candle with marked deliberation. Marked, in truth; — Miss Rowena saw it, and nodded to Melicent across the table; Mrs. Melbourne saw it, and grew sombre in the face. Now, Mrs. Melbourne had a favorite horse, which she was very tender of, all weathers. Moreover, this horse had not once been mentioned in course of the evening; and Mrs. Melbourne knew Madam was not thinking of it, and this worried her. Not but that this lady had a regard for the poor; she had, but she claimed an enlargement of sympathy even to the bounds of the mute creation.

Madam kept to her own thoughts. Turning to her grandchild, who sat in the corner, she said, "Alice Weymouth! Alice Weymouth!" But the child was asleep.

"Asleep!" exclaimed madam, "asleep, under such preaching as this? Asleep, when terror is calling, so hoarse and mournful? Asleep, when love is summoning all the elements to speak for it?" She did not say this loud and boisterously, but with that subordination of manner which never deserted her.

"I don't wonder the child sleeps," said Mrs. Melbourne; "she went half a mile, with a bed-blanket, before tea; and I scruple if the horse in the stable has a shred to his back."

There was a mixture of causticity and kindness in this observation; she wished to reproach her cousin, and the family in general, for their neglect of the brute, at the same time seeking to shield the child from the apparent severity of her grandmother. In all this, Mrs. Melbourne had the habit of flattering herself she was peculiarly, nay, in a double-fold, benevolent; and she took the flattery more to heart, because it was wholly a matter of her own contrivance, and no one helped her in it.

"Yes, yes," continued Madam, "bed-blanket is warming three, by this time; turkey sent yesterday stayed a whole table-full of stomachs." Here she raised her voice, as if she were squaring accounts with the weather, and the weather was a trifle deaf, and she meant her own side of the case should be fairly put: "Milk is served regularly every morning; have Peter's boys taken the cold meat?" Hereupon the wind lulled. This gave Madam an opportunity to declare there never was such a storm.

"We have had just such storms, every winter, for forty years," replied the Governor, quietly; "and you have said the same thing," he added, "this is now the fortieth time."

There was no point, no sharpness, in this rejoinder; it was only uttered as a pleasant reminiscence.

"Yes, indeed," she replied, twisting a little in her chair, but soon regaining her composure; "there is nothing new under the sun. What has been, shall be." Nor did she rejoin this out of servile deference to the Governor, or because she deemed the Scripture absolute authority on every topic that might be broached; but a moment's reflection recalled to mind those liberal views and permanent convictions that lay deep in her nature, and which exciting events, like the storm, seemed for the instant to obliterate.

These things passed with little or no notice. Miss Rowena laughed through her hand; a smile rose to the surface of the lips of Melicent, like a dolphin at play, and disappeared. The room was bright, and all were tranquil. The Governor went to bed; he went without a light, — he always did so. He said it facilitated sleep, to go to the place of recumbency through a long passage of darkness, and not flash into slumber too suddenly. Benjamin had one shoulder piled on the end of the table, and the paper as near his eyes as possible, and his eyes as near the light; — he was near-sighted, and wore glasses; — and his reading was intense, and was evidently fighting its way into something. Eunice had gone to the piano, and while the storm was dashing at the keys of her mother's heart, she was offering herself, eyes, ears, imagination, fingers, to the service of a couple of bars of music, and seemed unmistakably wishing that something would fling her bodily on to the keys of her instrument; but there was reluctance, or great short-coming, somewhere; there were but few reasonable tones to be heard.

Benjamin laid down his paper, and his glasses on top of it, and rubbed his right eye very hard with the knuckle of his forefinger. "There is something in it," said he, "if it could only be got at."

"I have no doubt there is," answered Eunice, "but who shall say what?"

"I have been thinking there might be," said Barbara.

"What if there is?" interposed Mrs. Melbourne; "who really cares?"

"Indeed, there is!" responded Madam; "and there are a good many that care."

"No doubt," echoed Roscoe.

What should happen, at this instant, but that all these persons were thinking of different things; Benjamin of California gold, Eunice of her music, Barbara of Richard Edney, Mrs. Melbourne of the horse, Madam of the poor, and Roscoe of the effect of the cold on peach-trees. The evening wore on, the lights dulled, the fire burnt low; and these folk were becoming languid, and relapsing into a half-stupid, half-unconscious state, in which the mind speaks out as it were in sleep, or in intoxication; and each of them, by a sort of hidden wire-pulling, exposed what had been on his mind for the last fifteen minutes. They were in a jumble, a laughable jumble; and when they began to explain, they fell into a greater jumble, and laughed a good deal harder; their thoughts twirled one another round, and tripped each other's heels, — all in play. Their thoughts, secretly controlled by the real harmony of their feelings, fell into groups and circles, and a sort of wild polka gallopade; but Barbara's thought, being the newest and strongest, got the upper hand, and led off, with all the others following it; and Barbara's thought was Richard Edney.

I dare say many of our readers have been having the same thought; and since Richard Edney's name is so near the Governor's Family, on the title-page, they are glad to have it get in there at last, and perhaps wonder how it will be treated. That is easily told; — it was laughed at. Miss Rowena loved to laugh, and to be decorous too. To unite these two things, she bit her lip. If we should say now she bit her lip hard — the fact — it would only be saying she laughed hard.

Eunice said she hoped he would find Asa Munk's; Barbara hoped he would find work; Miss Rowena hoped so too, and then he would not be out late evenings, frightening people in strange places; Melicent desired that his innocence and simplicity might not suffer.

"There would be great danger of it," said Miss Rowena, "if he had happened in St. Agnes-street."

"What! what!" ejaculated Madam, quickly and nervously. She folded up her work, and unfolded it. She rolled the edge of it in her fingers, and unrolled it. Just as she was going to bed, and the storm was subsiding, she was not prepared for the introduction of a stranger, or a strange topic; and while she commiserated any one in distress, she was not quite prepared, at that late hour, to go in quest of new objects.

"What is it?" she asked, emphatically; for all witnessed her agitation, but none answered her directly. There was a mixture of shame and suspense in their recollections of what transpired; and what they said was as confused as it was lively.

Alice Weymouth, the granddaughter, who had been of the party to the lecture, related that they had met a drunken man, or a tired man, or an old man, she hardly knew which; nor whether he was young or old had she any clear impression; and had left him to find his way, in an unknown town. Mrs. Melbourne hinted they might have offered him a bed. Madam, truly considerate as she was of the world at large, shrank from the idea of an utter stranger in the house; and in this very thing, Mrs. Melbourne, by pushing her benevolence a little further than the rest, contrived to keep up a little quarrel, and attain a brief triumph, on the gentlest of topics, and with people whom, from the bottom of her soul, she loved. It was her weakness. Miss Rowena intimated that he might sleep with the hired man, who would take care of him if he was likely to do mischief.

The young ladies drew their chairs about the fire; Madam turned down the solar lamps, sent Alice to bed, and admonishing her daughters not to make free with strangers, or light of misery, went to her chamber.

The young ladies lifted the smooth folds of their hair over their ears, undid their belts, and sat musing upon the embers on the hearth.

"A liberal, hopeful, wise human voice, anywhere," said Melicent, "anywhere, is something; but there," she went on, "there, in that darkness, that solitude, with the storm racketing and rending around it, and those weird shadows behind it, and the bitter, sullen cold piercing it, — how very strange it is!"

She thrust her fingers further under her hair, and raised it higher over her ears, as if she would hear more of that voice.

"Voices!" said Barbara. "Speech, a breath, a sigh, a prolongation of feeling, a flight of wish, an impersonation; without properties or relations; without the weights of flesh and blood; without the temptations of accident or position; without poverty, or ignorance, or vice; without ill-nature or ill-breeding; without folly or prejudice; without circumstance and without inevitability; — yes, voices are well enough, and there is plenty of them."

"I have no doubt there are some in my piano," added

Eunice; "and, like the woman and her goose, I should like to break it open and get at them."

"Eunice!" cried one from the chamber, "is it not time you were abed? Alice Weymouth would excuse you, but it would be a trial to her feelings, which are a little tender such a night as this."

"There is a voice for you," said Eunice, "right from the pit of your mother's heart. The weather, that has chilled every fibre of my fingers, has thawed out the great aorta of her sensibilities. How do you like it? How did you use to like it, when you were of my age, — snatching you away from pleasant company, breaking up your tête-à-têtes with the low fire, spoiling the pleasant feeling of your own independence and womanhood, blasting the enchantment of a novel or a moonlight, chasing you up stairs, and giving you no rest till you slipped away from it beneath three heavy coverlids?"

Eunice, as one of the younger children, still required, or received, some motherly looking after. She was an obedient child, and did what her mother wished her to do; she shut the piano, kissed her sisters, and retired.

The two sisters, by this time, were left alone; one by one, all had gone; the last footsteps on the stairs were heard, the last door was shut, the last muffled creaking in the distant chambers had died away.

But no gloom or sorrow remained, though but one candle burned, and but a handful of coals were alive. The storm was over; the atmosphere fell into repose; the moon looked down upon the hills sleeping beneath their robes whiter than Marseilles quilts, with a calm, gushing eye, like a mother upon her little children in bed; and the clouds, soft as summer, looked lovingly upon the moon. The parlor could not be empty; for the moonlight came in at the windows, and brought with it the shadows of the great elms that stood before the house, the branches of which went to extemporizing pretty patterns of things right over the figures of the carpet, getting up a smart trial between nature and art, and half persuading us of the superiority of the first. More than this, the spirit of love and the sense of a divine presence remained; parental and brotherly kindnesses and attentions kept their place good; gladness and joy still sat about the table; wisdom and reverence held its seat in the great rocking-chair; the words of the dead and the memories of the absent brooded among them; and voices, — a thousand murmuring voices of beauty, sweetness, ideality, ecstasy, — like a rivulet, flowed around the piano.

These sisters were alike, and they were unlike. They were about the same age, height and weight. Strangers often mistook one for the other. They were fully and symmetrically developed. Their constitutions had been reinforced by exercise, and nurtured by work. With every means of luxury, their habits were moderate. The features of both had rather a Roman than a Grecian cast. They were light complexioned, but Barbara retained throughout an infusion of shadow deeper than Melicent; her eyes were darker, her skin, and her hair. White was a becoming color for both; while pink was the favorite fancy dress of Barbara, and blue of Melicent. Melicent was the type of perfect women; Barbara was a perfect woman: the beauty of the one softened into the roundness of the whole; that of the other was concentrated into the sharpness of the individual. If you were acquainted with many excellent women, you would fancy you had seen a dozen Melicents to one Barbara. They had both been to the same schools, they read the same books, and belonged to the same church. In dietetics, Melicent drank coffee, Barbara drank tea. In recreation, Barbara liked to waltz, Melicent preferred the minuet. They were both Christians; but Barbara sometimes speculated on the miracles, — Melicent loved the Saviour; Barbara aspired after, and sometimes stumbled in pursuit of, the infinities of the universe, — Melicent delighted to yield herself to the serene, unconscious currents of the immortal life; Melicent bore her cross with the patience of a martyr, — Barbara carried off hers more with the ease of a strong man. Barbara had more ideality, — Melicent more purity; Barbara more impulse, — Melicent more firmness. Melicent possessed force of character, — Barbara power of manner. In filial devotion they were equal; but Melicent staid at home when her mother wished her to stay, and Barbara went abroad when her mother wished her to go. Barbara would make a sacrifice if her parents insisted; Melicent would make one after they had ceased to insist. Barbara was more lively, — Melicent more solid. Barbara could joke with the best of feelings; when Melicent had the best of feelings, she could not joke. In respect of humanity, Barbara was an Abolitionist, — Melicent gave herself to the cause of Peace. Barbara had great hope for the race, — Melicent a strong faith in it. Both excelled in music; but Barbara preferred Beethoven, — Melicent, Strauss. Barbara would create a deeper and stronger impression, — Melicent a pleasanter and warmer sympathy. Barbara would suggest a thousand thoughts to you, — Melicent would transfuse you with a certain stillness and serenity that would speedily fill with thoughts.

These sisters looked out on the moonlight; but they did not go to the same window, nor did they put their arms around each other, in the common glow of beautiful entranced feeling. One went to a window on one side of the chimney,

— the other to the other. They spoke to each other, as it were, through the chimney; each heart felt, and uttered, and reflected back, the glorious world without, not to itself, but that the other heart might hear. Barbara said, "O Spirit of Eternal Beauty, keep me this night!" Melicent responded, "O beautiful love of God, I am thine to-night!"

They set in place the chairs, wheeled back the sofa, removed the lamp and damask cloth from the table, that it might be ready for the servants to lay the breakfast in the morning; exchanged the elegant, downy hearth-rug for an obsolete, thread-bare one; raked up the fire, bolted the door; and they too went to bed.

We offer this chapter to our readers, not because it contains matter rare or striking; — it does not; it is of common and familiar things; — and because it is of common and familiar things, we write it. It is a simple picture of a worthy American family, that we would like to preserve, but which we are more anxious to present to our distant readers.

American family! Patagonian? Esquimaux? Nay; an United States of North American. Between a barbarism on the one hand and a falsity on the other, we adopt the falsity. A little euphuistic conformity is to be preferred to a broken pate. We are not puissant enough to throw the glove to national pride in favor of a proper nomenclature. The force of this observation will be felt when we drop down to the next.

Our *distant* readers. We mean the English, French, German, Swedish. But more, much more. Philosophy teaches that nothing is lost; and this tale must survive. Morality urges the illimitableness of human influence; wherefore we may calculate that some wave of kind appreciation will cast these pages on the remotest shores. Now, if license can be had from the Imperial Commission of Turkey, and our friend, Ees Hawk Effendi, of Constantinople, amidst other engagements, shall be able to complete the translation, we hope to publish the book in that celebrated metropolis.

But there are pirates in that region, who will undoubtedly be on the alert, and use so favorable an occasion to pounce upon the work, and translate it into the language of contiguous nations, — say the Tartars, — where its circulation, unimpeded by copy-right, must be immense.

Now, it is an established premise of history, that the Tartars, or ancient Scythians, peopled Europe; that the Anglo-Saxons and Normans came primarily from the banks of the Caspian. Whence it follows that we, soi-disant Americans, deduce our genealogy from a spot renowned as the home of Genghis Khan and Tamerlane.

Consider, then, the pleasure of introducing a work like this among our almost forgotten ancestors! With what delight must they hail intelligence from their long-lost, but still alive and well, trans-Atlantic and trans-Pacific children! With what eagerness will the ladies, God bless them! of Samarcand, that famous city, order the numbers, as they successively appear, done in silk paper — no other is used there — in the book-stalls of the great bazaar of the place! How exhilarating for the dear creatures, in loose, flowing costume, with this volume in hand, to stroll into the valley of the Sogd, where, says the old geographer, Ibn Haukal, "we may travel for eight days, and not be out of one delicious garden;" read to each other about their cousins, Richard and Melicent, and Memmy and Bebby, under the shade of the glorious plane-trees, and cool their transports in an atmosphere of musk, which is exhaled indigenously from the soil! How it must relieve the tedium of the caravan, to have something of this sort to peruse on the way!

Then, to retrace our steps a few degrees, let us imagine the ladies of Constantinople, in their frequent excursions on the Bosphorus, in those caïks, the "neatest and prettiest boats ever seen," reclined on soft and meditative cushions, and alternating the magnificent scenery around them with glances at these simple, domestic pages; — would it not be a fine idea?

But there is a cloud in this bright anticipation, — and that is the point we would impress, — a cloud arising from the misnomer just alluded to. Our Usbek relatives and Ottoman friends will not understand the term, "American Family." They would naturally associate the Governor, his kindred and contemporaries, with the Russians of Alaska. A great mistake. Why not call them a New England family? For the reason that they are not; but are an United States of North American one.

This note, addressed, indeed, to our cognates and fellow-citizens, will nevertheless fulfil its design as regards these distant literary circles, and explain what would otherwise be a kind of ethnical and geographical myth. And certainly, if this volume is to go among the Tartars, we cannot but be anxious that the introduction be as smooth and unencumbered as possible.

It will not only shed light on the interesting topic of the names of places, to which we may again refer; — it will likewise support the propriety of certain matters that may appear in the progress of these chapters.

CHAPTER III.

RICHARD FINDS EMPLOYMENT.

THE next day Munk went with Richard to the Saw-mills. There were many of these stretched along the canals leading from the River. They were large buildings; long, broad and low, and one story high. Busy, busy; so busy, as Richard looked into one and another, his first thought was, they must want assistance; but he soon found they all wanted work. In a great city, everybody seems to be doing something, and it seems as if there was something for everybody to do; but try it, just try it! They came to one known from its color as the Green Mill.

"Here is Captain Creamer," said Munk, "a great friend and patron of young operatives; I will introduce you. He rents two or three saws."

Captain Creamer was a man whom time dealt gently with, while advancing years served to ripen his person and graces; and with a few additions of art,—and art, we are told, is the interpreter of nature, as in this instance she labored to give most certainly the spirit of nature, and nature is kind,—additions of art, we say, as lunar caustic for his gray hair, and porcelain for his empty gums, he would pass for quite youthful.

"I hope," said the Captain, speaking politely, "you are very well, Mr. Munk, and that Mrs. Munk is well. Belle Fanny I need not inquire after; a bargain, that, Mr. Munk; she is the neatest trotter the city can boast. That is my judgment. Brother-in-law, you say; I am glad to see Mr.

Edney. I think I have heard of you. A new one seeking employment. They come fast. I think I have condemned ten applications within a week."

"Then you have no chance for him," concluded Mr. Munk.

"No, no; I did not say so. But it takes extra*or*dinary, I might say, mountaineous talents, to succeed. He has friends who are interested for him, and his own heart is interested for itself. As the poet has said, he has on the whole armor. Let me see you measure and figure on that stock of boards."

Richard took the rule and chalk, and in a few minutes reported an accurate and very neat account.

"Proficiency," replied the Captain, "proficiency. Considerable tact. Mr. Kilmarnok," — he addressed the head-stock man, — "let this young man take your place a moment."

The head-stock was the controlling and responsible end of a stick of timber on the works, and the head-stock man superintended the whole operation of sawing; so that Richard was put to a critical task.

"He sights well," said the Captain. "He handles the bar as if he had seen one before. He must have practised. Merit, merit, certainly. Talent in his bail-dog; his drop-down-feed, Mr. Munk, shines. It shines, as has been justly observed, like a hole in a blanket."

Richard stood in perspiration and trepidation. The severity of the eye that followed his movements was frightful.

Trembling and confused, when the log was run through, in attempting to stop the saw, he seized the "start," or handle of the lever that belonged to a "cutting-off" saw, near by, and set that going. The Captain was in an uproar; Mr. Kilmarnok stepped forward, and corrected the mistake.

"Lame," ejaculated the Captain, "and most unfortunate. What a pity! A most shuperior piece of work spoilt by these blotches! I am sorry for him. Let him attempt the tail-stock. No, no; he will only disgrace himself. I have no interest in this matter, Mr. Munk. I am only anxious that our young men should honor themselves and the cause. But they should confine themselves to what they can do well. Head-stock is nice business; and if he perseveres, we shall have the happiness of meeting him there, some time or another. Let him show his butting. I have no doubt he is a master there."

Richard took an axe, and very neatly proceeded to "butt" a log; that is, cut the end of it square off.

"A well-directed blow. A handsome calf. The swing of his axe is pleasing, — it is positively luxuriating; as Dr. Broadwell observed, the little hills of feeling within us clap their hands." So the Captain echoed the strokes.

Richard took breath and courage. The men in the mill were looking at him, and he did not know but he should be degraded before them; but these encouraging words of the Captain revived him. The Captain's teeth glistened with delight, and his arms shook applause.

"Do you think you shall be able to give me work?" asked Richard, quite hopefully.

"*Give* you work?" responded the captain, very archly. "We *pay* for our work. But it is necessary to begin small; you see that it is. In the little and common matter of chopping, you do well. But, alas! how many choppers there are! Why, everybody can chop."

"Then you do not want me," added Richard.

"I did not say that. I only wish you to know your own

powers. I wish you not to adventure too much. This is a great field. You see Mr. Kilmarnok; you think you can do as well as he does. It seems only a few steps there. It is a great ways from the butt to the head-stock. How would he do in the slip, Mr. Munk?"

"You can try him," replied the latter.

Richard, armed with a picaroon, descended the slip, some thirty feet, to the basin, where the logs lay in the water ready to be drawn in, and by aid of the tooth of the mill-chain dog, to be hauled to the bed of the mill. Richard, standing on one log, and aiming a blow at another, lost his balance and slipped into the water. Recovering himself, he pushed still more energetically the experiment on which he was sent.

"Tut, tut!" so the Captain expressed his disappointment to Munk. "That it should have happened! I feel for the young man. You recollect, Mr. Munk, at the lecture before the Mechanics' Association we had explained to us the difference between genius and doing. Now, your brother-in-law can do many things; I acknowledge that, — no man can deny that; but has he genius? I ask you. He can do, and do well, if he will only keep to his sphere. He has some axe-genius, perhaps; but he fails on the picaroon, — utterly fails. He fails on the head-stock. He may have some slight picaroon doing. He lacks self-oblivimy, and is too tiercy; not enough of the barrel and the tub, Mr. Munk. Ambition! oh, what a foe! I am sorry you spoke to me."

"We applied at several saws," answered Munk, "and they were full."

Meanwhile Richard was doing up his job very handsomely; and his brother called the Captain's attention to the fact.

Captain Creamer smiled,—he loved to smile; but with an air of melancholy.

"He can improve; I never questioned his capacity." The Captain shook his head, as if, while affirming so much, there were still many things he must deny.

Richard reappeared on the mill-bed, with a look of suspense.

The conversation that ensued will be better understood by a tabular word or two. The Saw-mills were the property of companies, or corporations; and the saws were let, and sometimes under-let. To each saw belonged, ordinarily, a "gang" of three men, both for the day and the night, six in all. These were the head-stock man, the tail-stock man, and a sort of servant of the whole, who tended the slip, and did the butting, and helped wherever he was called. Five men could manage two saws. Captain Creamer rented two; and, of course, in his double gang, employed ten men. This for the main work of the mill. There was a collateral business, as making shingles, laths, clapboards, which used up the slabs and refuse timber; and which also required a cutting-off saw. These operations employed several hands. If we reckon six principal saws to each mill, we shall have an aggregate of one or two hundred men in each; one half of whom were in constant activity, day and night. The subordinate branches were carried on below, under the "bed," or main floor of the mill, near the wheel-pit.

"Has your brother worked at shingles?" asked Captain Creamer.

"He has," replied Munk; "but I think he would not care to go down there."

"Natural, natural," answered the Captain. "As has justly been observed, we cannot die but once; and, Mr. Munk, allow me to say it, we do not like to. But, Mr.

Munk, how can one succeed without humility? without beginning low,—as Dr. Broadwell observes, taking one's place in the dust? Not be a shingle-sticker! Why, the Kilmarnoks, the Gouches, were all shingle-stickers."

"I had better return home," said Richard.

"Do not deem me unkind," responded the Captain. "Young men do not appreciate the necessity of industry, and acquaintance with detail. I fear me, I really fear, you are ambitious. Odious sin that, as the poet observes, winds like a hejus snake about the extremities! You see we are tolerably full on the bed; there is hardly room for a flea. But, Mr. Edney, it is not our interest, but the interest of our young men, which moves me to speak."

"You have no opening here," said Richard, decisively.

"I would do anything for you; I would, for your respected brother's sake. I know how friends feel. Nights—let me see. Mr. Kilmarnok, how is Clover?"

"No better, sir," answered the man.

"Clover is sick. Yes, there is Clover's night. He has tended the slip; he is a man of rare qualities, and can turn his hand to most anything. What would you say to his chance for a few days?"

"I can do anything," replied Richard.

"Bless me—that is it. What a spirit!"

"What wages can you afford?"

"We make no account of such things. We are only happy to bring the boys forward—to be the instrument of leading them to greatness. It is worth a world to us to see a head-stock man, and say, we carried that man forwards. Howd, the inventor of the patent wheel, was a shingle-sticker. I suppose Howd is *really* the greatest man in the world. Pierson, the improver of the shingle machine, has claims, and many fine points, and is sometimes named; but, to use the expression, he cannot hold a candle to Howd. To be associated with Howd in any way, even in the meanest capacity, might well fire the heart of a young man. He mounted from the wheel-pit to the bed, and went through the slip to glory!"

"Would you name a sum?" inquired Richard.

"I will be frank with you," replied the Captain, "and even lay bare our whole affairs. Laths feed themselves, but we find them; and so do shingles; but, in times like these, they are glad to pay us a premium for being — for the mere chance of being. What would you say to that?"

Richard shook his head.

"Ah!" sighed the Captain, "'t is Labor against Capital. Labor is ravenous; it scratches Capital, as the poets say, like a fowl on a dunghill. But we are generous; Green Mill is generous; it finds, and repairs, and makes its own insurance; it does everything, and gives all the profits to labor. We will offer you eighteen dollars a month, board yourself; Green Mill does not board. Or, you may form a gang, and take the saw. We allow two dollars a thousand, piled and stuck; oil and light yourself, of course; you understand that."

"I will go by the month," said Richard.

So he found employment for a few weeks, at least; he would work nine hours every night; and have fifteen out of the twenty-four, wherein to sleep, and do what else he liked.

CHAPTER IV.

RICHARD AT THE MILL.

It was an extreme night, and the mercury fell to a great depth before morning. One man, who raised the largest cucumbers, and had the most satisfactory children, and drove the prettiest carryall, said his thermometer, at thirty-eight minutes after seven, stood at five and three-quarters below zero. At any rate, it was cold enough; and Richard felt it, when he left the house, after supper. Its first onset was suffocating, like a simoom; then it began to cut, and sting, and flay, as if it would not only entrap but torture its victim. A delicate, thin, violet vapor, coming from we know not where, had clearly mistaken the time of the year, like birds arriving too early from a sunnier clime; benumbed and bewildered by the cold, it lay on the western hills, still, calm, hard, and dry. The sky was very clear, as if the cold had driven out of it all those soft clouds, and gentle zephyrs, and spiritual mists, on which our better feelings float through the universe, and by which our souls are indefinitely expanded, and our sympathies connected with unseen orders of beings, and left it the impersonation of intellect, — sheer, naked intellect, — intellect without love, without tenderness; awful, dismal intellect, in which the stars were so many iron, piercing, excruciating eyes — eyes which one did not wish to look at, but ducked his head, and hurried on. Or, if one could stand it, — if his fancy would have its way, in spite of the cold, — he would see the windows of heaven covered with frost, and the stars so many little crystalline sparkling points; and if he looked closely at Sirius, he would inevitably conclude it had been snowing there all winter; and the icy, glittering radiance of that star he would attribute to the reflection of interminable hollows, and mountains of snow.

There were no loafers about the mill to-night; and no boys skating on the river, with their cheerful fires, and the bell-like ringing of their merry voices. The great doors on the sides of the mill, that open on horizontal hinges, and are hoisted by ropes, were dropped. The wind drifted freely through the building; and the large, cylindrical, red-hot stoves, seemed to be an invitation to it to come in. Nor was it ceremonious, or hardly civil; it crowded about the stoves, and seemed determined that nobody else should have a place; and with a selfishness which nothing human ever paralleled, as soon as one windy troop got warm, it made way for another, and so left no chance at all for the workmen. Green Mill was a large one,—two hundred feet long, and fifty wide; and all the saws were running; not that they always ran in winter, but these were pressing times. It was one immense hall, where the saws were, mounting to the ridge-pole, and broken only by the tie-beams, and the frames in which the saws moved; and all the men might be seen, and their varied operations inspected, at a glance. It was a noisy, busy scene. Lamps hung on the fender-posts—lamps shaped like a coffee-pot, with a heavy coil of wicking in the spout, and producing so large a flame the wind could not blow it out; and the more it was attempted to be put down, the brighter it burned. But the lamp was provoking; it affected great nonchalance; it made feints of being beaten; it fell over from side to side; it treated the wind as a rope-dancer might treat his worst enemy, by capering on a slack wire, and jingling a tambourine in his face;

it was as insulting as a runaway monkey, that makes grimaces at his master from a chimney-top.

On one bed the men were butting; on another, hauling up the slip; on a third, dividing the logs by cross-cut saws; the creak of files, and the clink of iron bars, could be heard. The up-and-down saws sweltered, trembled, gnashed, hissed, as they made their way through the huge trunks before them. There was the piteous shriek of the cutting-off saw, and the unearthly rumbling of the wheels in the pit below. The rag-wheels patiently ticked, as it were time-keepers of the whole concern. The entire building, ponderous as were its beams and firm its foundation, seemed to throb and reel.

Richard was in a strange place, and among strange men, though he was at home in the business. There was not much talking, nor a very good opportunity for making acquaintance. The men were silent in the midst of the powerful agencies of nature and art; they were the silent Mind that wrought through these agencies.

Of the persons with whom Richard was associated, one, Mr. Gouch, the boss of the gang, was a middle-aged, middle-sized man, with a heavy face and a dull eye. He wore a white fur hat, of a very old fashion, — so old, indeed, it would be difficult to say when it was in fashion, — and which looked as if it had come down through all the fashions, and each of them had had a kick at it. He had on an antique surtout, with a very high waist, and an immense collar, riding the waist, as if it were the porter of a woollen factory. The lips of Mr. Gouch were large and rough, and kept up a constant twitching, as if affected with the shaking palsy. Not that he was a great talker; only his lips stirred, somewhat vacantly, somewhat timorously. Before he spoke, his lips moved, as it were getting ready for that effort; after he had spoken, his lips moved, as if the momentum of the effort did not immediately subside. Along with setting the gauge and minding the carry-back, another thing occupied a deal of his attention. This was the orders the mill had received, and which were nailed to the fender-post. Why did he dodge so around the corner of this post, and look at the schedule so often? Why did he point at it with his crow-bar? Why did his lips wag at such a rate, and all to himself? Why did he, from running the crow-bar over the list, like an overgrown lubber of a schoolboy, who uses his finger to fescue his eye from line to line, — why did he then jerk it towards his fellow-laborer, whose back was turned? Richard saw this farce, and was curious about it.

This other man seemed wholly indifferent to what was passing; he looked, indeed, more like a beast, who could not be affected by human interests, than anything else. He was short, and thick, and dark. His small cap, matted to his head, with its few filaments of fur, and its larger bare spots, did not look like a cap, but made him look as if he had a scrubby, stinted growth of hair. Running your eye down his person, you would imagine that his hair, deserting his scalp, had reappeared under his chin, and around his neck; for here it grew thick, bushy, luxuriant. He had no neck, apparently, but only a bed of hair, in which his head lay. He was not deformed, but he seemed to have grown, or been socketed, into himself; his hair grew into his head, his head into his neck, his neck into his shoulders, and his shoulders into his trunk. He wore a short frock, the ends of which were tied in a large knot on his back, as if it had something to do in keeping in place this singular structure that he was. His mouth, except in a strong light, was invisible; and then it opened and shut spasmodically, like a toad's; and then no teeth were seen, but a slight vacuum, filled with indistinguishable shapes; as one gets a glimpse through the fence at the charred stumps of new-burnt ground. Smoking was not allowed in the mill; but this man had a pipe in his mouth, whether he smoked or not. He would sometimes smoke of a winter night. This pipe, like the rest of him, had grown in, till there was nothing but the black bowl left. Ever in his mouth, it seemed to be a part of his organism; and he dipped his finger into the bowl as frequently when it was empty as when it was full. The name of this man was Silver.

Mr. Gouch, we have said, looked at Silver; but Silver did not mind it. Then Mr. Gouch read again the orders: "White, 4, hemlock 16, 7×9. Smith, 6, gray birch, 10, 3×12, Clover 9, plates, hemlock, 22, 6×8. Clover, joist, Clover, sills, Clover, furring." These things, from silently transcribing with his lips, he went on to articulating more distinctly, and finally spoke out quite loud. As he did so, he turned his face to Silver; and then, as it were, having caught the words on the end of his bar, he held that out for Silver to read; but Silver neither heard nor read.

During an interval when Silver was taking away the boards on one side of the carriage, and Mr. Gouch and Richard were at work with a cross-cut saw on the other, Mr. Gouch said, "He 'll get it! he 'll sweat!—he 's gone!"

"Who 'll get it?" asked Richard.

"He," replied Mr. Gouch, and thrust his head backwards towards Silver.

"Get what?"

"I tell you, Clover 'll build!" As he said this, he pushed the saw forwards, and leaned forwards himself, as if he were earnest that the communication should reach Richard. "Don't start so!" he said; "*you* are not concerned; you have just come; you need n't be frightened." Now, Richard could not conveniently help starting, since he held one end of the saw, and must needs retreat as the other advanced. Still Mr. Gouch kept operating the instrument, and endeavoring to impress certain truths on Richard. The first he did mechanically and skilfully; as to the last, he was in an absent state of mind, and continually blundered in the attempt to reconcile the ideal with the actual. "Don't be frightened," he said, as he again inclined towards Richard, who was again obliged to fall back. "I tell you, Clover 'll build; and he 'll get it," writhing towards Silver, "and we shall all get it! Plates, joist, sills and furring, — yes, furring, — that settles it, that does the business. *You* are not alarmed, I hope?"

"Why should I be?" replied Richard, laughing. "More work, more to do."

"Yes, more work; but how he will feel! how he will feel!"

"Capt. Creamer told me Clover was sick."

"Clover sick! The Captain done for, too! The Captain slabbed off, thrown among the reffige, flung into the river, like so much edging. And all through Clover. Clover sick! He is too strong to be sick. He would die before he would be sick."

"He may be sick, and die too," observed Richard.

"He can't die," returned Mr. Gouch; "you can't kill him. You might as well smite that saw with your fist; you might as well put a trig under the dam and stop it, as to practise on him."

They went to the stove for their lunch; and as they went, Mr. Gouch still muttered, "The furring fixes it; it will be a house. He 'll get it; Clover 'll build."

Silver said nothing, and Mr. Gouch said more, as if he would teaze Silver. In an instant, Silver seized the can-dog, and aimed at the head-stock man. Richard sprang between them, and Mr. Gouch fell backward over a log. Mr. Gouch laughed, and Silver snapped his lips together in a way that was intended to imply humor; and Richard, seeing that the demonstration was only a merry one, very quietly went to wooding up the stove. Mr. Gouch touched his fingers on the stove, to see how hot it was; then he applied them again, to see the hissing and crackling; and he at last got up a little cannonade, which he let off against Silver. Silver was not harmed, or cowarded. He knocked the ashes from his pipe, sliced a new charge of tobacco, ground it in the hollow of his hand, filled his pipe, and stooped to light it at the mouth of the stove. Mr. Gouch suffered quite a drop of water to explode close to Silver's ear, saying, "Haven't you got it? Won't Clover build?" Silver drew back, and groaned. He sat on the floor, and groaned. He made a few empty passes at the coals with his pipe, and thrust it, unlighted, into his lips, and groaned.

"He has got it!" said Mr. Gouch. "Did 'nt I tell you he would get it? Such quantities of furring! O, what a nice little house, and what a nice little bed-room, and what nice fixings!"

Silver took a pine stick and whittled it, sharpening and smoothing it. He then tried the point of it on the palm of his hand; then he pricked his cheek with it; then he made as if he would stab the stove and the saw.

"There will be family ways and family doings," continued Mr. Gouch, addressing Richard, who was quietly consuming his midnight meal; "and fires kindled where it is now bleak cold, and tables set for people that never ate together, and doors opening on new scenes and new operations. There will be another stopping-place along the street, and another yard to set flowers in; and by and by there will be children, and little ones will climb on their father's knee, and that father will be Clover; and little ones for the mother to put to sleep, and that mother will be ——"

Silver shrieked not out, but inside, and only a smothered explosion was heard. He thrust his stick wildly into the air.

"Don't do that!" said Mr. Gouch; "don't hurt Clover; don't attempt Clover; don't do anything to him!"

"It is not that," rejoined Silver; "it's myself."

He again tried to light his pipe, and now he was successful; and he sucked and whiffed, as if he would evaporate his sorrows, thoughts, and whole being, in the smoke.

"Clover'll build, and it is your treat," said the head-stock man; "and you need not take it so hardly; a couple of dimes will hardly be missed."

Silver blew the smoke from him, as much as to say, "That is nothing; I do not care for that." He sprang up with an air which seemed to add, "Bring on the boys! I am ready to treat."

The two men from the other saw came towards the stove. One of them advanced in a jaunty, tambourine sort of way, appearing to be playing on an invisible instrument of that kind with his elbow and knuckles, and shuffling to the tune with his feet. A red handkerchief was tied flauntingly on his head, and his waist was buttoned with a leathern strap. He was lively and talkative, and his name was Philemon Sweetly. "Pleasantly cold, Mr. Gouch," said he; "just enough to make a stove, ordinarily so dull, a very agreeable companion."

"An Indian could n't stand it," replied Mr. Gouch, rather solemnly; "a frog would freeze, a barn would be out of its element."

"I hope," rejoined Philemon, "the cold will bear kind of

strong on the Captain; just hold him down softly, freeze him gently, so he will not feel it, and let Helskill out. It is a precious night for Helskill; he deserves such a night, now and then."

"How is Clover, to-day?" asked Ezra Bess, the fourth man.

"Better," replied Mr. Gouch; "and Silver will be generous, — all gold, perhaps."

"That for Clover," added Philemon, heaving the hand-spike across the mill-bed; "Helskill is wanted just now."

At this instant, a man was seen entering the mill, and making his way stealthily through the shadows, as if he were afraid he might tread on them. And when a roistering lamp flared in his face, he started like a very polite man who had intruded too suddenly upon the light. He had on his arm a basket, over which he exercised incessant watchfulness, like a mother bringing her daughter into company. He had a broad, dark face, and eyebrows to match, and black eyes; but a timid look, — a remarkably timid, and almost slippery look; and a stooping gait, like one who has the misfortune to be continually seeing obstacles in his path. He signalized his progress, also, by a cough, — a small, hacking cough, — as a modest token of admonition to any one against whom he might come in the dark.

The approach of this man was regarded with interest by the gang.

"The Friend of the People is assiduous and devoted as ever," said Philemon, affecting a bow to the new-comer. "Shall I have the honor of introducing to you, Richard, Mr. Helskill, the Friend of the People?"

"I am the Friend of the People," replied the other, evidently brightening up and re-collecting his courage, in the cordiality with which he was received; "I look after the public good: I vote for it at the polls; I canvass for it before election; I harness my horse, and go in pursuit of it; I bleed for it, — yes, I do, — my purse bleeds, and my heart bleeds, to see how it is abused; I attend to it, in my own little way, at Quiet Arbor;" — he was still timid, and cast his eyes from side to side, but he waxed bolder as he went on: — "I am an advocate of the people: I defend their rights; I teach them their independence; I stand between them and monopoly; I take the brunt of oppression; I believe that men *are* to be trusted, — that they *have* discretion."

"Desput cold!" said Philemon, who, using the liberty which the timid man scattered broadcast around him, lifted the cover of the basket, and took from it a brace of bottles and glasses; — "but you are the chap for it. You must have been born in a bog, and nussed on cucumber juice. That was economical. When you was eight years old, your father sent you out barefoot in winter to catch titmice for poor people's breakfast. So you learned benevolence. A thermometer would have no effect on you; the mercury might plump down into the bottom and freeze, — you would n't mind it; you would buzz around your little Arbor, as chirk and bobbish as a fly in spring-time. And how, when it grew late, and your friends became tired and sleepy, and wanted to lie down, you would put them out of doors, using a little force, just to teach them self-denial! Why, you are equal to Captain Creamer, — you are the Captain! Has n't your wife a receipt for cold weather? You might send it South, and they could get up a little ice for their juleps, and kill off the yellow fever, now and then. You would n't do for a Methodist church, just now. You might answer for some other in town; they could set you up cheap, and you could do so much good! You love to do good, don't you?"

Men from all parts of the mill, having a respite from

their work, collected around Mr. Helskill, who seemed to be quite a centre of attraction.

"I knew he would come," said Mr. Merlew, head-stock man of saw No. 5, a burly, hulchy looking man; "he sticks to his word like a bail-dog to a log. He does n't mind the coldest night, any more than No. 5 does the knots of white hemlock."

"No. 5, No. 5," said Philemon, who was head-stock man of No. 2, "will want a little oiling; will be very thankful to the Friend of the People for a little help; will rejoice in the opportune kindness of that man, or I am mistaken."

The Friend of the People coughed, blushed, and looked down. So embarrassed was he by these compliments, he did not perceive that his glasses had escaped, and his bottles were being emptied, while the men were secretly trying the quality of his wares.

Mr. Gouch, meanwhile, with a medley of playfulness and timorousness, simplicity and cunning, slid to the door of the mill and looked out; hopped over the lumbered floor back again, and slapped the stove with his wet fingers, chattering to himself, "The Captain won't come; he can't come to-night. Clover *will* build; Silver 'll treat; he won't be happy, if he does n't." Silver muddled with his pipe among the ashes. Richard leisurely hacked the end of a log.

"The honor is Silver's to-night," said Philemon to Richard, holding a glass in his hand. "It is his to give merit an opportunity to distinguish itself, and to open to the Friend of the People a sphere of action. This ordinarily falls to the new comer; it should have been yours, as you are in that capacity; but it is Silver's to-night."

"I am truly obliged to you, Silver," said Mr. Helskill, making an effort to show his teeth, as if there resided in them a particularly pleasing and grateful expression, which he was anxious to communicate; "you must be a happy man."

Silver hurled a chip at the timid man's head, which he dodged, but manifested no indignation thereat. "Don't grin at me!" Silver added, very groutily.

"I must have declined the honor," replied Richard to Philemon; "and I think Silver has no satisfaction in doing it."

"But you will drink?" returned Philemon, tendering him a glass.

"I think I will not," said Richard.

"Drink!" growled Silver, with a quick, deep intonation.

"The laws of the mill forbid drinking, and the law of conscience forbids it," added Richard.

"Clover 'll build!" Mr. Gouch's lips began muttering. This was a magical word; it worked Silver to a frenzy; though Mr. Gouch certainly had no ill intents on his brother stock-man.

"You shall drink! you shall all drink!" screamed Silver, starting up.

"I am not afraid of Clover, and Clover shall not hurt you," said Richard.

Silver grew more quiet, and sat down to his pipe, saying, "Drink, Richard, only drink!"

"There is mischief here," said Richard, "and I do not understand it. And there is more mischief here, and I do understand it: and it is there; it is that man," — pointing to Mr. Helskill.

"I hope the young fellow don't accuse me of mischief," replied Mr. Helskill, picking up his bottles.

"You need n't hope anything about it," said Richard. "You may know; you may be assured."

"Well, accuse me of mischief!"

"I did n't accuse you of anything, and I do not. I said you *were* mischief; and you are! You are deviltry incarnate, and your stuff is the same incarnadined!"

"Not so fast," interposed Philemon.

"There is no time to be slower," answered Richard. "Our lunch is out; and we are here to work, not play."

"They would put on the screws," said Mr. Merlew; "they would make nigger-wheels of us, if they could, and keep us always at it; they would like to see us saw-dust under their feet!"

"There is no harm in fun," said Philemon. "Must spree it, these tremendous nights."

"Not a drop, friends, not a drop," replied Richard.

"He is no Friend of the People," observed Mr. Helskill; "he is a flinty and tyrannical character. I have seen such before. I have repelled their malicious attempts; I have defeated their mean operations; I have sacrificed a good deal to put them down."

"You are a very direct and unequivocal scamp!" said Richard.

"Drink, for my sake!" said Silver.

"I cannot drink," answered Richard.

"He is an unfeeling brute," observed Mr. Helskill. "I left my warm Arbor; I exposed myself to the weather. I knew I had comfort for you; I knew you needed it; I knew Silver wanted me to come. I defied the infamous statute; I ran the risk of falling into the hands of some skulking informer, and I have fallen into his hands, — I have fallen."

"I am no skulker," said Richard; "I am open-placed, and open-tongued. I will not inform against you elsewhere; I will tell you to your face what you are, and what you do. You bring in mischief here; you bring in fightings, ill-will, neglect of work; you bring in sickness and disease;

you come a good ways to do it; you brave the coldest night of the year to do it; you are desperate in the business; you would send these men drunk from the mill; you would drive them into a snow-bank to die; you would pitch them, reeling and staggering, into their own homes! Off with you, — off!"

"Presently, presently," said Mr. Helskill. "Alvin shall have his glass. Alvin shall have the ague taken out of his fingers." He inclined the bottle towards the person whose name he called.

"Alvin shall not drink!" replied Richard. "Alvin is a boy. He is too young to like it, and too old to be spoilt."

Mr. Helskill persisted. Richard, quite aroused, with a handspike, dashed the bottle to atoms. Carried forward by the impulse, he descended upon the other bottle, and treated it to the same end; and then, seizing the basket in which these things had been borne, he hurled it towards the door.

The confusion of this scene was heightened by what immediately followed. The basket, in its rapid transit, alighted in the face of a person entering the mill. It was Captain Creamer. Already agitated by what he overheard as he approached the building, he was exceedingly inflamed by this latter piece of impertinence. He blustered amongst the men in a way that boded no good to any of them.

"Don't *say* you did n't drink!" whispered earnestly Silver to Richard, as he saw the Captain approaching; "for my sake, don't *say* you did n't!"

The hands belonging to the other saws fled to their respective posts. The Friend of the People, already disheartened by the manner in which his intentions were received, had made an early exit. The Captain's own gang stood alone before him.

Captain Creamer could not find words to express his astonishment, his grief, his anger; and he was silent. At length, composing himself sufficiently to speak, he charged the men with violating the rules of Green Mill — their own promises, and duty. He enlarged upon the danger to which they were exposing themselves, and particularly on the risk to which the mill was subjected. "Mr. Gouch," he said, "my head-stock man, my trusty servant, I had not expected this."

"Clover 'll build —" began Mr. Gouch.

"Don't name Clover to me!" retorted the Captain. "I am not afraid of Clover; Clover does n't rule here. Who threw that basket at me?"

"I threw it," answered Richard; "but I did not intend to hit any one; I did not see you."

"Drinking! In liquor! Did not know what you were about! Could not discern an object of my size! I made no impression on you!"

"I cannot explain," said Richard. "I can say nothing about it."

"I presume you cannot," answered the Captain.

"Hoist the gate, Mr. Gouch! You will work an hour longer for this. In justice, I could demand more; I shall accept of that. I have suspected all was not right; I have had intimations of your doings. The mill is jeopardized, the whole corporation is jeopardized, by your conduct. Frightful as is the cold, I left my bed to look after you."

The men resumed their duties; the Captain, reädjusting himself in his bear-skin coat, strutted to and fro across the gangway.

Not many minutes after, approaching the door, he called to Richard, and pointing to an angle of the road in front of the mill, he said, "I see something stirring yonder. Be spry and easy; catch it, — do not let it escape!"

Richard, approaching the mysterious object, found it to be a man filling a basket with waste bits of wood. He trod catlike, and seized the man firmly by the collar. The latter dropped a stick he had in his hand, and fell back passively on Richard's knees. The Captain leaped forward, saying, "Hold on!" and also fastened himself to the culprit, who in a low voice replied,

"I did n't succeed, did I? Don't hurt me!"

"He is shamming," rejoined the Captain. "Let him not give us the slip."

They dragged him to the mill. The light revealed the face of an old man, thin and gray. He was shaking with the cold.

"Shut down," said the Captain to Mr. Gouch; "there are other matters to attend to. We have missed things from the mill; an entire pile of stuff has been carried off; — odd ends, to be sure, but such as there is market for, and without which the mill could not live, — nay, it could n't stand a day. I think we have got the knave."

"It is an old man," said Mr. Gouch.

"Old, is he?" asked the Captain, who had not noticed this feature of the case. "Too old to be stealing; too old to be in such bad business as this; too old to set such an example."

"Who would do it but me?" answered the ancient; "who but Grandfather? Who would get a pitch-knot in the cold, and the dark, that *they* might see the blaze, — that the young folks might be gladdened? I am not old, and they will see I am not." This was said with a sort of doting chuckle.

"What shall we do with him?" inquired the Captain.

"I would let him go," said Richard.

"Do you mean to insult me again, young man?" asked the Captain. "Has neither your own conduct nor my forbearance taught you decency?"

"I think the chips would do the man more good than he can do us harm," observed Philemon; "and I would not proceed against him."

"Who asked what you would do, Mr. Sweetly?" responded the Captain.

"You did, sir," answered Philemon.

"I asked what we should do with this criminal. I did not ask after your private sentiments. The world is full of them; we have enough of them. I have not been at all this pains to find them out."

"I replied to your question, sir, the best way I knew how."

"Call you that doing with the man? — to let him go — to take no notice of what he has done, — to set this villany at large?"

"Suppose we duck him in the canal," said Ezra, "then hang him on the jack-pole to dry."

"Don't do that," said the old man. "I could n't live through it. I have n't long to live; but I want to see the children in a better way before I die."

"If I could shake him, I would," said the Captain, and endeavored to suit the action to the word, but the garment on which he seized parted in his hand; — "but I do not like to take the law into my own hands; I should prefer bringing him before a justice. I shall enter a complaint, in the morning."

"He may abscond, in the mean time," suggested Ezra.

"Some one must stay with him," observed the Captain, directing an inquiring eye to his men.

"I will not," said Philemon.

"Nor I," added Ezra.

Silver was brooding over the fire, munching his pipe, and would not answer.

"It is no part of a head-stock man's duty," evasively replied Mr. Gouch.

"You will do it, Richard," said the Captain, "and I may think better of you."

"I will," replied Richard.

"Watch him close," enjoined the Captain, hooking Richard's arm in that of the old man. "He will be called for about ten o'clock in the morning."

Having given a right direction to the affairs of justice, he turned to the business of the mill.

The cold had increased. Midnight seemed to be gathering itself up for a final plunge upon the morning. The old man shook on Richard's arm.

"You are cold," said Richard.

"They are," replied the other.

"They need the wood?" continued Richard.

"I thought they did," rejoined the old man. "They seemed to. It may have been fancy; perhaps it was a dream. I get confused in my head, I have so much to do; and it seems sometimes as if I was all a dream."

"They shall have it," said Richard, with emphasis.

"It is too late now. It is over. I never thought I should do that. I never thought we should come to that; but a little blaze is so pretty. God's will be done!"

"I will pay for it," said Richard. "There shall be no trouble on that score." He went to the spot where the basket lay, which he filled; and giving the old man one handle, and taking the other himself, he suffered his attendant to lead the way whither he would go. This was in the direction of the Factory Boarding Houses. Richard inquired after the necessity of the fuel he was so unseasonably supplying, as a clue to the crime over which he was so strangely made sentry. He gathered from the old man that two girls, his grandchildren, had come to work in the Factories, and he had accompanied them; that one of them was sick, and the other lay exhausted at the bedside; that their means were short, and while the girls slept, he had slipped away for the wood.

As they reached the steps of the house, the voice of Captain Creamer was heard close behind.

"What does this mean?" he asked, angrily. "Have I set a thief to watch a thief? Through your means, young man, is the very thing consummated which I have wasted a whole night to prevent?"

Richard explained; — the Captain was not propitiated. Richard offered to deduct the value of the wood from his wages. How little did he understand Captain Creamer!

"The value of the wood! A basket of chips!" The Captain spurned the thought. "It was the wrong that affected him," he said; "the bad beginning of a young man." However, he could not easily reverse the course of events, and these accomplices in crime were permitted to enter the house with their ill-boding freight.

Richard followed his guide up stairs to a chamber under the roof, in the third story. A lamp in an angle of the chimney cast a shadow over the room, and faintly revealed the forms of the two girls on the bed. Weariness had folded the well one, and an opiate the sick one, in deep slumber; and they were not aroused at the entrance of Richard and his guide.

"We had better not try to make a fire," said Richard; "the room is not very cold, and the hearth is warm."

"A few shavings," whispered the old man; "just a little blaze. Junia loves to see a blaze. It is a comfort to her. And when t' other is gone, and I am gone, — and that will be soon, — there will only be a little blaze, and the memory of it, in all this cold world, for her to look upon." Richard drew some shavings from the basket, and soon had them lighted. In the flickering glare which they cast over the room, the old man looked and acted a little strangely, betraying a singular medley of imbecility, pathos and joy. He leaned over the bed with a deep and passionate interest. Then turning to Richard, with a playful, but sad infatuation, he pointed to the sleepers, and whispered, "That one, the sick one, the one with morning hair, — her child's hair, — is Violet. The other, with the evening hair, — she was born in the evening, and there are stars in her soul, — is Junia. Who called her Violet? I remember, her mother did, because she was born in spring, when violets blow. And she will die in the spring; it was then her mother died; she will die when the birds begin to come, and the weather is soft. If she could live then! But she had better not die *now*. God's will be done! I know it was spring, for I was sitting on the bank with the other when the nurse came. We called the other Junia, because she was born in June; and there is more summer in her; she is riper, and stronger, and can bear up better; and she is full of warmth and pretty life; her hair is darker, — they said it was then, and it is now, — and she was always amongst us like the smooth meadow, and her eye came into your heart like noon under the shady trees. I remember it; I have a strong memory, — a very strong memory. I remember a great many more things than I used to when I was a young man. This one was more tender, more frail, as the wind-flowers; she never seemed to get stronger, and we made a lamb of her. She hung like dew upon all of us, and all our feelings, — so her mother said, — only we knew she must go soon; and when the buds begin to burst, she will die. God's will be done!"

There was too much tenderness in the old man, too many cherished though bitter and confused reminiscences, too much vague but corroding sorrow, for Richard not to be touched. He was silent and reflective; and his whole spirit was concentrated on the beauty and the sadness that slumbered before him, and the unwearied, tottering affection that stood by the side of it.

Junia awoke, and, somewhat startled, said, "What is it, Grandfather? Has the doctor come?"

"Nothing has happened, dear," replied the Grandfather.

"I have no business here," said Richard.

"Yes, you have, — you know you have," answered the old man. "You cannot go."

"Let me make more fire," rejoined Richard.

"Where did the wood come from?" asked Junia, approaching the hearth.

"He brought it," replied her Grandfather, pointing to Richard.

"We are obliged to you," Junia said; "but so cold, — so late in the night —"

There was a mystery about the wood, which neither of them was ready to explain.

"Have you suffered much?" asked Richard.

"Yes," replied Junia, "we do, for Grandfather's sake."

"Have you suffered from cold?"

"Not much, — not long. Violet feels it sometimes."

"What is her sickness?"

"She was always slender, and after our father and mother died, she went to keeping school; but this was too much for her, and she had an attack of bleeding. One of our neighbors told us how strong her girls had become in the

Factories; and we must earn something — and we came here. She was better for a while; but she is worse now, — very bad, indeed. We are troubled that Grandfather should exert himself so much."

"They do not know me," said the old man, a good deal agitated; "they do not know how able I am, — how much I can endure. They do not mean I shall know how weak they are; they would keep it from me; they think it worries me. But they cannot hide it, and I know she will die when the season changes; — her mother did. I could have got wood alone."

"Did you go out for the wood, Grandfather?" asked Junia, with surprise.

"I helped him," said Richard, who wished to change that subject. "We will have a nice fire;" and he put on more chips and butts. He felt that his presence must be embarrassing; he knew that the matter of the wood was so; and he said, rising from his chair, "If there is anything I can do for you, I shall be glad to do it." "We are under obligations to you," Junia replied; "but we are not in need of anything." Richard advanced towards the door; but the old man laid hands upon him, led him to his chair, adding that he must stay.

"If Grandfather wishes it, — if it will make him happier, — we shall be glad to have you stay," said Junia.

Richard was bound to Capt. Creamer, and to the law, and to his own promise, to stay; and since he could not explain the real cause of his coming and staying, he said nothing.

"All for Grandfather!" The old man leaned forward, with both elbows on his spread knees, rubbing his hands before the fire, and repeated, with a dry laugh, "All for Grandfather! They do not know it was all for them, and that it has come to this all for them; God's will be done!"

"Tell me what has happened," said Junia, with an anxious tone.

"Nothing," said Richard, "nothing to speak of now. Your Grandfather was afraid you might suffer; and you will suffer if you do not keep quiet. Your sister is waking."

"Will God take care of us?" she asked.

"He will," answered Richard, solemnly; "and to God let us trust all things."

Richard's manner was so kind, and his words so soothing, that Junia, even if her heart had begun to work with some inexplicable evil, regained her composure, and said "I will," and went to the bedside. She raised her sister, and laid pillows under her head. The golden hair of the invalid, beneath her white cap, and above her pale, delicate face, was like a glowing cloud in the clear sky, and her blue eye beamed deep and far, like the sea beneath. "That is Grandfather's friend," said Junia to her. "Yes, my friend, dear, my friend," echoed the old man. "His name is Richard."

Violet nodded, and smiled a faint recognition to the stranger.

"Have you none to help you?" asked Richard. "Are there none in the house to take turns with you nights?"

"There is a number of girls," replied Junia, "but there has been a good deal of sickness this winter, and they have been called out often, and broken of their rest. Those that have strength and leisure are devoting it to Miss Eyre, getting her ready to be married. She is to be married to Clover, — you may know him; a Mr. Clover, who works at the Saw-mills, — and they say Clover will build, and that he expects to put up a fine house, and to live in style; and the girls are exerting themselves for Plumy Alicia. She is a fascinating girl, and has many friends; but I think she never liked us very well, and I suppose we get less attention, at this time, on that account. But so long as I have any force left, I can do without their assistance."

Richard felt another singular, strong twinge. The name that haunted the Green Mill had got into this sick chamber; that man, whom he had never seen, and never until to-day heard of, seemed to be chasing him like an evil or a mocking genius.

"We have had wood until to-night," continued Junia.

The mention of the wood troubled Richard, as he knew it did the Grandfather. He would have rushed out doors; but that would not help matters within. He struggled with himself, arresting the natural train of association, and repressing all sense of the strange complexity that surrounded him, and became calm.

The invalid, wasting under a seated pulmonary attack, coughed at intervals, breathed heavily, nor could she help disclosing the pains that invaded her frame.

"When the weather changes," the old man maundered, — "when the warm days come, when the violets sprout —"

Junia, tranquil as was her manner, lightly as she discharged the offices of the sick room, inured as she had become to the mournful chant of her Grandfather, and to the still sadder presages of her own mind, could not resist the perpetual sorrow that as a storm beat against her breast, and she wept.

"Have you no friends in the city?" asked Richard. "None," she said. "Has no clergyman been to see you?" "Not any." "Have no prayers been made here?" "Many, many," she said. "We have all prayed."

"Do you ever pray?" inquired the old man.

"Yes," replied Richard.

"Young men do not pray as they used to," rejoined the

elder. "In my day, they prayed. God was all about us, and our spirits were lively and growing; and the angels took prayers from us, as the bees and humming-birds draw honey from the flowers. The young men are getting old, very old, and dry, and blasted. I am young, — ha, ha!"

"I should like to have him pray," said the sick one.

Richard read the twenty-third Psalm, in its motion so full of spiritual and halcyon-like wafture, in its feeling so fervid, trustful and joyous; — and prayed. He collected into one earnest, sympathetic utterance, before God, the hopes and the fears, the anguish and the aspirations, of the hour.

The night waned. The Mill bells rang early, sharp, and clear; all parts of the house resounded with the clatter of the rising and the departing, of Work resuming its sandals, and going forth to its pilgrim's progress for the day. Some of the girls looked into the chamber, to inquire after the patient, and hasted away.

The landlady entered with a tray, furnished with such articles of food or nourishment as the invalid might require. She wore glasses, and had a gingham handkerchief thrown over her head, under which any quantity of grizzly hair struggled into view. She cast her eyes over her glasses twice at Richard, — once as she passed him towards the bed, and next when she had reached the bed. Addressing Junia and the old man, she said, "Breakfast is waiting." Did she intend, thought Richard, they should take their meal from the tray? She did not mean that, and they did not understand her to mean that. She meant that their breakfast was ready below. "Strangers are to be reported," she added; "that is the rule of the large boarding-houses, — front stairs carpeted, and Ladies' Parlor, — as one might see when they came up, and not act here as Charley Walter did. Perhaps he did n't know 't was Whichcomb's, — seeing he come in the night, — and thought it was Cain's, where they don't keep any hours; if they did, they would stop, some time or other, boiling their knucks. Velzora Ann Felty would cry when I spoke about it, and the things no more touched on her plate than if she had been at Cain's."

Both Junia and the old man said they did not wish for breakfast; and certainly that was the last thing Richard thought of. Junia took charge of what had been brought for Violet, and the landlady remained in the room only long enough to reconnoitre the person and purpose of Richard. "A cousin, Miss Junia?" "No," replied Junia. "Came in the night? — an old friend?" "A friend," answered Richard. "Been here all night — but I shall not be hard with you; the girls have their wills and ways, — I shall not provoke them." She retreated through the door.

Presently Mrs. Whichcomb returned for the tray, and to recover such portion of its contents as were not otherwise disposed of. Richard, who wished to communicate with the head of the house touching his rather equivocal and very unexpected entry into it, followed as she left the room.

He found her descending the stairs, and combining with each step a nod of the head, and an ejaculation of the numerals, as if the three things timed each other. "One, *two*, great plate, little plate; three, four, five, *six*, knife, fork, tea-spoon, and little jelly-spoon. Six, *six! little jelly-spoon;* gone!" She stopped, and looked back up the stairs, to see if she had miscounted a step. She beheld Richard watching her from above.

"O!" said she, "I was just thinking of you. No relation, — only a friend. Do you know your friends? — do you know them?" Richard replied that he had never seen them before that night. "I dare say," answered the woman.

"It is so in all the first-class houses, which Charley Walter knew all about it, for he pigged a month at Cain's, where they are all in a muss. And Velzora Ann Felty could n't have known it, for she was sick. Sickness is a bad thing in a house. I had rather have ten well persons than one sick, at any time." Richard observed it was not strange she should. "There is a great deal of viciousness in sickness; — vice brings it on." Richard said there was truth in that remark. "The eating and drinking is nothing, — they are welcome to the sugar, and jelly, and cream, — but when it comes to the things themselves that one depends on to get along at all, and purloining and putting out of the way, which our extra time does not deserve, it is too much. Many people are sick to gratify their wicked propensities. You may not know it and would not say so." Richard was silent. He did not know it, and he could not say so. "They take to their beds for the sake of being waited on; they linger along, that they may have more opportunities for imposing on the house; and they go to their graves with silver spoons in their hands!" This climax was awful, and the landlady felt it to be so; she staggered under the load of her conceptions, and would have fallen if the balustrade had not been a strong one.

It would have helped Richard to be put in possession of certain particulars relating to this woman. A catastrophe once came off in her house, from which she never entirely recovered. It was known as the Charley Walter affair, or the Velzora Ann Felty affair. This tinged her mind. She referred to it when she was speaking of other things, — she thought of it even when she was thinking of other things. It was a rock in the current of her being, around which her feelings perpetually eddied. In addition, she hated Cain's, a contiguous boarding-house. And, what was most remote from Richard's thoughts at the moment, she was anxious about her property.

But Richard, who was simply solicitous to be disencumbered of his confused feelings, and to unfold to the landlady the nature of his position, and why he was in the house, disgusted at her manner, returned to the chamber.

The officers would soon be there; the secret would be forthcoming, do what he might. The more he saw of Junia, the more he was assured of her true womanliness, and her capability of encountering evil; he stifled his repugnance to giving her pain, and resolved to acquaint her with the simple state of the case. Taking her one side, he related what had befallen in the night; how her grandfather was detected in theft, and he was appointed to watch him. He doubted if the old man would be convicted, though he did not know what Captain Creamer might be able to do.

In the mean time, he would take an instant and run to his brother's, that they might not be alarmed at his long absence. Returning forthwith, he encountered on the stairs the Captain, the City Constable, who was knocking at the door of the sick room, the landlady, and several others, women and girls, whom he did not know. "Out," said the Captain to him; "but is the old man *in?*" He said this with a violent glance at Richard, which he meant to be ungracious and stinging, and which should sever the young man in twain. Richard made no reply. The door did not open, and the Constable rapped again. He wished to be civil. He held his ear against it, to hear if it manifested any signs of relenting. He then looked hard at the door, as much as to say, "I give you a minute; and if you do not open, I shall break in."

The lips of this functionary were tightly compressed, and

his eye was vacant and dreamy; he did not notice the crowd that was about him; he did not feel the boys that, in their eagerness to be in with the foremost, trod on his heels. Klumpp was a man of one idea, and exactly suited to a painful or disagreeable duty. Nothing would prevent his arriving at his main object; nothing extraneous could divert his mind or mislead his steps. He had recently been elected to office; he felt his inexperience, but he wished to be faithful; he had often heard of the tap on the shoulder, and the look in the eye, and the whispered "Come with me;" he had seen the thing done, when he was a boy, and he had heard the old constable describe how he treated desperate offenders to it, and there was something magical in that tap, and that look, and that whisper; and he was now the magician himself, and he wished to conjure not only with success, but with dignity. Hence the uneasy, abstract way he had. The mercury, even now, stood nearly at zero, but he did not notice it; and when Mrs. Whichcomb spurted out her innuendoes, he did not notice her.

The mistress of the house had exchanged the gingham handkerchief for a black-bordered cap. She wiped her face with her apron, and leered at Richard. Her long, scant fore teeth, that looked like wheel-cogs, seconded the endeavor of her lips, and conveyed an expression of very vulgar satisfaction. Her manner betokened great intimacy with Richard, great understanding of his humor, great insight into what she knew would be his feelings on the occasion. "The world always turns out just about as we calculate," she said; "the world cannot deceive us long. He would not believe it, when I told him. But 't is worse, now. Was there any stealing, then?—ha! ha!" She laughed,—she giggled. "Miss Eyre, this is the young man that can tell about it. Have you examined your trunks and drawers, girls? I have heard Plumy Alicia say, says she, 'It was so,' says she. Ha! ha!"

A young lady in the crowd, whom this last observation seemed to arouse, and to whom it was directed, raised her hand, and shook her head, as if she would hush Mrs. Whichcomb, at the same time suffusing her face with blushes, that might have aroused the attention of anybody else.

This must be Miss Plumy Alicia Eyre, thought Richard; and he turned to look at her; and having looked once, he looked again. She was worth looking at, and she seemed even to exact an involuntary regard. She blushed, but in such a way as to make you blush, and then to set you to looking at her to see why she made you blush. So Richard found himself looking at her.

She was of good proportions, and of a suggestive and energetic countenance. Her hair was elaborated into streaming ringlets and flowing plaits. There were showy hoops in her ears, and glancing rings on her fingers. She had what are termed speaking eyes, — eyes full of animation, and brightness, and deliciousness, — and a pair of splendid dimples. Plumy Alicia, — we call her by the only species of titular abridgment she tolerated, — Plumy Alicia had no previous designs on Richard; but when he looked so earnestly at her, when he seemed so deeply interested in her, when she saw his handsome figure, and his intelligent face, some design took root in her. We do her no injustice in saying this, for it was evident to all who saw her; and her own conscience, if it were questioned, would have confessed it. But she had no time to pursue her arts, for the attention and person of Richard were called to other things.

Klumpp got into the room; but he did not see that it was a sick room, nor that one lay emaciated on the bed and another sobbing near her; nor that the old man sat bending over both of them, with their arms about his neck. He only saw the old man, and the white arms — the arms lying between him and the magical tap — interfering with Justice and Crime. Klumpp undid the arms, and executed the tap, and then drew back to see the effect. The old man did not stir. Klumpp then approached, and whispered the cabalistic words in his ear, "Come with me!" Still the old man moved not. He then raised him up, and looked in his eye. The eye did it. The old man went; and it was soon rumored, in all taverns and stables, and all lairs of boys and boyish men, what an eye Klumpp had; and everybody began to be afraid of Klumpp's eye.

The old man went to his trial. Richard, a leading witness, must of course go too. He fell in with the crowd that dogged the steps of Justice. The seat of judgment was the office of Benjamin Dennington, Esq., the Governor's son, — or Squire Benjamin, as he was called, — before whom the complaint was brought.

Captain Creamer testified to such facts as are in possession of the reader. It was a plain case, and the prisoner might as well have confessed his guilt; which in effect, though not in words, he did do. But what coloring would the facts bear? This was the important question, and the judge felt it to be so. Squire Benjamin reverenced justice, and he loved mercy. Richard spoke of some things that the Captain did not know. He alluded to the imbecility of the old man, to his affection for his grandchildren, to the straitened circumstances of the family, to the sick one, to the devoted Junia. Squire Benjamin had sisters, and his sympathies, — dangerous things in a judge! — were stirred. The Captain saw the danger to his cause, and exploded on the necessity of justice, strict justice, and of quelling the dangerous temper of the times. Richard was again questioned. He not only answered what was put to him; he enlarged on the subject; he glowed in depicting the extenuating circumstances; he was even eloquent in his enumeration of the several points of interest. The prisoner was acquitted with a reprimand.

CHAPTER V.

BIOGRAPHICAL.

Richard Edney was born of worthy parents, in an interior town of the state. Three things — the Family, the School, and the Church — contributed to the formation of his mind and development of his character. To the first, he owed his gentler feelings; to the second, his elementary knowledge; the last aroused his deeper thought, and determined his spiritual direction. He borrowed books from the village library, and newspapers from the postmaster, and had the reading of a weekly paper at his father's table. A debating club, maintained by the young men of the place, in which the topics of the times were discussed, aroused his invention, enlivened his wit, and while it inured him to habits of investigation, it directed him to some solid acquisition. At the Academy, he studied the ordinary compends of philosophy and history, and even made a slight attempt on the Latin tongue. Nor should it be forgotten that the reading-books in our common schools, comprising select pieces from the best authors, exert a permanent effect on the scholar, correcting the taste and enriching the imagination, affording at the same time many admirable sentiments, and suggesting some profound thought.

Besides, Richard enjoyed the ministrations of an excellent clergyman, a man of refined culture and earnest piety. Settled in a rural district, the recreations of this gentleman were gardening, fishing, hunting. In this way, he was able to pursue more satisfactorily his parochial duties, since in the fields most of his people found occupation, while in the woods some prosecuted their lumbering operations, and on the streams lay their mills. In these rambles, the youth of the parish sometimes joined their pastor; and no one was more happy to be thus associated than the lad who forms the leading character of this story. Richard was thus introduced to Nature. He conversed with the phenomena of creation; he learned the distinctions and varieties of the animate and inanimate world; his sense of the beautiful was heightened, and his love of being in general, to quote a phrase of the Schools, was developed.

Pastor Harold was not a Christian alone in doctrine and discourse; he aimed to be such in works. He believed that Christianity was designed to redeem mankind, and that the Church was a chosen instrument of this redemption. He sought to develop within the Church an Operative Philanthropy; and this principle he applied wherever it could subserve its great end. The evening religious meetings he divided into several sorts. In addition to what the Gospel could do for their souls, he urged it as a serious point upon his people, what it would make them do for others. In furtherance of this plan, different evenings were assigned to different subjects: one to Intemperance; one to War; another to Slavery; a fourth to Poverty: and the enumeration went on till it comprised the entire routine of Practical Christianity. He called these meetings the Church Militant; and any particular meeting was appointed as a Conference of the Church. At these Conferences, tracts, newspapers, circulars, that are apt to cumber a minister's study, were distributed, and the specific charities of the Church more wisely and easily apportioned. These meetings were of service to Richard; he gained thereby much valuable information, and was led to a clearer understanding, and a more vital impression, of his duties and responsibilities. He had access to his Pastor's library, and in some sense to his heart; so that in many forms he shared largely in that renovating, spiritualizing, and exalting influence, which this good man, from the pulpit, the fields, the evening meeting, and his study, shed over the town.

In the Sunday-school he learned the rudiments of the Gospel; in the services of the sanctuary he was carried through a still deeper religious experience; and the sermons to which he listened, and the prayers in which he engaged, brought him into nearer communion with the Father of spirits, and confirmed his progress in the Divine life.

It became not only the motto on the wall of his chamber, but the deeper aspiration of his heart, To BE GOOD, AND TO DO GOOD.

Yet his forte was rather physical than intellectual. He did not go to college, and adopt one of the learned professions; partly, indeed, by reason of pecuniary impediments. He had no desire to enter a store, and embark his all on the frail but exciting bottom of commercial avocation. His ambition was to be a thorough and upright mechanic. Manual labor pleased him; and he was skilled in many forms of it. His father, besides a farm, carried on a saw-mill, to both of which he trained his son. A well-regulated farm demands mechanical care, and is an ample field for the employment of mechanical genius; as, indeed, it furnishes scope for the exercise of almost every faculty of the human mind. Richard had spent one winter amongst the head-waters of the River, lumbering.

Suretyship, or loss of crops, or whatever it might be, excepting that it was no vice of his own, troubled his father in lifting the mortgage that had lain many years on his farm. One or two instalments were still due; — they were due the Governor, of whom the original purchase was made; and Richard came to Woodylin partly for the purpose of earning the requisite sum. He came, also, with the desire, not uncommon in the youthful breast, of seeing more of the world.

He came with good principles and good feelings; he was willing to meet the world on fair grounds; he neither expected too much, nor did he bid too freely. He sought to glorify God, and benefit man; yet was he ignorant, practically ignorant, of the many arts by which selfishness, vanity, and the false systems of society, disintegrate character, and undermine virtue.

He made engagements with Capt. Creamer in good faith; he brake the bottles of the liquor-pedler with a righteous zeal; he was irresistibly concerned for the Old Man and his unfortunate grandchildren; he did not know Clover or Miss Eyre; he loved the children of his sister, if the hyperbole will not be misunderstood, with his whole soul.

CHAPTER VI.

MEMMY AND BEBBY.

YES, Richard loved these children; and loved to be with them, and to amuse them, and to be amused by them. After his nap, — for he had had no sleep since the night before, and many things had happened, in the mean time, to excite and tire him, — after his nap, he came down into the kitchen, and sat by the stove. The children began their pranks, — they could not let them alone. Their mother was preparing for baking, and she could neither bear their pranks nor their presence; so she sent them into the middle of the room. They could not stop at that, but went clear over to Uncle Richard's knee, and rebounding thence, they fetched up with the other side of the room. They seemed to move together as we imagine the Siamese twins to have done, when they were children; having one will and one centre of gravitation, like boys in a boat, or leaves in a whirlwind. Then, again, it was evident they had separate wills, and sometimes a sharp individuality of will would show itself. Memmy was the oldest, and the strongest, and we should expect her to lead off. So she did; but not always. Bebby's little individuality was mighty strong when it got roused, and it made up in storming what it lacked in solid weight. It was like a cat frightening a great dog by demonstration, — sheer demonstration. But Memmy generally went ahead; and Bebby wanted to do what Memmy did. They climbed to the window, and entertained themselves with the frost that glittered on the glass. Memmy printed her hand in it; holding it there till palm, thumb and fingers, melted their image into the glass; and Bebby did the same. It was cold work, and Bebby's fingers were red; but she was persevering; and when Memmy called to Uncle Richard to look at what she had done, Bebby did so too. Not that Bebby could speak a word; but she had a finger that was full of the energy of utterance; and she had a scream, too, that needed no interpretation, and her lips quivered eloquence. And then, — as if she possessed neither finger, nor throat, nor lips, — there was her eye; that told everything. Poor piece of dumbness! she had a superfluity of organs; and her eye alone would have made way for her through the world, sans everything else.

Memmy laid down to it, as we say, and applied her face to the window, and she produced chin, lips, nose, eye-brows thereon; and turning to Uncle Richard, to show him what she had done, there glared, from the great ice-mountains which the frost creates on windows, this hideous ice-mask; and did n't Uncle pretend to be frightened? and did n't Memmy laugh? But Bebby got up something as good, and more humorous; for she laughed, herself, while she was making it; and then her mouth was so pinched with the cold, she could hardly laugh, and tears streamed down through what she did laugh.

Memmy then took a slate-pencil, and Uncle had to fit Bebby a sharp stick, and they set to work, scratching figures in the frost. Memmy effected rude houses, and ruder rings for heads, and triangular skirts, and points for feet, and called the whole boys and girls. Bebby scratched at random, straight lines, and cross lines; but it was all the same to her, and she meant it to be all the same to everybody else; and she, in her way, called it boys and girls and houses, and her eyes sparkled, her lungs exploded, her frame vibrated all over, when she told it.

But we must come back of what we have written, a little; we are overstating the case. We say Bebby could not talk; people generally said so, and we incidentally fell into the common error. But it would not do to say this before Memmy; she would be instantly upon you. "Bebby can talk; she can say 'Ma, Ma,' and 'No, No,' and 'dum, dum,' and 'bye, bye,' and 'there!' She has got teeth, now!" It was an old idea of Memmy's that Bebby could not talk because she had no teeth; she said the gums covered her teeth all up, and the words, too. But the teeth came, — at least, two or three of them got out of their entanglement, — and then she could talk; and she did talk. So declared Memmy; and when the Mother of the Child and the Father spoke of its defect and backwardness in this respect, Memmy always came forward with a stout demurrer.

We say this, that the children may have full justice; and we say it for Richard's sake, who took Memmy's side in the controversy, and always defended the ground that Bebby could talk.

Uncle Richard was reading a newspaper, but — the selfish imps! — they would not tolerate that; they would have no interference with *their* rights; they were news enough for him; accident and incident; hair-breadth escapes; wonderful discoveries; they were foreign news and domestic news; they had their poet's corner, and their page of romance. And they had some original thoughts on perpetual motion and the quadrature of the circle, and were crowded with pictorial advertisements of as many strange things as Barnum has in his Museum.

Bebby was more blond, and soft, and supple, than Memmy, or than Memmy ever had been. Memmy's hair was darker, and lay smooth on her head; but Bebby's was all in a toss, and always in a toss; it was not curly, but flocculent, and had a pearly lustre, and it hung on her like the fringe of the smoke-tree, and looked like a ferment of snow, a little cloud of snow-dust flying about the room.

Memmy pulled off her shoes and stockings,—this was not allowed, but mother's back was turned, and Uncle looked on so smilingly,—and Bebby's were off in a trice; and they went pattering and tripping barefoot. Memmy got into the bed-room, and hid, and cooped; and Bebby found her; and there were great bursts of astonishment and pleasure. Then Bebby undertook to do the same; but she cooped before she got to her hiding-place, and then she frisked round trying to find herself, and this made them still more obstreperous.

Mother went out of the room a moment, leaving a bowl of Indian meal on the table. No sooner did Memmy spy this, and see the coast clear, than she pushed a chair alongside the table, and fell to dabbling in the meal. Bebby must follow suit; she shoved a chair all the way across the room, and they both stood on the margin of the meal-bowl. This was rare sport; it was something new for Bebby,—she never had got so far before,—she had never thrust her hands into meal. Memmy had,—Memmy was used to it. But Bebby, she was awed, and she was enrapturcd; she was on Pisgah's top, and Canaan lay fairly before her,—only she was a little afraid of Jordan. Why should she crow so? Why should she be so all in a tremble? What did she want of the meal? But into it she dove both arms, to the elbows; she lifted it with her hand, she crumpled it in her fist, she sifted it through her fingers; she made piles of it, and scattered them. Then she looked at her fingers, and on her dress, and on the table; and when she saw the meal spilled everywhere, she seemed half frightened. Had n't she a conscience, and was n't some fiery young Nemesis scourging her inside?— Did she love the feeling of the soft powder? had she a passion for dust? would she wallow in the mire, if she had a chance? Inexplicable little meal-stirrer! Memmy sprinkled some on Bebby's head, and Bebby tried to reciprocate the favor. Mother came back. "Richard," she screamed, "how could you let them do so?" Richard had done nothing about the matter, except to look on. "Was n't that enough?" said she; "could n't you see it? did n't you see it?" Seizing Bebby by the shoulders, she held the child square round, for Richard to look at. "Her tire," she continued, "was span-clean this morning; her hair is full of it! O, I shall go off the handle! Have you no heart, brother? Could n't you feel, as well as see?" "It is nothing very bad, I hope," said Richard. "All covered with this dirty meal!" exclaimed Roxy. "Your meal is not dirty, is it, sister?" "Don't joke, brother! It is a serious case; the children are forming very bad habits!"

"Habits of what?" asked Richard.

"Habits of getting into things," she replied.

"That is not a bad habit, — is it?"

"Habits of getting dirty. And I always said, if ever I had a child, it should be kept clean. If there is anything in the world most disagreeable, it is a dirty child."

"The children are not disagreeable to me," said Richard.

"They are not to me," rejoined his sister; "but they are to other people."

"It seems to me," added Richard, "I would not trouble myself much about other people, if I was satisfied myself. 'Other people' are numerous; and if the little ones are to be adjusted to their caprice, I fear they will have a hard time of it in life, and will wonder what they were born for. Besides, 'other people' are a good ways off, and have really small concern in Memmy and Bebby."

"We do not know how far off they are, any more than we do death; and we ought always to be prepared, as Elder Jabson says. If Mrs. Mellow should call, — oh Richard! — Wash your face, Memmy! — I am expecting callers to-day. I want you to kindle a fire in the air-tight in the parlor."

Richard went on this errand, and the children followed him. But their mother drew them back, saying, "You shall not go into the parlor! I have often told you not to go into the parlor. I always said, if ever I had a child, it should not go into the parlor. I will have one place in the house fit to be in!"

The room, into which Richard had not been before, acquired all at once a singular consequence to his eye. He looked carefully around it; he walked softly over it, as if some rare mystery lurked in the midst of it. It was the largest room in the house, and apparently the most open and pleasant. It had windows enough, at least, to favor the notion of light and freedom; four of them, that must command fine views, — views, when the curtains were up, and the ice and snow were gone. In the mean while, as a substitute for these out-of-door objects, the curtains afforded certain attempts at scenery, — a yellow castle, a whittling of a stream of water; and on the west side, right in face of the sunset, was a picture of the sun setting in a botch of green paint. The room was well furnished with sofa, carpet, looking-glass, cane-bottomed chairs; a mahogany card-table stood under the looking-glass, containing books, a card-basket, a small solar lamp, and several daguerreotypes. The mantel-piece was decorated with plated candlesticks, a blue-tinted cologne-bottle, a bouquet of wax flowers, and a stromb shell.

Richard inspected the contents of the table. He found the books were gifts, gilded and embossed, — most of them old ones, and such as his sister received before her marriage. There were also little books, Christmas presents of the father to the children. On the sofa lay a cloak and shawl, and a leghorn bonnet, trimmed with green, and lined with flowers.

"Well," thought Richard, "nothing very terrible in this." Now, our friend was naturally of a serious turn of mind; but somehow, at this time, lighter feelings came over him, and he might have gone as far as a certain Methodist young man did, who was obliged to confess to his class-leader the sin of perpetrating a joke. At least, he went so far as to pretend to joke — pretend to see the ludicrous side of things. "What can there be in the parlor to render it so frightful? Will the chairs fall to pieces?" He shook a couple of them. "Are there trap-doors in the floor, to let the children through?" He tried two or three places, springing down with his whole weight on his heels. "Perhaps the harem-scarems will have the walls down on their heads!" He sounded different parts with his fist. "Would the curtain-pictures terrify them? That is possible, but it were easy to roll up the curtains, and there would be a fine view from the windows. Yes," he continued, "this must be very fine, in summer. What a lake the dam makes! it would hold a thousand like father's. The houses and gardens, trees and mountains, beyond, must be very fine." The world without sobered him, and so occupied him he did not perceive the entrance of the children. Somehow they had got into the room, and Memmy was running to show her Christmas present, and Bebby had climbed the sofa, and got her mother's bonnet on backside before, and her gloves palm side up, and was trying to wrap herself in the cloak.

Richard's humor had not so far evaporated but he enjoyed the sight of Bebby, and particularly when she thrust her hands through the cloak, with the thumbs on the off-side, and the fingers looking as if they would be glad to accommodate the little usurper, but had laughed themselves to death in the attempt, and had no strength left. But this was recreation at too great cost; too great for the mother, who bolted into the room, and soon had her ambitious child deplumed, and restored to its proper simplicity.

"It troubles you, Roxy," said Richard.

"It does," she answered; "and I think you and Asa are not considerate, — not considerate of what we women endure. You act as if we had n't any feelings!"

"You mean, the children act so."

"The children would not act so if they were only rightly governed; and there can be no government when the men do not take hold and help the women. — Get down from the sofa, Memmy! I have given you positive orders never to get on there."

"What is the sofa made for?" asked Richard.

"Not for children to dirty and wear out with their feet. We shall have nothing fit for company long, at this rate. — Put up that book!"

"It is my present," replied the child; "papa gave it to me."

"It is yours to keep, not to be torn up," answered the mother.

Richard began to think there was some fact in what he had regarded as fiction, and that there was danger to the children in the parlor. They touched the card-table, and their hands were snatched off; they climbed into the chairs, and were hastily taken down; they approached the walls, and were warned away; and presently, as if the floor itself might prove treacherous, and let them incontinently into the cellar, they were driven from the room.

The street-bell rang, and Richard was desired to go to the door. He found there two ladies, one of whom surprised him a little in the person of Miss Plumy Alicia Eyre. They were shown to the parlor, where his sister introduced them. The one whom he had never seen was Mrs. Cyphers. Miss Eyre had on a small white silk bonnet, with pink linings, and richly ribboned in the same color; a swan's-down victorine floated on her neck; her hands were quietly hidden in an African lynx muff. Mrs. Cyphers wore a straw bonnet, with plaid trimmings; a drab-colored sack, heavily fringed; and she was further insured against the weather by a genet muff and tippet.

What did these ladies want? To make a call; to discharge a ceremony; to demonstrate their friendly feeling; to talk about the weather, and say how cold the morning had been, but that it was growing warmer?

Miss Eyre inquired for the children, observing, at the same time, that Mrs. Munk had two of the handsomest children in town.

Now, Mrs. Munk began to be in her element; now she would triumph; now she would show Richard the advantage of keeping children neat. Uncle went for the darlings. Alas for the uncertainty of human expectations, and the probability that one will not conquer just when he thinks he is going to! The children had been to the wet sink, — then they had got the ash-hole door open, and poked out the ashes, and nibbled at the coals. But Uncle Richard, — hard-hearted man! — brought them in just as they were! What consternation! His sister would have gone into hysterics; but Miss Eyre and Mrs. Cyphers said the children were beautiful, — would take them into their laps, and would kiss them, and all that; and Uncle Richard would not take them away; nay, he seemed determined that Memmy should go into Miss Eyre's lap, and Bebby into Mrs. Cyphers'.

This scene was soon ended, and the children dismissed: and both Miss Eyre and Mrs. Cyphers seemed more lively than ever, after it. Both were delighted with the children; and to such an extent did they carry their good feelings, that even Mrs. Munk was willing to drop the subject from her mind; and she soon recovered from her humiliation.

"Little things," said Miss Eyre.

"Not worth minding," added Mrs. Cyphers.

"They are not little things," rejoined Richard; "and I do mind them."

"You are joking, Mr. Edney," said Plumy Alicia, who sat next to Richard, on the sofa, and turned her face towards him engagingly.

"He dotes on the children," observed his sister, who began to think they would account her brother a dunce; "and he has some strange notions about them."

"I thought our young men were not capable of serious emotion," said Plumy Alicia, — "that they had no deep feeling." The swan's-down victorine, falling from her shoulders and touching his hand, was very soft. There was tenderness in her words, that touched him too. Was he prepared to meet those fascinations, of which he had obscurely heard? Why did he look so at her? Would he fathom the nature of that power which had, like some invisible engine, shaken the Mill? Was he so ignorant of himself as to suppose he could handle that fire and not be burned? But Miss Eyre was engaged to Clover, and he would only look at her as a strange, singular being, who was soon to be married to an equally mysterious man.

Was she ignorant of the power she was capable of exerting? Was she insensible of the precise moment when it took effect? We should answer both these questions in the negative.

Miss Eyre was one who in certain circles would be reputed somewhat coarse, — somewhat unlettered. She certainly had not that refinement which a more thorough study, and traming in some other form of society, ordinarily impart. Yet Richard was not in a state to discriminate on these points; or, rather, so far as he was curious at all, he attended not so much the manner as the hidden force and character of the lady.

It had been rumored that Captain Creamer was a rejected suitor of Miss Eyre's; indeed, so much as this had been intimated in Richard's hearing at the Mill, — a circumstance that shed fresh interest on what sat near him.

But what were these things to Richard? Nothing, nothing at all; and he would probably have never thought of them except, — what we foreboded, — except for the swan's-down victorine, and that piercing, flattering eye.

"Did I not see you in the crowd at Whichcomb's, this morning?" she asked. Richard answered that he was there. "They said you were there in the night," she continued; "but I could not believe it." He replied that the Captain obliged him to keep guard over the old man. "You had pleasant prisoners," she said. "They are sadly in trouble," replied Richard. "Sad to be arraigned as common thieves," was the answer.

Richard dropped the victorine as if it had been a cold toad, and walked towards the stove. "Would you bring *that* against them?" he asked.

"Not that alone, — not that, without other things," replied Miss Eyre. "I know what poverty is; I am not ashamed to say I have been poor; my only boast is, that I have risen above difficulties."

Richard was again touched, but he did not resume his seat on the sofa.

"They are poor," he said.

"Yes," she replied, "but that is not all."

"Proud, perhaps you would add?"

"I am proud; I would not give much for a person that has no pride."

"What do you mean?" pursued Richard.

"I mean," she answered, "that they have felt above their work, — that they would rather do anything than work."

"You do not mean that they are vicious?"

"I do not mean to say that. They came here poor, and they have continued poor. But they could not find society good enough in the Factories, nor in the weave-room, nor in the superintendent's house; and they were but spoolers. Now, Mrs. Cyphers was the wife of a superintendent; and in alluding to a house of that name, Miss Eyre played off the glossy end of her victorine on the person of that lady, as much as to say, "You see what a woman they rejected. It seemed," continued she, "as if nothing short of Dr. Chassford's, or Judge Burp's, or the Governor's, would satisfy them."

"I do not know these people," replied Richard, "nor do I appreciate the distinctions to which you refer."

"You will know," replied Miss Eyre. "You have not been in the city long. They attended Dr. Broadwell's Church, as if they were as good as the people that go there."

"Is not the Church one?" asked Richard. "Are not all the Churches equal?"

"Mr. Edney surely cannot be so ignorant," rejoined the lady, with a smile. "The Church is not one; it is far from being one. It is a good many. Some of the Churches are aristocratic, while others keep on the level of common people."

"Is not Dr. Broadwell a good man?"

"He may be, for all that I know."

"Are not his people good people?"

"That is nothing to the point. They are haughty, fashionable, high-stomached."

"There may have been other reasons why these girls liked to attend there."

"I dare say there are; I dare say Junia could give you fifty reasons. She has a tongue of her own!"

"She did say no clergyman had been to see them."

"Nothing more likely," interposed Mrs. Cyphers. "They boarded a while at Swindler's; then they went to Cain's, and finally they got up to Whichcomb's; and no mortal could tell where they would come out, they rose so fast."

"Whichcomb's is higher than Swindler's?" observed Richard.

"Half a dollar a week higher," replied Mrs. Cyphers. "Pies for breakfast higher, — an extra course of a Sunday higher; to say nothing of Mrs. Whichcomb's jellies and cream. *I* boarded at Whichcomb's, I would have you to know, until our marriage."

"There would seem to be aristocracy among the boarding-houses," said Richard.

"Who would not try to keep above the mean, ignorant, stupid Swindler's?" asked Mrs. Cyphers. "And there is a difference, Sir, there is a difference between the weave-room and the warping-room, — between a dresser and a grinder; and, though I say it that should n't say it, between a superintendent's wife and the watchman's wife."

"All have the liberty to rise that wish to?" said Richard.

"All that *deserve* to!" replied Miss Eyre, casting a searching, but rather equivocal, glance at Richard.

But Richard did not notice it; he was thinking of the Orphans. "Violet is very sick." The ladies assented. "She needs attentions."

"If Junia does not engross them all," added Miss Eyre. She added this in a way that she meant to be playful; but Richard took it quite seriously.

"You are unjust to them," said Richard; — he said this sternly.

"We would not be," replied Miss Eyre, deprecatingly. Richard added nothing.

"We have other calls in hand," said Miss Eyre, "and must bid you good-morning."

They left the house; Miss Eyre went out with that calmness which dignified sorrow can so well assume. But Richard was not moved.

Having discovered where the Orphans were wont to worship, he would go and see the minister of the church. He found the reverend gentleman at home. Doctor Broadwell was of mature years, — indeed, a little past the meridian of life. But time, that crowned him with virtues and honors, had raised the summit so high, — if the little piece of fancy will be tolerated, — the top of it was covered with snow. He was gray. The lines on his forehead were marks of strength not less than of age; they indicated rather the vigor of thought than the corrosions of decay; like the furrows of the sea, which are large and deep only because the sea is large and deep. His face shone with benevolence, that cheered and vivified whatever object it alighted upon, and invited to its beams all sorrow, want and desolateness. The Doctor replied to Richard that two girls, with an old man, had been seen at his church, and partaken of his communion; that he had endeavored to see them, but could not trace them, and would be glad to be conducted to their room.

They went to Whichcomb's, where Richard parted with the minister, and returned home.

CHAPTER VII.

CLOVER.

In popular phrase, the back of the winter was broken. The weather became milder, the mornings grew a little longer, and the evenings a little shorter, and the sun at noon mounted a trifle higher. The vulgar distich runs thus —

> "When the days begin to lengthen,
> The cold begins to strengthen."

This is true of the few weeks immediately succeeding the Solstice. But in the latter part of February, and towards March, the change to which we have referred is so perceptible, that the popular voice changes, — "What mild weather! How warm it is!" though it is winter still; but winter maimed — winter inefficient.

At these times Richard went out more during the day. He had, indeed, turned night into day, and was obliged to sleep partly by sunlight; but he could secure what rest he required, and still have some hours to spare. These were his perquisites, and he employed them as he chose.

One day, as he entered the mill, he encountered Mr. Gouch, Silver, and Philemon, his fellow night's men, and he saw another person, whom he had not seen before, striding a log. "That," whispered Mr. Gouch, "is Clover; don't go near him!" But Richard could not be easy when he knew Clover was near; at least, he could not keep his eyes or his thoughts still. He looked at Clover; looked quite intently at him. "Don't let him see you looking at him!" said Mr. Gouch. Well, Richard must look at him all the more, — only he did it furtively, and by snatches. What did he behold? A man with a very careless, indifferent manner, bordering on malapertness and doughtiness. His face was one that could be easily identified. His lower lip rowdyishly protruded; it was a pouch containing a quid of tobacco as large as a pullet's egg. His upper lip was deeply indented at each corner, making two niches, where scorn and derision were seated. He held a cant-dog, with which he amused himself, drawing frightful figures in the saw-dust on the floor; then he teazed a butter with it, making as if he would thrust it under his axe. He had on a Shakspeare hat, with the rim turned up at the sides, and a silver buckle in front; and the hat was tilted so much on his head, it seemed as if it would fall off. His dress consisted of a blue-striped shirt with a large collar, a double-breasted vest, and a mottled Guernsey jacket. But what, perhaps, would chiefly arrest the notice of a stranger was his hair; — his whole head seemed to have gone to hair; it hung in long, coarse folds, like a mop; it came out along his cheeks, and under his nose and chin. It was bright red; and his small, gray eye gleamed in the midst of it, like a pig's eye. Not only did he annoy the butter with the cant-dog, but, intermitting this fancy, he would occasionally double his fist at the poor man, straightening his chest, drawing up and squaring at him, as if he would fight him. He bent his fist inwards and upwards, thus tightening the cords of his wrist, and stiffening the skin on his knuckles; and in this strained attitude he played it up and down, now inclining it towards his victim, and then thumping it against the log on which he sat; letting off, apparently, a vast amount of force and dismay into the insensible wood. The butter took all this patiently, either from indifference to Clover, or out of terror of him — Richard could not tell which.

Most of the hands were, or affected to be, afraid of Clover. Richard was inquisitive as to the secret of the man's power — whether it lay in his manner, or his character. Nor was his interest cooled by observing that Clover flung several significant glances at himself, and did some feats of fist, which he evidently meant Richard should give a personal interpretation to.

He asked Mr. Gouch to introduce him; but the timorous head-stock man declined the service. When Richard persisted, and said he would speak with Clover, Silver sprang at his throat, as if he would choke him, and told him to keep still. Philemon made as if Silver was in earnest, and said he had Richard within an inch of his life, and it was his duty to stop so dangerous an affray.

Clover himself started at this, and called out for fair play, or something of the sort. "It is all play," said Richard; "do not be alarmed." "I am not alarmed," replied Clover, resuming his seat on the log, and discharging the cavity of his lower lip, which ever, like a boiling spring, was inclined to run over. "I should like to see the man that tells me I am alarmed; new comer or old comer, — slip-tender or head-stock man!"

Richard, going towards Clover, replied, "Silver was in sport."

"*Of* course," rejoined Clover; "he dare do nothing else but be in sport, *of* course. You may make a mark there, if you will!"

"I believe I have your place in the mill," said Richard; "possibly you would like to take it again."

"I shall take it whenever I please," returned Clover.

"As soon as you are able to take it, I will relinquish it to you."

"Able!" he retorted; "I am able when I please to be able. Check that!"

"Have you entirely recovered?" asked Richard.

"Recovered!" He echoed the word with a very sharp sarcasm playing about his upper lip, which Richard did not see any necessity for.

"You have been sick?" Richard asked.

"Worse than that, — I have been indisposed."

"I thought you were sick."

"*Of* course, I meant you should think so, — I meant the Captain should think so, — I meant the whole Mill should think so. Trig that, and take breath!"

"I am ready to go on again," replied Richard, waggishly.

"Do you mean to insult me, Edney?" asked Clover, his eyes flashing fire.

"Do you mean to insult me?" replied Richard.

"How insult you?"

"By making me believe you were sick, when you were not sick."

"I can give myself to you in one word, Edney; I can convey the whole in a single phrase; I am a man of honor; I wish to be honorable. Tie a knot there!"

"I will," replied Richard; "and then I must ask you how you can call such conduct honorable."

"Enlargement, aggrandizement, glory, fame, are natural to the human breast; they are natural to my breast. Power, might, are honorable; and these I study to exercise. To make you believe I am sick, when I am sick, is nothing, — a child could do that; but if I can make you believe I am sick, when I am not sick, — if I can make the Captain believe it, and the whole Mill believe it, — I do something; I exercise power; I AM ENLARGED!"

Clover had the habit of talking sometimes apparently in Italics, sometimes in small caps, and occasionally mounting as high as canon. We would do him typographical justice.

"You would not lie?" observed Richard.

"Lie! lie!" replied Clover; "*lie!* hem! hum! You mistake. 'T is means, means!"

"It is lying," remarked Richard.

"If you were in an enemy's country, would you stick at what you call a lie, to secure your conquest? Did not our troops tell, utter, manufacture, publish, a hundred lies, in Mexico? Are they to be taunted with lying? I am in Mexico; I am in an enemy's country, and I shall lie to further my victories: but are you mean enough — have you no nicer sense of honor than to asperse my acts with the villanous epithets which a bilious stomach and morbid imagination know so well how to supply? Power is sweet; might is glorious; — it gives a man reputation; it affords him security; it protects him from assault. Look round you; there is not one in all this mill, from Tillington, of the Corporation, down to Jim Grisp, the shingle-sticker, that dares touch me. I have acquired this respect simply by the exercise of my power, — by demonstrating to the world the deep energies of my nature and character." In saying this, he gored the air, with his tense, vice-like fist, in the vicinity of Richard, and even extended it almost to Richard's nose.

Richard shook his head, not violently, not disdainfully, but rather abstractedly, as a man who is reading does when a fly alights on his face. Clover had a trick of snapping his fist, springing it suddenly in the joint of the wrist, as boys do the blade of a pocket-knife. He snapped it at Richard, who moved a little in his seat. "Perhaps you do not like the smell of it?" said Clover. "I cannot say that I do," replied Richard. "Very likely," he added; "and the taste of it would be still more disagreeable. But I design you no harm. The air is free; and what my arm can compass is mine. I know I am on the borders of my land. I do not wish to get up a fight with you, or any one; but if your nose happens to come within the radius of my fist, — that is, if you are lying within the proper limit of my power, — why, take care of yourself, Sir, take care of yourself! Forewarned, forearmed. I trust you will regard it an instance of my honorable disposition, that I give you this friendly precaution."

"I think you trespass on neighbors' rights a little," observed Richard. "At least, you are on disputed territory."

"I know I am," he rejoined; "I know I am; and where was Resaca de la Palma? WHERE WAS PALO ALTO? There is no great action except on disputed territory; no reputation is acquired anywhere else."

The fist continued to exhibit its feats, and to extend its familiarities a little too near Richard's sense of dignity. He laid his hand on the fist, — his open hand, — softly and modestly. He found it a hard and horny fist; and in other respects it had a bovine suggestion; for, like the horn of an ox, no matter how softly and modestly you grasp it, it is sure to toss, and wrench, and tear from your hand; — so this fist resisted the gentlest pressure; it grew more stiff, it hunched violently upwards, grazing Richard's nose, and hitting the forepiece of his cap, knocked it off."

"I would rather you should not do that," said Richard; "I should very much prefer that you would not repeat it. I must respectfully request you to attempt it again in no form whatever."

"I did not think of knocking up a fight," rejoined Clover.

"I am no brute, — I am a man of honor; I am ready to negotiate. Shall we adjourn to the Arbor? Helskill's is good ground for an amicable adjustment." Richard would not go to the Arbor. "Well," added Clover, "if you obstinately reject the only method of conciliation that I can with honor to myself tender, the consequences be on your own head. But I am not rash; I will not even take advantage of methods of redress which all usage puts in my hands. I can be lenient. Will you have a cigar?" Richard declined. "Don't be mulish," continued Clover. "Will you lift with me?" "I will," said Richard. "There is a good-sized hemlock stick; if you will manage one end, we will throw it on the stocks." "I am ready," replied Richard. The sawyers consented to the trial, and gauged the carriage to the log in question. "Take that end," said Clover. "This is the butt," replied Richard. "I know it is," returned Clover, "and I meant it should be." "All right," said Richard, "if you will take hold as far in from the other end as to make the balance good." "I will not be dictated to, in this affair," retorted Clover, and applied himself to the extremity of the smallest end. "You take the butt," said Richard, "and I will lift where the trial shall be a fair one." Clover refused.

By this time the mill-men had collected to see what was going on. Richard stated the case to them, and then repeated his offer to Clover. Clover disdained to concede, or to parley. "'T was an honorable proposal," said he, — "nothing said about ends, — I will have none of this whining, — he cannot gammon me!"

"Will you lift fairly, or will you not?" asked Richard.

"I shall lift it as I please," returned Clover.

"Then I brand you," said Richard, "for a cheat, a brute, and a coward; — put a pin in there! I cannot blacken you.

— you are too black already; I should only like to have you see how black you are; — put a spike in there! Your conduct is despicable as your principles are monstrous; — I recommend to you to drive a slide-dog there, and go home!"

The bystanders were a good deal excited. Mr. Gouch hopped from log to log, as if they were in the water, and he was afraid of sinking. Silver, in a paroxysm of astonishment and delight, let his pipe fall from his mouth. Some were amused; others manifested a disposition to rally for the defence of Richard, if Clover should attack him.

But Clover had no such intentions. He had not made up his mind to be offended. He seemed to recognize a rival in the field; and since he could not easily demolish him, he accounted it wise to come to an understanding of his quality, and ascertain his intentions.

"I applaud your spirit, Edney," said he, "though you misjudge me. I shall think the better of you. I should like to know more of you. Will you try a game of checkers?"

Now, it was contrary to immemorial and sacred mill usage to decline a game of this sort, when the men were at leisure. Richard might have foregone further intimacy with the man; but the others, desirous that he should not carry matters too far, hoped he would play. Perhaps he wished to know more of Clover, — for he had a good deal of humanitarian curiosity. He consented to the proposal.

They took a bench by the stove, with the draught-board between them. Clover was an experienced player, and so was Richard; but it soon appeared the minds of both were too much occupied for that deliberation which is needful either for the display of skill or the attainment of success. Their moves were made at random, and an accidental jar of the board served to confuse the whole plan of action, without, at the same time, awakening the surprise of either. In fact, they were thinking more of each other than of what was before them. "Where are we now?" said Richard. "I don't know," answered Clover; "my pieces are on the floor."

Richard nursed some questions that he wanted to put to Clover. And, as the loungers had left the mill, and he was sitting confidentially near him, he could not resist the opportunity of broaching what lay on his mind.

"What ails Silver?" he asked.

"*He fell beneath my hands!*" replied Clover.

"What do you mean by that?" asked Richard.

"His ambition fell, his affections fell, his excessive thirst for acquisition fell," rejoined Clover, who had lighted a cigar, cocked his hat, and made some effort towards getting his fist into operation.

"How did it come about?"

"I entered and took possession of a valuable prize he coveted."

"What was it?"

"Miss Plumy Alicia Eyre."

"Did he love her?"

"Of course he did; I should not care to meddle in the thing, if he had not loved her, and if she had not been an object to be loved."

"You cut him out?"

"That is the cant phrase. The simple truth lies here:— woman is given to man for possession on his part, and protection on hers. The man who can furnish the best guarantees in these two particulars, is the favored man; and the most desirable woman falls to the most favored man,— that is, to the strongest man. I am such a man, and Silver is not. Of course, Miss Eyre preferred to be allied to me, rather than remain in Silver's hands. She knew that her true dignity and glory lay in this breast, WITHIN THESE WHISKERS!"

"Had Silver no feelings?"

"What has he to do with feelings? Why does he not conquer his feelings? Why does he not let the will of God be done to his feelings?"

"Was she consulted in the premises?"

"Of course she was, — and she declared for me."

"Was there an engagement between them?"

"There may have been something of that sort. She came here a poor, defenceless girl, and was naturally interested in any one that would be interested in her. Silver attached himself to her, made her presents, and won over her ignorance and childishness. I took her under my protection."

"But Silver suffers."

"The weak always suffer; it is their misfortune; we can pity them. I see you have a noble nature, Edney; a nature that is not insensible even to what Silver may endure. It is honorable in you."

"He bleeds inwardly, I think."

"Bleeds! what is that? The Indians bleed when their lands are torn from them, — the slaves bleed when their children are sold. What hurt does a little bleeding do?"

"But is there no right in the case?"

"*Most* assuredly. Might makes right. Behold how that saw cuts through the heart and surface of that monster pine. Behold the majestic Scott cutting his way through the heart of Mexico; — veins, arteries, legs, arms, like saw-dust, lie on either side of him; he arrives at the Halls of the Montezumas in a foam of blood! that proud nation is humiliated at our feet! I have gone through Silver's heart. When I was in it, I felt that I was there, — I felt the warm blood spouting about me, — I knew I severed the tenderest part of his being; but, Sir, I attained my end, — I got Miss Eyre. They gave a dinner to Captain Bragg. I offer 'Clover,' as your next toast.

"Do you intend to build?"

"I may build, and I may not build."

"It is given out that you are going to."

"I know it is, — I meant it should be. The dimensions are on the fender-post."

"But would you deceive?"

"If I could make it honorable, I would deceive; if my interest were advanced thereby, if my power was augmented, I should deceive. Deceive! The Church deceives, when it can make by it. Edney, you don't know the dear, lovely, charming sense of power."

"How does the Church deceive?"

"Does n't it declare that St. Athanasius' Creed can be proved by most certain warrants of Scripture, and ought to be thoroughly received? Who believes that?"

"Possibly you would falsify your promises to Miss Eyre herself?"

"Falsify! I should certainly retreat from my engagements, if I found them difficult or disagreeable. I must be sovereign within my own sphere; and my sphere is what my abilities naturally comprise, or what my endeavors can conquer. I AM FATED TO SPREAD, — I AM FATED TO SPREAD, Edney! I might include even another with Miss Plumy Alicia."

"You are not so unprincipled. You would not pretend fidelity to Miss Eyre, and at the same time be making overtures to another."

"*What if I had two women in my train?* I should appear to the world in a more formidable light, as a man dangerous to be trifled with, and yet a perfect refuge for oppression."

"I believe you are a scoundrel, Clover, — utterly, and beyond redemption."

"You do well to tell me so; — it will not hurt you; it may relieve you. You do not know the deliciousness, the majesty of Power. See that saw, — behold yonder dam, — think of six run of stone in the Grist-mill, — enumerate all the engines in the Machine-shop, — contemplate nine hundred thousand spindles in the Factories, and understand what Power is. Meditate on this fist of mine, — look into my eye, — take the dimensions of my whiskers, — survey the expansiveness of my chest, and learn what POWER is. Imagine what it would be to be possessed of the same. Imagine yourself a Clover! What a wonder is that Tom Hyer! I have sometimes fancied myself a Hyer, and should like to find my Sullivan. I have toughened my hands, — I have employed two Irishmen to rub my body, — I have smeared my face with an indurating compound. I should like to have a Sullivan chasing me from saw to saw, from Mill to Boarding-house, from Quiet Arbor to Victoria-square! Undertake Sullivan, and your Hyer will be on hand!"

"I may prove a Sullivan," replied Richard; "I may chase you."

"If, then, you provoke me to it; if we come fairly to blows, — I must be plain with you, and use plain words, — you will get all-firedly licked; — take note, take note!"

"That is my look-out," returned Richard. "I shall be plain with you. You are committing an uncommon amount of rascality with Silver; you are equally perfidious in respect of Miss Eyre. And I shall pursue you in that matter until, most likely, we come to blows. Then, all I have to say to you is, 'Hardest, fend off!' I shall attempt to disgorge you of some of your ill-gotten possessions, and diminish the superfluity of your power. I am a stranger in the place, — a stranger to goings on here, — a stranger to all parties concerned. But you have introduced me to a measure of wickedness sufficient to move me, — sufficient to resolve me."

"I sought you as a noble antagonist."

"I do not intend to be a disguised or a mean one."

"Will you go with me to Quiet Arbor?"

"What for?"

"To exchange tokens of friendly understanding, and honorable emulation."

"Over a glass of sling?"

"Yes, and a game of whist."

"You gamble?"

"I recreate, recreate!"

"Who is with you?"

"A select company, of course; Captain Creamer, Webster Chassford, Glendar, — all worthy men, — all charming acquaintances, — the best families in the city. We meet in the Grotto, — a cool and pleasant retreat; Helskill is polite, gentlemanly, noble; yes, I would say of Helskill, that he is most noble, — that in him cluster every attribute and all the beauty of an honorable mind."

"I am obliged to you for this information," said Richard, "and I will make good use of it."

"That is well uttered, Edney. If I must meet you as an enemy, let us be fair enemies. But I must caution you on one point, — *Let Miss Eyre alone!*" He said this in a hard-breathed undertone. "Don't meddle with that, — don't go near that, — death catch you if you do! I will not touch my thumb to my nose, as modern writers recommend, in token that we understand one another; — I will rub my fist on your nose, to signify *that!*"

Richard brushed off the fist, and rising from his seat, said, "No symbols are needed; we *do* understand each other," and left the mill.

CHAPTER VIII.

A STROLL THROUGH THE CITY.

RICHARD, we have said, had leisure during the day. This leisure he would turn to account; he would look about the city. Richard, we need not say, loved to read; he had read not a little for a simple, agricultural lad, and he was always glad to get new books. Pity he should not have them when there is such an abundance. Richard had been over the world at some length, in his geographies and histories; he had travelled with attention and with profit; yet with his own feet and walking-stick he had measured but a few leagues of human affairs, — the merest crumb of the great ball. He had never been in the business streets of Woodylin, nor in its fashionable squares. So he sallied forth, one sunny morning, to reconnoitre.

Woodylin consisted of two portions, — the Old and the New Town, — divided by the River. The New Town comprised the Factories and Saw-mills, which lay in a graceful and polite bend of the stream. Yet both sides lived in harmony, and strangers used to say but one pulse beat there, whether in the head or feet. Nevertheless, fancy and caprice must dash this pleasant cup of unity with a little variety. As the New Town increased in size, and perhaps in conceit, since it possessed many picturesque spots, and indulged in much picturesque promise, its inhabitants called it the Beauty of Woodylin. It became a standing quip for one to say he did not live in Woodylin, but in the Beauty of it. If one side was the city proper, the other would seem to be the city improper. It would not stop at this; it meant to be the city more proper. It erected a School-house unequalled in the municipality. It hoped to do many more things; but it is not so easy to work with hopes, as with a well-earned fruition; it had nothing equal to Victoria-square. Elder Jabson's Church was on the Beauty side. Here was one of the Printing-offices, to which we may again refer. On this bank, also, was the Light-house,—a circumstance that originated innumerable smart sayings. The Custom-house divided its favors with both shores. The Beauty people built an Athenæum, founded a library, and supported a course of lectures, to match the Lyceum across the River. Here also a division of the Sons of Temperance had sumptuous apartments. Yet as the sun and rain, summer and winter, were alike on both sides of the valley, so the greater interests, affections, and preferences of the people, coalesced.

The Beauty side afforded less to engage the curiosity of a country youth, like Richard, than the other. So he crossed the stream. In a rambling way, he paused to look into a precinct, known as Knuckle Lane;—a dismal region, the sewer of poverty, filth and wretchedness,—a sort of Jews' quarter, where the cast-off clothes of the city—its old houses, old garments, old furniture, old horses—were collected, and if not exposed for sale, were certainly exposed to everything else.

Now, Richard's teacher at the Village High School inculcated this doctrine among his scholars,—that they should use in after life the knowledge they acquired at school; and to the Geography class he particularly addressed himself, and told them that when they saw new objects, they should associate them with the places whence they came; that if at any time they were abroad, they should recall, not only the origin, but the history and use, of what they saw. "For instance," — and thus he illustrated his meaning, — "this penknife is from England, — you know where England is; this silk cravat is from France. The tea your mother uses is from China; vain and extravagant dressing is from a wicked heart;" — he would laugh when he said this; — "rum is from the Devil." So he instructed them on various points, especially holding to the main one, that they should keep their eyes open, — ever be seeing, ever be learners, and have their minds always alive and active.

Recollecting this principle, Richard had a great many things to think of, as he looked up Knuckle Lane. Why this poverty? Why this meanness? Why are poverty and meanness so associated? Is there no remedy for it? Thus he questioned within himself. There is nothing of this sort in Green Meadow, — his native town. He might have stood there a month, in obedience to the direction of his teacher, Mr. Willwell, before he could get at the solution of the matter. So he went on into the street where wood was exposed for sale.

What quantities of it! How the loaded teams crowded the way!

Faithful to the principle just named, the first thought of Richard, when he saw the wood, was his own home. The oxen looked so like his own oxen, — the wood looked so like wood he had handled, every stick of it; — he knew the best kinds, and all kinds. But the oxen; — there came with them, to his mind, his own barn-yard, and stable, and hay-mow; he could have shaken the cattle heartily by the hand, every one of them. Then he knew their best signs, — the broad breast, the bright color, — and he could tell that there was a sprinkling of Durham in them, and he knew where Durham was.

And with the barn-yard was connected, in fact, and in his mind, a little path, and then an apple-tree, and then a well-sweep, a shed, and a kitchen; and so he crept along, till he came pat upon his old Father and Mother;—but he could stay there long.

The Surveyor manipulated with his scale on all sides of the wood,—inspected the ends, peered in among the crevices, rapped on the bark. "The sled is heavier than that," said the owner, looking at the bill the official gave him. "Short lengths," replied the latter. "We measure from the inside to the tip of the scarf." "There is a round cord, or my cattle may be ashamed of themselves, and never expose their sweat and hot flanks in Woodylin again." "It is not well packed." "It is well packed,—I'll leave it to any one that knows. Here, Captain," he called to Richard; "you have seen cord-wood, I should say, from your looks; you can tell what a load is, and when it's loaded. Is that merchantable?" "I should think it was," replied Richard. "Is he a Surveyor?" exclaimed that dignitary; "has he been sworn?" "I have handled wood," added Richard, "and I call that well stowed." "I shall not condescend to dispute with you," returned the Surveyor. "Nor I with you," echoed the driver, and he tore up the bill. "Your wood is forfeited," said the Surveyor. "It sells for a cord, or I will back about, and fling it into Knuckle Lane. I guess they won't dispute about it there."

Richard was called to apply his education in a way his school-master had not provided for; yet, after all, it was only an amplification of the general rule.

"I advise you, young man," remarked the Surveyor to our friend, with a sinister tone of voice, "to mind your own business."

Richard took the hint, and went on. He turned, without

method in his route, into Lafayette-street, — a broad street, with fine trees, fine houses, fine churches. This led into Victoria-square. With all his philosophy, it would have been difficult to pierce the mystery that lay about him now. He could, indeed, with his eye comprise the magnificence of the place, — count the stories of the houses, enumerate the successive blocks; but even to his eye, there was an inexplicable richness. How splendid those great elms would be in the summer! — that he knew. But the people, — the parlors, — the wardrobes, — the feelings; — he might as well be looking at the Moon.

He entered St. Agnes-street, where the Governor resided, and came to a halt in front of the Family mansion. There were the ornamented fence, the arched gateway, the deep yard planted with trees and shrubbery, the long piazza with its corinthian columns, the windows with rich caps, the heavy cornice, and the high walls of the building itself, that arrested his eye. Did he know what was inside? He did not — nor even who lived there. He saw what went in there; he saw two ladies, with stone-marten muffs, garnet velvet sacks, and one with a blue satin hat and bird of paradise feathers. These were Barbara and Melicent. They turned as they mounted the steps, and cast a leisure glance around, that alighted upon Richard, and passed to other objects. What account should he give of these to his teacher? What a distance between his home-spun and their French velvets! He drew back a little, as they looked towards him, and interposing between him and them a fir-tree, made good his escape. He came into a quarter of uneven pavements; he passed houses that had their basements new-furbished, and new-windowed, and let for grocery stores, while the upper stories remained dingy, brown, and dark; the improvement of the city being rapid and great, and flinging itself in haste into such parts of a building as it could most conveniently reach. What life, what animation, began to spread itself before him, in the long vistas of the business streets! How the sun poured itself down, cheerful and bright, on those syndromes of modern civilization! People complained of tight times, a dull season; — there was no dulness, no tightness, to Richard's eye. Gayly varnished sleighs, puffed and pranked with silver-furred robes, and streaming with a whole pack of tails behind, flashed by. Pungs of butter, oats, mutton, defiled along. Four elegant horses, attached to an elegant van, with seats for twenty, and having a dasher as high as a barn-door, on which danced an Hungarian girl, under an arch of gilded flowers and vines, attracted his gaze. He saw men in buffalo coats, and scarlet leggins, and very red faces, moving to and fro rather heavily, with the chin sunk, as if in deep thought. These were stage-drivers, executing their orders. People from the country were continually arriving, and hitching their horses at the stone posts by the walk; — the females crawling out of their fur beds, then squinting at the signs over the doors, and darting forwards, as if their health and salvation were staked on getting in at a particular door.

There were men with pale faces, and white cravats, and gray hair, who walked a little stooping and leisurely; — these were the ancient and venerable fathers of the City. Young men, well dressed, with bits of paper and little blank-books in their hands, passed him, walking fast and straight forwards; — these were clerks. Others, in loose paletots, with one arm folded round the breast, and cigars in their mouth, were the gentlemen of leisure.

He came to a store that had an ancient goose hanging

one side of the door; — he knew where geese came from. A pair of denim over-hauls mated it on the other; — he knew where such things came from, but he looked more closely at them, — not philosophically, but economically, — for he wanted a pair. He saw in the shop barrels, — rows of barrels, — piles of barrels; and on the heads of the barrels he read, N. E. Rum. Devil! thought he, what a Devil is here! He remembered the words of his Teacher, — "Rum comes from the Devil." There were men in the store drinking, and other men serving drink. The Devil, he thought, had set up business for himself there. He turned hastily away.

He came into a street of new stores, with high brick walls, and great windows; and every window, — oh, it was a realm of enchanted vision, — a gulf opening into Paradise, — a portal of Dream-land! There were oranges and lemons in the Fruiterer's windows, that brought to Richard's memory what he had learned of Sicily, Cuba, and the evergreen Tropics. There were golden watches and bracelets, diamond rings, pearl brooches, in the Jeweller's, spread out in full view, on terraces of black velvet; and Potosi came to his mind, Golconda and the Arabian Nights. At the Confectioner's, glass globes of candies and lozenges, and all kinds of colored sugars, stood a-row, and there were sugar dogs, and sugar houses, and sugar everything, —a whole microcosm of pretty ideas in sugar; and what should he think of, —what did he think of, but Memmy and Bebby?

Richard was a parvenu; he was fresh from the country, — this everybody saw; the way he stared at things showed it, even if his red shirt, and snuff-colored monkey-jacket, and striped mittens, did not. But Richard knew where everybody came from, and he had no inquiries to make about them. But he did not understand the mystery of all the things he saw in the windows, and he wished the friend of his youth was there to tell him. This instructor had a pin that he took from his coat-sleeve, on which he used to dilate, and spent hours talking about it, and telling how it was made; then he illustrated all sorts of things by it. A pin and a pencil were a whole armory of apparatus for Mr. Willwell. At the Jeweller's, he longed to ask the artist some questions; but there the man sat, right behind this beautiful display of work, brushing a bit of brass, and never looking at what was before him, — never looking at Richard, — but very vacantly laughing and joking with an idle fellow that stood near by, with his thumbs in his breeches pockets. Richard was almost bursting with philosophical admiration and inquisitiveness, and the man was so stupid! How different from his Teacher!

But when he faced the many-tinted and many-shaped wonders of the Confectioner's, he wished, he only wished, *if* the window should fall out, and those piles of fascination be tumbled to the ground, Memmy and Bebby might be there!

As if his fancies were just turning into realities, he heard a thundering over head, and a crash at his side. The snow, sliding from the high roof, had fallen to the ground. It struck among the horses, and frightened them. Richard attempted to compose them. One beast, frantic and fiery, broke his halter, and plunged backwards, dragging Richard after him. Richard was thrown to the ground, but without relinquishing his hold. The horse turned to run; Richard, by a strong jerk of the rein, and a dextrous application of one foot to the flank of the animal, cast him, and had him lying quietly on his side, before the people, who rushed to his assistance, had time to be of much service. It was the Governor's horse, and in the sleigh was the Governor's daughter, and the Governor himself appeared in the crowd. The daughter overflowed with thankfulness; the Governor took, with his thumb and finger, from his vest-pocket, it might be a cent, or a dime, it was a gold piece, which he quietly dropped into one of the flaring pockets of Richard's jacket.

The crowd dispersed, and Richard resumed his studies. He reached the Booksellers' quarter. An immense wooden book, suspended at the corner of the street, over the walk, caught his eye, and large pictorial advertisements on the door-posts held it fast. He read the advertisements; he went from door to door, reading what was emblazoned at each, — reading the posts from top to bottom. There were books by authors familiar to him, and more by those of whom he had not heard; there were titles of books that conveyed no meaning, and some that aroused all his curiosity to know what they meant; and others still, so full of meaning he could hardly keep from clutching the bills and running home. These doors of the Booksellers' Shops, with their typographical enigmas, were mystic entrances to the enchanted palace of youthful hope and intellectual idealism, and to what he had wished to know, and to what he thought some time he might know, and to those visions his Teacher unconsciously kindled in his mind, and to things of which his Pastor spoke. If he could not enter this palace, he could look into it through the windows; so he ranged along from window to window, up and down the street. May no worse impediments to aspiration and desire ever be offered than transparent glass! Richard did not feel that he was denied anything, though he stood outside, and though it was cold weather; he thought he had a feast. He was thankful to the kind people that put these things in the windows. It seemed to him that the panes of glass were very large, and very accommodating. He saw the backs of many beautiful books, and the inside of one great landscape book. He saw many more things, the nature of some of which he understood, while others puzzled him. On the broad shelf of one shop he saw porcelain gentlemen, in antique costume, standing very erect; — what they were for he did not know, but he supposed they were toys, and he knew toys came from Germany; so Germany was in his mind. He saw pearl-handled penknives, and all that Teacher and books had said about Sheffield was remembered. There was a little marble dog, with a gold chain about its neck; — he did not comprehend that. There were boxes of toilette soap, hidden away in silvered paper; — here he was out, too. There were quantities of Valentines, to which he could get no clue whatever. A box of gold pencils revived his confidence. There were patent inkstands, and patent pickwicks, and patent table-bells; — good a mechanician as he might be, he was totally confused. In the broad alcove of the bay window of another shop, in addition to all this glitter and richness below, over head were a whole choir of little white angels, and a bevy of cupids, venuses, and innocent white children. O Memmy! oh Bebby! where are you now? And more still! there were beautiful pictures, Madonna faces, tenderest looks of childhood, many a sweet human expression, verdant landscapes, quiet pastorals, some of the deepest affections of the heart. Germany, Sheffield, Art, Mystery, — good-by! They all vanish; nothing tempts his curiosity now; his spirit is ravished by a new enthusiasm; — these simple pictures sink into his soul, and his imagination swims in ideal feeling.

On the door of this store he read NEFON'S. By this time, also, he recollected that he wanted some paper and pens; and especially were his thoughts quickened, when, among the many things that garnished the door-way, he saw the words Circulating Library; for he remembered his Pastor told him to seek one out, — " that is," he added, " if you can find a good one, a good one." Did Nefon keep a good Circulating Library? What was this NEFON'S? He looked again at the inscription. Then he looked at the window; he even stepped on the sill, and looked through the glass door. Was Nefon's so small that one word sufficed to cover it? Was it so large that that same pair of syllables was all the hint it needed to give? Of whatever size, it was big enough for Richard. He had studied grammar, and he knew the apostrophe indicated the possessive case; he saw at a glance that Nefon possessed what, to his eye, appeared so grand and magnificent; and Nefon must be a large man. He was mistaken in this; Nefon was a small man, — small in stature, though he had a large heart, and a large head. Why was not Nefon on the alert, and when there stood on the walk a stranger who had such interest in his wares, why did he not open the door and invite him in? That was not Nefon's way of doing business. Yet, if he had known who stood there, and what the feelings of the young man were, and how near that young man's feelings were like his own, he would not only have invited him, but even seized him by the collar and snatched him in, and saved him the trouble of getting in as he did; for Richard's heart beat smartly, — so smartly it might have answered for a good knock, if there had been any but himself to hear it, — and he tried the latch twice before it yielded. But he entered. Did the inside of the shop fulfil its out-door promise? Was Nefon equal to NEFON'S? This is the truth of the matter: if Nefon's face — that is, his show-window — looked bright and attractive, his heart — that is, the interior of the store — was less lustrous, but more solid;

darker because it was deeper, and more quiet because it was more substantial. This Richard felt; and if he wondered in the street, he was awed within the walls. What quantities of books! Now, within those books, that filled the shelves on either side, and were piled on the counters, lay many of the purest and profoundest thoughts and feelings that Richard ever had, and many more which he expected to have; and it is not strange that he gazed at the books, and forgot Nefon. Nor did Nefon notice Richard; there were other persons with whom he was engaged.

Richard had heard of great libraries; — of the Alexandrine library, that was burned; of the National Library, at Paris; — but if all the libraries in all the world had been flung into one, and opened to his view, his emotion could not be much deeper than it was now. Not that Nefon had so many books, but Richard had never seen so many.

But before he could set his eye steadily to work, his imagination must exercise itself a little; and there passed, as in a trance, before his mind, many a rosy-colored youthful vision of books, and, as it were, a sea of literary mist, in which floated whole islands of flower-reading; and calm, shady coves of solid intellectual progress opened in the scene. These things over, he could observe more literally the nature of what was about him.

It is an observation of Dr. Johnson, that no place affords a more striking instance of the vanity of human hopes than a public library; for who, he asks, can see the wall crowded on every side by mighty volumes, without considering the oblivion that covers their authors? Yet, had these authors known what eye was upon them now, — how that heart coveted them, — how this young man would have gloated over their dullest lines, and carried to his closet their most neglected tomes, — they would have smiled within their leaves, and, in their own joyous thrill, shaken off the dust that lay on their lids. The meanest author on Nefon's shelves was immortal in Richard's feelings; Richard was fame, fortune, posterity, to all of them. How much suffering, neglect, and toil, was recompensed in that single moment!

But as he gazed at these rows of books, reaching higher than his head, and extending, in shadowy files, far into the rear of the building, the pleasant sky of things became a little overcast. He had this feeling, — that he knew nothing, and never should know anything.

He had the feeling which a young and ardent author may be supposed to have, who enters a book-shop with a basket of books on his arm, to dispose of his wares, and try his fortune in the general market. He sees such a multitude of other authors, with their bright, glittering titles, — some in pretty blue muslin; some in prettier brown goatskin; some arabesqued in gold; others fragrant in Russia: here one, urgent for a purchaser, in two volumes; there one in three: here one reposing in princely folio; there one gemmed in 18mo: one recommended by his engravings; another by his type: some calling attention to the originality of their style; others to the importance of their matter: some pushed forward by backers; others buoyant in their own reputation. He feels that he has not written anything, and never shall write anything; and contemplates the books in his basket as a collection of apes, that he had unwittingly sought to introduce among polite and respectable men, whose chattering he had mistaken for speech; and he would fain set them adrift in the first piece of woods he can find.

So Richard, the admirer of all authors, — so many an author, — is, in a sense, killed by those authors whom Dr.

Johnson summarily consigns to oblivion. This bibliothecal dust, after all, has some power in it.

So, we say, Richard, with these treasures, endless granaries, of wisdom, genius, art and science, before him, felt he knew nothing, and never should know anything. He forgot even the Circulating Library, and paper and pens; and was half resolved to leave the premises, and go home to Memmy and Bebby, and the Green Mill. But ere he had time to execute such a purpose, Nefon accosted him with a cool, How do you do, Sir? Richard could hardly tell how he did.

Recollecting himself, however, he asked after a Circulating Library. Nefon replied that he kept one, retailed the terms, but added, it was an unprofitable part of his establishment, and, moreover, that he had been obliged to adopt the rule of not lending to strangers, — that was, to people out of town, and to such as had no ——. He was at loss for a word; he said credentials, or something of that sort. He meant, to irresponsible persons; to those, in a word, who looked as Richard did.

Ah, Nefon, how could you do so? But Nefon was busy; he had many customers, and many cares, and he did not regard Richard attentively. He had a glimpse at him, and, not thinking but that he might be a prodigal, good-for-nothing fellow, like many in the city, who wanted a novel to read, he answered him as he did. Why did he not look into Richard's gentle, truthful eye? why did he not observe his earnest, honest face? What did he see in the glimpse he had? A red shirt, coarse coat, and rustic manner. The truth must be told, though Nefon falls. The suit which Richard's mother had spun and wove for him, which she had bade him good-by in, and which she had thought, with a strong motherly feeling, "None will be ashamed of my son" in, — that suit well-nigh ruined him with Nefon. Nefon will deny this; but we will put it to him thus: Suppose Richard wore a fine linen shirt, a Cremonia doeskin paletot, and one of Bebee's castors, — would you have answered him as you did?

But Richard possessed a last resort. He took from his wallet a piece of paper, which, after some hesitation, he gave to Nefon. That paper was a sort of cosmopolitan passport for Richard, from the hands of his Pastor. It ran thus: —

"*Green Meadow, Dec.* 18—.

"To whom it may concern.

"This may certify that the bearer, Richard Edney by name, son of John and Mary Edney, of this town, whose birth has been duly registered in the town records, and his baptism in the records of the Church; having arrived at man's estate, and profited of such occasions as his native village affords, being desirous to see other places, and visit cities and towns more remote, is a member of the Church of Christ in this town, and has maintained a good walk and conversation; that he is a lover of truth, and a friend of humanity; is a practical agriculturist; ingenious in the understanding of mechanics, and industrious in the fulfilment of his tasks. He is believed to be a youth of honor and trustworthiness. As such, he is recommended to the fellowship and sympathy of the good, the true, the noble, everywhere.

(Signed) "TIMOTHY HAROLD,
"Pastor of the Church."

This was nuts to Nefon; or it would have been, if he had forthwith cracked them. But between interruptions on the one hand and those first impressions on the other, he dallied. He looked at Richard, — looked as if he had not seen him before, though he had been in the shop twenty minutes. He looked again; and Richard, embarrassed and aggrieved, took the note, and turned away.

Now, why all this? Could not the three thick volumes of Lavater outweigh the short jacket? Why had not Nefon been appointed Head Phrenological Custom-house Inspector, — and he might have determined in a trice that Richard contained no fraud in his composition. We have said Nefon had a great head and a great heart, though he was a small man; but all his greatness would have melted with kindness and run over, had he imagined how the case stood. He will not do so again.

He did offer his library to Richard; he asked him after his business, and where he lived, and said he should be glad to see him again.

Richard took a book, and left the shop; but he could not go home and face the children with empty hands. So he got candy and toys, as a sort of ammunition with which to encounter the onset of their affections.

CHAPTER IX.

SUNDAY AND SUNDAY EVENING.

SATURDAY night the Mills did not run, and Richard enjoyed a regular sleep. Sunday he went to Church; he went with his brother's family. He wore his strong surtout, and his warm red shirt. He had cotton shirts but at this season of the year he did not like to risk a change, and at home he always wore such a shirt to Church in winter.

In the afternoon he said he would like to go to another Church; he named Dr. Broadwell's.

"That is aristocratic," replied his sister, "and your shirt will not be tolerated there."

"I might sit in a back pew," added Richard.

"I would be as good as anybody," rejoined his sister, "or I would not go at all."

"We are as good as anybody, at your Church, Roxy?"

"We stand with the first class, there, and have a centre pew."

"They are better than we are, at Dr. Broadwell's?"

"They *think* they are; that is their conceit, — that is their silly pretension."

"The real difference between us is the shirt."

"I guess," said Munk, "that is about all. There may be a slight odds in the thickness of the hand, but not much. At any rate, the advantage is on your side. Your shirt is as clean as theirs, and it is certainly warmer, and it cost more; and there is quite as much human nature in your hand, brother, as in theirs."

"Well, Richard," — so his sister appealed to him, — "if you will drag the truth out of me, and excruciate me to tell the whole, Mrs. Tunny, the grocer's wife, goes to Dr. Broadwell's, and she has invited us to her house, and I should not like to have her see you at Church in such trim."

"You did not use to talk and feel like this, when you were at home, Roxy."

"The city is not the country, Richard, and you cannot do here as you do there. I have learned many things since I came here; I have learned more of the deceitfulness of the human heart. Elder Jabson is a very different preacher from Parson Harold. You cannot be so independent here, with everybody looking at you, and commenting upon you, and so many slanderous tongues about, and so much depending on propriety and taste. I have changed in some things, and I hope for the better."

"I will compromise matters," replied Richard; "I will not go to Elder Jabson's, for, in fact, I am not accustomed to such a service, nor such discourse. Nor will I go to Dr. Broadwell's, lest my shirt should give *you* offence. I will find some other place."

Richard joined the currents of people that came from every direction, and went in every direction, — as if nobody wished to have it known where he was going, as if everybody was in pursuit of something which he would hide from everybody; — up this street and down it, plunging into that lane and coming out of it, avoiding one another on the crossings, plumping into one another round the corners, disappearing in large doors where nobody else went; — as if heaven was a gold mine, of which each one had had a dream, and snugging the dream in his own thought, he followed its secret intimation; or as if religion were a game of hide and coop, which the whole city was out playing;

and presently you would see these people, joyous and loving, rushing from their retreats to some central spot of Christian feeling!

Richard, with no intelligent bent of his own, except to keep clear of Dr. Broadwell's and Elder Jabson's, adhered to a bevy of people in which he happened to find himself, and in their wake entered the first Church he came to. It was a large Gothic door into which he went; and in the porch whom should he see but Nefon! Now, Nefon had evidently repented him of his sins. It was Sunday, and it was sacrament day, and there was good reason for his doing so. The glare of life was gone, and the encroachments of traffic had abated; and his feelings were calmer, purer, truer. He had found his heaven of enlarged, humane, all-encircling sentiment; and he was stirred with great kindness and brotherliness towards Richard, and took him cordially by the hand. "Show me a back seat, — the negro's seat, if you have one," said Richard. "Come with me," replied the Bookseller, in a quick but significant way he had, meaning more than he said; and most likely haunted by the recollection of his former dereliction, he led Richard to his own pew, which was as conspicuous as any in the Church. Richard could not have appeared to better advantage in Nefon's eye than he did, with his cap off, in meeting, that afternoon. We speak not now of how he appeared to the Omniscient eye, or to the eye of the simple Spirit of Truth. But Nefon saw that his manner was devout and earnest, his expression spiritual and intellectual, and that in worship and instruction his heart was engaged. He saw, moreover, that in the distribution of the sacred elements, Richard was a recipient and he was touched, Nefon was, and he loved Richard more than ever. There was little sectarianism in this, — little of mere wonder or admiration.

The religious tie is perhaps as strong as can bind two hearts together; the tie that comprises time and eternity, God and man; that has for its basis the most solemn and liberal, the most simple and magnificent, exercises of the soul: that sweeps the earth in quest of objects to pity or to save, and still finds in the nearest and homeliest duties the repose of contentment, the affluence of satisfaction, and the lustre of fame; that moves with Destiny, and reposes on Providence; that loves Love, exults in the Pure, and swells in the Light as the new-starting bud of the spring anemone.

Nefon saw no more of Richard's red shirt; it had disappeared utterly, — the flame of his virtues burned and consumed it. We will not say Richard stood naked before Nefon; rather he appeared in the glory and the amiability with which Christ clothes his disciples. Nefon remembered Richard after this; not that he had entirely forgotten him since he saw him in his shop, but he had thought of him by inch-meal and flittingly. Now he appeared to him more as an incarnate, well-favored tangibility.

The after part of the Sabbath, and the twilight, and the evening, are very pleasant. It is a free, tranquil, cheerful time. It is an hour favorable to domestic reünions and social communion. The laboring classes — and that, in fact, means all classes except professed vagabonds — make great and very reasonable account of it. The hurly-burly and wish-wash of existence it visits with a genial humor and purifying serenity. It is a zephyr that fans the feverishness of the week, and soothes excitement and replenishes exhaustion. In the most boisterous weather, when no one goes to meeting, the whole Sabbath has a summery feeling, and many flowers and green leaves of piety, hope, repentance, show their tender faces, which Monday morning is too apt to nip as an untimely frost. There is a reconciliation with God and with one another, at these times, which it is delightful to experience and painful to lose. Heaven then lets down a golden chain, on which every one loves to fasten a prayer, and see it drawn up. Even Memmy felt something of this, for she said to her mother, "How it seems Sundays, don't it?"

Asa Munk was of the firm of Munk and St. John, and their business was with horses. They kept a livery-stable, did some teaming, owned hackney-coaches and an omnibus, and were interested in a stage-route. Their stand was near the Factories, and their business grew naturally out of the rise and increase of the New City.

It will be supposed Munk enjoyed his Sabbaths. He loved to be at home with his wife and children. He loved the enfranchisement and the comfort of the Sabbath. Munk took life easily, though he worked hard. He used to say, "I am always happy, and Prince Albert can't say more." "Bless God for Memmy and Bebby!" he said, this afternoon, as the children played round him. "Bless God for Papa!" echoed Memmy.

The heads of this family could not both be absent to Church at the same time. One must stay with the children, and it had been Munk's turn to do so this afternoon.

"You should have heard the Elder," observed his wife; "he was solemn." "I have great peace of mind in my children," replied Munk. "Children cannot save your soul," said she. "They have been preaching to me all day," said he. "We need something more powerful, more searching," she added. "Children are eloquent, — so Pastor Harold says," interposed Richard, "for the Scripture declares 'out of the mouths of babes and sucklings Thou hast ordained praise.' Children, he says, are standards; for Christ instructs that we must become like them, in order to enter the kingdom of heaven."

"I hope you will not compare Memmy and Bebby with Elder Jabson," returned Mrs. Munk, with a slight tartness of manner, that betokened considerable internal roil.

"The Elder," answered her husband, in a patient, peace-making way, "is meat, strong meat; and the children are nuts and raisins, after it."

There was a point in which Munk was lame, — at least, his wife and Richard both thought so. He let horses on the Sabbath. He qualified this statement, indeed, and extenuated it. Richard replied, quoting Pastor Harold, that the use of horses on the Sabbath should be confined to occasions of necessity and mercy. Munk said the factory-girls and mill-men had no leisure except Sundays; and hinted at their need of recreation. Mrs. Munk said scores of them had been to dancing-schools that winter. Richard observed there were ample woods, the margin of streams, and pleasant roads, where they could walk. Munk said they must visit their friends. Richard asked if they did not go to taverns in the neighborhood, and squander the sacred hours in dissipation. "Even," he continued, "has not Clover had one of your horses to-day for such a purpose?" Munk had not reflected. Munk would not permit such a thing again.

Mrs. Munk was getting tea. Memmy could toast the bread, and so could Bebby; at least she could play at it, — she could hold the empty toast-iron to the fire, and her father put a chip in, which he said she did brown. Memmy could set up the chairs, and so could Bebby. There was a dispute whether Bebby could carry a plate from the closet to the table. "There is one thing we can all do," said Munk; "we can eat. Let us bless God for that!" "Can't everybody eat?" asked Memmy. "No," replied Munk; "some folks can't eat." "I should think it was very funny," answered Memmy. "If you could eat properly," said her Mother, after they were seated at the table, "I should be glad! You have slobbered your bib, and spilt milk on the table-cloth! It was span clean this morning! I should like to keep a cloth clean, one day! I should like to see such a thing, where there are children! It should be published in the newspapers! I would send the cloth to Barnum's!" Memmy could feed herself, and Bebby could want to; and she got a spoon and held lustily to it, in spite of her Mother's efforts to remove it. "Do you feed her, Asa," enjoined the Mother; "I always said, if ever I had a child, it should not feed itself." "You seem to have laid out pretty largely beforehand," added her husband. "I have had experience enough to teach me, at any rate," she rejoined. "Perhaps our children are precocious," suggested Munk in his pleasant way; "who knows? — and we can't expect them to do as other children do." "You have got them into the pulpit," returned his wife, with a demi-sarcasm, "and of course they must be masters of themselves at table. Elder Jabson says we can't be too strict with children." "The Elder," said Munk, "has driven the children from the pulpit, and possibly he would not let them come to the table at all. He never touched a child but he seemed to be taking up a caterpillar."

Munk took things by the smooth handle; but sometimes the handle was rough, and sometimes there was no handle at all then he seized the vessel bodily. So now, after tea, he put his arms about his wife, and drew her into his lap, and kissed her. But the children — munificent little sly-boots! — thought this was not enough, — that his pitcher might be a little more brimming; and Memmy climbed up after her Mother, and Bebby, betwixt lifting and scrambling, got to the same spot, and Munk had his pitcher overflowing; and it was so large he could hardly get his arms around it. But it was all nectar to him, — a glass of joy and hope, that hummed and chirped, — and he crushed it handsomely. "Let us be good, and happy," he said to his wife; "let us not borrow trouble; don't keep your spirits spotted as a painter's shop, but clean and bright as your own little kitchen. God has given us many comforts; let us be grateful and enjoy them, as Pastor Harold used to say. Let us be just to ourselves, by wisely improving what we have, and not eat the crib when we have plenty of sweet fodder." "O!" sighed his wife, "it is such a responsibility!" "It is heavier," he rejoined, "because you let it weigh on you. Put it out of your heart a little; it gets water-soaked in your feelings, and sinks. We have house-room enough; let it play about now and then. We have chairs enough; see if it will not sit down and rest itself. Try and make it stand on its own feet, dear, and you will be easier, and just as good." His wife threw herself on his neck, and cried; he pressed his arm about her very softly and warmly, and kissed her cheek, and the little ones kissed their Mother, and then their Father kissed them.

Richard, meanwhile, went to visit the Orphans at Whichcomb's. Here he found a lady to whom he was introduced as Miss Dennington, daughter of the Governor's. It was Melicent. She was dressed in a blue satin bonnet with bird-of-paradise feathers, and a purple velvet sack. Did he recognize this dress? He had seen it before. Did she remember having seen him? — That she was on an errand of mercy, appeared in her sitting by the sick-bed, and laying her hand on the head of Violet, to whom she spake in soft, low tones; and likewise in the fresh oranges and an unbroken glass of jelly on the small table at the head of the bed, which she must have brought.

Violet was no better, and she would never be in this world; but she was without pain, mental or bodily, and she had that look of transparent, moon-light repose, which, if it be ominous of death, is beautiful as life. Junia, pale with waching and confinement, was still of patient, perennial, sisterly love and devotion. The Old Man romanced with the fire, making it seem how he could graduate it exactly to the necessities of the room, and the state of the wood-box; showing his skill in using from the scant pile, and not diminishing it.

"You achieved a great deed in the street, the other day," said Junia to Richard.

"I owe my deliverance to you," added Melicent, "and I know not but my life. Father said it was a narrow escape."

"I did not know who it was in the sleigh," replied Richard. "The horse showed good pluck. I never had the handling of one before so set on making music out of my bones."

"Were n't you hurt?" asked Melicent.

"I should have been," he replied, "but that my mother, probably anticipating some accident to her son, had encased his flesh in stout wrappages."

They were interrupted by the entrance of the mistress of the house with the tray. "How do you do, Miss Dennington?" she said. "How is the Governor? We heard he was unwell; we could not afford to lose him. Elder Jabson is having a Reformation; well, there is need enough of it, — we are all bad enough. I do not expect to get to Heaven on my own merits, according to Parson Smith's doctrine; —

I hope I may have none of that sin to answer for. I am ready to help the sick and the destitute, though they are ungrateful. Madam has sent some jelly; my own is most gone, we have had so much sickness, and there is so much call for chicken-soup, and nice steaks, and arrow-root, and lemonade, and jellies, which we never mean to be out of for a moment; for who knows when another will be taken down, and all the things in the house called for?" She took the paper cover from a jelly-glass that looked as if Noah's wife, in her haste to disembark, had put it away unwashed in a closet of the ark, and it now made its appearance for the first time in Mrs. Whichcomb's tray. But no—it was not its first appearance; three times a day, for as many months, that identical glass, with its identical contents, had been brought into the chamber on that tray. "I do feel for the unfortunate," she added, as she offered the venerable cordial to the sick one. "Would your sister, Miss Junia, relish a slice of ham, and a few griddle-cakes, or a dish of stewed oysters, which are so innocent? or must we still keep her on the cracker-water the Doctor recommended? It is not easy, Miss Dennington, to know what will agree with the sick, which I have had some experience that way for thirty years."

Mrs. Whichcomb was complaisant and deferential in presence of Miss Dennington, and she forebore her gibes and quirks with Richard. And when she saw Melicent and our friend freely conversing together, she even went so far as to commend Richard to her ear. "The coldest night that ever was," says she, "this young gentleman brought wood to these poor folk; and many is the time since, he has taken their basket to the Saw-mill and filled it, which he did not know that we had a plenty of it, and country boys is apt to do. And he has sent his sister, Mrs Munk, to watch; and he has got other women to come and spell Miss

Junia; and he is almost a stranger in the city, himself; which shows goodness, if it does not lead to pride, which is apt to be, as Charley Walter could not think."

Mrs. Whichcomb retired. Melicent, with an ill-suppressed smile, said to Richard, "Is Asa Munk's related to you?" "Mr. Munk is my brother-in-law," replied Richard. "Did you find it, that night?" she asked. "I found it," he answered, "the night I came to Woodylin." "You must be the person we encountered on the Bridge," she continued. "And you of the party that was frightened by a drunken man," he rejoined. "We were in quite a gale. The darkness of the Bridge is wont to create a giddy, rattling reäction in the spirits of all who cross it." "You must be Transcendentalists, if I understand Pastor Harold's account of that thing," said Richard. "Very likely we are," she added. "Have you attended the Athenæum Lectures?" she asked. Richard said he had not; that he did not know of them. "Have you ever worshipped at the Church of the Redemption?" she asked. "What is that?" Richard queried. "In which Parson Smith officiates," she replied. Richard answered that he was there this afternoon. "This must be the young man," she said, turning to Junia, "that defended your Grandfather so ably at his trial." "I have no doubt of it," replied Junia. "He has been as a brother to us, and that when we were entire strangers to him." Richard replied that he had only done what he felt to be his duty. Melicent commended his generosity, and hoped he would persevere in the practice of usefulness, and ever maintain those principles of virtue which he seemed to have adopted.

Richard left with a new impression in his heart, — that light-spirited, lyrical impression, which the approbation of a refined, high-bred, religious woman is fitted to produce.

At the foot of the stairs he met Miss Eyre, who drew

him into the parlor, and seated herself near him. She had been weeping; her face was flushed, and her eye swollen. She was subdued by an apparent melancholy. She looked at him tenderly and beseechingly. She said, "Mr. Edney, you have shown the goodness of your nature by your attentions to the sick; you will exhibit the greatness of your spirit by commiserating the distressed. Some have disease, some have sorrows. You know this, — I need not assure you of it. Have I ever appeared harsh, or resentful, or haughty, may God forgive me. I can be depressed, — I am depressed. But why should I say it? Yet how can a woman help being weak at times? I would dash away this tear, but it is best you should see it. You do see it, and none but you shall see it. Have you pity, — can you pity?" Richard replied that he could, though clearly he did not know as an answer was expected. "I have then only to ask your friendship. I cannot relate my sorrows; 't is no matter what they are. You will be my friend." "Certainly," said Richard; "I am your friend." "I can rely on you, then." She rose as she said this, and stood like one on the point of departing. "I shall appeal to you, — I shall have confidence in you." With her face towards him, she slowly retreated. "Remember," said she, raising her jewelled finger, "that you are my friend." "Of course," rejoined Richard, "I am your friend."

The pleasant impression which Melicent had left in his soul was not effaced by this rencontre with Miss Eyre; albeit a slight confusion of thought was thereby engendered; but not sufficient to prevent the calm serenity of the setting Sabbath sun exerting its full effect, or to darken the many-tinted, lustrous dew-drops that glittered through the green wood of his sensibilities.

That affair was like a high suspension-bridge over a dark

gulf; but he crossed it rapidly, and was soon on the safe side of his home. And here he was very happy; not happier, indeed, than when he went away; but it seemed as if the lamp of his feelings had been turned up a little, and he gave a little stronger light; or this may have been the mere reflection of the light and happiness that was about him; for his sister was more heartsome, the children more blithe, and Munk was always sunshine. Moreover, they had opened the parlor, and the little air-tight was busy as a bee in summer, filling it with sweetness and pleasantness. The neighbors, and others, were dropping in, including Tunny, the Green Grocer, and his wife, Mr. Gouch, head-stock man, and Mrs. Grint, an aunt of Munk's. There was a heavy stamping in the entry, and an audible wheezing; and Munk said it was Winkle, and the children knew it was Winkle, and Winkle it was. Now, there was not, probably, on all this polyzonal orb, a pleasanter, we mean a more pleasure-giving face, and coat, and hand, than Winkle's; and whip too, — for he brought his whip into the parlor, — and cap, and muffler. He was one of Munk and St. John's drivers, and was employed on a mail route that extended some fifty miles into the country. He was inclined to corpulency, and his face was full-blown, and so were his lips, and red as a tomato; and his skin was varnished with the cold and the storms he every day encountered. He wore a blue, shaggy, lion-skin overcoat, margined with black. But face, coat and all, were radiant with delight, — we mean everybody felt delighted where they came. The totality of the man was a self-working decanter, perpetually discharging satisfaction into the breasts of all whom he encountered. There was this difference between Munk and Winkle, — the first was a subjective, the other an objective, delight. Munk was always happy in himself. Winkle made everybody else happy. In other respects they had a good deal in common. But we cannot say all we ought of Winkle here. What a man he was, and how he communicated so much joy, and how people liked him, are matters that would cram a dozen pages; and none that knew him would be satisfied with what we have now said, and we must compound with these friends of his by a promise of more hereafter.

But, sakes alive! what are we doing? We are in the midst of Memmy-and-Bebby-dom; and what have we to do with Winkle, or anybody else? Winkle has gone, disappeared, swallowed up in a teknocratical tempest. The children control the parlor, and the hour. They are sovereigns, — they are empire. Under the guns of their fort every vessel that enters must lie to; they are as big as Cæsar Augustus; all the world pays tribute to them; you can't approach them without bowing as many times as you do to the Chinese Emperor. Attractive as Winkle is, dry as Aunt Grint is, proud as Mrs. Tunny is, strong as Mr. Gouch is, and selfish, independent, consequential, vain, preöccupied, as everybody is, all cotton to Memmy and Bebby. Even Winkle's great whip, that four as smart horses as there were in the county ran from, and all the cows were afraid of, and dogs leaped stone-walls to get out of the way of, yielded to them. Winkle himself, weather-seared, porpoise-limbed as he was, went capering and rigadooning about them, as if they were tarantulas, and had bitten him, and kept him dancing for their amusement. Aunt Grint, chromatic, grum, hard-mouthed, who looked as if she had been kiln-dried, and all her natural juices evaporated off, — how she sweetened to the children, and tiddled them, and caroled to them! She was always believing something was going to happen; — she had seen a strange-looking, corpse-shaped substance in the yolk of an egg; and when a member of the family had died a while ago, they did not hang crape on the bee-hive. But the children *had* happened, and there was no help for it; they were the event, and Aunt Grint was confounded before it. Then she thought Munk was no Christian, because he let his coach carry ladies to balls; but good a Christian as she was herself, she could not help loving him when she looked at his children. Then there was Mrs. Tunny, a sleek, round, fubby piece of mortality, with bunches of ribbons in her hair, and bunches in her neck, who owned a broad-aisle pew in Dr. Broadwell's Church, — had been to a party at Judge Burp's, — hired a piano for her daughters, — boasted of a cousin in New York, — who exchanged bows with the Mayoress, whom she did not know, and who would not bow to a great many people that she did know; — even she, all engulfed in a huge cotton-velvet sack, paid her duty to the children, — stooped to them, and toadied about them.

So we might go round the room, and tell how these dear despots worked their cards, lording it everywhere; and nobody could look at anything else, or talk of anything else, or do for anything else, but them.

Richard and Munk were of course in their glory, for their countenances seemed to say, "See there! Just what I told you; the children are mighty little things; no matter what Elder Jabson says, they have a masterly power on the human heart."

There was Tunny, a little man, diffident, white-faced, as if he had grown up under the shadow of his wife, — how richly he colored when he held Memmy in his arms, — how his lank knees puffed and swelled when he trotted her! Mr. Gouch, who seemed never to have been properly kneaded, so loose he was in his joints, so tripping in utterance, so quivering in the muscles of his face, as if he had done nothing all his days but hop over logs, dodge Silver, and peer after Clover, — came completely into requisition, and displayed the education of his life in leaping over the children on the floor, bopeeping to them behind the sofa, and mouthing with Bebby.

The children, of course, did their best; and being in state, it behoved them to magnify it. Memmy got on the floor, on all fours, and Winkle trod on her, and tickled her with his foot; and Bebby got down too, like a frog, on the floor, and, like the frog in the fable, she swelled up under his feet; and he repeated all he had done to Memmy; and how archly she looked up to him, and how she laughed, and how they all laughed! Memmy whispered something to Uncle Richard, as if he was her Prime Minister; and Bebby likewise sought his ear, and mummed at it; then she retreated, and came back again, and mummed some more; and there were additional peals of laughter. Bebby could not talk; but she could dummy and warble and crool and caw, and look with her eyes and point with her finger; and this was a sort of high-born language, which the commonalty around her were not expected to understand; but it puzzled them, and set them to surmising and gossiping, as the actions of the great are wont to do.

Uncle Richard got the singing-books, and they sang psalm-tunes; and Memmy and Bebby sang too, — and did n't their singing attract more attention than all the rest? Bebby, one would think, had learned to sing in that other state of existence in which metempsychosis places us all; and she was not yet familiar enough with our modes of utterance to make herself intelligible; but all agreed that it was very wonderful. While the others were singing, Memmy got up little concerts of her own, and introduced, with an originality peculiar to herself, a medley of stanzas, beginning, "My Bible leads to Glory," "Get out of the way, Old Dan Tucker," "Mary had a little Lamb," "Wild roved the Indian Girl, bright Alfarata."

"I fear we are too happy," said Aunt Grint; "oh, I do!"

"You don't?" answered Mrs. Munk, startled.

"Jabson preaches at the school-house to-night, and we are not prepared for it," continued the Aunt.

"I know I love the children too well," replied Mrs. Munk.

"There 's it," rejoined the other. "You make idols of them, and something will happen to them. Jabson looked very solemn when he went by our house to-day, and I know it 's a death. It must be a death. He looked so the night John Creely was taken."

"Come, Aunt," interposed Munk, "let Roxy alone this time. She has not digested all you have told her before; and it is n't best to overload, body or mind."

"I only want you to attend to what I tell you, Asa," she rejoined, "before it is too late, and not let the children draw off your affections so."

"I see through you, Aunt," returned Munk; "I understand it all, and you know how 't is, only you are modest, and won't say so. The more my affections are drawn off, the more they keep pouring in; and I have such a pile of them here, I don't know, Aunt, but I should go crazy, if I had n't you to love. Bring in Jabson; I would love him to-night. Roxy has been so bad here, this afternoon, getting into my lap, and kissing me, and looking so smiling, and being so happy," — he pinched his wife's ear, — "oh, if she had n't any children, how good she would be!"

"Bad man!" replied Aunt Grint; "bad Asa, you won't believe anything till you see it; and when it comes, you say it is n't there."

"I could see better if it were not so dark, Roxy," he said;

"you must light the solar, — then it will be all as plain as a pipe-stem."

No sooner did Memmy hear the clinking of the glass shade than she said, "I can light the taper," and was permitted to demonstrate her ability. She thrust the taper through the register of the air-tight; but when she attempted to draw it out, the flame was sucked in and extinguished. She burned her face, and almost her hand, in the undertaking, and had to give it up. Memmy-and-Bebby-dom was over! Their reign was ended. It is the misfortune of greatness that, like the Legalist, if it fail in one point, it is guilty of all, and can indemnify its blunders only by retirement. The children must go to bed. Papa unhooked and untied Memmy, and Mamma undid Bebby; but even now, in disgrace, as it were to show the true imperiality of their natures, before they could be reärranged for the bed, they slipped away, and recommenced their tantrums about the room. But they were pursued, seized, endued with the costume of obscurity, and thrust into the truckle-bed.

Aunt Grint exhaled a long sigh, and breathed easier; and expressed her sense of relief in these words, "I am glad it is over!"

"What is over?" asked Munk.

"The children," she replied.

"That is not over," rejoined Munk; "it has only begun. I go at it to-morrow, and keep it up all the week."

"If you would only go to the meetings," said his aunt; "the Reformation is commenced, and they are to be held every day, as long as the Lord will."

"I am going to the meetings," added he; "Roxy is going, Winkle is going, — we are all going."

"Not Tunny and I," exclaimed Mrs. Tunny.

"Yes; Tunny and you," replied Munk.

"Not Tunny and I," retorted the lady; "they are noisy, riffraffy, and smell of cowheel and codfish, — uncomfortable to polite minds, disrelishable to respectable society, and dangerous to genteel young ladies. Faustina shall not go, nor Theodoric. Dr. Broadwell does not approve of them, nor Parson Smith, and they are men of taste."

"Yes, all," continued Munk; "we have begun to-night, and we will go on, press on, pray on, sing on. Come, Uncle Richard, help us to some more music."

"I can't let the chance pass," said Aunt Grint, "without saying to Mrs. Tunny that what the Lord approves is good enough for her to approve, and that the souls of the righteous will shine at the last day, when some other souls will not look quite so well."

Mrs. Tunny nodded to Aunt Grint, and smiled.

"All," pursued Munk, as he turned the leaves of the Psalm-book, "all go to meeting, all sing, all good, all happy. Bless the Lord for what we have, and are, and can be, and is always a being, and a happening; bless him for Dr. Broadwell, Parson Smith, and Elder Jabson, and Memmy and Bebby!"

They sang, and softened down; and becoming very musical they sang more. Aunt Grint thought they might have some praying; and if nobody else would pray, she would. Richard prayed, and they parted.

CHAPTER X.

A CHAPTER RESPECTING WHICH THERE IS A DOUBT WHETHER IT OUGHT TO BE INTRODUCED. N. B. — NONE BUT THE PRINTER OBLIGED TO READ IT.

THERE is one point which, as faithful historian of Richard, and his times and place, we shall be obliged to mention. Yet, since it connects us with a controversy of a nature equally intricate, obscure, and exciting, involving such numbers of people, and one many of the parties to which still survive, we would gladly omit it. Still, as the narrative cannot proceed without allusions thereto, we address ourselves to the task before us.

It was a question, in a word, of Cats and Dogs; yet, insignificant as this may appear, there are few things in the course of human affairs that have attained so much consequence, or threatened so serious results. The origin of the dispute it is not easy to trace, but its principal elements are more readily deduced. Many years anterior to this tale, a respectable individual of Woodylin had his cat worried by a dog. A dispute arose with the owner of the dog. Families were inflamed, neighborhoods took sides, and at last the whole city was drawn into the controversy. One party would have all the cats killed; the other denounced the dogs.

There was no harmony of purpose. Those who sought to destroy the dogs wished to preserve the cats; on the other hand, whoever was friendly to a dog became the determined enemy of a cat. Two parties were formed, and officered, and drilled, and propagated. The newspapers espoused one doctrine or the other; and when Richard came to the place, there were two dailies, discriminated according to the sentiment of the times. One of these was called The Catapult, a name borrowed from an ancient piece of ordnance which was understood to have been employed against cats. The other bore the name of Dogbane; the sense of which is obvious. The people were sometimes called Dogs, or Cats, according to their respective preferences. The subject-matter was ordinarily denominated "Phumbics." The origin of this term cannot be discovered.

Phumbics, if I may so say, formed much of the spirit and temper of the city, — became part of the popular feeling, and entered into many public acts. It opened various and lucrative offices. It determined the election of Mayor and Aldermen; and sometimes, even, it was whispered that a Clergyman owed his living to his peculiar phumbical sentiments. Phumbical meetings were held; processions instituted, and flags hoisted; there were phumbical Reading-ing-rooms and Hotels.

Whenever the Dogbanians came into power, you would perceive a violent tremor in all the streets and thoroughfares of the city. Men, armed with stout clubs pursued the objects of their fury; the yelping of dogs tormented the ear; their blood glaired the sidewalks, and their carcasses filled the docks.

These measures were of course retaliated, in the event of a change of administration; the Dog-haters were hurled from place, and the Cat-killers assumed the reins of affairs. The hour of their operations was partly in the night, and the scenes of their attack were chiefly the neighborhood of houses. They scoured wood-sheds and barns; they chased their victims through yards and gardens. Wherever a mewing was heard, to that point scores of men were seen staving and hallooing.

Of the merits of this controversy we shall not speak. The leading arguments were these. The Dogbanians asserted that dogs were dangerous; that they frequently bit people, and dispensed that terrible malady, canine madness; and were at all times the terror of the women and children. The other party declaimed on the great annoyance of cats; their terrific screams in the night, so detrimental to the sick, and so hostile to the repose of every one. In addition, their pilfering habits were portrayed, and elaborate tables published showing the quantities of meat, poultry, pies, etc., they annually wasted. The number of their incursions into the larder and the cellar was reckoned up. They allowed, indeed, the usefulness of the cat as rat-catcher and hearth-rug companion; but their aversion chiefly vented itself against so many foreign cats, and the endless multiplication of cats. Foreign cats, they said, injured the utility of our own cats; spoiled their habits, and prevented the proper end for which the cat was designed.

The other party, again, commended dogs for their watchfulness and sociability, and were willing that the race should be preserved; and only sought to impose proper restrictions upon it, and lessen its liability to evil.

They might have discriminated, and discrimination was a word ever on their tongue. Yet, practically, were they always in extremes; excited feeling, in this, as in most human affairs, sweeping off the deliberateness of judgment.

Were there not some who perceived whatever advantages and disadvantages pertained to both races, and who would apply protection wherever it was deserved, and practise extermination to the extent it was needed? There were; and these were called fence-men, and had no repute. They were accounted persons without decision and without judgment. Whifflers, temporizers, trimmers, were the softest epithets allowed them.

Let it not be implied that Phumbics was the sole-absorbing topic of Woodylin. It was not; and only at critical intervals — just before an election, or something of that sort — did it rage.

It was, also, tacitly understood among the people, that there were many subjects, occasions, and places, where it was not admissible. For instance, it was a part of the constitution of the Lyceum, that the question of Cats and Dogs should be touched by no lecturer. The Sons of Temperance, by solemn vote, decreed that it should not be named in their halls. From the Pulpit it was supposed to be excluded, and one Clergyman gave great offence, and was charged with violating the comity of the times, by reading a portion of Scripture, in which the exhortation occurs, Beware of dogs. It was said he emphasized the words, and uttered them with a peculiar snarl of the voice, whereby the friends of that race were aggrieved. It was an interdicted topic in schools; social parties were not expected to be disturbed by it, and it was considered no ground of divorce between man and wife.

It did determine the course of trade somewhat. Catapulters transacted business with Catapulters, and Dogbanians were expected to patronize Dogbanians. Yet a merchant did not ordinarily ask after the Phumbics of his customer, when a good bargain was on the threshold.

The even tenor of things, whether it be that of aversion or amity, however, was interrupted by the rise of another party who called themselves Hydriatics, or Water-men. They said the questions that had so long agitated the public mind were trifling and useless, — that weightier issues should be considered. Their doctrine was, that more water should be used; that men ought to be washed,—the city cleansed and purified. On these principles, they gained many adherents; held public meetings, diverted men from the old parties, and appeared with considerable force at the polls. Their numbers were composed of simple and well-meaning people. They established a paper, called The Rinser.

Now commenced what was called a triangular fight, each party having to shoot two ways. But the old parties did not unite and expel the new sect,—a thing which might easily have been accomplished; rather they became more and more embittered against each other. Still the Hydriatics were the subjects of not a little abuse from both quarters. It was said that it was not their real object to benefit the city, but to arrive at its emoluments. "They would clean it, indeed, by rifling its offices! Spunge the inhabitants! Undoubtedly." If a member of the old parties joined the new, he was said to be a disappointed man, and reviled as a traitor.

The anti-dogs were, at one period, greatly excited. It was mid-summer, and the Hydriatics were very active. It got bruited that it was the object of these interlopers to introduce water into the city, and set the dogs mad, and fill the place with confusion and death; and out of the general distress and alarm extract personal benefit, by plunder or usurpation.

Diabolical plots and mischievous artifices were continually discovered.

If we dwell at all on matters that are familiar to any of our readers, it is that our distant friends, the Turks and Tartars, may have a more complete insight into Life in the New World.

The Editor of the Dogbane, a keen-eyed man, earnestly devoted to the interests of the city, but quite sensitive to innovation, writes, one morning, as follows: "A new ruse of the Catapults! — The leaders of that party, who scruple at nothing where their own interests are concerned, have been known to be busy, for a long time, about the Hatters' and Furriers' shops; and it is understood those trades have consented to vote the opposition ticket. The secret is out. These unprincipled demagogues, in case they come into power, have bargained to make a free-gift of the skins of all the cats that are killed to those artificers, who work them into muffs and tippets."

The Editor of the Catapult, likewise keen-eyed, very Woodylian, but perhaps too much concerned for party, replied, the next morning, in this wise: "Our neighbor, across the River, need not attempt to pull wool or fur over our eyes. He discloses his own baseness. The Apothecaries have been bribed to desert the only principles on which the good of the community depends, by a promise of a monopoly in the sale of strichnine. The city, which is already largely in debt for that article, is to pay whatever price infamy and treachery shall demand."

We clip the following from the papers of the time.

"COALITION! — ANOTHER PLATE OF ABOMINATIONS!

"The Butchers have joined the Hydriatics, under a bargain that if they carry the election the ordinance for the throwing of the carcasses of cats and dogs into the River shall be revoked! A more abominable device to ruin the credit of Woodylin with the eating public could not have been got up in the conclave below!"

"———, who vociferated in the Catapultian caucus last night, true to his instincts, is offended by the loss of a favorite dog, which had bitten a horse and two children, before it could be destroyed. Such selfishness is worthy of the Catapults, and may they make the most of it!"

"———, whom the Dogbanians have taken into favor, is seeking reparation for injury done to his garden, in the attempt to break up a nest of cats, whose hideous cries, under the window of a sick neighbor, caused the patient to relapse into fits. Pay the wretch!"

The Tanners, having got a charter for a Dog-hide Tanning establishment, applied to Congress for an increase of duty on that species of merchandise. This measure provoked a singular hash in the public feeling. A violent debate arose as to whether it would diminish the number of dogs. Some said, of course it would, — it will kill them off; others said, Nay, it will be a premium for their production. Some, who hated high tariffs and dogs with equal acerbity, went almost frantic with doubt and uncertainty. Certain Catapulters, who were alike attached to high tariffs and to dogs, were on the point of committing suicide. The parties criminated and recriminated. Again, Catapulters were seen electioneering for Dogbanians. Then they charged all the evil on the Hydriatics, who had introduced the project, they said, for the purpose of weakening both the old parties, and aiding themselves. What gave color to this suspicion, was the fact that the Tanners had negotiated with the Hydriatics, in case they succeeded in their plan of bringing an aqueduct into the city, for a supply of water from that source for their establishment. The Butchers, who had already gone over to the new party, it was reported, were combining for the purchase of the carcasses. The Tanners had, also, won over the Shoe-makers, and the Leather-dealers. It was rumored that the Farmers in the neighboring towns were making extensive preparations for the raising of dogs; and such as had bark to sell, were all agog in anticipation of a lively market. Then it was suggested that Cat-skin tanning would come into vogue, and works for that purpose be built, and new duties demanded; and this created fresh consternation.

Where the matter might have ended, we cannot say, if the dogs had not betimes taken the decision into their own hands, and in mortal dread of the fate that awaited them, wasted away, so that the Butchers would not have their flesh, and their hides became too dry and crisp for the Tanners.

We repeat that Phumbics, except at brief periods, was not an absorbing theme, save with those who made it a profession and trade; and at the time Richard came to the city, the excitement had materially exhausted itself. The great interests of life, the diversified occupations of human beings, the Family, the School, and the Church; trade and manufactures; the farm, the factory, and the ship-yard; wooing and marrying, preserved their balance, and exerted their supremacy.

CHAPTER XI.

A PARTY AT TUNNY'S.

THIS was to be a grand affair. The note of preparation sounded long and loud: it rattled at the door of many houses; it purled in the ears of Judges and Clergymen; it whirred about the Confectioner's, and rebounded to the Fruiterer's, and darted away to the Milliner's and Fancy Goods Dealer's. Munk and his wife and Richard went. Richard fairly struck his high colors to the persuasions of his sister, and ran up instead a white collar and bosom-piece.

The note of preparation, like the wind to which we thoughtlessly likened it, passed by many persons unheeded. But there were enough there. The two parlors, connected by folding-doors, swam with guests. The Milliner's and Fancy Goods Dealer's had evidently come. Clover was there, and Plumy Alicia; Mr. and Mrs. Xyphers, Captain Creamer, and Judge Burp; and there were many other persons from the Factories and the Mills, and all the region about. And Mrs. Tunny was there, — indeed she was, and it seemed as if half the Milliner's and Fancy Goods Dealer's clustered in her single person; and what she could spare had gone to her daughter Faustina. Mrs. Tunny curtsied to Richard so stiffly, so amazingly, it embarrassed the bow he was executing, and converted it into a horrid bungle. Richard himself blushed; and his sister, who was truly proud of him, — proud of his fine figure, and fine face, and proud too, I must say, in justice to her, of his noble heart, —

blushed also. And by the time he had finished Tunny, and got through with Faustina, he was in a truly shocking state. He lost his rudder, his feet, foundered on his hands; and made for a blank place on the wall, as a haven, like a vessel in distress. But here was Plumy Alicia, glittering with jewelry, and beaming with sensibility. Ah, wicked, wicked Plumy Alicia! how could you exert your art to reassure Richard so? How could you take advantage of that moment to show him that you did not mind his awkwardness, but only regarded himself, so? And when you got him to face the room, right in the midst of the lights, right in the midst of the Milliner's and Fancy Goods Dealer's, there stood Clover, with the fingers of one hand thrust in his vest, and dispensing perfume with a bouquet of flowers in the other, — so cool, so steady, so strut, and with a snake-like eye, looking down on Richard so triumphantly; — and you knew it all, — how could you do so? You are a medley of elements. And so Richard thought; at least, you laid the seeds of that thought in his memory, which was to spring up by-and-by. There was also Captain Creamer, who looked resentful and surly, even when he did his best to salute you in a polite way. And there was Mrs. Xyphers, with whom Clover was talking; and when Richard would have exchanged with her the compliments of the evening, you even drew him back; you pouted, in a quiet, but stealing, very stealing manner, your pretty lips, and Richard only half did what he set out to do. Then you had him all to yourself; and you were so amiable, so round-cornered, so genteel, — what did you mean? Would you make Richard love you? Let me tell you, Plumy Alicia, Richard could not love you; — I mean, the depths, the teeming crypts, the abeyant longings of his nature, you could not thrill; — and I believe you knew it.

Yet, you could exert a magical power; and that you did know.

There sat on the sofa, quite unobtrusively and unseductively ensconced behind the jam of people, a woman plainly dressed, with dark eyes, and bands of rich black hair. Her face was comely, but not handsome; her eye was small and retreating, but expressive of great earnestness, thought and animation; so much so that Richard looked at her twice. Miss Eyre, kindly attentive to the motions of our friend, said it was Miss Freeling, a dressmaker. At Richard's request, she presented him, and he took his seat by the stranger. If Richard had been flurried by Miss Tunny, and ravished by Miss Eyre, he was quite restored by Miss Freeling. They talked about the weather, as everybody else on first meeting must do; and spoke to the mooted question, whether after so severe a winter we should have an early spring. The thought of spring, when it did come, gave to Miss Freeling the same sort of halcyon, saltatory, juvenescent feeling that Richard had, and this made them seem like old friends. Moreover, Miss Freeling expressed the hope that she should be attacked by no more snow-storms, since, she said, it painfully suggested her inferiority to nature; and she related how, a little while before, she had been worsted in such encounter, and was rescued by some angel-man, she would be glad to know who. Now, this angel-man was Richard, and this, of course, transformed them into the very best of friends.

Then Miss Freeling knew a great many people; and she knew Asa and Roxy, and Aunt Grint, and Memmy and Bebby; that was enough. But if she had known a deal more, — if she had known whether Pope was a poet, or where Captain Kidd hid his money, or who the man in the Iron Mask was, — she would have been obliged to stop; for every one in the room stopped, and Richard turned his head, and she turned her head, to see Mrs. Tunny advance to receive Dr. Broadwell. Yes, that lady advanced several steps, when that venerable form was seen entering the door, having on his arm one of his daughters.

"Mrs. Tunny mistakes her part," observed Miss Freeling; "she should keep her standing, and wait for the guest to approach."

"I am not expert in the rules of good society," replied Richard.

"Mrs. Tunny should be," said Miss Freeling; "she tries hard enough to be."

"The disdain of the woman is more reprehensible than her want of manners," added Richard.

"She was a dressmaker, and I was apprenticed to her; and I know her sufficiently well."

"She must have some good feelings, as Pastor Harold says."

"She has, but they are buried beneath a mountain of worldliness and ribbons."

"Elder Jabson is no favorite of hers."

"He was once, until she discovered that Dr. Broadwell's Church was richer and more fashionable."

"She visits at Mr. Munk's, and his family go to the Elder's meeting."

"She would forget them speedily, but for her interest. Munk and St. John are customers of her husband's, and help to keep her plumes a nodding. For the same reason her entertainment to-night comprises many from the Factories and the Mills, whom she draws not in the train of her feelings, but her necessities. Her dress is not in taste, — indeed, she never had any taste; her cap is a mile too small, her tunic is unsuited to her figure, and her white skirt terminates in yellow slippers."

"At home, we had but one Church, one people, one rank, one intimacy."

"Here there are many; and I know something of them all. I have worked in every family, from the summit to the base of the social frame. I have made brocade dresses for Governor Dennington's daughters, and muslin ones for Tunny's; Dr. Broadwell's daughter was under my fingers before she came here, and so was Mrs. Xyphers."

"What is the difference?"

"All women look pretty much alike to a dressmaker. There is but little odds in waists, upper ten or lower ten. What we study is forms, and what we aim at is a fit."

"Are they alike?"

"They are not; but the difference is not perhaps what you would think. It is *good sense*, more than anything else. Lacking this, some aspire to what they cannot reach, — others tread on what they cannot depress. With it Munk and the Mayor are equally princely. Differences! There are the Gum-chewers, — all backlotters, and vulgar. But why, my good Sir, is gum more base in woman than tobacco in a man? There are the Rocker-footed and the Square-footed; the vulgar, in stepping, go over from the heel to the toe, like the rocker of a cradle; the genteel tread square. These are some of the wonderful differences!"

"The other night, at our house, Mrs. Tunny berated Elder Jabson's people and meetings; lessening their characters and deprecating their influence."

"They were vulgar, she said; and added, I suppose, that Dr. Broadwell did not approve of them. The Doctor is her cue; and she alights about him, and follows his track, as birds do a ploughman, for the worms that are turned up in the furrow. But the forms of religion, or the modes in which it is applied, do work characteristic and deep-seated changes. Into whatever family I go, I can very soon perceive what Church they attend, and what is the turn of their religious views. Elder Jabson seems to me like a silly dressmaker, — and I am sometimes that one myself, — who, instead of studying becomingness, aims at effect; he produces nothing beautiful, — his labors result in jauntiness, incongruity and distortion. He does not clothe the soul, but finifies it. His flounces are enormous, and he compresses the chest so that it is almost impossible to breathe. He does not enlighten the mind, or refine the feelings, or restrain the prejudices, or enlarge the humanity, of his people. He addresses the darker passions, — not the tenderness, or the love, or the aspirations, of our being."

"Yet," replied Richard, "I should prefer Aunt Grint to Mrs. Tunny."

"Dr. Broadwell," continued Miss Freeling, "is a most excellent man; he has good sense, and, so to say, good taste; he understands the soul, and how Christianity applies to it, and endeavors that the robe of righteousness shall be a seemly one. But he has one fault; he makes his people think too much of their dresses; and he has a freak which I cannot bear, — that there shall be just five rows of quilling on the border. Parson Smith has the most perfect theory of soul-costume, but he does not always succeed in working it; or, rather, some of his people are so wild that, like savages, they will not wear their clothes when he puts them on."

"Is there not good sense," asked Richard, "among the lower orders as in the higher?"

"It is good sense," replied Miss Freeling, "that creates the higher orders. Joined to this, — sometimes leading it, sometimes enforcing it, — are education, opportunity, industry, self-denial. It is his good sense in law, politics, business, life, that gives to Gov. Dennington his distinction. If Mrs. Tunny had more of it, she would be a respectable and worthy woman. She does not make her own daughter's dresses, as the busy-bodies report, lest the prick of the needle should appear on her fingers. Faustina is a sensible girl; — she is pursued by a young man, a Sailmaker, whose attentions she discards, as his friends say, because of her aristocratic feelings; as her mother unequivocally declares, because he is a mechanic; but as I certainly know, simply and solely by reason of his habits."

Dr. Broadwell, who was exchanging a word with those he knew, recognizing Richard, took him cordially by the hand, presented his daughter, and inquired after the Orphans. Ada deeply commiserated those unfortunate ones, and was pleased to know that Richard had so kindly befriended them. These attentions of the Doctor were the signal for attack from other quarters, and several persons shot at Richard. Mrs. Tunny bestowed herself upon him, and thrust Faustina into his face and eyes, adding Tunny gratis. Captain Creamer, though having some scores against Richard, was more complaisant than usual, and rejoiced Richard could have a taste of good society. It was a fine thing, he said, for our young men to imbibe a little polish as they were coming on to the public stage. Mrs. Tunny attempted a blush, and with her feather-edged fan tapped the Captain on the cheek, and called him roguish. A pair of stern eyes, under a beetling brow, capped by a short tuft of thick hair, were seen working their way up over the shoulders of Captain Creamer, and scowling at Richard. These belonged to Measle, the wood-surveyor. "I think," said he, "that our young men, and all other young men, had better attend to their own business." "An undoubted truth," replied the Captain, "and I am glad you have mentioned it; but we must allow them moments of relaxation." "I shall make no reply," rejoined the Surveyor; "I have said something, and let those take it to whom it belongs."

Now it happened that the Surveyor was joint-suitor of Miss Faustina with the Sailmaker; and of course disagreeable to the latter, who conceived that this something aimed at himself, since he was the younger of the two. He instantly retorted, "I take it, and will hold on to it, and remember it; and it may be you will see its picture again!" Richard, perceiving the misunderstanding, said, "The gentleman does not refer to you, Sir. He recalls a little matter between himself and me. But I hope it will not prove serious." "No," interjected Munk, who stood by, "not serious, — jocose, lively, playful as a kitten." The Surveyor was a Catapulter, and a violent partizan; Munk was a Hydriatic. This feline allusion of the latter was more than the other could bear. His back seemed instantly to crook, and the hair on his head to rise; and he glared on Munk, and a faint hissing could be heard. The Sailmaker, a Dogbane, instantly contracted his neck, grated his teeth, and emitted a distinct growl. In this way they stood gnashing alternately at each other and at Munk, who laughed at them both. "Now is your time, Tunny," said Mrs. Tunny to her husband; "show your patriotism; snarl, bark, or I shall do it for you!"

Scenes of this description were of too common occurrence either to engage curiosity or excite alarm, and Richard was glad to make his escape. Threading his way through a dædalian intricacy of cords and starch, where his breathing was impeded by a dense vapor of cologne, he encountered Miss Eyre. She put her arm into his, and drew him towards the hall. "I should not have left you so long," she said, "but I knew you would relish your own reflections in a place like this; and I have had my reflections, — too sedate, too grave, for such an hour. You have said you were my friend. You will be glad of an occasion to prove that you are my friend, though I am afflicted that it should be such an occasion. It is but a trifle I ask of you, and that I know you will do. Come with me up stairs."

He went with her to the upper entry, and she conducted him to a sort of recess that overhung the stairs leading to the rear of the house, and motioned him to listen. Voices were heard on these stairs, which were clearly distinguishable as Clover's and Mrs. Xyphers'.

"Edney is out of the way," so Clover was heard to say. "I vanquished him to-night; he knows he is a fool, and he cannot recover."

"But Plumy Alicia —" Mrs. Xyphers replied.

"Is disposed of," answered Clover. Miss Eyre clasped both hands on Richard's arm.

"Xyphers," rejoined Mrs. Xyphers, "I do not value, — I cannot value. His name is his nature; he is nought, and the additional *s* only doubles his emptiness."

"Xyphers is something," replied Clover; "his nothingness is something, or he would not be game. Then he was interested in you, and that shows that you are an interesting woman, and that you deserve protection; and I should be false to my own honor, if I did not rescue you from such imbecility. You can rely on my honor."

"I think I can," answered Mrs. Xyphers, with some hesitation, as if a new thought had struck her; "you said you had money of Plumy Alicia?" Clover, flustering, said, "I wish not to talk of irrelevant matters." But Mrs. Xyphers insisted, and said, "I must talk about it." Miss Eyre took one of Richard's hands in both of hers. Clover replied,

"Plumny Alicia was lavish; she would have conciliated me any way. She knew the value of my friendship; she deposited with me two hundred dollars; — a mere tribute — a sort of hostage."

"How can you repay it?" asked Mrs. Xyphers.

"Repay it!" sneered Clover. "She feared my anger, she appreciated my ability, she knew what my alliance was worth; she feed my discretion." Miss Eyre throbbed on the breast of Richard.

"Xyphers' money is his own," rejoined that lady, with emotion; "it is his own earnings; he has worked for it; he never denied me *that;* but he had not *heart*, and could not give it. Nay, I will not touch his money."

Dancing being called for below, Dr. Broadwell and daughter would retire. Mrs. Tunny followed them to the dressing-room up stairs, and servants were summoned to assist them off. Clover and Mrs. Xyphers fled from their retreat. Miss Eyre, releasing herself from Richard, said, "Do not remain here; go to the drawing-room. I will digest my sorrow alone." Richard went down.

The dancing lasted till supper, the announcement of which silenced music and dissolved partnerships. While the mass crowded up stairs to the eating-room, some stayed below and felt of the muslin curtains, looked at the pictures on the wall, and turned over the burnished books with which Mrs. Tunny freely loaded her tables. Among the loiterers were Richard and Miss Freeling.

Now Richard longed to ask Miss Freeling, "Do you know Miss Eyre? — what sort of a girl is she?" — but he knew more about her than Miss Freeling did, and he had come by his knowledge in so confidential and secret a way, and it was so sacred a matter withal, he did not dare to put the question.

But Miss Eyre herself appeared, roaming pensively across the room, like a mourning shade; traces of sorrow descended down her face and dress; a band of hair lay pathetically loose on her forehead, and her look was tender and irresistible,—full of that sort of beauty with which misfortune, when it has taken everything else away, seems sometimes to renovate its victim.

Miss Freeling, taking up the subject very nearly where it lay in Richard's mind, said, "Miss Eyre seems to have been born out of her place. She has powers, but no sphere. She is certainly unfortunate; I should not dare to call her wicked, until I knew more of the human heart than I do now. She has some education, but no discipline; she observes, but never reflects; she hides defect of character with a certain brilliancy of temper. She insinuates herself by tact and talent, where most people would commend themselves by prudence and discretion. The attentions of the coarse and illiterate she cannot reciprocate. The flattery of what I should call super-sensualism inflames her vanity, while at the same time she can discern its motive. She creates a sensation wherever she goes, and contrives to be essential to a good many persons. Yet modesty condemns her, and rank will not tolerate her. She might have drudged in Silver's kitchen;—her destiny, I fear, will be to expatiate in larger and more questionable fields. She might have married Capt. Creamer; but he lacks sincerity, which, after all, she loves. Clover has more art, more power, and more audacity, than she has, and he may outdo her in her own line. She had a portion of her bringing up in the Governor's family; but she imbibed not the principles, but only the consequence, of the family. Mrs. Melbourne had her in charge; and the notions of that lady, to my thinking, are very—singular—bad.

She has the gift of fascination, but cherishes no ideas of usefulness; nor is she fitted by culture for stations which she might otherwise adorn. Where is the home that shall offer her happiness, contentment, and repose? A man under these circumstances, if he does not relapse into drunkenness, will keep his virtue, vindicate his capacity, and find his place. What shall a Factory-girl do?"

Richard was oppressed; he knew too much, and he knew too little, to say anything, and he kept silence. Besides, Plumy Alicia turned to him so smiling, sad indeed, but so grateful and azure a face, that what he would like to have said was snatched from his tongue's end.

Miss Freeling, without observing these pantomimic passages, continued. "Yonder," said she, pointing to a man on the opposite side of the room, "is Mr. Cosgrove, a carpenter, and a member of Parson Smith's Church, which you have heard is aristocratic. He came to the city a poor boy. He possessed intelligence, energy, and ambition. He pursues a useful trade, and strives to perfect himself in it. He has good sense, withal. The defects of his early education he has repaired by later application. He is a large contractor for houses, and advances to opulence. He visits among our nobility, and is welcome in the most polished circles. His powers have been not only developed, but employed. Would you like to know him?"

She introduced Richard to Mr. Cosgrove, and he liked his new acquaintance very well.

Those who had gone first to the supper beginning to withdraw, opening was made for the others. Mr. Cosgrove squired Miss Freeling; Richard, seeing Miss Eyre standing alone and aloof, offered his arm. But she declined, and said she would not eat. So Richard proceeded alone to the rendezvous of attraction. If the Confectioner and the

Fruiterer had been there, so had the Eater, and there only remained the fragments of a sumptuous fare.

Mr. Cosgrove handed Richard a glass of water, which he drank. The Surveyor and the Sailmaker, whose frenzy a liberal drench of wine had not reduced, were at once aroused. "Mr. Cosgrove dare not offer it!" said the one. "The young man dare not drink it!" said the other. Having uttered this, they both underwent the beastly metamorphosis, one growling and the other mewing. Clover, a violent Phumbician, approached; he had one arm devoted to Mrs. Xyphers, the other he presented to the attention of Richard, giving it the fisticuff form and the snapping motion in which the expert delighted to display itself. He said, "The barbarian will do it; he is mean enough to chip off an insult into the eyes of the City's honor; but here is the power that shall chastise his insolence!" Richard laid hold of the arm, and lowered it, and held it down; and Clover could not raise it. It was Clover's left arm, and Richard used his right. It was a strong arm, indeed; it labored like the piston of a steam-engine, but it could not be disengaged. "There is its place," said Richard; "and this is mine."

"Tunny!" cried the female head of the house, "Tunny, speak!" "Water," said the little male, answering the call of his spouse, in a thin, child-like voice,—"water is wholesome, it is respectable; I am for water, myself, [a hiss,] but I would not make it an absorbing topic; we are in danger of getting one idea on the subject; I should say half an idea was better! Shall we break up the city with water? What danger of falling into the ditches, and losing our lives! I am for reasonable water, and will never countenance these sanguinary measures! But, gentlemen, allow me to say, our troubles are not water; but—shall I say it? I must say it — Rats! I do not allude to Cats and Dogs, [mewling and growling,] I do not, — I will not, — I dare not! But I must speak the truth. The tightness of the times, — the numerous failures we mourn, — the unsettled state of the market; — I might name cabbages and turnips; — oh, fellow-citizens, it is owing to Rats!"

"You know I had the honor to be appointed chairman of a Committee to investigate. We are prepared to report. I have the schedule in my pocket. There are three thousand tenements, inclusive of stores, manufactories, barns, wharves, vessels, &c.; we estimate ten rats and mice to each tenement, making the enormous aggregate of thirty thousand of these mischievous non-producers! [Hear, hear.] Can the expense of supporting them be less than fifty cents per head, annually? Fifteen thousand dollars, then, is our yearly rat-tax! Consider some of the items: —

Perforations of meal-bags, doors, drawers,	$50.00
Attacks on cheeses, loaves of bread, joints of meat,	200.00
Eggs sucked,	40.00
Corn and grain pillaged,	300.00
Fruit-trees annually girdled,	80.00
Turnips and apples munched,	35.00
Nuts carried off,	10.00

The cost of preventives: —

Rat-proof cases, tubs, jars,	250.00
Cementing cellars, and pointing walls,	400.00
Sinks in drains,	90.00
Damage to cellars by water coming in at the holes they make,	50.00
Ratsbane and potash,	5.25
Traps of all sorts,	18.00
Annual bill of joiners for repairs,	325.00
Board of 1000 Cats,	2000.00

At this point, there was an outcry, soon hushed, however,

by the overwhelming interest of the topic. The little man continued, wiping his brow. "I need not go on. You see the astounding disclosures, and I see your alarm. But we approach the great question: Is there no remedy? These thirty thousand rats, it is estimated, would support sixty missionaries to foreign lands." "Cats is the remedy!" cried a Dog-hater. "A plot, a plot!" shouted an enemy of Cats. There was a scuffle about the table.

"Gentlemen, fellow-citizens, brothers and sisters!" Tunny began, again. "Let me be heard! bear with me one moment! I am magnanimous, — I hate incendiarism, and will spit on a traitor! There is hope! I have allowed myself to receive a consignment of rat-traps; — a new article, cheap and safe. They will hold every rat that gets into them, and there is a large size, the A. A., that will hold more. A child can manage them. Could not a Rat-trap Stock Company be formed? Shall not the Common Council be petitioned to purchase the patent? I propose this as a measure of conciliation."

"I did not agree to the report," rejoined Draff, a rival Grocer, "and I should oppose the plan of Tunny's. The fact, which all overlook, is here, just here, and nowhere else. The more there is eaten, the more there is sold; this is the law of trade — and it matters not who eats, the merchant makes by it."

There was a storm of suppressed sputtering. But Munk cried, "Yes, all eat, all sell; I buy a trap, you buy a trap; catch them if you can. Domestic turkeys, foreign grapes, some of Mrs. Tunny's nice custards; nobody can beat Mrs. Tunny in custards. Catapulter, Dogbane, all like good things, — all love to be happy." At the same time, he distributed the viands, and coaxed the belligerents to a softer mood.

The party broke up. Miss Eyre contrived, as young ladies always will contrive when they undertake it, that Richard should beau her home. But she was considerate; she did not distress him. She said, "You are my friend; I retain you by the strongest tie, — that of confidence; I have shown my estimate of your character, by imparting to you the profoundest affairs of my existence. Good-night."

CHAPTER XII.

RICHARD AND CLOVER UNITE.

AN Anti-Slavery meeting was gathered at the City Hall. It comprised men and women from Victoria Square and Knuckle Lane; from the Factories and Saw-mills; from Taverns and Alehouses.

The lecturer had perhaps more of truth than love in his composition; he was one who would not receive a cotton shirt from a slaveholder, lest, like Edward the Confessor, when a tax he had imposed was brought before him, he should see a little devil jumping about it. He seemed to feel, in regard to Slavery, as is related some of the Puritans felt about Popery, that a thwack at it was the best cure for the heart-burn. Possibly, acting on an old notion that enchantment cannot subsist in running water, he thought that the spell whereby that direful evil infatuates the popular mind might be broken by setting in motion the currents of popular feeling.

He was earnest and vehement; quite Pauline, quite Savonarolian. His words did not exemplify so much the rain on the new-mown grass, as the fire and the stubble. It seemed as if he would burn the grass, rather than be at the trouble of mowing it.

The audience listened patiently a while; many with a deep conviction of the justice of his cause, — others overpowered by the terror of his language. But uneasiness manifested itself, either from fright or from offence. The speaker no whit faltered. He seemed like one who was used, as the Prophet says, to threshing the mountains, and making them small as the dust. And though these mountains were, like Olympus, covered with gods, it made no difference; the gods must come down. Presently there was hissing, and scraping, and groaning. Diana *was* great, but old, and gouty withal, and she could not be ousted suddenly.

He spoke of the recent War, and its connection with his subject, and with national affairs generally. And now the gods rallied, and particularly Clover, and his confreres, young Chassford, Glendar, and others.

"That war," he said, "is the disgrace of the nation, and the triumph of Slavery. Both are a curse, cleaving like leprosy to the comeliness of the Republic; both are a wickedness of such magnitude that perdition is not deep enough to hold them!"

"Repeat those words!" cried Clover, springing from his seat. The speaker repeated them in such a way there could be no possibility of misapprehending them.

"Drag him from the desk!" "Pitch him from the window!" rang from different parts. Timorousness took the alarm, and some would have left the house. Dr. Broadwell arose and said, "Be quiet, friends; if the lecturer's truth does not hurt us, his rhetoric surely will not. There is no danger."

Clover, with two or three others, leaped forward to the platform on which the lecturer stood. "I wish to speak," he said. "Certainly," replied the other. "This fellow," so Clover harangued, "assaults the nation — he assaults the people! He mocks at our institutions — he scoffs at our government! He would wrench the flag from the mizzen-peak of our glory! he would break the band-chain of our destiny! Might is right; Might rules; Might gives law; Might blew up the fort of Moultan; Might thrashed the Chinese; Might burned Little Berebee; Might captured Osceola; Might punished Sullivan! Great is Might! Who will join in that shout? Who will cheer Might?"

The response was vociferous, but sparse. There could not have been more than a dozen individuals, out of three hundred, engaged in it. Yet it sounded large, and seemed to fill the house; and as with stentor lungs the sentiment was repeated, "Great is Might!" there were those who thought it prevailed. Some weak and nervous ones yielded to it, and fell in with it; some who were opposed to it, adjudging it to be the sovereign voice, were disposed to acquiesce in it; and if a vote had been taken on the instant, it would probably have carried the house.

"I question the response; I repudiate the sentiment!" cried the lecturer.

"Woe be unto you!" responded Clover. "Might rises; Might blots out its enemies; Might crushes you!" He laid his arm heavily on the shoulder of the speaker, as if he expected to see him vanish through the floor.

Instantly there was a bellowing from all sides, "Do him, Clover!" "Devour him!" "Take him up with a pair of tongs!"

Meanwhile, Richard, backed by some friends, mounted the dais, and while Clover was adjusting himself to the undertaking of despatching the lecturer at a single swallow, he swung his cap, and shouted, "Great is Truth!" and his comrades vibrated the cry; and by deep, pulmonary thunders, it rolled through the Hall; and the Might-voices, bemazed by the Truth-voices, fled screeching away.

But Clover, not a little incensed, darting his skinny eye at Richard, said, "Who are you, that dares cross the path of Might? Who are you that presumes to lift your puny finger against the victorious, awe-spreading march of this powerful, this tremendous nation?"

"I am Richard Edney," replied the other.

"You are a traitor's whelp!" pursued Clover; "you are the dregs of an indigo-tub! You are a swag-bellied sniveller, a coop of half-starved chickens, a milk-blooded son of a cow! You are rot in the timbers of this hurricane Republic, — the sappy edge of our all-scaring Institutions! O, admirable baby-jumper! run home and tend your pigsneys!"

"I am what I am," replied Richard; "and if you do not know what that is already, you may know by and by."

"Am I to be bullyragged by you?" retorted Clover. "Is Might to have its whiskers pulled by a spinster's lackey? Is the career of national glory to be turned back with a cant-dog? BEWARE OF CLOVER!" To give piquancy to his words, Clover let loose his fist, which had long fretted in the leash, at Richard, and dealt him a violent blow in the face. Richard reeled, and put his hand to his face, as if he would feel whether it was there or not. His friends hastened to him, but he shook them off. His blood was up, — it was up very high for him. He turned towards Clover, both of whose fists were levelled at him; he leaped upon these fists, as one would upon a long lever under a mired wagon-wheel; he clenched one in one hand, the other in the other, and sought to lower them. He bent them down, though they were refractory as an elephant's tusk. He straightened them out carefully and squarely on Clover's thighs; then he crossed them on Clover's back; and Clover could not stop him. He writhed, and throbbed, and fumed, but to no purpose; and though every nerve in his body had been wrought of Damascus steel, it would not have availed him; and Richard embraced Clover, giving him, in rural phraseology, a bear's hug. Then he lifted him from his feet, and swinging him lightly, very lightly, in his arms, laid him backwards on the floor, and bade the lecturer proceed. Clover did not wince nor stir. The audience, who had risen in expectation and alarm, resumed their seats. Without further disturbance, the lecture was finished, and the people dismissed.

Richard and Clover left the Hall together. Richard drew Clover's arm into his, and they went towards their homes, both of which lay in the Beauty of Woodylin. Few words were interchanged. Only we can affirm that Clover went to bed that night soberly, — quite soberly.

CHAPTER XIII.

RICHARD EXHORTS AT A RELIGIOUS MEETING.

ONE Sunday evening, Richard went, with Aunt Grint and his sister, to Elder Jabson's meeting, in a neighboring School-house.

A hymn was given out, the first stanza of which is as follows:

"Am I a soldier of the Cross,
A follower of the Lamb,
And shall I fear to own his cause,
Or blush to speak his name?"

The chorister was gone, but Richard, knowing the tune, and loving the words, led off; and he threw such life and unction into the singing as never was seen before. It was as if *tutti* had been written on his understanding and his spirit, his lips and his eyes; and his throat was equal to any *tuba mirabilis* that was ever invented.

A brother spoke in this wise:

"I feel to bless God that I am here. I think I have known the Saviour; I was brought to see my wretched and lost condition, it is now twelve years gone; it was in just such a meeting as this I closed with the offers of mercy, and light fell on my mind. But I have backslidden since; gay companions and vain amusements drew off my attention; I know I have not borne the cross as I should do; I ask your prayers. At the last Reformation, I was enabled to come out from the world, and set my face toward Zion anew. You know, brethren, how it has gone with me since; the business of this world got the upper hands, and speretual realities were shoved one side. I feel to be thankful that my life is spared; and I think I can say I rejoice in this evening."

Richard, thereupon, spoke, and said: —

"We will pray for our brother; we will help him to a confirmation of his wishes, and a renewal of his assurance. But, my friends, is there not a radical defect here? Are we building on the Rock of Ages? Is it possible that the ordinary winds and floods of life could so easily subvert our foundations? Our temptations and besetments, our hindrances and cares, are as nothing compared with those to which the primitive disciples were subject; yet they endured unto the end. If one has pure and deep love to God and to man in his heart, I should urge that he cannot lose it. What is the world but a grand theatre for Christian usefulness; and how can contact with the world deteriorate our virtue, or diminish our zeal? If Christ be truly in us, he is a well of water, springing up unto everlasting life; a source of spiritual vitality, that can neither intermit nor be exhausted. Are we not depending too much on mere impulse and gladness, without grappling with the cardinal principles of Christianity, and planting them low in our natures, and working them into the frame-work of our characters? Are the laws of the religious life more variable than those which regulate every other human concern? A peace-man does not lose his interest in peace, nor does an anti-slavery-man backslide from abolition; a lawyer perseveres in attachment to his profession; and what mother present grows lukewarm towards her children?

"Are we careful of our bodies, even? Do we make them fitting temples for so glorious a guest as the Holy Ghost? When we approach the throne, do we come not only with hearts sprinkled from an evil conscience, but also, as the Apostle directs, *with bodies washed with pure water?*

"Our brother has spoken of amusements. Recreation, in the present state of being, is needful as food and clothing. If we enter upon sportive scenes with right feelings, — if we pursue what is innocent and joyous in the spirit of innocency and joyousness, — if we derive what advantage is afforded by a free and unreserved intercourse with our fellows, we shall be better prepared for the graver duties and severer events of life."

The Elder here reminded Richard that this was a religious meeting, and that he should not digress into other topics.

Richard replied, that it was only of what had a supreme religious bearing that he wished to speak, and continued:—

"The trouble seems to be that we get religious feeling without acquiring evangelical principle. We amass the hay, wood and stubble, of momentary enthusiasm, and have not the true life of God in the soul. We look for sudden changes, and have no maturity of growth. The dew of an evening meeting is speedily exhaled, — the sun of gospel love mounts to the perfection of the day. We cry, lo here! and lo there! lo this meeting! and lo that church! while the infinite gifts of Providence and of the ages, of nature and of grace, are ever offered to our hands, ever pouring into our hearts!

"Our religion is like a saw I have seen, which was respectable on bass-wood, but birch or a knotty hemlock discovered its weak points, and condemned its brittleness. It is a glow-worm religion, that fails by day-light, and disappears in the glare of occupation. It is a parlor religion, that shifts its dress and loses its temper when it goes into the kitchen. The pursuit of salvation in the midst of excitement is like gunning in a strong wind; you cannot distinguish your game nor steady your sight. Why hurry your converts into the water, plunging them through the ice in mid-winter? — true spirituality, like the witch-hazel, having blossomed in the fall, will bear its fruit the next summer. We need a piety like the plantain, which will flourish even under the feet of mankind; and like the sandal-wood, that bestows its sweetness on those who bruise it most hardly. Trees flourish where corn dwindles; — you ought not to expect the same description of holiness under all circumstances, nor refuse a fruit of the spirit because it does not happen to be your favorite crop.

"I am very frank with you, my brethren and sisters; I love you all, — I desire that we may each attain to the stature of perfect ones in Jesus. You invited me to speak; I thank you for the opportunity. May God bless us all!"

After the meeting, several of the people spoke with Richard. One said he had hit the nail on the head; another, that he had driven it home; a third thought he had clenched it; a fourth hoped he would bring some more nails.

Returning, Aunt Grint said, "Well, I do believe something is going to happen."

"Why?" asked Roxy.

"Our Richard," replied Aunt Grint, "has really got waked up."

"I am usually awake at proper times," observed Richard; "and I sleep my eight hours every day. But my soul never sleeps."

"You do not know, for all the world," rejoined the Aunt, "what feeble and uncertain creeturs we are; you have no experience of the dreadful natur of man. I wish I could feel as you do, but I can't. Nothing but sovreign grace will ever save *me*. Why, a salt-cellar will upset me; and there is spots on the finger-nails that make a body so dismal; and when a dog howls in the night, I have n't the least mite of faith that ever was."

"Your Bible," answered Richard, "would correct these superstitious fears, and lead you to a constant, unfaltering, filial faith in God."

"Ah's me!" added the Aunt; "I sometimes am afraid to open my Bible, for who knows on what verse I may pitch?"

CHAPTER XIV.

RICHARD CALLED TO NURSE A SICK MAN.

This was Bill Stonners, a man belonging to one of the other saws. He was a person of rude manners, intemperate habits, and solitary life. He practised log-booming in summer, and sawing in winter. Richard knew but little of him. His disease was malignant erysipelas, a fearful form of St. Anthony's fire. Symptoms of this malady had appeared in different parts of the city, and an impression prevailed that it was infectious. Moreover, this case of Bill Stonners' was represented as the most shocking imaginable; and many who would not hesitate at a common instance were intimidated by this. Bill had no family, and what was worse, he had no friends; none were moved by affection or love to look after him, and so deplorable was his condition, that even the sense of duty in the strongest minds was overborne. His home was a miserable hut on the bank of the stream, within the woods, about half a mile above the Dam. It had no comforts; none for the sick man, none for his attendants, none even which the most indulgent benevolence could find any satisfaction in applying in such an emergency.

It may be that corporations have no souls; but the city undertook what individual charity shrank from. It provided a physician, medicine, emollients, and went in pursuit of a nurse. The Overseer of the Poor came to the Mill on this errand. He encountered great reluctance; — some had watched with Bill, and were rightly excused. He addressed

Richard. But Captain Creamer interfered; he thought it was flinging away a valuable life on a worthless one. Mr. Gouch opposed even his tears to the idea, and said, with extreme emotion, that he should never see Richard again. Silver who had become strongly attached to Richard, planted a picaroon in his collar, and declared he should not go.

But somebody must go; and the city would remunerate Captain Creamer for the loss of Richard's time, and also give Richard such compensation as was just.

So Richard went. "O God," he said, "spare my life, if it pleases thee; but if thou takest it, let it be in the service of my fellow-men!"

He reached what, under the circumstances, was a dreary place, and one sufficiently revolting. The house, a rude shantee, was perched on a rock, overlooking the frozen stream below. It might have been deemed a picturesque spot, but only so to life and health. It was dismal to solitude, and sickness, and death. The roof covered two apartments, in one of which lay the sick man; the other was the repository of his stuff and tools, comprising spike-poles, raft-pins, raft-rigging, augers, a draw-shave, etc. But the sick man, — we shall not describe him. He was past consciousness when Richard arrived; his head was swollen to a preternatural size; his features had all disappeared, and were submerged in a chaos of whatever is most shocking in the ravages or the deformities of disease. Bill was intemperate, — he had been irregular every way; and his blood was corrupt, and vicious humors in incredible quantity, and with frightful swiftness, determined to his head.

Nor need we describe the room where such a man, without culture, without piety, without a friend, had lived. We have said he lived alone; — this is not quite true. There was frequently with him one who was called Bill's Boy; the soubriquet of this creature was Chuk. Richard found this fellow sitting on a block before the fire, nursing his ears with his fists. He did not rise when Richard entered,—he did not speak; he only gave a sort of hunch with his head. His dark visage — dark with hair, and beard, and grime —was freaked by that dull redness which intemperance and exposure impart; and intermixed with this were traces of a huffy despair,— a state to which we might suppose a human heart, uninfluenced by refined affection, unenlightened by religious truth, would arrive. One might fancy that Chuk had tended upon Bill,— that he had set up with him all night, and had ministered to him there in the day; that he had done this all alone; that he had continued to do it till hope had fled, and his strength was gone,—and out of sorts with himself and with all things, now surlily grinning at and daring the issue, had gone to brooding over the fire; and such a fancy would not be far out of the way.

Did he not speak? He did not employ much of what is understood to be human speech;— he swore. His every word seemed to be an oath; his sentences began and ended and were sealed with oaths. He could only converse in oaths. And he swore at Richard in the first reply he made to him, when he asked what he should do; and he damned Bill, soul and body, to hell; yet, if we shall be permitted to say so, he loved Bill.

What should Richard do? There was little else to be done, except to foment the blasted, bloated face of the patient with alcohol. Richard thought cold water would be a better lotion, and said as much to Chuk; who, having first sent Richard to eternal perdition for intimating anything of the sort, took a pail, and descending to a hole in the ice, filled it, and brought it to Richard.

The Physician, Dr. Chassford, called. He was a quiet man, of few words, but gifted with pleasant manners, great professional fidelity, and much flavor of gentle feelings. His replies extinguished expectation, and provided for a speedy termination of the sickness; Bill could not live twenty-four hours longer. Chuk did not swear at the Doctor; he bit at him, he touseled him, he burnt him alive with oaths.

The Overseer brought candles, food, and such things as the living might require, but which could have no pertinence to the dying.

Chuk laid a large heap of drift-wood on the hearth, and then bestowed his wonted blessing on what he had done. Richard ventured to expostulate with him; but it was like spitting against the wind,—rather like raising sail in a hurricane.

Having drained a flask of liquor, the Boy doubled himself into a coarse blanket on the floor, and went to sleep.

Richard was left alone with that sick man, and that Boy, in that room, for the night. He needed no candle, for the resinous stuff that Chuk provided emitted an illumination quite sufficient. The sick man breathed hard and hoarsely; but he made no motion as if he were in pain. He could not speak, nor hear, nor understand. Richard's employment was wringing out the rags afresh in the water, whenever they became hot; and this was very often. He could hardly pray for mercy on the soul before him,—he could commend that soul to the Infinite Mercy.

If there was anything to qualify the gloom of the hours, it was the roaring of the Dam. All the winds played on it, and it took advantage of all the winds to exhibit its peculiar powers. The sound rose and fell,—it was plaintive and it was harsh; it died away in the distance, and directly it reäppeared under the windows of the house, and filled the adjacent high-embanked stream with its tempestuous clamor. Anon, as it were breaking away from its proper source, the fall of the water, it leaped into the woods, — it fled through the forest like a detached volume of smoke; it whispered miniardly to the hills, — it howled, goblin-like, in the gullies; it trapsed out of hearing, to strike up some new and strange vagary, in an unexpected quarter of the heavens.

It was now the beginning of spring, and the crows attempted the poetic office of heralding the dawn; and from many a tall pine, and many a bleak rock — and occasionally facilitating the matter by a short bout on the wing — they shrieked the pleasant news.

Their noise awakened Chuk, who, with such utensils and in such way as he was accustomed to, went about getting breakfast.

The eastern sky was bland, prismatic, reviving; and the sun came into the room with warmth and peace, if not healing, in its beams, and Richard was tempted to the window.

"Don't look out there!" said Chuk; "that is Bill's window; eat, if you want to, and go to the dogs, but don't sit there! The city gives the vittles, — it did n't give that! Don't you see Bill's boom, just below, norward of the Pint? No, — he can't see it, and you shan't!"

Richard drew up to the rude table. Chuk poured out the coffee, and handed him the sugar and milk; and while Richard was eating, the boy tended his master, and chowtered about the room.

"There is not a boom on the river like that," he said, "and there 'll never be another; for Bill will be dead, and in the lake, where no timber grows. In three weeks the ice will be out, and the logs will run; and they will all curse

Bill, as they go by, for not catching them. He knew the marks as far as he could see them; and he never beckoned with his picaroon at a stick, though it was big as thunder, that it did not mind him and come in. None could manage a rip as he could; and the logs were proud of him, — wan't they, though? and they would n't quit him, though every infernal rock in the River was tearing at their bellies! He ought not to die; he is an old fool to die, after such a winter as this, when there has been such a cramming of the Lake, and such jobs are laid out for us!"

All at once the Boy seemed to soften; he changed his tone, and leaning over the bed, he said, "Did you speak, Bill? It's Chuk, — Chuk is here. For God's sake, don't die, Bill! Shan't I caulk the boat? Shan't I overhaul the rigging? Swear at me, Bill! knock me down! once, only once, before you can't!"

Richard had been to the Lakes; he had hauled timber to the head-waters of the stream; he had once, in a stress, helped "drive the River," as the idiom is, and knew about the catching of logs in booms; and he understood a little of the Boy's feelings, and truly commiserated him, and tried to cheer his heart. But Chuk would listen to nothing, — he would be persuaded by nothing.

A low tapping was heard at the door. "That's Mysie," said Chuk. "Plagues light on her old pate! why does she come asking after Bill? She knows he an't any better; she knows he never will be!"

Mysie entered the room; and as Chuk did not tell Richard about her, and as Richard, when he afterwards knew her, was interested in her, we will venture a word or two for her.

She was called Mysie; but Mysie what, or what Mysie, nobody knew. She was quite old; she might have been near the allotted period of human life. She was wrinkled, even beyond the extremest age; yet her face had a fresh and vigorous look, and her wrinkles did not seem to be so much a symptom of natural waste as a part of her constitution. She was tall, straight, and bony, yet she had nothing of the Meg Merrilies stamp, nor of any other but her own. Her costume was shabby and neglected. She wore an old and dirty straw bonnet, with an immense rim, and a green plaid cloak, of a kind that was common twenty years before; and she towed herself through the mud and splosh in a huge flaring pair of India-rubbers, like a small boat. She was not stern, or sharp, or prying, or malevolent; her reigning expression was that of quiet good-nature, and innocent self-complacency.

Mysie, too, like those upon whom she called, lived alone. She occupied the spare end of a tumble-down house, not far from the Point. Nor was she wholly alone; she kept cows and cats; having five or six of the former, and a dozen of the latter. In the summer it was her vocation to wait on these cows; and having no regular pasture-ground, she drove them into the woods, and led them by the road-side, wherever she could find grass. The cats constituted her immediate domestic circle.

Mysie was never at church. She never entered a house, she was never known to change her dress; she claimed no relatives. She sometimes went into the city to sell butter.

She was never sick, and though always exposed, she was never injured. She would be out all day in the rain, tending her cows, but she took no cold; she frequented the loneliest woods, and sauntered in the most out-of-the-way fields and lanes; — she was not afraid.

She had led such a life forty years, as she was wont to say, and was never hurt yet.

The children saw her as a grotesque, bug-bearish, sprawling-looking woman; a kind of ogress, emerging from the depths of the forest, or traversing, with an idle, vacant step, the sludgy swales and courses of the brooks, and were afraid of her; yet, when they came near enough for her to speak to them, so pleasant was her smile, so soft her voice, she easily composed them, and sometimes made them love her.

She had a fondness for trees and wild-flowers, and some taste for natural beauty; and she did all her worship beneath the sun and the open sky, which she used to say was as good as a Meeting-house.

In a cold and dry winter, springs of water fail, and the domestic supply of that essential aliment of life is cut off; aqueducts freeze, and brooks and wells give out. This misfortune befell Mysie, and she was obliged to take her cows to the River to drink.

For such a purpose had she come down this morning, and for such a purpose had she come a good many mornings, by Bill's.

We have said she had no relatives. Nobody knew that she had any; there were not five persons, out of eighteen thousand in the city, to whom she appeared otherwise than of Melchisidechian origin, without father or mother. She seemed like a rural anchorite, a social fungus, a tame female Orson. Yet it was sometimes said, — not that there was any reason for saying it, or any malice in saying it, but merely because something must be said — a sort of buzzing conjecture, that a man must lift his hand and brush away, — that Bill was her son, and that Chuk was Bill's son; but of this nobody knew, and nobody will know.

Chuk swore at Mysie when she entered, and branded her with many abominable names; but she did not mind it, and it neither quickened nor slackened her wonted heavy, slow-forward gait, nor did it disturb the placid folds of her wrinkles.

She brought a mug of milk, which Chuk, of course, damned when he took and emptied; and she poured from her apron a quantity of poppy-seeds, which, she said, were for poultices. She turned from the bedside, and, as if it were a foregone conclusion, said, "He is past being better; he is gone too far for that! He would like to have seen the red heifer when she changed her coat; but he 'll not care; and there are not many to care. Everything is best when it is ended. This going on so without stopping is the only thing *to* care about."

Mysie took her mug, and was going, when Chuk caught at her cloak, as if he would rend it from her shoulders. "Don't pull so," she said, very gently. "Mother!" he cried; he did not cry it at once, or as if he was used to crying it. He strangled with it; he wharled it out; he yelped it, as we might suppose a wolf to do in some attempt at filial agganition. "I would n't call for mothers," replied Mysie; "there an't any mothers now, and no children. We are alone. There is Line-back, that had as pretty calf as ever you see —"

"Give me something!" replied the Boy. "He is gone, and the business is gone, and all is gone. Who was a child? Who got into somebody's lap? Who kissed him? Did n't she die? Did n't they put her in a grave? Where is that? who is that? Don't tell me nobody cares! don't call me Chuk! Had n't *he* another name? Did *she* swear?"

"I would n't speak so, if I was you," replied Mysie. "It is a big world we live in, and God Almighty has n't made us for nothing, I guess."

Had n't the creature any emotion? She did n't express any. She was inflexibly bland. Had she no hopes, no regrets, no memories, no sympathies? She called after her cows, — each of whom had a name, and knew her name, — who, having come up from the water, were nuzzling amid the seared herbage that appeared about the doorway.

Three ladies approached the house, who addressed Mysie with a friendly freedom, as if she were an old acquaintance. These ladies were Ada Broadwell, Barbara Dennington, and Mrs. Judge Burp. When the Boy saw them, he retreated from the door, blaspheming like the screech of a steam-whistle. "More to kill Bill," he said; "more to tell me he can't live; more stuff to help him die!"

Richard went to the door to answer the inquiries of the ladies. He thought Barbara was Melicent, and spoke to her as a friend, and extended his hand to her; but she did not know him, and her manner showed that she did not. But Ada knew them both, and set them to rights with each other. Barbara said she had heard of Mr. Edney, and was glad to see him; and Mrs. Judge Burp, or the Lady Caroline, as she was generally called, said the same. The Lady Caroline was very glad he had come to Bill Stonners'. "Poor wretch!" she said; "he is rejected by all; and what is worse, he rejected himself. He has no friends abroad, and none in his own soul. But it is a Christian duty to minister to him, and make his situation as comfortable as may be."

They had brought cordials, and fruit, and rolls of linen; but, except as to the last, they were too late, Richard replied.

They would go in. The Boy had flung himself into the chimney-corner. The Lady Caroline did not hesitate to apply the fomentation to the sick man's face with her own hands. Richard feared she was exposing herself; but she would do it. Richard beheld her, shall we say, with astonishment. She had thrown off her bonnet, and seemed to act as if she were the chosen nurse of the hour.

And there were other reasons why Richard should regard her with interest: the Lady Caroline was a noble woman to look to; she completed the idea of what is called an elegant woman; and she exceeded it, in that she added thereto great beauty of spirit, and the charms of religious self-denial. She was tall and proportionate, with hazel eyes and hair, arched brows, and a very perfect mouth; and in the excitement of action, her face kindled with the hues of spiritual and deep sensibility.

Barbara turned to the Boy, whose distress startled her tenderness. She spoke kindly to him, — he did not look up; she laid her hand on his head, — he hunched it off; she offered him an orange, — he hunched at that.

Ada talked with Richard; she ventured to say the room seemed lacking in comforts and care. Chuk let fly at her a salvo of oaths. "Bill could n't live anywhere else," he said; "and you want to bring in your handyjingledoms here, and kill him before his time! If you touch a thing, he 'll die! That block is where he used to set; that coat is just where he threw it off, when he took to his bed; there is where he spit his tobacco, — he could spit against any man living; them shavings he whittled from a new paddle: but he 'll never want it, — he 'll never ask where it is; and its there, — there, in the corner, right before his eyes, and, curse him, he can't see it!" He swore himself into a sort of blubbering yex, and brayed his eyes with his fingers, as if he was angry with them for their ability to see, and would grind them to powder.

It was easier to minister to the dying than the living. The ladies did all they could do, and left. Richard was not detained in that place a great while. The disease ran its course that night; and Bill Stonners died, and was buried.

The Boy clung with fang-like tenacity to the old spot. Bill had no other heirs, and Chuk became sole proprietor of the estate and the business. Every day, Mysie carried him a mug of milk.

CHAPTER XV.

RICHARD VISITS QUIET ARBOR.

CLOVER had been fairly beaten at the Anti-Slavery Meeting, but he knew his antagonist was an honorable one ; nay, he thought that Richard, like one having got a large advantage, might be disposed to make some deduction ; and he was sure he was rich enough in spoils to offer a handsome present. "You can't refuse the favor of going with me to Quiet Arbor." Of course, Richard could not ; it would give him compunction to refuse Clover even a larger favor.

Quiet Arbor was in the basement of an extensive block of buildings, lying on the margin of a small stream, called the Pebbles, a tributary of the River. Red curtains shaded the windows and the glass door, just to show to the world how quiet it was ; nothing glary, nothing dazzling, nothing that should disturb the serenity of the passer-by, or seem ostentatious to anybody.

And Clover and Richard entered it very quietly ; and the Friend of the People — the man of the timid eye and a small hacking cough — was very quiet behind the bar ; very quiet in pouring out liquors, very quiet in stirring the glasses. Only when a new customer called, or when Helskill dropped the silver in his till, he vented this small, hacking cough. There were men in the room who had drank, and men who were going to drink ; men in different stages of drink, and men in all stages of drink ; but they were quiet ; — perhaps because it was early in the evening, and like other gatherings of the human species, they were not yet waked up, — the fervor of the occasion was slow in mounting. There were young men, and some gray-headed men, and, as well as the dim light and clouds of tobacco-smoke would allow him to ascertain, there were some whom Richard knew. But Richard, participating in the spirit of the place, was quiet also, and said nothing.

Helskill's whole soul seemed to start out from under his heavy eyebrows, and to shrink into a most fearful glance at Richard, and finally to be cracked off in a quick short cough, as he saw him advance. But this was soon over, and the people in the room, who had been aroused by that sudden cough, relapsed into repose.

Clover led Richard through this room, towards another, which he gave him to understand was the Grotto. When Helskill saw Richard approaching that door, he hacked three or four times in rapid succession, but Clover winked him into silence. The apartment into which they now entered was quite subterranean, and hence the pertinence of the name. Ventilation must have been supported by mysteriously arranged conduits, the course and outlets of which were invisible. It was well lighted by a brace of solar lamps suspended over two tables. At these tables sat men playing cards. There were stakes of money, watches, and jewelry. Decanters of high-colored beverage adorned the retreat.

Capt. Creamer was there; he did not hack when he saw Richard, — he put his hand to his eye, as if he would correct his vision, — as if he was not right at first. But he was right: it was Richard, his slip-tender. And how it pleased the Captain to know who it was! Dropping his finger to his lips, he kissed it to Richard; and jumping up, he seized him both by the hand and the shoulder, and leading him forward with a double gripe of honor, introduced him to young Chassford, son of Dr. Chassford, and Glendar, nephew of Mrs. Melbourne.

"Play?" said the Captain, snapping a card in a very confidential sort of way. "I do not play," replied Richard, affecting a pun; "I take it more seriously." The Captain, pretending to understand him, laughed very hard, while Richard quietly ensconced himself in a seat by the wall.

Tunny was there, and so was the Sailmaker; and these were playing against each other, and so thoughtful of their sport, they did not notice Richard.

Yes, Tunny was there, and he knew he was there; even if Mrs. Tunny did n't know it, and Dr. Broadwell did n't know it, he knew it, and felt it. He felt it in his forelock, and was trying to hetchel it out with his fingers; he felt it in his chair, that seemed to burn under him; and he felt it in his conscience, where the facts in the case were at work like a *miserere mei* with an hundred hands, wringing, grinding, taughtening, till he seemed paler, and thinner, and smaller than ever.

And the Sailmaker knew Tunny was there, and meant he should be there, and would not have him elsewhere for the world.

Richard saw another man there, whom he had also seen about the Saw-mill, and who he knew had a young wife and small children to support, and who, he was well assured, had better be anywhere else. It was Cornelius Wheelan, a River-man, who owned a flat-boat, and conveyed lumber from the Mills to the ships that anchor in the Harbor.

"You were at Tunny's the other night," said the Captain to Richard. "A pleasant party; it takes some of our young men from the country a good while to get the hay-seed out of their hair; but no one would imagine, Edney, you had ever seen a barn. Why did you not dance? Ah, you are afraid of Dr. Broadwell, I see. I cannot blame you for that. Yet, between you and me, I think the Doctor carries matters a little too far. Our young men need recreation; perhaps we are too fond of it. Chassford drags me into it. But one has now and then a spare evening on hand, which he must, so to say, bolt down, and get rid of. I never will back out when a noble-hearted fellow wants company. Cards are perhaps too fascinating for you. We 've a new kind, — the Merry Andrews, — most comical objects."

Richard replied that they were all alike to him.

"I presume so," rejoined the Captain, affectedly laughing; "I presume so."

In fact, Richard was not only ignorant of cards, but so unconscious of the pleasure of gaming, that he quite abruptly rose to leave the room. On his way out, he looked at Tunny and tapped him on the shoulder. O that he had Klumpo's eye! — but he had n't. Yet he had an eye, that operated on Tunny worse than his internal gripes; and as if he was as thin as some of our newspapers, that look seemed to annihilate what there was left of him. The Sailmaker resented this interference, but Richard had no controversy with the Sailmaker. Tunny revived sufficiently to whisper in Richard's ear, "Don't tell Mrs. Tunny." Richard passed on to Cornelius Wheelan, and did not tap him, for he was a stronger man, but thumped him on the back. Now, Cornelius was partly in liquor, and did not take the sense of the blow. He drew upon Richard; but Richard whispered something in his ear, — something of his wife and children, we guess, — and he was still. Interlocking with him, Richard led him from the room. When he reached the other apartment, he found the calmness somewhat broken; and the Friend of the People, when he saw Richard, and knowing how he loved quietness, and fearing that the pleasure of his visit might be marred, said, "Let us be quiet, friends." These were the very words he said.

But Richard manifested no uneasiness; only, clinging to Cornelius, and followed by Clover, he left the Arbor.

Clover followed him, we say, and asked him to go back. He said there was a private entrance to the Grotto, and they could reach it unobserved. But Richard went on, arm in arm with Cornelius; and Clover himself returned.

Was Clover disappointed in Richard? Did he not understand him? Did he suppose he would game, or that he was game? If he did, he was very stupid.

Richard went with Cornelius to his own home. It was now near midnight; but there sat his wife waiting for him — there were his children in bed sleeping for him. Cornelius fell at the feet of his wife; he rolled on the bed where the children lay, stinging with remorse and shame, and overwhelmed by a tumult of recollections.

CHAPTER XVI.

THE ICE GOES OUT.

THAT which Chuk looked forward to with so sad a heart; which thousands of people up and down the valley anticipated as the opening in the midst of their towns and villages of a new, radiant, beautiful realm of existence; what the travelling public were on tip-toe for, and merchants and customers, and mill-owners and log-drivers, were so interested in; what many a coaster from sunnier climes was spreading all sail for, and hundreds of fond souls, awaiting union with other fond souls, in distant places, had almost despaired of, was at hand, — the ice began to start. The warm weather, the dissolving snows, the powerful rains, generously combined for this end.

All who had occasion to use the "Free Bridge," as the ice was called, hastened to do so. The wood-mongers got their loads over; those who had bulky articles of any sort to transport fidgeted lest they should be too late. One of the last incidents was what befell a gentleman in his ardor to avoid the odious wooden structure to which we have referred, — he drove a valuable horse through the ice, and drowned him. Of course, everybody said the ice must be very rotten.

Large rocks, that had been hauled on the ice for the construction or repairing of booms, were seen to sink. Merchandise that had been deposited in store-houses on the wharves was removed, against the possibility of an inundation.

17*

The Bridge too, the reviled Bridge, with its great wooden eyes, reposing on its immense stone piers, looked on very quietly, — it was quiet as Helskill himself; it did not resent the "Free Bridge," — it did not laugh when the horse went down, — it did not shake its head when sleighs galloped by on the ice, and frumped at its slow walk; it seemed to fold its arms and say, "I can bide my time. You will perhaps sing another tune, by and by."

These things were done, and with unacknowledged impatience all waited for the issue.

First is the cracking of the ice. This is generally instantaneous and universal. The rise of the water, the confluence of the stream above with a high tide from below, produce the effect. The entire field is on the instant traversed with innumerable irregular lines, and divided by a rude polyhedral fracture, and the whole mass is gently agitated.

There were many who heard the cracking, and some who saw it, and would asseverate stoutly what time it was, and where they stood; and knots of men and boys who hang about the docks would get into a vociferous scuffle because they had seen so much.

But the ice is not discharged in a minute. That lying between the Bridge and the Dam, where the water runs very swiftly, is first set adrift. This sails with moderation and dignity, and stops on the piers of the Bridge, awaiting events. It sometimes lies there three or four days. Below the Bridge the stream expands in a broad basin, interspersed with islands, and constitutes the Harbor. Beyond this, and about a mile from the city, are what are called the Narrows. These are not yet free, and the loosened ice of the Harbor, like a fleet of boats ready to put to sea, rocks leisurely on the current; the abraded fragments are thrown into heaps, — the cakes careen and expose their bright edges, — the water bubbles up in many dark fissures; boys go out and stand on the large cakes, with their hands in their breeches pockets, — a cool way they have of taunting the ice; some creep to the edge of the cakes and look into the water, so rejoiced are they to see it; some find the smallest possible lump that will bear them, as much as to say to the ice its reign is over; one or two get dumped into the stream, but this only shows how near at hand is the long wished-for crisis; some set off with billets of wood and thump on it, to wake it up, and set it stirring.

Presently the Narrows were pronounced clear; and there, between the dark, pine-clad hills, on a shining mirror, the light of the sun was reflected, silvery and exultant; and an opening of light and joy glistened in the heart of Woodylin. Then the loosened pieces next above drifted off; they went in shoals, platoon-like. In the afternoon another division followed. The next morning beheld the Harbor without a vestige of its winter bands.

At the Saw-mills these things created their wonted interest. The water lay in a broad, level plain behind the Mills, now turbid indeed, and beginning to seethe and surge, by reason of the increased volume pouring over the Dam. The hollows in the bed of the stream were filled, and the "rips" concealed from sight. The icicles that form on the fall of the Dam, — glacial stalactites, a columnar veil extending nearly the whole length of the structure, — these Richard saw give way and tumble into the stream.

But the end was not yet, — hardly the beginning. The ice above the Dam, where the waters form a vast pond, had not started. At the head of the pond was probably also a jam of ice. And likewise up the River, like the locks of a canal, rising one above another, and each having its own level, were other dams, and ponds, and jams. On numberless tributaries, the ice, swathed by narrow, winding shores, stagnated in marshes and on flats, arrested also by frequent petty dams, had made little progress. Then, quite likely, as you approached the sources of the stream, in a higher latitude, the waters still slumbered in their wintry solitudes, and gave no vernal intimations whatever. So that there were hundreds of miles of substance, solid as the earth itself, and seeming to be a part of its rocky crust, yet to slide off, yet to mount the crest of the Dam, to be compressed within the piers of the Bridge, and pass through the city.

But such a finale would require another rain, or more heat.

Then what might happen? This: that the ice would be choked in the Narrows, a dam extemporized, and a jam created, having at its back these hundred miles of fluent blocks; and that the water, indignant at this detention, recoiling, striking on the right and left at the shores, which it supposes to be accomplices in this attempt at subjugation, shall engulf the lower parts of the city, deluging stores, and barricading streets; overflow the Pebbles, and disturb the repose of Quiet Arbor; and lifting the ponderous Bridge from its abutments, and the strong mills from their beds, toss them both into the torrent. Such things were dreamed of.

But the rain, impatient at the dilatoriness of the heat,—black in the face, swollen in its veins,—just tightened its girdle, and began its task. For two days and two nights it labored like a steam-pump, without once losing its wind. It created a flood on its own behalf, independently of the River, in barn-yards and wood-yards, in cellars and drains; the streets were a freshet of mud.

But the eviction of the ice and freedom of the River

was its great object; and this the rain did by a gradual process of undermining, beginning at the Bridge, and carried on to the tips of the fingers of the tributaries, and to the hairs of the head of the stream; insinuating itself beneath the superincumbent mass by millions of sluices dispersed over millions of acres of soil.

The Mills, to be technically precise, hung up; the gates were shut; the hands scattered, — some busy on repairs, others idly observing the course of the flood.

Richard saw the first ice flake over the Dam; then an immense sheet, many rods square, parting in regular sections, like snow sliding from the roof of a house, came on. Then acres of the crystal, so long in suspense, plunged forward, and the broad expanse of water was full of ice, — like all the blocks of granite Quincy ever produced or ever will produce, set suddenly afloat. Intermingled with the seething shoal were peeled logs; trees that had been ravished by their roots from the banks; small buildings, which the flood picked off in passing, and the wash of all the woods and fields. It would take twenty-four hours for the whole to run by.

Night came on apace, and the people of Woodylin went to bed with some degree of uncertainty as to what the morning might disclose, inasmuch as so sudden a rise was not often chronicled. In the middle of the night the Church-bells rang, and the people hurried to the River. Some said it was flowing back, and, of course, a jam was formed at the Narrows. Lanterns gleamed; anxious voices and hurried steps could be distinguished. The riparians must strip their houses; destructibles must be hoisted from the basement of the stores; the Timid Man fled to the rescue of his bottles. The Bridge was thronged: beneath it crunched and rumbled the burdened current; upright beams, which the flood bore on its surface, were hurled against it, making its own beams creak and tremble.

Where was Richard? Where he ought to be, — helping Mr. Gouch, who lived on the shore, save his furniture. Where was Tunny? Sweating over the hatchway of his cellar, hoisting up potatoes and a rat-trap. Where were Memmy and Bebby? Fast asleep in their trundle-bed. Where was Chuk? He and Mysie were out together and alone, in that horrible time, trying to secure his boom. Where was the Governor's Family? Down on the Bridge. Let us not particularize.

Up the waters came, — up with a rush, — up like a race horse, up the landing-places, and the passages between the stores and the end of the streets leading to the River, and the Pebbles. There was a frightful hiss in the stream, as it swept under the Bridge, and a melancholy roar in its fast accumulating waters above, and the darkness of the night was awful. People's hearts swelled as the waters did, and were as dark as the night was. Now the ice was so high that it struck the bottom of the Bridge, and every man's heart seemed to be thwacked and going. Some ran as if the Bridge was falling; others clenched themselves into silence.

The Governor, with his hands in his side-pockets, attended by his two oldest sons, walked leisurely across the Bridge.

"Do you think she will stand?" said one to him. "I do not know," he replied; "if it goes it goes, and there is no help for it." The same question he was asked forty times, and he made nearly the same answer. Did he not care? He was a share-holder in the concern. O, it was a way he had. But the people did care. "It rises slower," said one. "But it is still rising," rejoined another. "Two inches more, and we are gone." It was as if their hearts would go, in two inches more. "Horrible to think of!" they exclaimed. "The worst thing that could happen." "The loss of the Bridge would ruin a whole season's business!" "What could we do without it?"

All at once a voice might have been heard, as of the Bridge speaking, — a voice that sounded gruff and sepulchral, from end to end of the dark, timber-teeming vault. "Ye are scared, ye are troubled," it said, "sinners that ye are! How often have ye taunted and scandalized me! How often have ye scolded at your tolls, and abused the gate-keeper! What conspiracies have ye hatched against me! What mutterings have filled your streets about me! Year after year have I listened to your complaints, and borne with your revilings. Year after year have I aided your passage across the stream, and received in return your ingratitude and scorn. Every beam and rafter is witness to your maledictions; every plank in my floor is worn with the foot of your contempt. What will ye now, ye poltroons? Too dark, am I, for your ladies? Too exorbitant for your poor ones? What means your consternation?"

The people were aghast.

"Ye have wished me out of the way," the Bridge continued; "ye have denounced me as a nuisance. Shall I leap into the water?"

"Mercy! mercy!" cried the people.

A voice was heard from the River. "I know those fellows," it said. "They thought they had me under their feet, when the ice was on, and they could cross for nothing. They thought I was of no consequence, and grudged the pennies they paid for getting over me. Every curse on you, my good friend, I have felt as a slight on me. I have not said much about it, but I have felt it. I am glad you have spoken; I am glad the ice is broke. It was you, Mr. Bridge, that gave me a sense of my dignity and importance. When I saw your piers going up, and your sills laying, and the heavy couplings entering into your superstructure, I felt that I was something. I am getting ready a jam of ice. I will help you off, and punish these impudent bipeds."

"Oh! oh!" screamed the people.

"Down upon your knees, every man of you! down into the dust ye have hated, and ask our forgiveness," rejoined the Bridge; "and we will see what shall be done with you."

While the Bridge is dealing with the malcontents, let us follow the Governor into the streets. When he saw how the water was rising, he bethought him of a widow that occupied one of his houses on the margin of the Pebbles. He hastened thither, with his sons. He found the woman and her family up and alarmed; but the water never before, so far as the Governor could recollect, had covered that spot. The River had lost its recollection too, and on it came, rushing, like a mill-tail, over the sills of the house. Roscoe seized one child, Benjamin another, and the mother followed with a third. The Governor set off with a bed. But the River, though it was the Governor, and everybody reverenced him for his wisdom, thought he might still be taught a few things, and poured upon him breast high, and threw in, to increase the weight of its impressions, a boulder of ice. The Governor, never easily thrown from his balance, never yet prostrated by adversity, clung to the branch of a tree, and defended himself with the bed, against the ice.

Now, quicker than this pen can move, Richard was there, and Munk, and Silver, and the gang that had been relieving distress elsewhere, and they dashed into the water and rescued the Governor.

Now, also, the River, having concluded terms with the backbiters, fell off as suddenly as it had risen. Down it went in the twinkling of an eye; the jam had broken, and the peril was over.

Now, also, since the suspense is ended, and we can speak of it, it will be expected we should say that Richard was the first to leap in after the Governor; that in his young and athletic arms he grasped the bruised and exhausted magnate, and bore him to dry land. Poetical justice to Richard, and to the Governor's Family, and to the whole scope of this book, and to the hearts of its million, polyglottal, deeply interested readers, requires this. Well, it is so: fact coincides with fancy, and Richard, who, by the way, was a very accommodating youth, did just what poetic justice and all our readers would wish him to do.

The Governor was not much hurt, — he never was; he went home, and to bed, and all the city did the same.

The next morning the people turned out to see what had happened, and to mangonize on what might have happened. The ice still flowed, and the river luxuriated in the calm magnificence of inundation. The Dam supplied the principal attraction, and hither many came.

The water passed the crest at a height of fifteen feet greater than its common level, and the whole structure seemed to have suddenly mounted so many degrees. The entire volume of water had swelled in proportion, and the River seemed like a vast lake that had broke out within the precincts of the city. The Dam, a thousand feet long, poured like a Niagara in its teens. At its foot was the rabid "boil" and terrific undertow; caverns were hollowed out in the liquid rage; smooth arches sported over the exacerbated surface; the spray rose soft and beautiful; jets of sparkling crystals spurted from the dark depths beneath;

an occasional ice-plateau, like the deck of a man-of-war, was precipitated down the fall, and borne, a shivering, scattered wreck, across the field of view.

To Richard this scene was new, and he sat at the back-door of the Mill looking at it. Many gentlemen and ladies came to the same spot, among whom were Melicent and Barbara Dennington, their little brother, Sebastian Rasle, and niece, Alice Weymouth. With them were Webster Chassford and Glendar.

Now Chassford and Glendar had seen Richard a few nights before, but they did not remember him. The Denningtons remembered him well, and talked with him. The River repeated its wonders every year, but the beauty and the grandeur of the scene were continually revealing a new shape to the minds of these ladies, and awakening fresh transports of delight; and while the whole was comparatively novel to Richard, they could meet him quite half way in the enthusiasm of the hour. Water is always quickening to the spirit of the beholder, and such water was very quickening. They had much to say and to feel about it, and, as it happened, their three sayings and feelings, like the subject thereof, ran in the same channel. Glendar dipped in his oar, and rowed with the ladies a while; finally, so to speak, he got them into his own boat, and rowed in another direction. Richard, with his pocket-knife, was carving toys, out of a piece of pine, for Memmy and Bebby. So he kept at his work, and let his boat run whither it list. He tried to talk with Alice Weymouth, but she blushed deeply, and said little. She was a black-eyed girl, about twelve years old, with a quick, sensitive face; and every time Richard looked at her, she half laughed and wholly blushed; and, clinging to Aunt Barbara's hand, she seemed quite unable to support conversation. Melicent did ask what Richard was making, and he told her; and she even dropped a question or two about the children, and he could have answered a folio volume. But she was polite, and he was polite; and she had other friends to listen to, and he had no wish to inflict the children upon her.

Barbara asked Richard if he had seen the Boy, Chuk, since Bill Stonners' death. He had not. She would like to go and see him. So would Richard and Melicent; and so would Chassford and Glendar. And they all started for Bill Stonners' Point.

Rasse ran everywhere; but little Alice Weymouth kept in the rear, and little though she was, she seemed to be laboring with a mighty large arrision all the way up; and every time she looked at Richard, she laughed the more; but all to herself, all within her own thoughts. If the others happened to look back, she coughed and blushed, and seemed to be trying to cover up her laughter with her blushes. What was there in Richard so provoking, or so titillating? He wore his red shirt, and snuff-colored monkey-jacket, and had mounted a new Rough and Ready glazed hat; but these she ought not to laugh at. They had to cross a small brook; and while Chassford and Glendar were attending to the ladies, Richard would have helped her over; but she shrank from him, — she seemed to feel as bad to have him touch her as Tunny did to have him look at him.

They found Chuk in trouble; his guys had parted, and his boom-sticks were broken. Richard promised to help repair the disaster when the water fell. The Boy flung his pole into the stream, and himself on a rock, and acted quite desperately. "You an't Bill," said he, "and you need n't try to be! You can't swear as he could; and the ice never crowded so when he was alive, and could swear!"

Melicent told him not to feel so bad. But he would feel

so bad; that was his prerogative, — it was his duty. Mysie brought back the pole, which she went along the shore and rescued, and gave it to him. She said, "Bill would not do so; and I would not do so, if I was you. You can mend the boom, and there 'll be a plenty of logs by and bye. We did the best we could." Mysie alone seemed to have power over the Boy; but her power did not always prevail. Chassford put a silver dollar into Chuk's hand; he heaved it from him, — he flung it with sarcastic swiftness into the water. "We did n't want money," said he; "we wanted life; and your father would n't give that, and he shan't give t' other. Let the River have it! See if you can't buy up its good-will!"

The road to the Point went by Munk's; and when the party returned, the children, who had probably already espied them from the kitchen window, stood on the front door-step, jiggling, and hooting, and clapping their hands; and before Richard could get to them, Bebby had backed half way down the steps. Their uncle took them both in his arms, and turned towards the ladies. These were Memmy and Bebby! these were the lords paramount of that mighty dom! He did not say so, but the fact was so. Melicent dotted one, with her smooth kid-gloved finger, on the cheek; Barbara chucked the other under its chin. Alice Weymouth — the tyke! — laughed outright. It was all day with her; she began to splurt, and had to let it go. And the children laughed too; this was a god-send for Alice, since it put her own laughter into countenance, and she could go ahead without restraint; and she laughed herself high and dry. Indeed, they all seemed to have a merry minute, till Mrs. Munk appeared in the door, calling after the children, and reproving them for being out, and saying they would certainly catch their death of a cold to be there without their hoods on.

Alice Weymouth laughed no more till she reached home. But when the Family were sitting at dinner, she began again, or rather the imp inside of her began again; she herself blushed, — she tried to drown the imp with a glass of water. But it was n't to be drowned; it dashed back the water, — it scattered it over the table. "Why, Alice Weymouth!" said Madam. "The child is choking!" exclaimed Mrs Melbourne. Cousin Rowena had already begun to bite her lip, a sign of suppressed emotion; not that she knew of anything to laugh at, but only out of an unconscious sympathy of joyous feeling. "It is nothing," said Alice Weymouth, rather in reply to Mrs. Melbourne than anybody else "You should not drink so fast," said Madam, quietly The more attention was drawn to the child, the worse she acted; if she had been alone, she would have got through with it well enough. "Why don't you speak, if you have anything to say?" asked Roscoe. "It is nothing," she said "only I saw Richard Edney." "So did I," sang out Rasle. Miss Rowena laughed outright, now; in fact, they all laughed. "He did n't hurt you, did he?" inquired Cousin. "I was only thinking," replied the child, "it was he that scared us so on the Bridge, that he was the one that stopped the horse when Aunt Melicent like to have been run away with, and that he dragged Grandpa out of the water last night. I did n't mean to laugh, but I could n't help it." It was out, now, and the child was easier. "Nothing to laugh at, I am sure," said Mrs. Melbourne. "You are at leisure to attend to other matters," added Madam; "will you have some cranberry?" "How did he look?" asked Miss Rowena. "He is real good-looking," replied the child. "He has an intelligent look, and a noble bearing," observed Barbara. "He looks the same as anybody looks, out of his eyes," added Rasle, who had the reputation of being a smart boy. "I do not know how he looks," said the Governor, "but he carries a pair of stout arms. — Let me give you a thin slice of beef, Mrs. Melbourne."

"It was so funny," pursued Alice Weymouth, "to see him talking with Aunt Melicent and Aunt Barbara, and to see him try to help them over the brook, with his queer hat on, and his red shirt!" "Where have you been? what has been doing?" asked Madam, rather quick, rather nervously. "We went up to Bill Stonners'," responded the child, "to see what had become of his Boy." "This Richard Edney," said Madam, "must be a good youth," — here she laid down her knife, unconsciously, — "a very good youth," — her fork dropped, — "and you should not laugh at goodness, Alice Weymouth; nor you, Rasle." "I did n't, Mother," replied the boy, "and I shan't be likely to laugh at anything again very soon, with this pickled pepper in my mouth. I wish peppers was sweet." Madam stirred her tea, and looked at her spoon, — she had tea at dinner. "Goodness," she continued, "is too rare in this world to be treated disrespectfully when it does come." "I will try not to laugh, next time," replied Alice Weymouth.

So fared Richard in the Governor's Family, to-day.

He, in the mean time, had displayed his toys to Memmy and Bebby, and I guess they laughed as hard as Alice Weymouth did. He had made them a little wagon, and a little old man that he called Uncle Squib, and a very little chub of a baby that he called Tuckey, to sit in it; and the way Uncle Squib and Tuckey were whisked across the room was a caution to rail-roads, to say nothing of Winkle, and the four best horses in his team.

If we wish to run a further parallel between the heroic elements of our book, we should say, that at the precise instant Melicent and Barbara were setting back the table in their dining-room, Richard was helping his sister, Roxy, with the same office in her kitchen, and that the two tables struck the wall together.

As Richard returned from the Mill at night, Clover walked on with him. "Fine girls, those Governor's daughters," said the latter. "Chassford is engaged to one of them and Glendar expects the other." Richard made no reply.

Richard was more thoughtful than usual after tea that night. The children were rampant as ever, but he did not seem to notice them. He had been in the habit of rocking Bebby to sleep in his arms. She climbed into his lap, — she lay on one shoulder, then tried the other; nothing suited her. She pointed to his pocket for his handkerchief, with which he sometimes cushioned her head; then she pointed to the mantel-piece for the match-box, which she was wont to go to sleep upon, holding it in her hands; but he did not attend to her; — she pulled his lips for him to tell her a story; he did not answer; then she cried. "She wants you to tell her a story," said Memmy. Her mother took the child away. "You are getting her into very bad habits," she said. "They are always wanting things, and you get them." She pacified the child, and put it to bed.

But Richard kept on thinking. Munk was smoking and reading, his sister was sewing, and he thought. His thoughts went down into the neighborhood of his feelings, and his feelings, like fishes about a ship, kept edging about his thoughts. He feared Chassford and Glendar were bad men. He believed the Governor's daughters were the best of human beings. At least, if he never imagined so much before, it seemed to him so now. Set off against bad men, they appeared to him good, very good indeed. The contrast brought them into strong relief,—their goodness took a most palpable, glorious form to his eye. And this got down into his heart as a sort of divine impression,—a something that stirred his deepest reverence,—and he could almost worship it.

At the same hour, while Richard sat by the stove at Munk's in a sort of brown study, Chassford and Glendar were making a call at the Governor's. "That fellow," said Glendar, alluding to Richard, "has an off-hand way, rather uncommon among his class." "He has true courtesy," replied Melicent; "the transparency of a gentle heart through a gentle demeanor." "He is a strong man," observed Roscoe, "a very strong man." "Melicent and your father can judge best about that," added Madam, looking very sharply at a needle she was trying to thread in the light of the candle. "I mean," added her son, "he is very strong every way." "His demonstration at the Abolition meeting was rather weak,—rather a failure," answered Chassford. "It was superb,—perfectly ecstatic!" exclaimed Barbara.

CHAPTER XVII.

TROUBLE IN QUIET ARBOR.

Not many days afterwards, Richard might have been seen, at mid-evening, in close conference with Nefon at the store of the latter. They seemed to have some private scheme in hand. What it was will better appear in the history of its execution. Only this we are prepared to say, — that Nefon was a great friend of Temperance, and so was Richard; and they had often spoken together of the increase of drunkenness, and the means of quenching that evil.

They left the store, and proceeded to a building in which was a Hall of the Sons of Temperance, where this fraternity were then in session. While Richard waited on the walk, Nefon ascended to the Hall, and in a few minutes returned with a half-dozen sturdy Brothers, in their white collars, including also a W. P., with his scarlet ensigns.

Richard led them forthwith to the Pebbles, on the shore of which Quiet Arbor was snugly located. Leaving his accomplices at the door, he entered this sanctuary alone. Waving ceremony, he abruptly accosted the obliging but modest head of the establishment in these words: — "You are the Friend of the People?" said he, interrogatively. "I am," responded the Timid Man, hacking. "You are willing they should be befriended, and that their best friends should exert themselves for them, and that their liberties should be achieved?" "I am," he hacked.

Richard opened the door, and the six Brothers approached.

"These are the Friends of the People," he said. If another flood had made a sudden onslaught on his bottles, Helskill could not have been more alarmed; but he was more than alarmed, — he was incensed; he set his teeth, and he set his eyes, so that they did not play up and down, but looked straight forwards. But there the white-robed phalanx was, and he had to see *them*, and receive them, and behave as mannerly as he could under them; and when he tried to hack, he could n't; and when he had got a little hack half way up, it slipped back, in spite of him.

There were the customary tarriers in this abode of leisure; in a sort of mirage of smoke and dim lamp-light, loomed up a motley group of shabby beards, slouched hats, blub-cheeks and blistered noses; men, who looked like an old sheet-iron stove that has been burnt out and dented in; men, who lay coiled up in their repose, as a grub lies in the earth; men, some of whom retained the power of capering about in that soothing atmosphere, like a hog in a snow-drift.

Richard proceeded with his plot. He addressed those men: "Ye are slaves," said he; "slaves to your appetites and habits, — slaves to this spot and this hour, — slaves to sin and shame! You have no liberty of thought or of feeling,— none of money or of time. You know not the freedom of health or of strength, — you have no independency of hope or of happiness. You propagate the evils you suffer. You, Weasand, have enslaved your wife; you, Fuzzle, have broken the spirit of your mother; you, Horn, have sent your family to the Alms-house. We come to-night to give you liberty. We proclaim your freedom. We have brought the Temperance Pledge. Sign this; it is the covenant of your Redemption, — it is the Constitution of your Independence." "Make out the papers," cried one. "Mr. Nefon," said Richard, "pass the pen and ink." "One more bouse, and I 'll sign," exclaimed another "a stiff one, Helskill; I must wet both eyes, for I want to see sharp into what I am about." The Tapster could not so far overcome his friendly feelings as not to favor the man in this his last request. Emptying the glass to the dregs, and sweeping his lips with his hand, this man advanced to the table and wrote his name.

"Worthy Patriarch," said Nefon, addressing the scarlet-robed Brother, "witness the signatures."

"I am so infernally drunk, I can't sign," swore a third. "Drunk or sober, it makes no difference," replied Richard. "All sign that will sign."

"If I could get up there, I would sign," jargled one from the floor. "Brothers Bisbee and Sloan," said the Patriarch, "lift up Mr. Fuzzle, while he signs."

"I can't write," said a fourth. "The Worthy Patriarch will witness his mark," responded Nefon.

In this way they canvassed the entire room. "Here is one too stiff to stir," some one said. "Four Brothers carry him to the Division Room," enjoined the Chief, "and thither let us all proceed." These Liberators, with their captives to freedom, departed, and Richard and Nefon were left alone with the Keeper of the Arbor. If this man was surprised, he was also stunned. That his guests had taken their well-being into their own hands, or even committed it in trust to the Sons of Temperance, was a fact which he could not gainsay, and a virtue that he dare not revile; and he stood behind the bar, looking like one who had just seen his grandmother's ghost.

Now Nefon was tart — tarter than Richard; and he longed to rub the dram-monger's ears a bit, just in an easy way; and he could not forbear a little pleasantry, even if there was a needle at the point of it. So he said, "Your Arbor will be very quiet now, — still as a nether mill-stone; and you will have nothing to do but whirl round on it, and grind out your meditations at your leisure."

He had better not have said this, for it made Helskill mad, very mad; and it did no good. Besides, it came near frustrating part of their plan, which embraced the Grotto. Richard tried the door that led to that apartment, but Helskill sprang forward and locked it; and Chuk-like, he would see them, and himself, and the whole premises, in the ashes of perdition, before they should go in.

They retreated to the street. "There is a private entrance," said Richard, "and we will find it." They did find it, and went in, and were hazed in a labyrinth of passages and darkness. The little Bookseller might have been frightened, but he was not. "We are in for a job," said he, "and for a broken head, for all I know. I could not have done this yesterday. I am warm, very warm; and we must strike while the iron is hot."

They felt their way onwards, and at length came to the door of the wizard-room. They entered quite abruptly; and their arrival seemed to betoken unusual pertinence. The occupants of the room, — Captain Creamer, Chassford, Glendar, Tunny and the Sailmaker, — felt this. The Captain glavered, the Sailmaker blustered; Glendar, leaning over the table, shuffled cards very vacantly. Tunny, — what did he do, what could he do, when there was so little left of him the night before? If he could have vanished, he would; but he had to be there, or let his shadow be there, and take what might befall.

"I am indebted to you, Sir," Richard said, addressing the Captain; "you gave me occupation when I was a stranger in the place. As your servant, I might hesitate in what I am now upon. But there is a higher relation between us than that of employer and employed, — the relation of humanity, of Christian fidelity. And this obliges me to say that you are in a bad way. These practices are destructive of all that you value in life, or that you would have me value. I shall not take advantage of what has come to my knowledge; but I must affectionately, and very positively, admonish you."

The Captain, for once in his life, lost his self-possession, his gay ease, his oily grace; and he seemed in an instant to sink into his proper age, and reäppear in the furrows and the palsy of an old man. He stammered, and tripped; and, with Glendar and Chassford, hastily left the room.

The Sailmaker was not to be interrupted; he had got too valuable a prey in his clutches to admit a rival. He declaimed against interference, — he snuffed at this meddling with other folks' business, — he fanfaronaded on sentimental benevolence. "I do not mind that," replied Richard; "but you must give up Tunny."

"Any man that comes between me and Tunny is a dead man!"

"I am between you and Tunny; and I am alive, and tolerably well," rejoined Richard. "Tunny," he added, "go home." There was so slender a remnant of the Grocer on hand that it did not seem to hear, — it lay passively in the chair. The Sailmaker stooped to seize it. Richard elbowed him off. "Go home, Tunny," he repeated, in a still louder voice. Nefon took the relic by the arm, and led it to the door "I will have it out of you, body and soul, for this!" added the Sailmaker. Richard and Nefon supported Tunny to his house.

The Sailmaker sought to be as good as his word. He came to the Mill and detained Richard one noon after the bell had rung the others to dinner.

"I demand satisfaction for what you have done!" he said. "I will give it," replied Richard; "what shall it be?" "One of us must *die!*" he answered, with an emphasis of pathos and frenzy. "Not so bad as that, I hope," rejoined Richard. "Just as bad," said the other. "Choose your weapons, and your own way." "Very well," answered Richard, "and prepare yourself to meet an antagonism that comes with weapons not carnal, but spiritual." "You canting hypocrite, you!" sneered the Sailmaker; "sliverly coward! you mean to avoid me, — you mean to hush away! You won't do it, — you are too late for it!" He drew a dirk, which he might have done mischief with; but Richard took it from him, and breaking the blade, threw the fragments into the wheel-pit.

The Sailmaker, slackening in physical rage, calmed down to argument. "You do not know," said he, "what I have endured. It is not Tunny's money I want; it is revenge. I scorn him and his dust. But his family have insulted me, — his wife has planted her flat-footed pride on me, his son has lost all recollection of me, because I am a Sailmaker, — because I am what my father was before me. Who are they but mangy skip-jacks, half-baked upper crusts? Did n't Tunny drive a fish-cart? Has n't he tooted his carrion by our own door?"

Richard replied, "My friend, I think I understand you,— I believe I know to what you refer, and I may be deeper in the secret of your affairs than you are yourself."

"How is that?" eagerly asked the other.

"You allude to a disruption of intimacy between yourself and their daughter, Faustina." "I do," answered the other. "Well, let me tell you," continued Richard, "that was not owing to your birth or vocation, but to your habits."

"'T is false!" answered the Sailmaker. "Mrs. Tunny

forbade my visiting her daughter. She said my hands soiled the door when I entered. I heard her say so."

"That may be," responded Richard; "but Faustina never said so, did she?"

"Is there any hope for me with her? If there be, I do not mind a farthing that soap-bubble of a mother."

"There may be," said Richard, "for all that I know. But, in my opinion, all depends on one thing."

"What is that?"

"That you repent of your sins, — that you reform your manner of life, and by God's grace renovate your spirit. Avoid the haunts of vice; consort with what is good and pure, and come to appear, and to be, a new man."

"I will think of what you say," replied the young man.

CHAPTER XVIII.

THE JUNE FRESHET.

So it was denominated, because it commonly happened in that month; but it sometimes anticipated its period. In this instance, it was announced about the middle of May.

This flood was both spring-time and harvest for log-drivers, boom-gatherers, and lumber-men generally. The gates of the Lake were opened, and vast deposits of logs that had been accumulating on that inwooded realm of ice during the winter were turned into the River. Gangs of men were despatched to break up the jams that formed on shoals and rips. Others scoured the banks of tributaries, and launched whatever logs they could find into the current.

A portion of these logs, unlike their predecessor, the ice, were retained above the Dam; yet many thousands must attempt that pass, and be hurried across the Harbor, and through the Narrows.

Now little boats are seen darting out from the shore, sylvan buccaneers, in chase of their prey; each manned by two men — one to row, the other to strike the picaroon. Where was Chuk? What should poor Chuk do, all alone? The water was very smooth and still where he operated, and his boom was sheltered in as quiet a little nook as the whole stream afforded; indeed, it was generally conceded by those whose habits would render them competent to form an opinion in the premises, that Bill Stonners' privilege was one of the best in the County.

The Boy made his picaroon fast to his boat with a rope,

and then put into the stream, with the double office of rowing and striking. He cried when he did so, — cried like a spoiled child. He had nobody to swear at, and nobody to swear at him, — and he cried. There, under the shadow of the rock that formed the shoulder of the Point, and of the great trees that overhang it, and under the blue sky, and over the clear sky-and-rock-and-tree-embosoming deep, he wept while he worked; and there Mysie, whose broad, gaunt form stood folded and calm on the high shore, saw him weep as he paddled in and out, and never looked up; striking and trailing all alone, without Bill, and with nothing in the wide world to comfort him.

The logs swept over the Dam just as the ice had done, and people came to the Saw-mills, and stood on the shores to see the feat, just as they did before. The logs, with the bark bruised off and the ends "broomed" up, by reason of the roughness of their passage, — some of them discolored and black, from long exposure in the shallows, — many of them large, now and then one six feet in diameter, — were the monsters of this deep. They slid tranquilly and gracefully down the swift, limpid fall. But now their danger commenced. They must seethe in the "boil," and be absorbed by the undertow. Descending to the bed of the stream, they rebounded, and leaped into the air. Some, forty feet long and weighing four or five tons, were tossed like candles the water played with them on the ends of its fingers, as a juggler manœuvres with a broom-stick. They thrashed about as if they were the arms of a giant, who was strangling underneath. They would be piled one upon another, drawn under the fall, and then spurned into the hideous regions below. Still afloat, — still struggling to escape. One, that had got away, as it supposes, into clear water, is deliberately drawn back; a second one tumbles upon it from above; a third, rising from beneath, forces their groaning, aching, battered bodies into fresh catastrophes. In this commotion hundreds are engaged at the same moment. In a light mood, you would imagine them whales or porpoises at their gambols, or beach-bathers rolling in the surf. They might seem to you instinct with a certain life, which was to be acted out in that spot. A more terrific suggestion is that of humanity arrested in its progress, and Faith, Hope and Charity, writhing in the cataract of evil, — springing to regain a serener surface, and yet at every instant overpowered by a relentless destiny; or of a single heart, stricken by calamity, panting, pleading to be free, yet doomed to an irrevocable anguish.

But this did not propose to be a dramatic spectacle of admiration or of terror; it had more serious matter in hand. There was a weak spot in the Dam. So the Man of Mind in the city said. He whispered it to newspaper editors; he wrote information to the Dam Corporation about it; he nudged it to the Sawyers and the Log-drivers; he nodded it to himself, as he walked past the Dam. Some people believed him. It got to the ears of the logs, and they would see if it were so. In their submergence, like prisoners in a dungeon, they found out the defect in the walls, and matured a plan for breaking through. Certain of the stoutest of them, rearing concertedly their enormous shafts, fell, battering-ram fashion, on the structure that detained them. One broke the cross-ties; another dislodged the ballast-stones; several, diving out of sight, unearthed the foundations; and, before any one but the Man of Mind saw it, the erection gave way — the bulwark of the River fell. These resolute logs did not enter the breach they made, but, having effected their object, they sailed tauntingly away. In an hour the entire pond was drained to the natural level of the stream.

One way, it seemed, to get out of difficulty; one way for Hopes and Hearts to liberate themselves, — turn, full-butt, on the evil that beleaguers them!

The Man of Mind stood immovable and frowning, and pointed to the spot; and as they ran from all quarters to see what had happened, he seemed to have the entire population of the city on his finger's end, and they went just where his finger directed, and believed just what his finger indicated; and *as* he stood, immovable and frowning, everybody was abashed by him, as a man of mind, and gave it up that he was a man of mind.

But the Mill-owners and the Factory-companies cared nothing for minds; they wanted water. Their canal was emptied, and their wheels were silent in the pit. The work-folk were dismissed. It would take three weeks or a month to effect repairs.

But the people, whose employment failed so suddenly, did not grumble, so far as we heard. The girls would have a vacation, and visit their friends; Mr. Gouch and his family would not starve, for he had a little laid by for a rainy or an idle day. More than all, the indomitableness of "our people" would be exhibited. The wounds of Young America heal quick. A breach in a mill-dam, — fie! it is no more than a bird-track through our incalculable sky. Then there were repairs in the Mills that would occupy a number of hands. Tunny felt bad, because such an event dispersed his customers. But Chuk was as large a sufferer as any. His boom was ruined; the sudden cessation of the water carried it off, logs and all. He and Mysie held on to the guys, and retarded the catastrophe, by main strength, as long as they could; but when nought availed, and the fabric of his heart and hope was being swept into the rapid current, he flung his paddles into the boat, and sent that down too. Mysie was only afraid he would follow suit himself, and clenched his arm to prevent such a piece of folly.

Richard was at work in the Mill when these things took place. There were ladies there, and Melicent and Barbara. Richard, cant-dog in hand, would now and then go to the door and look at the logs, and exchange a syllable with his new acquaintance. But Captain Creamer, who, however he might behave at the Grotto, was, reasonably, master on his own premises, deemed Richard too young to have much to do with the ladies, kept him engaged in fresh tasks, and, as if he himself was of an age when such conversation would be harmless, he monopolized it altogether.

When the accident was announced, it appeared that even this sort of intimacy had not softened the Captain; he stormed at his men. The saw was half through the middle run, and it seemed as if he would make them urge it to the foot by their own strength of arm.

Of course, Richard and all hands were afloat, as well as Chuk's boom. The Captain said they would not expect wages to go on when nothing was doing, and when he, perhaps, might find himself a ruined man to-morrow. Of course they would not. They put on their coats, and went home.

Munk had employment for Richard at the stable; in fact, his brother-in-law could be of real use to him. The steamboats and rail-roads were running, and people were hastening to overtake them, and these people must have horses; so that Munk & St. John's business was good. Their business depended on that of the world at large, and this was good. The stable was neat as a penny, with its whitewashed walls and well-swept floor. Each horse had his name fairly inscribed above his stall; there were Fly, Black Maria, Beau Savage, Belle Fanny, and many more. A small office was attached to the establishment, where hung the harnesses and whips, all in Primlico style. Here, also, was a stove, and a bunk where the boy, Simon, slept. Into this office a newspaper was dropped every morning. Mr. St. John, the partner, was a nice man, and Simon was a clever boy. Simon had an interesting peculiarity. It was the snatch of a song he sung, that went thus: "O, the break down, on; O, the break down!" He sung this when he groomed the horses, and when he swept the stable; when the carriages came in, and when they went out; indeed, at all times. What it meant, nobody could tell. It passed as a mystery of human nature. Moreover, Winkle appeared every other afternoon, with his four horses all a-reek with perspiration, and his face a-reek with good-nature.

There was in the stable a rare animal, Belle Fanny: so sleek a skin, so arched a neck, so bright and cheerful a countenance, such fleetness of foot, and gentleness of spirit, were not often the perquisites of a single horse; but they were hers. How readily she started; how freely she moved; how quick to stop; how easy to turn! — and with her never shying or stumbling, she was a wonder. Then the little wagon that belonged to her, — what an equipage was that! Ho! Memmy and Bebby will ride to-day. Queen Elizabeth, when she started on her Progresses, — the green and blue Chariot-races of ancient Byzantium, — are nothing compared with the excitement got up when these young Imperialnesses went abroad.

We forbear to describe the ride. We can only say, the weather was pleasant; the roads were good; the grass was green; the birds were songful; and Uncle Richard never was happier, nor the children either.

Sometimes Richard drove the hack to the wharves and

the depot; sometimes he went on family and social excursions with the omnibus.

Munk had a garden, which Richard spaded and sowed. Munk's lot extended from the street to the River, and comprised a quarter of an acre. This Richard resolved to ornament and improve. He applied to the woods in the neighborhood, where were all varieties of evergreen and perdifoil. He knew how to dig deeply round the trees, to sever the roots carefully, and prune the tops judiciously. He was thoughtful enough, also, to choose a humid day for this operation. He studied grouping and curves in the arrangement of the trees. He supplied their roots with well-rotted manure. Against the kitchen window, where was the sink, and Roxy did her work, and the summer sun burned like an oven, he planted a good-sized maple. He ploughed and graded the rear portion of the lot, and laid it down to grass. He induced his brother to purchase a quantity of fruit-trees, for which he discovered an abundance of suitable locations. On the River-side of the estate was a gully tufted with willows and alders, and vocal with birds, where also flourished a willow of remarkable size. Hence he called the place Willow Croft.

Was Richard in advance of his age and rank in this? He may have been: but he was not in advance of the newspapers, nor of Pastor Harold, to say nothing of his own taste.

Then, as if he had purposely designed that we should write his history, how much prettier it is to say Willow Croft, than Munk's, or his Brother-in-law's. I think there is no person of refinement who will not rejoice in the new terminology.

He had assistance; — Mysie and Chuk volunteered their services. There was not, probably a clean-bodied, fair-topped staddle within six miles, that Mysie had not taken particular note of. Then she recollected a thorn that she had seen in its full snow-bloom, and when it dripped with red apples; and she thought there was nothing so handsome in the whole world, and Richard must have it. Chuk dug, and pulled, and lifted, with amazing good-will.

But the Boy would take no pay. He seemed to recognize no other currency than that of the River; he made all his drafts with the picaroon; the use of the spade was real bankruptcy to him; and Richard had behaved so wickedly at the Point, Chuk deemed his tender of money a sacrilege on the memory of Bill and the boom; and even his thanks he rejected as a device of the adversary.

But Chuk got his pay, and Richard took his receipt, in the children, who applauded what was done, and condescended to disport amid the trees; Bebby indicated her royal interest in the scene by upsetting one of the shrubs.

Chuk, as if he had inhaled magic gas, began to frolic with the children; he acted as if he were a mere child, and had never been anything else. He keeled over on the grass, peeked through the trees, cock-a-whooped to Uncle Richard, strutted behind Bebby. "This," said he, "is it; it was just so, then — there was toddling and skirling; it huv stones, it rolled in the dirt. But where is the woman with the blue tire and the lasses cake?" He repeated this question, and turned towards the door of the house a wild, haggard stare. He presented a comical, not to say pitiable picture; — bare-headed, with long, tangled black hair, in the native luxuriance of which neither comb nor shears had interfered for many a month, and a voluminous pepper-and-salt shirt, that flared wide in the neck.

Roxy appeared in the door with a dry lunch in either hand for the children. "That is the woman with the blue tire and the lasses cake!" shouted Chuk, and ran forward with the children, flapping his arms like a new-fledged chicken, to receive what the good dame would bestow.

Richard noticed, during this metamorphosis of the Boy, that he dropped his customary oaths, and that his tone was milder, and his language less rough and churlish, than at other times.

CHAPTER XIX.

VIOLET DIES.

RICHARD was laying out his vegetable beds one morning, and the children were to their knees and elbows in dirt, preparing for baking, — moulding pie-crust, stirring puddings, cupping cakes, out of the damp earth. Looking towards the street, he saw the Old Man, the Grandfather of the Orphans, urgently bent upon something, as it were star-gazing, — now lifting his face into the air, now peering across the fields, anon putting his hand to his ear. Advancing to the gate of Willow Croft, he entered it, and came with an excited step towards the garden. "Did you not hear it? Did you not see it?" said he to Richard. "My eyes and ears are trying to cheat me out of it, because I am an old man; but I am too old for them." "What is it?" asked Richard. "The hang-bird," he replied. "I see it!" said Memmy, whose eyes were sharp as a razor, pointing with the bit of a shingle she was at work with; "it is there on the fence." "That is a robin," answered Richard. "No," said the Old Man, "it is a hang-bird. I have been out every morning after it. I know its trump. It carried off her mother, and now it has come for her."

Aunt Grint, who was making an early morning call on Roxy, overhearing the conversation, appeared, exclaiming, "Sakes alive! what is going to happen now? Death everywhere, — death all around us, and who is ready?"

"Did you see it?" asked the Old Man.

"See it!" she recoilingly answered. "How can you see it, when a body is frightened to death hearing it?"

"Which way?" eagerly inquired the other.

"It has n't any way. It is the most invisiblest thing that ever was. You look right where it is, and it ain't there."

"I heard it in the lot."

"Pshaw!" she exclaimed, "you can't hear it in the lot; it is in the chamber. It was there just before our Roseltha died. I heard it last night. God have mercy on us! what is a coming? O!"

"There it is on the tree!" said Memmy. And Bebby knew it was there; she could see it, and she screeched at it.

"For the love of heaven's sake!" cried Aunt Grint, "don't be noisy such a time as this. Who knows but what it may be one of the children?"

"It was a hangbird," said the Old Man.

"No, it was n't," rejoined Aunt Grint; "don't you suppose I should know, when I sat up in bed half an hour, a hearing it? And there the wretch kept at it on the left wall, right over my shoulder, and none of us prepared. It was a death-watch, as I was telling Roxy. O! the poor children!"

"I would not talk in this way here, Aunt," said Richard. "Such ideas can do the children no good. It may be you are both right. This man's granddaughter is very sick, and I have not thought she could live long."

They were both right. Death was near; Violet was dying.

That afternoon there were assembled about the final bedside of the Orphan, Dr. Broadwell, the Denningtons, the Lady Caroline, Richard, Miss Eyre, and one or two other girls from the Factories. The Grandfather held the hand of the dying one, and seemed to be counting the pulses, as if he had precisely calculated the last one. Junia leaned over the pillow of her sister. Respiration waxed rarer and fainter, and all was over.

Dr. Broadwell said, "Our friend, we have every reason to believe has gone to her rest. She has been received by her Saviour. She gave good evidence of reconciliation, and a spiritual life, during the few months that I have been acquainted with her. When our last hour shall come, may it find us as prepared as she was."

From every eye gushed the silent, irrepressible tear; every bosom heaved with the tenderness of funereal anguish. The Old Man, now that his watchings, his predictions, his little duties were ended, and all that he had so carefully planned was so entirely fulfilled, and there was nothing left, moaned, and wept, and trembled;—forlorn decrepitude, bereft of its staff, bereft of all on which its heart or its limbs could lean! Junia supported herself in Melicent's arms.

It is, in common language, hard parting. However joyous or certain may be Immortality; however undesirable, in any instance, may be the prolongation of this earthly existence; however certified we are of the salvable condition of our friends — still, it is hard parting. Not the immediate prospect of Heaven, not the presence of the Angel of Bliss, can prevent the bitterness of emotion. We weep from sympathy, and we weep from sorrow; and sympathy makes the sorrow of many one. In a moment, as by electric communication, all hearts coalesce; and Miss Eyre wept as purely, as deeply, as Barbara.

It is hard parting: the cessation, the giving over, the farewell, the last view; the absence, the being gone; nothing for the eye to look upon, or the hand to feel, or the tongue to speak to; the withdrawal of the spirit, the burial of the body; the silence, and the lonesomeness.

It is hard parting: the room is bereft, the table is bereft;

old clothes and old utensils are bereft; the trees are stripped, the landscape is lonely. There is a ceasing to talk, when the thought is full; a ceasing to think, when the heart is full; a ceasing to inquire and to communicate; a ceasing to gather reminiscences and to revive attachments. The subject is gradually dropped from speech, and from letters; dropped from the countenance and the manner; it passes into an allusion, it withdraws from the world, it cloisters itself in the eternal sensations of the loving soul.

It is hard parting: — but it is not all parting, — there is a going, too; there is an elevation of spirit, as well as depression of the flesh. The parting takes us along with it. It raises us from the limitable to the Illimitable. It gives to Faith its province, and to Hope its destiny. Beyond this vale of tears, our friends await us in the eternal Bloom!

It is hard parting: — but there is a remaining, too. All does not go. There are blessed memories and sweet relics still in our hands, still sleeping on our bosoms, still sitting by the fireside, still coming in at the door. Beauty, Holiness, Love, are never sick; for them is no funeral bell. That face visits us in our reveries when we wish to be all alone with it; an Ascended face, it shines on our despondency, and smiles on our love; it peoples the solitude with a sacred invisibility; it introduces us to the realm of the departed, to converse with spirits — to commune with saints. The medium between us and the dead is a purifying one. It cleanses the character; we see nothing bad in what is gone; there is no remembrance any more of sin; we are ravished by virtues perhaps too late recognized; we adore where we once hardly tolerated; — a departed friend is always an image of pure crystal.

And the body, the transient tabernacle, the clayey tenement, has its wonderful mission. It hastens to repair the rent in our hearts, by its look of angelic peace; as, in the forest, a prostrate tree hides its decay in a vesture of green moss, so the body endues the pain and the waste of sickness with an expression of health and repose.

When the last agony was over, the features of Violet resumed their wonted composure;—beautifully on the pale cheek lay the long, silken eye-lashes; on thin lips flickered a smile, as it were a shadow reflected from the ascending, beatified spirit. The Lady Caroline crossed over the silent breast the lily hands, and smoothed on the forehead the flaxen hair; and the well-defined eyebrows were still that western cloud, floating between eyes that had set forever and the azure expanse of the forehead above.

Mrs. Whichcomb, and the tray, came into the room, more quietly than usual, not to minister to the sick, but to remove the traces of sickness, and gather up sundry medicinal vessels, for which there was no further use.

Richard left the room; and Landlady followed him.

"It has come to this!" said the latter. "Yes," replied Richard, mournfully. "You would hardly have thought it," she added. "I have feared it a long time," he rejoined. She was behind him when she said this. Reaching the landing, he turned towards her, and saw her eye drooping over the tray, loaded with empty bottles and sundry trifles, the wrecks of a vain Hygiene. To that tray, as he had nothing else in particular to look at, his own gaze gravitated. "How much is gone!" she said, while a tear swelled in her eye, which she tried to suppress, and her voice thickened with emotion. "Yes," replied Richard, touched by her emotion. "How little comes out of the sick room!" she went on; "but to remember how faithful you was, and you are kept up under the heavy blow. Then there is the going up and down stairs, seeing to everything that is wanted, and with a weak back and so many others to look after, — if I was n't a Christian, which I sometimes fear, I could n't have got through it all. Who knows what death is, till it comes into a body's house, and that a boarding-house, right amongst so many, who all have their own feelings? They will not use the things again, and it takes a good while to get them back into the room, which we have to do to raw hands, and never tell them. Then there is the Doctor's bill, and the Undertaker's, and the grave-digging, which must be paid; and you never know where the money is hid." Richard heard enough, too much for his peace of mind; and he retorted, with reasonable severity, "How can you so harrow the sensibilities of the living, and insult the memories of the dead!"

"So-ho!" snapped the woman; "you would fob me off, — you would shirk me out of my dues; when I have been in the business thirty year, and stood between myself and ruin six months at a time, which death always produces, and the friends afterwards have no more hearts than a stone! You shall pay for it; this sickness shall come out of you!"

Richard escaped into the street. He provided for the obsequies; he took charge of the services on the burial day. It was a scant procession, but it comprised the elements of tenderest sorrow. In a quiet lot, in the city burial-ground, the remains of Violet were laid.

What should become of the Old Man and Junia? They were without resources. The expenses incident to what had transpired more than exhausted their little store. There was a balance against them of a few dollars, which the generosity of the Factory Girls, and some others, removed.

They could not remain at Whichcomb's, for two reasons, — the head of that establishment would not have them there, and Junia had no wish to be there.

Nor was Junia inclined to resume her labors in the Factory. The Old Man had a son-in-law in one of the neighboring counties; thither they would go. Meanwhile they were invited to spend a few days at Willow Croft.

But how should they reach that distant town? Munk & St. John's stage-route led part way to it, and it occurred to Richard, as it probably would occur to half our readers, that a free passage would be offered them.

But there was an obstacle. Mr. St. John was a right-angled man; he liked to see things square. He would have the way-bill square with the passengers. He was wont to follow the stage to the suburbs of the city, to see that the footings squared with the seats. And he had introduced a rule into the firm, possibly suggested by the laxity of his associate, to have no free seats. A good rule, indeed, when we reflect how a stage company is liable to be pestered by mendicant applications, or imposed upon by fraudulent ones. "If men are really poor, let the towns to which they belong, or their friends, pay their passage. Why are we the sole public benefactors?" So Mr. St. John argued.

Richard was compromised with Junia. He had said there could be no doubt about the conveyance. Munk contributed half a dollar towards the fare, and so did Winkle, and so did Aunt Grint. As much more was needed. There were the Denningtons and others, but Junia was already insolvent to their kindnesses. What should Richard do? What should Junia do? They were both in that pain in which little things will sometimes involve pure and benevolent minds; — Richard overleaping his means in an attempt to do good; Junia sorely perplexed by the trouble she gave her friends.

Deliverance came in this wise. Munk and St. John desired to send an agent into the country to purchase grain, and look after stables and other things incident to an important stage-route, and Richard was deemed a suitable person for such a trust. He wished to see the country, and was glad to go; but stipulated, as a consideration for his services, that his unfortunate friends should be carried likewise.

So, one morning, after collecting passengers from all the hotels, and taking in the mails from the Post-office, with his clean-washed, newly-painted, and highly-enameled coach, and his team of mettlesome, pawing, bright-haired bays, Winkle drew up at Willow Croft.

CHAPTER XX.

THE STAGE-DRIVER.

We promised to say something more of Winkle; and this is the chapter to do it; and what we would say is, there was no such man. This statement is quite true, and quite false. Such is the nature of human language. The truth will be understood by Winkle's friends. Is it convertible in the Tartar tongue? Let us explain. We suppose, and the calculation is based on an unanimous popular sentiment, that if all the Stage-drivers on the North American Continent were recast and made into one, that one would not be equal to Winkle. Or thus, — if the essence of all good stage-driverism on the aforesaid territory were extracted, it would not compare with what could be got out of the smallest fragment of Winkle.

In the first place, Winkle knew everybody, and everything and every body and thing knew Winkle. He knew all the girls, and the school-children, and the old men, and the young men; and bowed to them all, as he rode by, and they bowed to him. For forty miles, he knew where everybody lived, and who everybody was that lived anywhere. He knew the tall, white house on the hill, and the large house with pillars in front, among the trees, and the little black house over in the field; and there was always somebody standing by all the houses, to whom he bowed. Sometimes he bowed to the well-sweep that happened to move in the wind; sometimes to a dog that sat on the door-steps. How many smiling favors he got from the girls, who, after dinner, and after dressing for the afternoon, sat by the open front windows! how many from the children that swarmed about the school-houses! In fact, everybody smiled and bowed when he passed, — black and hard-favored men; muggy and obstinate men; coarse and awkward men. Every day he had a sort of President's tour.

Then, he pointed out the tree where a man hung himself, and the woods where a bear was shot, and the barn that was struck by lightning, and the stream where a man was drowned.

And this, in the second place: because of his unbounded good-nature. He did errands for all those people; he ran a sort of express to the city; an express, too, from one neighborhood to another. Then, he did his errands so correctly, so promptly, and so genially. If those for whom he acted were poor, he charged but little. He knew every place in Woodylin, and could execute any order, from getting iron castings to purchasing gimp, and matching paper hangings, and delivering billet-doux. Furthermore — and herein the beauty of Winkle was seen — he ran express between Hearts. Nothing pleased him better than to have a love-case in hand between two persons on different parts of his route; there was such a carrying of little notes, and little remember-me's, and little nods and signs; and then he could drop a big bundle of tenderness in a single look, as he passed the sweetheart, hanging out the washing of a Monday morning. Then of the widow's son, whom he carried to the city some five years before, and who had been all this time at sea, he got the first intelligence; and as he walked his horses up a long hill, and the mother sat rocking and knitting by the roadside, he told her that her boy had been spoken off the Cape of Good Hope, or that his ship had been reported from Rio. When anybody was sick along the road he bore the daily intelligence to friends, who stood at their doors waiting for it; by what divination it was communicated nobody could tell, but the effect was instantaneous; so, by an invisible, and, as it were, omnipotent hand, he dropped smiles and tears, joy and sorrow, wherever he went; and his own heart was so much in it all, none could help loving him. In addition, and notwithstanding Mr. St. John, he gave little gratuitous rides; he let the boys hang on behind; and in the winter we have heard of his taking up half a dozen school children with their mistress, and helping them through snow-drifts. Then he carried the mail, which is itself a small universe in a leather bag; — here sweet spring to some bleak and ice-bound soul, — at the next turn a black thunder-storm on some tranquil household; — now singing at one corner of its mouth, as if it was full of Jenny Linds, — anon tromboning out its melancholy intelligence; and, like a Leyden jar on wheels, giving everybody a shock as it passes, making some laugh and others scream. Winkle carried this, and it was as if Winkle himself was it; and some people, notwithstanding they loved him so, hardly dare see him, or have him open his mouth; they did n't know, any more than Aunt Grint, what had happened, or what might happen. In addition, he brought people home; and as he drove on, *he* got the first sight of the old roof and chimneys; *he* got the first sight of the rose-bushes and the lilacs in the yard; he saw, too, from the quietness about the house, that a surprise was on hand; he knew perfectly well that the daughter whom he was bringing was not expected, — that she meant to surprise the old folks. He did not hurry his horses; he did not make any sign. He landed the young lady at the gate, and was taking off the baggage, when he heard a scream in the door. He had expected it all, and looked so sober, as he pulled at the strap, with one foot on the wheel, and his back bent to the ground. "Naughty, naughty Winkle!" cried the mother; "why did n't you tell us Susan was coming? You have almost killed me." Winkle loved to kill people so.

In the third place, there is magic in the calling of a Stage-driver. Everybody knows and aspires to know the Stage-driver; everybody is known by, and is proud to be known by, the Stage-driver. The little boys remember it a month, if the Stage-driver speaks to them. There is a particular satisfaction to be able to distinguish, among drivers, and say, it was Winkle, or it was Nason, or it was Mitchell. The Stage-driver is Prince of a peculiar realm; and that realm consists of the yellow coach he drives, and the high seat he occupies, and his four mettlesome horses, and forty miles of country road, and the heart of several principal roads, not to speak of ten thousand little matters of interest and pleasure, business and profit, news and gossip, with which he is connected. Hence, he, like a Prince, is held in reverence by the populace. Of all the people on the earth, *he* is the one who rolls by in a gilded coach; he is the one who sweeps it high and dry over the world; he is the one who rides through his immense estate with the most lordly and consequential air, and all the rest of us seem to be but poor tenants, and gaping boors. It is something to speak to a Stage-driver; it is a great thing to be able to joke with him. It is a sign of a great man, to be recognized by the Stage-driver. To be perchance known by one who knows nobody, is nothing. To be known, to be pointed out, to have your name whispered in a bystander's ear, by one who knows everybody, affects you as if Omniscience were speaking about you. The Stage-driver differs from a Steamboat captain, in that the latter is not seen to be so immediately connected with his craft as the former.

We meet the Captain at the breakfast-table: he is nobody; he is no more than we; we can eat as well as he can. But who dare touch the Stage-driver's ribbons? Who dare swing his whip?

How rapidly and securely he drives down one hill and up the next, — and that, with fifteen passengers and half a ton of baggage! Then how majestically he rounds to, at the door of the Tavern! What delicate pomp in the movement of the four handsome horses! In what style the cloud of dust, that has served as an outrider all the way, passes off when the coach stops! How the villagers — the blacksmith, the shoemaker, the thoughtful politician, and the boozy loafers, that fill the stoop — grin and stare, and make their criticism!

How he flings the reins and the tired horses to the stable-boy, who presently returns with a splendid relay! How he accepts these from the boy with that sort of air with which a king might be supposed to take his crown from the hands of a valet! There are his gloves, withal; — he always wears gloves, as much as a Saratoga fine-lady, and would no sooner touch anything without gloves than such a lady would a glass of Congress water.

There is, moreover, a mystery attaching to the Stage-driver, — a mystery deeper than the question, Why the carcasses of elephants are found imbedded in the ice-mountains of the Arctics? — even this, Why the Stage-driver is not frozen to death in our winters? His punctuality has something preternatural in it; — how, in the coldest weather, in the severest storm, in fogs, in sleet, in hail, in lightning, in mud, when nobody else is abroad, when Madam Dennington hardly dare look out of her windows, when even Helskill expects no customers, — then the Stage-driver appears, rounding the corner, just as regular and just as quiet as the old clock in the kitchen.

It is no wonder that the height of the ambition of multitudes of young men is to be a Stage-driver. This was for one month Simon's ambition; but it was clearly seen he had not the necessary genius, and he gave it up, and went on singing as abstractedly as ever, " O, the break down! O, the break down!" The wonder is, that in this world of uncertainty, and deception, and sin, where the temptations to wrong are so frequent, and the impulse to it so easily aroused, so good a driver as Winkle should be found.

Shall we say that Richard had all these thoughts about Stage-drivers, and Winkle in particular? He had many of them; — he could not help having many of them, for there he sat on the box with Winkle, and saw whatever transpired relating thereto.

They drove on through a well-cultivated, deep-soiled, gently undulating country. The landscape did not mount to the sublime, nor was it remarkable for boldness; the sky-line was agreeably scolloped, — quite subordinate dome-shaped hills ever and anon arose into view. They crossed frequent ravines. The road was skirted with Ponds, — those beautiful collections of water, that singly or in groups challenge the regard of the traveller in every portion of the country. Winkle, as he knew the inhabitants, so also knew the hills, the ponds, and the streams.

He told Richard the names of many of them, and they were bad enough to be dismissed in silence; but it is because they were so bad, Richard could not be silent, neither shall we be. Many of the places were distinguished by the name of some man who lived near by; thus, there were Vail Hill, Squier's Corner, Sills's Mills. Possibly, in a country where Man is so respectable, any man may dignify any spot whereto he is neighbor. There is, however, this difficulty. Man changes, moves away, dies, while the spot remains, and then it is christened into the next comer. So it happened that Vail Hill was sometimes called Water's Hill, and sometimes Wrix's. They passed through "South Smith," and "Smith Corner," and "North Smith." "Why was this so called?" asked Richard. "From one of the Heroes of the War, who shot a man — or a man shot him, I forget which," replied Winkle. "What is this?" asked Richard, as they stopped at a lovely hamlet on the margin of a pond. "Mouth-of-the-Klaber Road," answered his companion. "Old Squire Klaber, some years ago, built the road; and this was the mouth of it, and it has gone by that name ever since. And that is Twenty-five-mile Pond."

A town would sometimes be thus discriminated: La Fayette, La Fayette Centre, La Fayette Bridge, La Fayette Ferry. There were "Forks" and Cross Roads. A favorite classification was "Corners." One town had eight "Corners,' — not on its edge, but in its middle.

Consider the effect of this arrangement. In John Gilpin's race, substitute Stubb's Tavern, or Peacock's, for Bell of Edmonton, and Cowper would have had a more dolorous time than his hero. Make some other changes thus: for "Banks of Air," read Banks of Teagle's Brook. In the following passage —

> "More pleased, my foot the hidden margin roves
> Of Como, bosomed deep in chestnut groves;"

for "Como" introduce "Long Pond," which is as fairly bosomed in oaks and beeches, and overhung by as stupendous hills. How could "Foss's Stream" be wrought into any stanza like this, "Thou sweet flowing Dee, to thy waters adieu!" "Think of coming," says a recent traveller, "into Eskdale, and Ennisdale, of walking four miles on the bank of Ullswater, of looking with your living eyes on Derwent Water, Grassmere, Windermere!" Now,

Richard rode through a beautiful valley belonging to Sam Jones and Isaac Seymour, and along the margin of a stream remarkable for its contrasts of thickets and clearing, wildness and repose, known as "Eight-mile Brook;" and while the horses were changing, he went upon an elevation called "Tumble-down-Dick Mountain," from which was a view of unequalled tint and variety, rimmed around with those bright waters, "Spectacle Pond," "the Matthew Paxson Pond," and "Smith Corner Pond!"

But in the midst of these reflections, where was Junia? She sat on the back seat, with the curtain lifted, leaning on the side-strap, rapt in her own thoughts. Winkle knew he was carrying Sorrow that day, and he was graver than usual. Richard relapsed into frequent reveries. All places, independent of their names, were beautiful to Junia, — beautiful, too, was what might be called the Spirit of the road coming forward to greet Winkle. But this beauty was shaded with grief. The stage was a teeming News-teller dropping its items and its bundles of information into hands that stretched up all along the way to receive them; but it would bring no news to her. It was carrying her further and further from the sacred spot of affection; and as often as it might return over the same ground, it would bring no word to her of the absent and the loved.

Richard offered her water, but she could not drink; at a hotel, where they stopped to dine, she could not eat; and when Richard would have walked with her into the streets of the town, she could not go.

They reached the terminus of the route about sunset. The Uncle of Junia lived a few miles distant. Thither, Richard, taking a horse and wagon belonging to the Company, drove his friends, and arrived late in the evening. This family he found very glad to see Junia and her Grandfather, and in very comfortable circumstances. The man had indeed married a second wife, but a woman who exhibited the tenderness, and preserved the recollections, of the immediate Aunt of Junia, and daughter of the Old Man. They were certainly open to affectionate appeal, and some hidden, strong sensibility could alone have prevented Junia's having recourse to them sooner. Early on the morrow Richard returned.

Having attended to the business of the route, in a few days he came back to the city.

CHAPTER XXI.

A DOMESTIC SCENE.

"WHAT is the matter?" said Munk, coming in to his supper, and finding the children in a snarl.

"So much for gratifying the children!" replied his wife; "Mrs. Mellow told me never to gratify children, and I always told you it was not a good plan."

"I hope there is no harm done," rejoined Munk.

"Mamma made us two dough-nut babies," said Memmy, "and Bebby has eaten hers up, and now she wants mine."

Indeed, she did want it, and screamed lustily for it. "She may have the head," said Memmy, — but that would not do; it was the whole or nothing.

Munk, meanwhile, had taken his seat at the table, and was stirring his tea, looking at the lumps of sugar as they turned up in his spoon. Mrs. Munk put Bebby up to the table in her high chair. The child wanted a cooky. "Eat your bread and milk first," enjoined the mother. The child reached forward, and purloined the cooky. "Put it back!" cried the mother. The child did not obey. "Put it back!" the mother called out, still louder. The child delayed. "Put it back!" the mother screamed. The child yielded, and began to cry. "Stop your crying!" — so the mother pursued her. "You shall be whipped! Asa, will you take the child and whip her?" Asa relucted. "We must be obeyed, — we must be firm," — so the wife expostulated and instructed, — "and I am too weak, you know I am." Munk was not moved. Again Bebby began to cry for Memmy's dough-nut. "The children shall never have another dough-nut in the world!" threatened their mother. "Don't say so," replied Munk.

"I shall go off!" bitterly exclaimed Roxy, and covered her face with her apron.

"Don't do that," said Munk.

"No, no, I may never do anything, only be crazed by the children!"

"Yes, Roxy, you may do everything, — everything you wish to do, everything you ought to do. Did n't you love to make the dough-nuts for them?"

"I did; but we are not to be ruled by our affections, but by a sense of duty, or we shall ruin the children. Have n't I told you so before?"

"Were not you happy in doing what you did?"

"Surely I was. Memmy asked me, and Bebby pleaded so, and I was happy; but I had no right to be. I yielded to it, and this comes of it."

The trouble of the parents only seemed to increase that of the children, whose noise and altercation it became more and more difficult to bear.

"Give her the whole," said Munk to Memmy.

"That would not be right, I think," interposed Richard. "Bebby has not been very well to-day, and she has appeared more fretful than ordinary. You had better look into the matter, and see if it is not something besides the dough-nut that ails her."

"She ought to be whipped!" said Mrs. Munk. "Mrs. Mellow says a whipping, now and then, does children good."

"Don't say that again, will you, Roxy?" rejoined her husband.

"Let me see what can be done," added Richard. He took the child into the rocking-chair, sang songs, and soon had her fast asleep.

CHAPTER XXII.

RICHARD AND THE GOVERNOR'S FAMILY AGAIN.

THE Governor was in the practice of taking his family, in a festive way, sometimes to "Spot," sometimes to "Speckle," — names of ponds, of which there were several in the neighborhood of the city, — where they spent the day, and returned at night. This year he would go to "Spot," and "Climper's," Mr. Climper being the proprietor of "Spot," and its hotel, its boats, and other recreative additaments. The family, in this instance, meant more than it does in our title; it included married children and grandchildren, and it did not include Roscoe or Benjamin.

The Governor's carriage was too small, and he ordered Munk & St. John's omnibus, and Richard was commissioned to drive it.

Alice Weymouth, emerging from under the trees in the front yard, was the first to discover Richard Edney on the box. She smiled and blushed, and turned to Miss Rowena, who laughed and turned to Barbara; who did the same to Melicent, by whom the drollery was conveyed to her mother and Mrs. Melbourne, where it stopped. And for a good reason, — these were the last out of the house. "What are you laughing at?" asked Mrs. Melbourne. Madam laughed just because the others did, and said, "This is a pleasant beginning, and we shall have more sport before the day is over."

Notwithstanding Barbara and Melicent were so much alike they were often mistaken for each other, they had their peculiarities; and one was this, — that Barbara could not ride on the outside of a coach, and Melicent disliked the inside. So, when the rest were seated, Melicent mounted the box with Richard. It had indeed got whispered all through the party that it was Richard; but Madam, who hated an ado, hushed the folks, and Richard drove on without molestation.

He took the same road that, a few months before, in mid-winter, he had come to the city on. Grass was sprouting where the heavy drifts lay. Cattle luxuriously fed in fields from which they had gladly retreated. Barn-yards that had been so variously and thickly stocked were open and empty. Buds that folded themselves from the storm beneath the bark of trees were abroad and wantoning in the sun. Doors that had been doubled, listed, bolted against winter, were waltzing with summer. Men, whose every look and step, whose every article of dress, and posture of body, indicated a struggle with the old temperature, sparkled and sped in the deliciousness and congeniality of the new.

Richard remarked these changes, and spoke also of the woman whom he extricated from a snow-drift. Melicent knew Miss Freeling well, and liked her much; and they talked of that.

Richard went on to thinking of his first coming to the city; — of the Bridge, and the lively people from the Athenæum; of the man with the umbrella, and his solemn warning; and of other things that had befallen, in many of which Melicent herself had borne a part; and now he sat alone with one of the objects of his thought, and he wished to know more of her, and she was ready to know more of him.

How he could talk at random, and think of remote

things, and mind his four horses so well, she would like to be informed. It was habit, he said, and the horses were well trained. But attention to the brake now and then interrupted conversation; and she was not sorry it did, for going down hill on the top of an omnibus inclines a woman to silence. How could horses be so courteous? Why should they not, in some rude moment, jerk the coach into the ditch? This brought up the whole question of horses, and domestication, and the power of the human over the brute; all which topics Richard handled very sagely and instructively.

As they were walking slowly up a hill, Melicent observed, for the second time since they started, "It is a fine day." "Exquisitely fine," added Richard. There must have been something in Richard's mind, or education, or association, to suggest this expletive, which he pronounced as if he was used to it, and deeply felt it. And there must have been something in the day to revive the memory of such an expletive. And Melicent looked again at the day, and thought of Richard. "A very blue sky, and very white clouds," added he. A common remark. But Melicent herself had hardly noticed the intensity of the blue and the white, and she looked at them again. "How beautiful an opening into the sky those two mountains make!" she said, inclining her fan carelessly in the direction indicated, and letting it rock back on the pivot of her hand. "How fine a promontory the sky makes down among the mountains!" Richard rejoined. He was ahead of her this time; but he instantly apologized by saying, "My teacher, Mr. Willwell, used to instruct us that there was an earth-line of the sky, as well as a sky-line of the earth. Instead of calling a mountain high, he said we might call the sky hollow." "He must be an ingenious man," observed Melicent. "He is," answered Richard. "He told the class in geography there were harbors in the sky, and capes, and peninsulas; and took us out and showed them to us. The sky, he said, was like a great ocean overhanging us, and bounded by the earth, and having its shores along the hills and plains. He showed us clouds at sea, and in a storm, and at anchor in the harbors. Then he showed us how this earth-line of the sky varied its height and distance relatively to our position and to surrounding objects. Here was a hill fifty feet high, and sky above it; and the sky was fifty feet high, apparently, he said, and the clouds were the same; and it looked as he said. On each side was a range of mountains a mile off, and there the sky and clouds appeared to be a mile off. The sky, he said, was not like an inverted bowl, having a regular edge in the horizon, but rather like a bowl full of water, that took all the forms of the irregularities of things about us. — Here the road goes through a piece of woods; let us see what is there."

"The sky," said Melicent, "is like a river above us; and there is a cloud before us, that seems to rest on the trees, and is just as high as they are, — rather it is a bridge across the river. Were we spiders or spirits, we might walk on that bridge, or sail on that river. Your teacher's theory," she added, as they drove on, "is a good one. As we ascend, the sky recedes; as we descend, it comes nearer."

"At the bottom of a well," remarked Richard, "the sky, he said, would appear to rest on its mouth. We went down into one, and found the fact to be so."

"A cloud," resumed Melicent, "appears to be stranded on the top of that pasture-ground, and the cows look as if they might tear it with their horns. Yet, if we were up there, I suppose we should see the same cloud on the summit of some higher hill. — Have you seen paintings much, Mr. Edney?"

"I have not," replied Richard.

"I have often thought what studies the clouds might be for painting; yet how much better they are without painting!"

"They are better than pictures, Mr. Willwell said; and I doubt if any picture can exceed them."

Melicent wondered that a mill-boy and hack-driver should be so well informed. There was no wonder about it. He had had a good village school education, and improved on what he was taught.

A scream was heard from the inside of the coach. A bonnet had fallen. Melicent would hold the reins, while Richard jumped down and recovered it, — she really would. This pleased Richard, and it pleased Melicent, both equally.

Here was sympathy, harmony, a certain piece of never-to-be-forgotten mutual good feeling. That Melicent should offer to hold the reins, that Richard should think she could hold them, that she did hold them, that she had held them, — the reins, and the four horses, and the coachful of people, — oh, these are trifles, but they are such sort of trifles as helped while away a mile of the road, and such as have their place and mission all along the road of life.

Let us look at this ride, and in fact this entire tale, in one point of view: — that Richard Edney now had the Governor's Family under his thumb, or, more literally, in his two hands; that there they were, closely stowed under his feet, in a tight vehicle, — a mere box, — and four stout horses in front. If Richard were evil-disposed, how easy to do them an injury! If he were vain, how natural to feel exalted! If he were wanton, how pleasant to tease and scare them! If he knew the dignity, extent, and value of the Family, how readily he might manage an advantage out of them! But his Father told him to treat everybody respectfully, — to behave properly in all relations. If he were a servant, to be faithful; if he were a master, to be kind; and if he drove, to do it carefully, — to reverence life, and be tender of sensibility, human or brute. Almost the last word his Mother said to him was, "Richard, be a good boy. I need n't say it, I know; but it is all that is in my heart, and all that is in your duty, and I will say it again, Be a good boy." Richard was a good boy, and of course a good driver, and treated the Governor's Family becomingly, and drove them securely.

So he got the party, in good shape, to "Spot," and "Climper's." The hotel overlooked the water, and commanded a picturesque horizon. Climper was fat, and gruff, — Giles to the contrary notwithstanding, — petulant, and slow; and one would think he neither understood the arts of courtesy, nor the tricks of trade; — and, furthermore, that he had been set up in life at Spot Pond, by some cynical school of philosophers, on purpose to prove that our theories, touching the effect of beauty and goodness on the character, are moonshine. Every coach that darkened his yard was not half so dark as he himself was all over his house. But somehow Climper was the proprietor of "Climper's," and of the fine view therefrom, and of the best side of the Pond, and of the boats and bowling-alley; and everybody liked Climper's, while everybody had an idea of hating Climper, but did not do it.

This shows there is a difference between a man and his attributes, — between quality and substance; for there might be a Climper's, and no Climper.

So Richard thought, when Climper wheezed forth to let down the steps and hand the people out. He scowled, when he did so, and scolded because Richard had not driven a few feet further, and worried because word had not been sent that they were coming. The grandchildren were intimidated by the man, but Madam urged them along. Still, Melicent would not be squired by such a grumbler, and tried to find her way down from the box alone. Her foot caught, and she would have fallen, if Richard had not caught her. This brought around him the whole Family. Madam had an inkling as to who the driver was; and when she saw him in such near proximity to her daughter, she cast a searching sidelong glance at him, and thanked him. Miss Rowena, who, on a former occasion, had really sneered at Richard, was awe-stricken. Melicent introduced Richard in form to her several friends.

When this ceremony was ended, Richard proceeded to look after his team. Climper's boy had already unhitched the horses, and was leading them to the stable. Richard took from the box a coarse frock he wore on such occasions, and followed. While he was rubbing down the horses, Climper appeared in haste, and said Mrs. Melbourne wanted to see him. Richard would take off his frock. No! The lady could not wait, and Climper drove him off with his fists. Richard went to the drawing-room, where were Madam, Mrs. Melbourne, Melicent, and Rasle. "You wish to see me," said Richard, looking rather indefinitely. "We are very glad to see you," answered Madam, yet rather dubiously. "Mrs. Melbourne wishes to see me," particularized Richard. "I do not," answered that lady; "I am far from it." Richard was quite blanked. "Mr. Climper said you did," he explained. They all smiled, and looked knowing, except Mrs. Melbourne, who looked knowing, but did not smile. Richard neither smiled nor looked knowing. "A little pleasantry," said Melicent. "How are your horses, sir?" She wished to turn the subject. "There was n't anything pleasant about it," spoke out Rasle. "Aunt Melbourne said she wished to see you punished for sweating the horses, and she did n't care how quick." "Never mind, young man," said Madam, coming kindly towards him, and as it were moving with him towards the door. "Mrs. Melbourne has a way, and Mr. Climper has a way, and we all have ways, you know." O yes, Richard knew; and went back, very pleasantly, to his work. It was a trick of Climper's.

Having finished the horses, he threw off his frock, went to the house, where he washed and combed, and loitered to the verandah; where were Madam and Mrs. Melbourne. Madam beckoned him to her side. "We owe you an apology," she began. "Do not speak of it," said Richard. "We owe you something—" "Nothing," he persisted. "We owe you," she went on, "for the deliverance of the Governor in one instance, and our daughter Melicent in two, which makes three." "I only did my duty," answered Richard. "And in that," interposed Mrs. Melbourne, "we all come short. Why, Cousin, make such account of trifles, when a whole life of sin lies against us?" Madam was silent; she never argued. This silence was interrupted by the dashing of the Governor through the hall, followed by the little ones.

"Hurra for the boats!" he cried.

The Governor was a grave and reverend man; but he could unbend,—he could be quite relaxed,—and with children he was playful as a child. Perhaps he remembered a certain great one who was detected in his library playing leap-frog with his children.

They scampered to the Pond, and after them puffed and fretted the head of the domain. When they were well seated in the boat, Climper shoved them off; and he did it after a fashion as if they were a cargo of small-pox.

Richard took the oars. He had seen that article before, on the River, and the Lakes, to say nothing of his father's mill-pond; and he pulled dextrously and strong. They rowed to the middle of the Pond. The children dropped hook; had much gayety over their glorious expectations and their insignificant success. They heard the rattle of the king-fisher; they descried the black heads of loons floating upon the surface, like pieces of charcoal; they saw the tall firs on the banks, standing base to base, and spiring substance and shadow, into the skies. There were little holms, and large islands. On one side, a dark schistous bluff faced the sky and darkened the water. On another, parallelogramic farms, with white houses and capacious barns at the head, and corn and grass lots at the foot, sloped to the shore. "If sky is like water," said Melicent, "what shall we do with sky in the water?" "Sail on it," answered Richard. "Un-spidered, un-spirited, we can do it, can't we?" she rejoined. "I wonder," said Barbara, "how the fishes relish the arrival of a boat from the air-world, passing like a cloud over their pleasant prospects. How should we like to see a galley, having its sides lined with sharp-shooters, sail out from the Moon, and hover over the city?" "I wish I was a fish," spoke out Rasle. "Why?" asked Melicent. "I would bite Aunt Rowena's hook." That was Rasle all over, and he made it all over with the rest. There was great concert of merriment, and great disconcertion of purpose. Miss Rowena had been soberly watching her line, and calculating her luck, for half an hour; and some others had, too. As it is considered a semi-crime and a certain disgrace to go a-fishing and not catch fish, this sally at once aggravated and decided their failure, and they concluded to return. "The fish are at the hotel," said the Governor, "and I have a hook in my pocket that will catch them." "What was that?" the little ones asked. "The round O hook, with a white face," said Rasle, addressing one of his nephews that was beginning to go to school.

Rolling nine-pins was part of "Climper's," and a considerable part to the children.

Who should choose up with Grandfather? Mr. Edney, he said; and what he said, everybody said; and some of them thought so, and some of them did not think so. It was Richard's first choice, and whom should he choose but Madam herself? The Governor took Mrs. Melbourne; Then Melicent was matched against Barbara, Eunice answered to Rasle, and so on to the very baby end of things. Miss Rowena kept the tally. Now commenced the solemn pauses, and the obstreperous outbursts; the spurrings on to the alley, and the banterings off; the flourishes of attempt, and the blankness of defeat; the young ones jumping up and spatting their hands, the old ones heroically staid; complaints at the unevenness of floor on the one hand, and quips at the awkwardness of the roller on the other; mock condolences, answered by mock applause; such screamings after some little runaway partisan, and such cautions when he was found; such shouts when Grandfather got a spare ball, and such shouts when Eunice got one pin; the intense excitement as to who should beat,— the little ones beating and annihilating each other a dozen times, with their joyous tongues, before it was decided which side had beat. Richard led off handsomely, and Madam was no mean player; but the Governor was a great ball, and so was Mrs. Melbourne: but Richard beat, or his side did; and such Yankee-doodling as the little ones, who had beaten Grandfather, set up, was never heard this side of the Revolution.

Some staid, and rolled longer; some rushed to the swing, and tore at it like a house-a-fire; others chased one another, like a troop of dogs, over the grass; a portion betook themselves to the seclusion of a pine grove; a few explored the edges of the pond for lilies.

They were summoned to a dance; and the Governor asked Richard to join them. But Richard, imagining the invitation to spring more from politeness than cordiality, — that it was rather from consistency's sake than any singleness of feeling, — declined. Now, Climper, fat and mulish, always on the off side, always plaguing people, declared Richard should dance; and, pushing him into the hall, said if he did not dance, he would make him, and rendered excuse abortive and retreat impossible.

Madam was tired; so the Governor led out Miss Rowena, Melicent paired off with Barbara, and Richard bowed to Mrs. Melbourne. This lady could not refuse, and Richard could not but advance; so he and Mrs. Melbourne danced together! There may have been contrivance in this; and, judging from the way Cousin bit her lip, one might conclude she had something to do with it.

There was one advantage in Climper's, — it levelled distinctions. Here the Governor's Family bowled and danced with their hack-driver. The same thing might not happen anywhere else; but here, in this out of the way place, where mirth and good feeling were the presiding genii, the common sensibilities had free play; and those tastes and inclinations, which of themselves know no rank and belong to all men, were spontaneously developed and harmoniously exercised. They could all be merry, Richard and the Governor alike; and Mrs. Melbourne had to be, albeit she did not like to be; besides, among the oddities of Climper was the practice of jumbling all sorts of people together, — a practice, indeed, that might not seem suited either to the decorum or the policy of a respectable landlord; but it was a way he had, and all who went to Climper's must put up with Climper. More than that: this very way he had, so repugnant to certain standards of feeling, accomplished the end every one aimed at in going thither, — to be merry.

After the dance, Richard stood with Melicent on a knoll overlooking the very pretty sheet of water that formed the nucleus of the interest of the place.

"I have not thanked you," he said, "for the pleasure I have had here."

"You have been a part of the pleasure," she replied, "and may take a portion of the credit to yourself."

"How could such an one as Climper have selected this beautiful place to dwell in?"

"It was one of his oddities, I imagine; he knew that natural propriety would assign to him a plainer residence, and out of sheer opposition to his destiny he came hither."

"The love of the Beautiful," continued Richard, "may have captivated his heart."

"Did you say that?" rejoined Melicent, in a way rather abrupt, but earnest.

"Did I say what?" inquired Richard, as if he was startled at something he might have said.

"About Beauty and Climper."

"I said what I have heard Parson Harold say."

"Then you do not believe it?"

"I believe and feel it."

"Repeat what you said."

"You banter me."

"I never was more serious."

"I said the beauty of the place may have captivated Climper."

"In that Pond," interposed Mrs. Melbourne, who had not been far off during this conversation, "is plenty of slime and eel-pouts, and the garbage of a thousand years."

"The slime," replied Richard, "is one of the best of fertilizers; and eel-pouts are a grateful dish to some people."

"Who told you so?" asked the lady, quickly.

While Richard seemed to be refreshing his memory, Melicent, laughing, said, "Parson Harold, I suppose."

"Very likely," answered Richard. "The Parson often says everything in God's world has its use."

"Who is Parson Harold? — and what does he know about the wickedness that lies under all this fair surface?"

Mrs. Melbourne delivered this slattingly, and then pulling at Melicent, she said the little children wanted help in getting strawberries; and she asked — she only asked — Richard if his horses had been watered; she could not bear that the poor, dumb beasts should suffer through the folly of men.

Richard went towards the stable.

"I must water my team," he said to Climper, whom he encountered in the way.

"Don't pull wool over my eyes so!" replied the latter. "I smell dogs."

"Dogs!" echoed Richard.

"Yes, dogs. And if it ain't dogs, it 's pups; and I won't have one here! They bring them out in their coaches, and hide them under the straw. Climper's is not to be imposed upon, — Climper's has no hand in it; when they go up to the polls, they shan't say, 'Climper's is against us, — Climper's harbors dogs.'"

Richard laughed outright; but the more he laughed, the more Climper blared, until he consented that the carriage should be overhauled. The straw was ransacked, shawls and tippets were thrown out, but to no purpose, — no sign of a dog appeared.

"You belong to the anti-dogs?" asked the landlord.

"I am of no party," replied Richard. "There is some good in all parties."

"There is n't some good in all parties!" replied the other, doggishly.

"Indeed, there is some good in you."

"No, there is n't any good in me! Don't tell me that!"

"You love cats, don't you? Kitty, Kitty," he called to his fingers an amiable and womanly looking Maltese, and taking her in his arms, stroked her back, in face of the wilful man, and added, "That is good; I love cats, too."

The strange Phumbician was touched, and, smiling good-naturedly, he struck Richard smartly on his shoulders, and bade him look after the horses, and went with him towards the barn.

"You love cats," said Richard; "and do you love nothing else?"

"I love to be odd, — so get along!"

"And nothing more?"

"I love to hate dogs and plague folks."

"Do you not love this spot, this hill, this view, this water?"

"Yes, and because it plagues folks so to climb the hill, and because they don't catch any fish, and because they get ducked in the water. I love to have Mrs. Melbourne come here, because she finds so many things to fret about; the children will get cold, or they will get drowned."

"You love cats, and to plague people?"

"I did n't say I loved to plague people; but to see them

plague themselves, if they have a mind to. It is no business of mine. I only give them the opportunity."

"That is why you settled here? Come, now, tell me the whole."

"I never told anybody."

"Tell me."

"I lost my wife and my children, and I had none to love; and I bought here, where I could love God alone, and let the world craze about me as it liked."

"Can't you love me?"

"Get along!"

"Why hate dogs so?"

"My child was bitten by one; don't ask about that. She died; don't speak of that; let me alone of the dogs."

Climper helped Richard lead his horses to the pump; he gave them their full measure of oats, then drove our hero back to where the Family was.

But Richard could not find it, or come near it; for the whole group was concealed, and monopolized by certain strangers, young gentlemen who had just arrived from the city, among whom were young Chassford and Glendar. The entire aspect of things indicated to Richard that his company was not wanted, and he strolled to a distance. He did wish to see Melicent, and make, as he thought, a great communication to her.

Nor was Melicent indifferent to Richard. She saw his disappointed look, and watched his retreating steps. She presently took the liberty to leave her friends, and go where he was sitting.

"I have discovered the secret of Climper," said Richard, with considerable enthusiasm; and related what Climper had said. "He has been smitten by adversity, and makes of this spot a refuge to his spirit."

Melicent looked at Richard incredulously, and then with an expression of wonder.

"Do you doubt what I say?" asked Richard.

"I am only surprised to hear you say it."

"If it be true —"

"Yes; — but that you should discover it."

"Why should I not?"

"Why should you not? Only I did not think it of you." She gave Richard another direct look, — one of so fixed and searching a nature, that he started and said, "I hope I have done no wrong."

"None at all," she replied, and caught a twig of the tree, which she tore off and flung away with great apparent indifference.

Richard, not wholly at his ease, was yet sufficiently disembarrassed to say, "This place is a Hermitage, — a queer one; but shall we not call it so? My Teacher used to say we ought to give pleasant names to pleasant places."

"Call it Mystery," she said.

"Nay," replied Richard, as the little children chased their Grandfather in and out among the trees, full of gambol, and breathlessness, and joy, "let us call it Merrywater."

"Climper will not like that."

"I will make him like it. He shall pull down his present sign, and run up another."

"Will you be kind enough to see that my horse is rubbed down, and grained, and put into my phaeton, when we start, young man?" said Glendar, who approached at this moment, and threw a quarter to Richard. "I will," replied Richard, picking up the money, and going off.

The bell rang for supper, and the party was soon seated around the sumptuous tables of Climper. Chassford took care of Barbara, Glendar of Melicent, and the Governor and

Climper of the whole. There were nice fried, white perch, and crisp, savory pork; piles of bread, white and light; yellow and sweet butter; bowls of strawberries, and pitchers of cream; cake of all sorts; and the Family were hungry and merry. Climper loved to plague people; and Mrs. Melbourne eschewed gingerbread, but Climper would make her eat his gingerbread. Madam was sometimes delicate in her meals, but he made her eat; and those that loved to eat, he would force to eat more than they ought to; and so he plagued them all. If mouths watered for the strawberries, the strawberries seemed to water for the mouths, and the cream foamed for the strawberries; the bread was piled up high, on purpose to fall easily into the hand; and the pies were in large plates, on purpose to go off in large pieces. Climper's servants were at hand, with smoking cups of tea; and it was as if Climper, out of this abundance of good things, had determined to destroy them all.

The sun was going down when Climper shut the coach door, flung up the steps, and cried to Richard to be off with his load.

Barbara was timid, and did not like the omnibus, and was persuaded to resign herself to Chassford and his buggy.

Glendar attempted the same arrangement with Melicent, but failed; and she rode home as she had come out, — on the box, with Richard.

They returned safely to Woodylin. Melicent, with apparent sincerity and good intention, invited Richard to call at her father's. Nay, more, — Madam herself, to the amazement of all, asked him to tea on a specified evening.

CHAPTER XXIII.

WE DO NOT KNOW

WHAT is before us; and Richard did not know what was before him. Yet Miss Plumy Alicia Eyre was before Richard; her dark, thrilling eye was before him; her pale, pensive, earnest face was before him; so was her searching, pleading, piteous heart. But did Richard really know what was before him? Was not the future hidden from him, and was not the present even partially veiled?

But with his body's eye he only saw Miss Eyre; and with his mind's eye, if he had striven to look another way he could not, for she tyrannized over that too.

Miss Eyre was intimate at Munk's, and she brought fruit and candies to the children. Moreover, Richard had been sick two or three days, and Miss Eyre frequently called, exhibiting the gentlest sympathy. She brought cordials to his bed-side; she spelled Roxy in the kitchen, while she watched with her brother.

But Miss Eyre, as these pages have had occasion to record, was unsphered, unhomed. In this she was to be pitied.

Moreover, she lacked a contented mind; she would not submit to the orderings of Providence, or the inevitabilities of fortune. She was too ambitious to be useful; too confident to be wise; too bad to be good. She was too reckless either to improve advantage or support evil. Here she was to blame.

A little true humility, — even common candor of feeling,

— a grain of piety, would have saved her from the agitation she was in, and the extremity to which she was tending.

Even now, Miss Eyre, with all that you have suffered still burdening your memory, with all the lacerations of sorrow yet fresh in your heart, may we not ask you if you ought not to have been more considerate, — if some suggestions of reason, humanity or religion, ought not to have restrained you? Do not lay all the blame on others, but ask your own soul if you can fully justify yourself.

Plumy Alicia appealed to the sympathies of Richard; she thrilled every commiserant fibre within him; her anguish, like a troubled wave, beat upon him, her description of herself awakened his tenderness, while with consummate nicety she concealed her design to do so. Her ministry to Richard when he was sick, she knew, had established a place for her in his gratitude; she had imparted some intimate matters to him, — a movement which, while it secures confidence, inspires self-esteem. She laid her hand upon his; he could not repudiate the familiarity, because by that act she seemed to be discharging upon one stronger than herself a load of sensation too heavy for her to bear. She looked into his eye, but only to assure him how sad and heavy her own was.

"Do not say that you love me," she said; "I do not wish you to say that;" — she did wish it, nevertheless. "Kiss me, and I go, — go with one assurance of friendship and happiness, which, if it be all that is allowed me, will be a precious keepsake forever." She said this with her warm breath pulsating on his face.

CHAPTER XXIV.

RICHARD RETURNS TO THE SAW-MILL.

THE Dam in due time was repaired; the Factories and Saw-mills resumed operations, and the life and activity, rattle and clatter, that attach to extensive mechanical works, once more resounded.

But Saw No. 1 — Richard's appropriate field of action — was dead. Captain Creamer had failed; the breach in the Dam ruined him. Richard, Mr. Gouch, Silver, and the rest of the gang, gathered at their old resort; but there was no one to employ them. None appeared, to rent the saw. The Corporation, rather than that the instrument should lie idle, offered to stock it, and let it by the thousand, if the original hands, of whose ability and fidelity they had proof, would take it. A bargain was soon struck. Mr. Gouch and the others retained their several posts, whilst, by unanimous consent, it was arranged that Richard should assume the supervision of the concern. An honor to our hero! For this office, it was evident to his fellows, he was well qualified, and to it all were happy in raising him. His readiness in figures, his judgment of timber, the accuracy and economy with which he could answer an order, his familiarity with the several branches of work, — what had become obvious during the winter, — united to never-failing vigilance and sagacity, and great kindliness of feeling and urbanity of intercourse, rendered the choice of the company as easy to themselves as it was flattering to him. His wages advanced with his responsibility; and, if his labor was less manual, his duties were not less arduous and exacting.

Clover was missing, — an absence which none regretted.

Affairs moved on harmoniously and prosperously. Mr. Gouch, unabashed by the presence of Clover, grew a firmer and more resolute man. Silver was silent and glum, but not spiteful or rude. All the men had their weaknesses, as well as their strength, and sport was too nimble and too needful to be subdued by toil. There is no humor so genial, no gayety so inspiring, as that which is awakened among good-natured, hard-laboring men.

Summer was upon them, with its softening and expanding influences; — the great doors stood open, — the breeze was welcome, — the roar of the Dam, which had been sharp and hard in winter, grew round, limpid, melting, — the rumbling of the wheels in the pit, the screeching of the saws, all acknowledged the return of a milder dispensation.

The signs of business about the premises were not a little pleasing; teams hurrying to and fro, the cries of the teamsters, wheels laden with boards, carts filled with refuse, and whatever indicated rapid exchange and a thriving season.

In transacting the affairs of the concern, Richard came in contact with a variety of individuals in the city, — lumber dealers, carpenters, and such as were engaged in the erection of houses. He did a large amount of what is called custom work.

In all things his honesty and intelligence were of use to him. He had been in the forest, studied trees, and investigated the kinds and properties of wood. The hard and the soft, the new and the seasoned, — what will bear the weather and what must be protected, — what is adapted to one end and what to another, — were familiar matters. In manifold particulars, his opinion was sought, and his advice followed.

During the summer, Richard and Nefon, the Bookseller, became better acquainted; and the more they became acquainted, the better they liked each other; as if the non-acquaintance of man with man were not at the foundation of nine tenths of mortal dislikes! Now, Nefon applied to Richard to take a class in the Sunday-school, of which he was Superintendent. Richard, with natural distrust of his abilities, yet obedient to the rule he had adopted as the supreme guide of life, TO DO GOOD, replied that he would be glad to do so. But an obstacle intervened, which seemed at first sight not easy to be surmounted. His sister feared such a step would alienate him from the church she attended, and consign him remedilessly to Parson Smith's. Richard declared that no position of this sort in the Church of the Redemption should bind him to its authority or its influence, beyond the plain teachings of the New Testament. Rozy promised him her prayers, — albeit she could not yield him her blessing, as he entered upon this novel duty. To his class he added certain boys, whose abodes were the shores of the River, the Islands, and the neglected quarters of the New Town, and whom he had seen playing the vagrant or the thief about the Mills; and had the satisfaction of finding them punctual and interested, and of recording their progress in divine knowledge.

CHAPTER XXV.

HE VISITS THE GOVERNOR'S.

Among the events of not a little interest in this season's experience was Richard's appointment with Madam Dennington. He ascended the Governor's piazza and pulled at the bell-handle with a slight palpitation of the heart; and the servant who ushered him in might have noticed a certain rusticity in his manner.

Madam received him with grace and dignity. Melicent and Barbara took his hand in a cordial way. With the Governor, whose greatness of mind and force of character were always at the command of courtesy and kindness, and replete with the minor social instincts, he was quite at ease. Cousin Rowena was particularly complacent. There was cause for this. Mrs. Melbourne rallied strong against Richard, when she found attention to the Sawyer going so far as a summons to a social family gathering. Not that she had anything against Richard; only, — she could hardly tell what. This was enough for Cousin, who thought the aversion unreasonable, and was easily inclined to protect Richard from it.

Tea was carried round. Were Richard's nerves a little wanton, and his hand a little clumsy? What with cup and saucer on his knees, and waiter with sugar and cream, waiter with sandwiches and cheese, waiter with dough-nuts and cake, and the gradual filling up of the narrow rim of the only receptacle for this endless enumeration, and his own desire to be polite, and his fear that he should not be, and Mrs. Melbourne and Miss Rowena both watching him so closely, — it was not strange there should be a downfall both of bread and of feeling. But Cousin Rowena picked up the fragments, and bit her lip.

The Governor's Family owed something to Richard, and they were disposed to requite in full, and that in modes at once delicate and honorable. Roscoe talked with him on farming; Rasle joked with him; Barbara showed him the library and pictures; Eunice played to him; Melicent walked with him in the garden.

But would these parties square accounts, and be off? Was this the purpose and upshot of their interview? Was there no common ground of humanity or religion, — no consentaneousness of thought or feeling, — no grandeur of moral aim, — no depth of character, — no aspiration for ideal progress, — no accidental revelations of approved state and being, which might suggest a perpetuity of acquaintance, and even protract remembrance when calls were ended?

In evidence that the invitation to Richard did not spring from merely personal and private regards, but belonged to a more expansive and general circle of social sentiments on the part of the Family, other guests, obviously by invitation, came in the evening. There were the Mayor Langreen, the Redfernes of Victoria Square, the Lady Caroline, young Chassford, Glendar, and other ladies and gentlemen.

Richard was in the centre, and, we might say, in the centre of the centre, of the nobility of wealth, office and culture, and, if the worthy Dressmaker aforesaid is to be trusted, of the *common sense*, of Woodylin. How did he carry himself? He had heard his beloved Pastor speak of God's and nature's noblemen, and perhaps sometimes thought he was as good an one as any. He had heard from the lips of his respected Teacher, and was himself sufficiently versed in geography and history to know, that in some countries the nobility are distinguished by feathers in their caps, in others by riding in coaches; in some by a red patch on the cheek, in others by a gilt sword; and that it was once the law that any man who had made three voyages round the world should be knighted. But what did his knowledge and convictions avail him now? His favorite feeling, that he was as good as anybody, — his indomitable resolution to cower to no man, and be confounded by no woman, even Pastor Harold with his sacred gown, and Teacher Willwell with his impressive spectacles, — vanished from his recollection, and wavered in his hold; and he felt himself amidst these people, shivering, like a ship suddenly brought to, with all sails in the wind. He was fidgety, wandering, purblind. He stood face to face, and shoulder to shoulder, with these people, not one of whom wore a sword, or had more feathers in his cap, or rode in better coaches, or had made more voyages round the world, than he; yet he was not at ease. To be in the centre of the Family and its appendages, and compose one of its associates at an evening reünion, was a different thing from having them, as we have said, under his thumb, and driving them in an omnibus. With entire self-possession, leaning on a cant-dog, he could talk with Melicent and Barbara in the Mill. Having nothing for his muscular hands to clutch, how could he talk in that drawing-room? Calm and cool, on a certain occasion, he seized the Governor, and lifted him bodily out of watery peril; yet an introduction to the Governor's niece made him shake like an aspen. He could take his turn at bowls or a dance with the best of them; but, alas for the imperfections of human nature, he was not adequate to the demands of this social hour!

Still, Richard's weakness was sustained and relieved by

the intelligent and charitable experience of the Family, and he was borne in tolerable condition through the shoals and breakers of first encounter with high life.

The cardinal maxim of his Teacher, that he must inquire the use of, and derive wisdom from, every new thing he saw, he was too agitated to apply. It was as much as he could do to be there, without asking why he was there. If he had gone on to asking questions, he would, peradventure, have startled points of a still lower deep, that would choke and flurry him far more than the superficial aspects of the case did.

In that something which goes by the name of high life, or good society, is what pesters inquiry as much as it eludes attempt. When it is said of one, he is aspiring, or of another, he looks down upon us, what is implied but that there is a something above, which the first has not reached, and which, to the last, is an attainment and a power? There is an Idea in it; — that idea is supreme excellence; or, in that height is centred, and by it evermore is symbolized, the sum of what, in a given community, or country, or age, is deemed most valuable. There is a divinity in it, — it is an order of God. Wealth and office are not it; they are subsidiary to its plan, and typify some of its results; and are, remotely, a means of reaching it. Height, excellence, superiority, are indeed tantamount and convertible terms; and imply, respectively, that precious something, which makes us feel poor and mean without it, and evermore hangs out to us its banner of hope, and is an ultimate desire of the mind. If my neighbor slights me, he makes me feel he has something which I have not; and I either sink into a brutish state of envy, or resolve to gain that which shall make me his equal. Dr. Broadwell is in good society partly by position; his position being that which implies the requisites of good society. Mrs. Tunny means to get into it by the wealth of her husband; but that will depend wholly upon how he uses his wealth. Melicent — no thanks to her — is born in it; therefore her responsibility is greater. If Richard shall be established in it, it will be by his virtues. Fashion sometimes sets up for good society in its own name; but this is simply a mimicking of the great Idea, and an attempt to get in by some other way. In America, since what constitutes the best society is not determined by Court, it is determined by ideas; and around and toward these ideas is the community in city and country always gravitating. Primary instinct will in the end be found as absolute as historical precedent. That is a wise and righteous government which affords to ability the free opportunity of rising to its proper height. Good society is therefore not only a measure, but a crown, of exertion.

After all, that is the best society which God loves most; and among a depraved people much will pass for good society which is really bad.

Richard was at his ease in the Saw-mill, and at Mrs. Tunny's party, and at a public meeting; but he was not at the Governor's. That mystic something which others possessed, he was conscious of lacking; and he might have retired in great disquiet, if Cousin Rowena had not supported his flickering courage. He told her that he loved music, and she ordered the young ladies to sing. This tranquillized him, because it equalized him with the rest. He had a good voice, and well modulated, not to troubadour songs, but to pieces of a different description. Sacred melodies were familiar to him; and he sang one, popularly known as a pennyroyal hymn, — a measure that combines unction and vivacity. It was well received, and he was pleased.

But, ever and anon, in course of the evening, — whether it was owing to the heat of the room, or the proximity of unfavorable comparison, or the rapid transition of unaccustomed persons and topics, or his own effort to divest himself of what he most dreaded, — his perceptions clouded, and his language tripped; his hands swelled, and his face burnt. He was glad to find an open door, and disburthen himself to a draft of air. Blessings on the wind, that did for Richard what the Governor's Family, with its opulence, its beauty, its breeding, could not do! Melicent joined him on the piazza; and Richard, being himself again, could converse and behave more to his satisfaction.

Richard was honest, and had a heart, and spoke of things that he loved most to those who loved to hear them. Melicent answered to the same description; and as there were many things in both their hearts alike, it was natural they should get up quite an interchange of sentiment on cherished and pleasant topics.

Correspondence of sentiment, connected as it often is with correspondence of aim, is wont to lead to harmony of feeling and mutuality of interest; and Melicent left Richard, with a strong desire to know more of him, and be more with him

Richard went home that night burthened with reflections; at one moment reproaching himself for pusillanimity and weakness, — at another, questioning the authority of that which exerted so strong a spell over him during the evening; but after vibrating between several disagreeable and disjointed subjects, he settled at last upon thinking about Melicent. In her he saw exaltation without arrogance, purity without demureness, tenderness without insipidity, piety and no cant, beauty and no affectation, common sense and yet great ardor and hope.

For the second time was he brought to the direct and intense contemplation of Melicent; and that in the night, —

that with the glare and surroundings of the day withdrawn. He had formerly thought of her as the Governor's daughter, — beheld in her a wonderful instance of human and female excellence, and admired the contrast she afforded to what sometimes appears a dark back-ground of aristocracy, pride of wealth, and meanness of station. He now thought of her as Melicent; she was individualized to his imagination, — she was beginning to stand out alone in the universe to his eye; vapors or shadowy emptiness separated her from all others, — an embarrassing, a hazardous state of affairs to a young man. But, before he slept, the natural order of things was restored,— her own proper world surrounded and absorbed her; and his own world, — his Saw-mill and his rusticity, — came and took him off.

CHAPTER XXVI.

HOUSEHOLD WORDS.

RICHARD's chief joy was his nieces; and his Sundays, and meal-times, and evenings, that gave him to them. He played with them, and they made a child of him; nay, they made less than that; they used him as if he had been a giant moppet in whiskers, and tumbled him about like a man of straw. He was the child, and they were the masters. He must listen to their wants, obey their commands, bide their caprices, go where they wished, do what they ordered; they climbed up his chair, tore at his legs, rode on his back, pilfered his pockets, hid his boots. He brought blocks for them to build houses with, allotted a quarter of the garden for their agricultural operations, put up a swing for them on the willow-tree. Sundays, after church, he went with them to Bill Stonners' Point, to see Chuk, and through the woods to Mysie's. He filled their baskets with box-berries and partridge-berries, and adorned their hats with bellworts and laurels. To Chuk the children were an intelligence, — an incantation, — a glimmering of long-lost ideas. Mysie showed them her cats and cows.

To add to the wonders, — a wonder it was to Memmy, and a real wonder it might be to the universe, — Bebby began to talk! The teeth came, and the talk would soon follow. This was Memmy's philosophy; and is it not as good as anybody's? Who can explain the mystery of speech? Is it not God's miracle? To witness this dull clay putting itself into tune, — to see unconscious muscle adapting itself to articulation; ideas seizing upon corruptible flesh and blood, and converting it into a living organism; to hear the short words, and the half-uttered long words, and the endeavors after impossible words; and how innumerable things seem, like bees about a hive, to fly about the lips of the child, — some going in, some crawling on the edge, and some falling back, and all keeping up such a buzz; — oh, these *were* new things, and well worth reporting to Master Willwell! And how Bebby's eyes would strain when she tried to say something, and twinkle when she had said something; and Memmy's would twinkle too, and so would Roxy's and Munk's, and the twinkle would be contagious, and go all round the room. This was pleasant.

And *what* would the child say? what would be the first utterance of that which from eternity had been silent, or which from other worlds had come to take up its abode in this? What incipiency from the mystic depth of things would start into being? It was "mamma" and "papa." These were the first shoots from that thaumatergical seed-bed, which was ultimately to produce such harvests of prattle, ratiocination, poetry, and newspapers; — whereon would that the dews of divine grace might descend, and adorn them with heavenly beauty and sweetest charity!

She ere long perpetrated those dreadful words, "I will," and "I won't;" as if it were a crime to practise volition, and presumption insupportable to be supposed capable of the prerogative of free-agency, or to have any preference or aversion. "Say 'I had rather not,'" enjoined the mother. "I won't!" answered the child. "You will, won't you?" pleaded the mother. "I wont!" reëchoed the child. Roxy turned to her husband, and seemed to relieve her sorrow, saying, "It is just as I always said, and what Elder Jabson teaches: Children are wicked." "Bebby wicked!" said Munk, stopping what he was at — washing his face at the sink — and looking round.

"Bebby *is* wicked." Roxy said this, and was serene again

There is the nativity of ideas as well as words; and Richard, being bound to inspect everything new, considered of this also. Whether our ideas, for instance, of love and of goodness, have a spiritual or material source, was a question on which Master Willwell philanthropically descanted. "You love Papa and Mamma," said he to Memmy, in a sort of leading way; "and whom else?" "I love," replied the child, "Bebby, and Uncle Richard, and — and — pussy, and peaches." He had a peach in his hand. "Why do you love peaches?" He asked this in a playful manner, indeed, but with earnestness of thought. "Because they are good," was the brief, yet, to the child, very complete, reply. "And you love Papa because he is good?" The child assented. This was a poser to Richard. Vainly did he invoke the lessons of his Teacher. Was it one thing to the child, — peaches or Papa? Was it the same goodness, or the same sense of goodness? Both yielded pleasure. May it not be that God awakens the sentiment of goodness, by affording to sense and contemplation that which pleases us? But there is a spiritual susceptibility of pleasure, as well as material; both sets of instincts were stirred in the child, — only she was not old enough to distinguish between them. So Richard found, on inquiry, that she hated badness, whether in Turkey rhubarb, or the neighbor's yelping dog, or drunken Weasand.

Still, vast as these problems were, the children cared not a straw for them; they had rather play hide-and-seek among the trees than among abstractions. They loved play, and nothing but play, Roxy insisted. "I love Mamma," said

Memmy. "Me lub Mamma, too," echoed Bebby, as she stalked, with a made-up air of mixed pomposity and roguishness, out of the room. Under the trees that Richard had planted was their play-ground, and there they acted out what their mother seemed to feel was their unhappy destiny, — play.

Richard had set the trees, not at the corners of the yard, not in straight lines, but in groups and curves; thus creating many little in-and-out places for caprice and pastime to practise in. "Look at the children among the trees," he called to his sister. She did look, and smiled. They were nothing but her children, and these were nothing but trees; they were children too, who, in the house, were so often a sigh on her heart, or an annoyance to her hands; but now they were pretty, — simply pretty, exquisitely pretty. She felt this, and so did Richard; and they showed it by their looks, since neither spoke.

Trees, considered as an avenue for the eye to traverse, enhance the beauty of objects at the end of it. The reader has looked through trees at water or the sky, and witnessed this effect. Nature, like Art, seems to require a border, in order to be finished. The dressmaker hems and ruffles; the carpenter has his beads and pilasters; the painter never rests till his piece is framed. This appears to be an ultimate law. Whether Master Willwell attempted to explain it, we know not. We do know he was wont to tell his pupils there were such laws; stopping-places of thought, — dykes in the seams where inquiry is ever mining. "Bread," said he, "is bread; and that is the whole thing. We may say, indeed, it is a composition of flour, and yeast, and water; but that is not it. Your mother's bread, that you get, fresh and warm, every Wednesday afternoon, so sweet in milk, — why, it is a primitive idea; it is bread, and that is all we know about bread —" he looked down on the bench of little children, who were agape to see whereto so much wisdom tended, and added, "except to eat it." So, likewise, he would expatiate upon toads; "A batrachian reptile; batrachia, naked body, and two feet; what is a toad?" "We are all toads!" cried the class. "Clumsy, harmless." Here he paused. "Little babies are toads," answered one of the scholars. "Body warty and thick," continued the teacher; "now who is a toad?" "Peter Tubby!" cried a bright boy. "Yes," said the teacher, with an innocent smile, "Peter Tubby is a toad. Nay," he added, "a toad is a toad; — repeat this in concert." So the class repeated it, and some went home singing, "A toad is a toad." If we should say, Nature loves a bordering, as it used to be said, she abhorred a vacuum, we might state the whole truth. An uninterrupted plane, — continuity of similar surface, vast, monotonous, silent, — is intolerable. So a column must have its cap, and a house its cornice; so along the edge of the highway spring innumerable flowers, and on its margin the forest is lavish of its foliage; so the sea is terminated by the sky, and we look at the sky through vistas of embanked and woofy cloud. Were you ever in a pine grove of a bright moonlight night? How different from standing upon a mountain at such a time! We recommend to any one on an eminence, to go back from the brink thereof, and stand in the forest, and look out through the breaks and crevices. A moss-rose is an instance in point, — beautiful because it is bordered; it is a landscape seen through trees. A house in the midst of shrubbery is an instance; so are islands in a pond; a view through half-raised window-curtains, and distant scenery through a long suite of rooms; so are light on foregrounds and shadows on backgrounds, in all pictures. Glens, valleys, a flower in the grass, a star in the sky, belong to the same category. So did Memmy and Bebby, at this present speaking; they were bordered by trees, — cedars and birches were about them, like curls on the face of fair maiden; and one of Master Willwell's primitive ideas turned up, — bread was bread; a toad was a toad; the final sense was reached, and Richard and Roxy were pleased. Then, in this case, the children were on the go, while the bordering kept still; they were the picture, dancing up and down in its frame; they were the blue sky, crisping and rippling behind the clouds. This great beauty, which they were, was now in the shadow, now in the shade; now its straw hat and ruddy face gleamed through the green spray, — now its silver, healthful voice carolled in ambuscade. It ran round the trees that made it so beautiful; it halted in front of that which set it off so behind; its fluttering was seen through the depth of the little copse. A chipping sparrow sang in the trees over it; Munk sat on the steps, and pressed his arm very tight about his wife's waist as he beheld it; passers-by stopped and leaned on the fence to look at it.

Lo! now Bebby stands between, and partly screened by, two little cedars, about as tall as she; — and how beautiful she is; what a joy in her father's heart; what a glistening in her mother's eyes; what a ravishment to Richard, all over, she is, or the thing that she is! She is a moss-rose, — a rose mossed, — bordered. Is the beauty herself, or her circumstances?

What is the principle herein involved? Some refer the interest of this class of phenomena to ideas of Infinity. It is a glimpse, an opening, into the vast, they tell us. But why, if vastness be the ultimate sentiment, is partial vastness more attractive than entire? Why curtain it, to heighten the effect? What has Bebby's head, stuck through those trees, to do with Infinity? I should call it, rather, Limitation. It is rather the reduction of the Infinite to palpable bounds, than an elevation of the Finite to the immeasurable. Bebby runs away. Bebby is the same Bebby; the trees are the same trees; but how different apart! The rose has lost its moss; the view its border. Run back, little additament! Throw yourself into the middle of the picture, or what will be a picture when you get there! Consent to be bordered. Those happy, blue eyes, — those flocculent, foamy locks, — were they ever so pretty? The pea-green, crinkly little cedars, — what enchantment they suddenly assume! How the beauty flashes from one to the other, and centres in the whole! How it vanishes when Bebby quits! Memmy had gone to crawling in the grass, full of frolic and laughter, and Bebby must do so too.

"You will green your drawers all up; come into the house!" cried their mother.

This ended the scene.

Parson Smith's and Dr. Broadwell's Sunday-school children and teachers were planning a union picnic, combined with a rail-road ride and a sylvan meeting; and Richard was going, and he wanted to take Memmy, and Memmy wanted to go; but Roxy clouded. She feared what might be the effect of her children associating with Parson Smith's and Dr. Broadwell's; — they were aristocratic children; they would slight and deride hers; Parson Smith's and Dr. Broadwell's people felt themselves above Elder Jabson's, and so on. But she said to her husband, and here she was more positive, "They have n't clothes fit to go in, and you know it!" Munk need not feign ignorance, or affect to poh the matter off; he was sufficiently conscious of the state of affairs. "Always," continued his wife, "something is a happening, and you are not such a man as you should be!"

"Do you want me to change into another man? — say into Tunny, or Clover, or, if you like, into Elder Jabson?" Munk did not say this in his usual, that is, a pleasant way, but in an irritated way; he was roiled. Roxy flung her apron over her eyes, slatted into a chair, and began to cry. There seemed to be no coming to terms now. Munk knocked his pipe on the andiron, and looked into it, — cool, — rapped again, — stinging, — and when the ashes were all out, he refilled and lighted it, and went to smoking, and reading the evening Catapult, — past endurance. "You wicked man, you!" His wife seemed almost to gnash at him. Munk did not stir. "I guess Memmy's clothes will do," said Richard, in the way of oily interposition. — "I wish you would ever have your shoes on!" Roxy addressed this to the child, who, insensible to what was going on overhead, was down on the floor, busily divesting herself of what clothing she had. "She shall have a new hat," said Munk. "It was a black beaver, with plumes," rejoined his wife. "That was last winter!" explained the other.

"What if it was? It was all the same then as now. We don't have anything! I wanted a Thibet shawl, small figured, and you were not willing. Mrs. Xyphers had an ameline at Tunny's; and what was I, what was I? Bobbin & Shally advertise forty kinds of silks; and all of Dr. Broadwell's folks are in there, — I have seen it with my own eyes! The parlor curtains I am ashamed of! Mrs. Tunny says, have silk damask and tulip pins, and would have if you were worth as much as you are; and you are! Memmy might have a China pearl!" An explosion; Munk stood the shock tolerably well. "Memmy shall have a China pearl, if that will satisfy you." "If that will satisfy me, — as if you had no feeling, and no sense of things, of yourself, — as if all the blame must fall on me! Mrs. Mellow is a woman and a Christian, if there ever was one! And her house don't look like this; and I know what she thinks when she is here, though she don't say anything!"

Here was a cloud, and a shower; and Richard was afraid the children would get wet. "Do not say all this before them," he interceded.

"Yes, before them!" rejoined his sister. "They shall know what a suffering mother they have! I wish I was dead!"

Memmy screamed, and Bebby screamed in sympathy; Munk groaned, his wife sobbed. Richard took the children out doors.

The upshot of the matter was a compromise; Roxy consented to let Memmy go to the picnic, and Munk agreed that his wife should have a fashionable dress.

In great spirits, of a clear morning, the children filed to the depot and entered the cars. They rode on the banks of the River, that now afforded lively glimpses through the trees, now exposed its broad Siloam face, now withdrew behind leafy headlands. They passed lumber-laden sloops, steamboats, and merchandise packets. They went through pretty towns, fruitful farms, and cool woods. They unloaded at Sunny Hours, a grove so called. Here recreation enforced itself; charity found its sphere, harmony attended freedom, innocency sanctified mirth; clean grass and breezy shades inspired exertion, and invited to repose. The children were kind to Memmy, the teachers affable with Richard. Memmy could run among the trees with any of them, and there is no aristocracy in eating. Unitary sentiments were exchanged; congratulations of mutual good feeling made; many hopes of childhood, the Church, and the world, echoed. They sang exultant songs, made earnest speeches, and returned.

Memmy got home safe, with her palm-leaf hat prettily wreathed, and her gown soiled and torn. Roxy was not sorry that she did not wear China pearl, and Munk promised the child a new gingham; and going with Dr. Broadwell's and Parson Smith's children turned out not so bad a thing, after all.

The parlor at Munk's was a hidden room, — an inner sanctuary, — a Blue Beard's chamber; and Richard longed to get into it. It was the largest and the pleasantest room in the house, and he longed to enjoy it. But it was stepping on corns to say anything about it. The room was not open long enough for ventilation, and Richard declared the straw under the carpet was musty, and smelled damp and close. The buzzing of a venturesome fly alone relieved the stillness of the spot; and a spider, not having the fear of Roxy before his eyes, was setting his traps to catch the fly. But the children would litter the carpet, soil the sofa, scratch the chairs, disturb the things on the table.

Munk was satisfied with the kitchen, because he could smoke, lean against the wall, put his feet on the stove-hearth, sit in his shirt-sleeves, — in a word, be what he liked to be, a free man, — better there than in the parlor; and he did not mix with the controversy.

The street-bell rang, and Richard answering it, encountered Mrs. Mellow, the lady to whom Roxy so often referred. She was the Secretary of a Home Inspection Society, and distributor of its tracts. She was well dressed, had a patronizing air, a soft, gentle voice, blue eyes, and her face seemed all made up of tender-line and goodness. When Roxy knew who had called, like a dozen girls let loose from school, she dispersed in all directions at once; she chased the dust-brush, washed the children's faces, swept the hearth, shut the table-drawer, and hurrying into the bed-room to adjust her toilette, rapped and righted the pillows on the bed, and smoothed the window-curtains. Not that Mrs.

Mellow was in the bed-room, or likely to be; but she was in the house, and Roxy acted as if she felt she was all over the house. These matters being attended to, she presented herself in the parlor. Honored as she deemed herself by the call, she was in no state to do justice to it. Nervous, bungling, confused, as if she feared the walls of the room would fall in and crush her visiter, and she had no power to admonish her of the danger, she stiffly returned the salutations of the lady, who took her sweetly by the hand, and went so far as to kiss her. The customary domestic inquiries ensued in routine, until the children were reached. But these were on hand to report for themselves. They bounced into the room, and like captives set free, they made a wild and rude demonstration of their joy. "Come to me, little one," said Mrs. Mellow, holding out a blue-gloved hand on her silken knee. But Memmy was busy with a gilt-edged book she had snatched from the table, and Bebby was urging a chair towards the same forbidden height. "They act so!" said Roxy, making vicarious confession for the young transgressors, at the same time taking the book from Memmy, and the chair from Bebby. "Won't you go and see the lady?" she besought them. Bebby was rolling on the carpet, pulling at Memmy's gown, who screamed to free herself. "They always behave worse before company," explained their mother. "I always said —" "What have you said?" asked Mrs. Mellow. "Nothing," answered Roxy, "only I used to think how children ought to behave in company. I do believe we have the worst children that ever was!" "That depends a good deal on circumstances," replied Mrs. Mellow. "Do you teach them obedience?"

"I endeavor to," said Roxy, "but they beat me out of it. I am not so well sustained as I think I ought to be." She glanced at Richard, who, having been requested by Mrs. Mellow to sit, had remained in the room.

"One should never give up to children." Mrs. Mellow said this positively.

"Never?" asked Roxy. "Never. When you have laid down a rule, adhere to it."

"What if the rule is a bad one?" queried Richard.

Mrs. Mellow, unlike herself, bridled at this, and looked sharply at Richard. But Richard was not pierced; and perhaps because he was not, the lady remarked, as if it was the most effective thing she could do, she was sorry to see our young men, and laboring men too, imbibing transcendental notions; at the same time tendering Richard a tract, which she said she hoped would teach him humility and the fear of God. Richard accepted the tract, and unceremoniously left the room.

"I fear for that brother of yours, Mrs. Munk," said Mrs. Mellow.

Now, Roxy, however she might view and feel some things, loved Richard, and was proud of him, and was wont to hear people speak well of him; and though she sometimes blamed him to his face, she had no idea anybody else would do so to hers; and while she entertained a profound regard, and an almost servile reverence, for Mrs. Mellow, the language of that lady served to jar the awe in which she stood, and set her upon a train of independent thinking. Still, she made no reply, and in a short time her caller left. Moreover, she thought Mrs. Mellow reflected on her condition in life, and that of her brother, as belonging to the laboring class; and this was grievous. Mrs. Mellow had never done such a thing before. She was rich, and she belonged to the best church, and the best society, and lived in an elegant house; and Roxy thought she was an uncommon Christian, and never before, through the suaviloquy of patronage and condescension, had the sting of derision appeared. It was as if the dove concealed a serpent's tongue, and Roxy felt herself bitten.

Still the sentiment of Mrs. Mellow, "Never yield to a child," and the query of Richard, "What if it be a bad rule?" weighed in her mind.

The subject of the freedom of the parlor came up in conversation, a short time afterwards. "I always said I would have a best room," observed Roxy. "That is the best room," replied Richard, "which answers its purpose best, and contributes most to the enjoyment of the family. Sometimes the kitchen is the best room." "Yes," said Munk, not looking from his paper, "be good and happy,—only be happy, that's all." "The best room," continued Richard, "on the present basis, is the worst room — one that affords the least satisfaction of any in the house. You are obliged, Roxy, to defend it as it were with a broomstick against your children, from morning to night."

"But," answered his sister, "I have made it a rule that they shall never go into the parlor except we have company. They will remember this rule, and I shall seem to yield to them."

"What and if you actually yield to them? It will be, as Pastor Harold used to say a concession of arrangement to affection,— of economy to happiness. It may be an exchange of what is purely whimsical or fashionable, for what is useful and salutary. How the children are tried and tempted by that room; how often it proves too strong for their virtue; how their inclinations are teazed, and their humors blackened, by your regulation! Take rainy days, and washing days, and busy days, — the kitchen is too small for the children and you, and the parlor is full of sunshine, and green-sward, and blithe freedom to them; but they must forego it all, and stay here in the suds. Would it be right to set a plate of cake on that chair, and keep it uncovered before the children for a week, and forbid them to touch it, and punish them for touching it? That parlor is a great plate of cake, and peaches and pears besides, to them. You say they spoil things. That is because they are not used to them. Familiarity with the contents of the room would moderate the excitement of novelty. It is the rarity of entrance that leads the children to abuse it so. This is according to Mr. Willwell, who says, the more you hide things from people, the more they want to see them."

"But I have said they should n't," answered Roxy.

"What if you said wrong? That is the question. May a parent never do wrong, or impose a wrong command? If he has done so, he ought to retract, I think. In doing wrong, you violate God's law, disturb your own feelings, and confound the moral perceptions of the children. On the other hand, while you seem to stoop to the children, you are really rising to the heights of absolute rectitude; and if they appear for the moment to gain a triumph over you, they would soon find they had only arrived at a natural and simple position; and instead of using it as an advantage, it would rather humble them by its responsibility. Parental concession is provocative of filial obedience. That is Pastor Harold again; I have his sermons by heart."

"You will 'Pastor Harold' me to death!" rejoined Roxy.

"He would kill you by love, as he did me once. But that is the true Resurrection. Die to sin, that we may live to holiness. Be firm in what is right, reasonable in what is doubtful, but give up in what is wrong, — that is his doctrine. Look into your own heart, Roxy, and see what your motives are, in this thing. Do you keep the parlor shut for the good of your children, or for the prosperity of your house, or even for any reasons of comfort or edification? Is it not solely for the world, — because you are ambitious to have as good a parlor as Mrs. Tunny, or from fear of what Mrs. Mellow will think, or from a prurient desire to have the reputation of keeping a handsome parlor? You talk a good deal about the aristocracy, and pride-and-vanity folk, and worldly-minded professors; and you think you belong to a very humble and self-denying church; but it seems to me you commit more sin, and betray more folly, about your parlor, a hundred fold, than the Mayor's wife, in allowing dancing at her house, for which you censured her so; or the Redferns, in taking the fine house in Victoria Square, and who, you have said, were so abandoned to the idolatry of this world."

Roxy oh-deared; and Richard, not knowing but he was pressing the subject too closely, dropped it.

Roxy was easily persuaded; and perhaps that was one source of the infelicity of her life. When she left her country home, the city persuaded her; when she began to assume a church relation, Elder Jabson persuaded her; when she went into society, Mrs. Tunny persuaded her; — sometimes it was Aunt Grint; sometimes it was a thunderstorm. Her husband once had great influence with her; but she had got used to him, — he had lost his seasoning, his piquancy, his forcefulness, to her; a word from Elder Jabson outweighed whole sermons of Asa's. But Richard was a fresh ministry, — there was at least the raciness and edge of novelty to his words, and she was disposed to be persuaded once more.

It was agreed that the room should be thrown open, and all rejoiced in the prospective enlargement.

CHAPTER XXVII.

KNUCKLE LANE.

During the year, there arose in Woodylin a movement, which ultimately embodied itself in what was called the Knuckle Lane Club. Its object was to remove degradation from the city; and no person was deemed fit to join it who was not willing to spend an evening in Knuckle Lane. This precinct, extending along a deep gorge, was sinuous, jagged, damp and dark. It was a result of the city. Its waste measured the improvement of the city. It was the slag and dross of the city refinement. Its houses were the old city houses, that had been replaced by better ones; and they looked as if they had been brought to the edge of the gully, and one after another pitched into the receptacle below, where they lay, in all shapes, at all angles, and in all predicaments.

This Club did not, however, confine itself to that locality; it had a more comprehensive aim. It was a sort of subterranean method of doing good in general. It proposed to look at vice from beneath. Like the sewers of London, there are moral sewers in all our cities, extending many miles, in the labyrinthine passages of which one may travel days. It would go into these.

The Club resolved, not merely to berate vice, but to follow it home, — see its bed and board; talk with it, and find out what was on its mind; listen to its arguments; make a stethoscopic examination of it, and trace to their source some of its streams.

The enterprise required tact, strength and faith. A number of individuals were combined in it. Some ladies acted with it, — others sympathized. Some families in Victoria Square contributed furniture and clothing; some rich men gave money. But there must be workers, — Putnams of this den.

The plan had been for some time maturing. There was no secrecy about it, nor were there any attempts at publicity. There was no desire to provoke opposition, or to be impeded by prejudice; therefore, those were chiefly spoken to who, it was thought, would be interested in the matter. Richard and Nefon were particularly interested.

In the course of this business, Richard made new acquaintances, and, as he thought, with nice people. Among these was Augustus Mangil, one of the Brokers. No one dreamed of Augustus Mangil in such a connection. At his capacious office window lay all day long piles of gold and silver, and passers by, seeing the man through the window, and, as it were, breast-high in the precious stuff, supposed him a sort of monster, — half a knave, half a fool. He was reputed to shave notes, get up panics, disturb the street; and, with a shark-like voracity, devour railroads and factories, and orphan patrimonies. He had a pleasant, smiling face, — but that was to win your money. He played on the flute, — that was to decoy the unwary; his head was partly bald, and some said the widow's tears scalded it; yet he was fat and sleek; — still, there were hundreds who knew where his marrow and oil flowed from.

But Nefon, who prided himself on his insight into human nature, knew his man, and knew this man. He looked him in the eye, somewhat as Klumpp would, and said, "Gus," — he called him Gus, — "you must go with us." "Go? go? go where?" "Knuckle Lane." "I know

Knuckle Lane. I have just sold some Knuckle Lane stock." "Don't speak of it. We must try to improve the stock."

"Not speak of it?" exclaimed the Broker. "I have saved five dollars for the poor dog. He put all he had in a railroad share, because they told him it would help his trucking. Frightened, horse dead, wife confined, and all that, — would sacrifice. I never stand about such things; cashed the bond, divide the profits; and five dollars is his, — that goes into Knuckle Lane."

"Come along!" said Nefon; "you are a man, and the man, and our man."

In addition, Richard was introduced to a worthy lady, of whom he had heard, a sister-in-law of the Broker's, Mrs. Helen Mangil; and as there was another lady in Woodylin of the same name, and whose husband bore the same name with that of the first, this one, in certain circles, was called Helen the Good.

This Knuckle Lane became a cause; it counted its friends and supporters, — it grew into a spirit and a feeling.

Mayor Langreen was its President, Parson Smith its Secretary, Nefon its Treasurer; then it created a Do-something Committee, or might be said to resolve itself into such; and this comprised men and women, among whom were Richard, Mr. Mangil, Broker, Elder Jabson, Munk, Mr. Cosgrove, Carpenter, Mr. Horr, Collector of Customs, Mr. Lawtall, Pianoforte-maker, Ada Broadwell, the Lady Caroline, Helen the Good, Melicent, and others.

It will be recollected the condition of membership was willingness to spend an evening in Knuckle Lane; and this, in the estimation of many good people of Woodylin, was narrow and exclusive. It savored of bigotry; it was a reflection on excellence. Mrs. Tunny was shocked at it;

the Redferns in Victoria Square sniffed at it. "But now," said Nefon, "we know who is who; if anybody has got quills, here is a chance to show them. Every man's eyes must be his own chap in this business."

There must be first a reconnoissance, and a report. Richard, Mr. Mangil, Elder Jabson, and Nefon, were commissioned to this task. It was a thick and misty night when they sallied forth. From the height that overlooked Knuckle Lane, that region, with its pent lights, appeared like a gully cut through Hades by some deluge, along the hideousness of which a dim phosphorescence luridly gleamed. "We must peel and go at it," said Nefon. Not peel, but wrap up, oh valorous man! — pull on gutta percha boots, to wade through that mire and dirt; clothe breast and arms in faith and hope, to meet that sin and shame. It was the rendezvous of theft, the resort of bawdery, and a creek into which whatever is unfortunate in human condition, or depraved in human nature, daily set, like the tide.

"There are children there!" ejaculated Richard. "There are souls there," said Elder Jabson, with pious eagerness. "I have a customer there," answered the oily, laughing Broker, "and I think we had better corner him."

They entered the house of the truckman, where they found a sick wife, and a sorrowful looking man vainly attempting to fill the office of nurse, and keep his infant child alive. "Where was the Lady Caroline?" bethought Richard. It had not been deemed safe or prudent for the ladies to come out that night. Mr. Mangil had in his hands a balance of money due the truckman. This was opportune. It enabled the man to buy a horse; a horse would restore him to his business, — his business would support his family. "A transaction," said the Broker. "I negotiated his share, and put five dollars into my own pocket; if he has any more dealings of the sort, I should be happy to act for him."

They went next to Fuzzle's, one of the men who had been induced to sign the temperance pledge at Quiet Arbor, the winter before. He had been, in his own language, "off and on" abstemious. His wife was an acetate of bitterness. He spent most of his evenings out; drank to enjoy himself; cursed the License law.

They visited a washerwoman, who cared more for others than herself, and seemed to absorb in her own family all the dirt she took from the world at large.

Whimp's was a vile and villanous spot, — no culture, no ideas, no hope, no God.

Slaver's, they attempted to inventory, but it was an endless task; it stood plus nothing, and minus everything. Yet there were cats, and a pig, broken stools, smoked walls, unseemly beds, and some of Elder Jabson's "souls," staring out, wild and savage, through uncut hair, bronzed cheeks, and shaking about in rags and dirt.

No. 6 was a rookery, — music and dancing, drinking and swearing, the Satyrism and Bacchantism of modern civilization.

Our Heroes stood their ground at all points, patiently investigated, kindly counselled, and carefully remembered. Sometimes the Elder prayed. Nefon had with him tracts, little picture-books, and embellished cards, which he distributed.

They made due report of proceedings. The Club was surprised, horrified; they inquired, What shall be done? They passed resolutions; they adopted plans; and all with an honest purpose at the bottom.

Committees were sent out by twos; not Knuckle Lane alone, but other similar spots were visited. They explored the shores of the River, picking their way through drift-wood, hulks of boats, drag-nets, hog-styes, hen-coops, and went up the bank to tenements that hang down from many stories above, where the freshet and the cholera sometimes enter, — where squalidness and destitution are always entering, — where children, like bank-swallows, are seen entering, — inhabited by Canadian French, and Connaught Irish. They traversed the Pebbles. They searched the purlieus of hotels and stables. Eating-houses on the wharves, and boarding-houses in the same vicinity, were remembered. They risked the most in the rum-shops. It was voted that two members of the sacred band should sit out an evening in these retreats. The thing was done. They entered the curtained door, took chairs in the midst of *that* congregation, saw what was done, heard what was said, — staid from eight o'clock till midnight. Some members of the company chose gambling-rooms, dancing-halls, and the gallery of the Theatre, for their field; others frequented the circuses and menageries, and entertainments promised by negro mimics, mesmeric mountebanks, and jugglers of all sorts. Some spent a portion of the Sabbath at the various Lazy Poles, and Paradises, and the Islands. The Alms-house and Jail were rummaged.

Not that this was done at once. Summer hardly sufficed, and winter was upon them before even their preliminary operations were concluded.

But Knuckle Lane flourished. Judge Burp joined the society. Alanson M. Colenutt, the millionnaire, signified his approval. The Editor of the Dogbane said in his office, one day, in the presence of a large number of most notable and keen-sighted Phumbicians, in an earnest but whispered under-tone, swaying a great newspaper in both hands, he believed it was a good thing. "I say it, — I will say it; I say it not as a Phumbician, but as a man,—I believe it is a good thing." Tode sprang from his chair, and leaving the office, said, "Stop my paper!" "Mr. Tode," cried the Editor, "I am a Phumbician; every drop of blood in my veins boils with Dogbanian fire. I know what is due to our cause. If they dare to meddle with that, and bring the curs about our ears,—if a single whelp is heard to bark in consequence of their movements,—no indignation, no scorn, no blasting, is too great for them!" Tode resumed his seat.

It was rumored, the same day, on the opposite side of the River, that the Dogbane had caved in, having announced in favor of Knuckle Lane, and was making capital out of the new enterprise. The Catapult wauled, "What if some poor man's dog was saved,—it was his comfort and defence;—he shared with the faithful creature his bread and butter: and when he dies, who watches his grave,—who, if we may so say, sheds a tear for the departed?—who, who, but his dog? But that is not it; we warn our readers, it is not hatred to dogs that inspires the cunning of our amiable contemporary;—it is a covert design to encourage amongst us that spawn of perdition, the cats. *The meat that was conveyed by worthy members of this Club to a certain poor family is known to have been fed out to a cat!* Driblets and bones, they say! But driblets and bones are nutritious. CATS ARE THE MOTHERS OF KITTENS!! This is a momentous truth, and one we hope the people will duly ponder."

A deputation, consisting of the most respectable members of Knuckle Lane, headed by Judge Burp, visited both offices, and explicitly assured the editors that Knuckle Lane had nothing to do with Phumbics; and the matter was dropped from the public prints.

It went on, however, in the hearts of the people. It gained the affections, and silenced the scruples, of multitudes.

Richard was indefatigable. He had not so much leisure as many, but he had faith and patience. One evening every week and, in emergencies, two, he assigned to Knuckle Lane

In these visits he was often aided and directed by Cornelius Wheelan, whom he had rescued from the Grotto and ruin, and who, so to say, having been pickled in vice and crime, took a long time to freshen; but as it is said beef freshens better in salt water than fresh, so it seemed to take all this man's humors out of him to go around among his old associates and haunts; — and he became not only a better man, but useful to those who were better than he, and also to some that were worse.

Richard's special beat was the New Town; yet sooner or later, he visited almost the whole of the city. He went down among the roots of many of its evils. He got into the bosom, and, so to say, blossom, of much of its sorrow. He sat by the bed-side of its remorse. He made himself at home in its dens of iniquity.

It was a rule of Knuckle Lane to give no offensive publicity to discoveries they might make. As the historian of the society, we are bound by the same reserve, and cannot relate all that fell under the observation of our friend, albeit they were matters of interest and moment, both to him and his co-laborers.

We shall briefly advert to one or two results. The Club had gathered facts and statistics enough, — the map of the thing was definitely drawn and pretty deeply colored before their eyes. Some were overwhelmed, — some disheartened, — but the majority seemed to derive illumination from afar, and clearness, on the whole, came to the relief of obscurity.

Knuckle Lane, having disentangled itself from Phumbics, came near falling out with Polemics. What was the Church to it, and it to the Church? — that was the question. One or two Clergymen said it interfered with their labors, — usurped the prerogative of the Church, and drew off communicants. But Clergy and Laity, on the whole, favored it. Still, among the adherents of the cause, the inquiry arose, Shall the Church go to Knuckle Lane, or Knuckle Lane come to the Church? But Knuckle Lane was too dirty and too ragged to go to the Church. Shall the Church wash and clothe it? It may not stay washed and clothed. Shall the Church support external Knuckle Lane organizations? Not agreed. Prosecute the rum-shops? General shaking of heads. Knuckle Lane itself would take it in dudgeon. Furthermore, the Church is represented partly in Victoria Square, and La Fayette-street. What have these to do with Knuckle Lane? Shall these streets go down to Knuckle Lane? Shall Knuckle Lane, the Docks, the Stables, the Islands, go up to Victoria Square? "Rather a tight squeeze," said Nefon. "In plain language," observed Mr. Cosgrove, Carpenter, "shall the Redferns and the Fuzzles meet in one another's parlors and kitchens?" "In the existing state of human society," said Judge Burp, rubbing the palms of his hands, "I should deem it impracticable. I doubt if Mrs. Redfern and Mrs. Fuzzle, on first introduction, would not deem it a very awkward and disagreeable piece of business."

Why should not Victoria Square deputize its interest in Knuckle Lane? "A good plan," whispered Mr. Lawtall, Pianoforte-maker, to Nefon. — Nefon drew his hand hard over his face, and was still. — Create deputy almoners of its bread, deputy carriers of its compliments, deputy communicators of its instruction? But who shall bring back the thanks, the love, and the evidences of good, from Knuckle Lane to Victoria Square? Shall Knuckle Lane have its deputies, too? Shall the whole business of Christian intercourse and human duty be a matter of delegation? Shall the Redferns, and the Tillingtons, and the Tissingtons, of Victoria Square, — shall Governor Dennington, and Mayor Langreen, and Judge Burp, of the city generally, — be doing and acting, — sending bread, and sympathy, and encouragement, to the Fuzzles, and Whimps, and Slavers, of Knuckle Lane, and these parties never see each other? Shall the Widow Droop, who lives by the Pebbles, receive a basket of meat, a bed coverlid, a jacket for her boy, from the Mayoress, and never see the Mayoress, — never give vent to her glad feelings, which else are quite a-bursting her, — never kiss the hand that is so open and soft? Shall the warm-hearted Mayoress even not know where her beneficence goes, or whom it blesses? — Great commotion, and a deal of anxiety. — How shall the rich and poor meet together, and the Lord be the Maker of them all? "That is *the* question," said Nefon. "That points to the ring-bolt, I tell *you!*"

A plan was proposed and achieved somewhat in this wise.

A building was erected, called The Griped Hand, from a device of that sort, cut in stone, over the entrance. It was a three-story house, and divided into a Coffee-room, a Reading-room, and an Assembly-room. It was a large building, of freestone, tastefully designed, and standing in a convenient spot. It was a contribution of the Church, Victoria Square, and other parts of the city, or of various individuals in the city, — or, more systematically, of Religion, Wealth, and Common Sense, — to Knuckle Lane. The Coffee-room supplied cheap refreshments of various kinds; the Reading-room was well stocked with newspapers, magazines, and comprised also a library; the Assembly-room was devoted to miscellaneous gatherings, collations, reünions, lectures, etc., etc.

All who were able paid something for its privileges; those without means were admitted gratuitously. Its ultimate support was chargeable to the charities of the Churches and individuals.

At the dedication, Dr. Broadwell preached an eloquent discourse, and the combined Church choirs added excellent music.

The people of Woodylin were invited to unite freely in the Griped Hand, and what it could afford. Members of the holy brotherhood visited Knuckle Lane, and other places, and extended the graciousness of the Griped Hand to those people.

Would Fuzzle enjoy his evenings as well at the Griped Hand as in Quiet Arbor? He did. Sailors, stevedores, river-drivers, teamsters, came to the Griped Hand for their cups of tea and coffee. Victoria Square and Knuckle Lane did meet in the Assembly-room of the Griped Hand. Evelina Redfern and Sally Whimp did shake hands, and converse together, and appear like two Christians, at a Fourth of July pic-nic in the same room; and Evelina and Sally bowed in the street the next day, and certain people did not know where it would stop, this intimacy of those two; indeed, it would probably go on through this world into the next.

"Victoria Square is on the way to Knuckle Lane, and Knuckle Lane is moving towards Victoria Square, actually!" So Nefon exclaimed, thrusting down his right fist emphatically on the counter, — his store full of people, — and no man dared say aught against it.

The Church lost nothing. Indeed, the whole world belongs to the Church, through Christ Jesus, and has been bought with a great price, and paid for; but how many briers and thorns, how much sour bog, how much gravelly drift, there is on the farm! The Church gained in the improvement of Knuckle Lane. It was so much muck, and decayed vegetation, and corrupted life, hauled out and mixed with Gospel lime and sunlight, and Woodylin culture; and it became excellent soil — and it was all clear gain to the Church.

The rich and the poor met together; benefactor and beneficiary looked each other in the face. The willing hand and the relieved want poured out their feelings in common; the sick man saw his kind physician; penury and hopelessness beheld the eye that had been moved to tears over the story thereof. And were not many glad to see the Lady Caroline, so free-hearted, so ready to do, so anxious to know what she could do? Many knew how she went up to Bill Stonrers' when nobody else would go, and staid by that disease when nobody else would stay. She was the woman that many had heard of, and she was sometimes pointed out as the woman that was not afraid of Bill or Chuk, or sickness or death; and the Fuzzles, and Whimps, and Slavers, stood in awe of her, as a god. Were n't they glad to speak with her, and see her smile, and to have her elegance, and wealth, and fashion, about them, as an atmosphere which they could breathe, — as a little garden right in the midst of their bleakness and meanness, where they could play, and pluck a flower or two? — and this they had at the Griped Hand. Then how many crowded about Helen the Good, with eyes, and hands, and hearts, all brimming with delight.

What of Religion? There are Churches enough in the city, and preachers enough; let Knuckle Lane go where it chooses. So it was decided. After meeting in the Griped Hand, and getting better acquainted, and loving each other more, Knuckle Lane was more ready to worship with Victoria Square. "Our Church is open to all," said Dr. Broadwell; and so said Parson Smith, and so said Elder Jabson.

What of Education? There is plenty of public schools; let Knuckle Lane, and the Islands, be drawn into them.

Well, in process of time it was found the rum-shops were a good deal thinned out. The Coffee-room, and kindness, and cordiality, had superior attractions. "Men have feelings as well as appetites, and a longing for home amidst all dissipation," Richard used to say, quoting from Pastor Harold. Then he added, — this he got too from the same reverend source, — what St. Pierre relates, how the European settlers in the Isle of France said they should be happy there if they could see a cowslip or a violet. Let us send, he said, to these wanderers from virtue and peace, a cowslip and a violet.

The Theatre lost some of its charms, and much of its perniciousness. The Griped Hand furnished cheap amusements for the poor. Knuckle Lane would be amused, and cannot we amuse it? So asked Benjamin Dennington. "Happy and good, — good and happy!" cried Munk. Elder Jabson started, but Nefon held him to his seat. "Can't go, my man, can't go; it is rather hot for you, I know, but you must stand fire."

Popular lectures were had in the Assembly-room, and singing concerts; panoramas and wax-work were exhibited; that large class of people who itinerate through the country with their wisdom and their shows found it for their interest to employ the same Hall, where indeed Knuckle

Lane was admitted *ad valorem*, while Victoria Square paid enough to keep the revenue good.

Did this redeem Knuckle Lane? It went some ways towards redeeming what was redemptible in it. Would any one refuse the blessings of the Griped Hand? He must indeed be reprobate. Did it Christianize the Church and Victoria Square? It helped their Christianization.

Were there no drawbacks? Yes, a plenty. One or two of the Clergy and their people drew back. They said there was no religion in it, — that to introduce the subject of Knuckle Lane and the Griped Hand into their pulpits was a desecration, — that they ought to preach the Gospel, and not exciting topics, etc., etc. I need not enumerate all they said. Miss Fiddledeeanna Redfern drew back; — didn't she, when her sister Evelina came in from the picnic aforesaid? And when she knew her sister had shaken hands with Sally Whimp, very facetiously she seized the tongs and made as if she would throw her sister's glove into the fire. Mrs. Mellow drew back, because she said the friends of the enterprise, in their distribution of tracts, refused to accept those of which she was agent; while, in fact, they only said they did not wish to be confined to them. But the knowing ones declared the true cause of this lady's opposition lay in an unwillingness to have her children meet with Knuckle Lane children at a juvenile celebration to be given at the Griped Hand. Zephaniah O. Tainter, Jr., general clacquer and spy of the Catapult club, held back, because he said he could see a cat in this Knuckle Lane meal. Mary Crossmore, nurse, ditto, because this movement had fished up two or three excellent nurses out of Knuckle Lane, and her business might fall off. Mr. Squabosh, Superintendent of Sewers and Drains, ditto, because it would interfere with his contract. Mr. Catch, philosopher, suspended opinion until it should be ascertained whether it recognized the true theory of capital and labor. Mr. Gresney, reformer, could not assent to it, because it did not begin with the distinct enunciation of a principle. The Man of Mind stood at the corners of the streets and looked wise.

But why recount expressions and feelings that would fill a volume, and which would reduce Richard Edney and the Governor's Family to a very small space in their own book, and which, in truth, gave Richard and his friends trouble enough, without being employed to obscure the narration of events in his story.

What did the Knuckle Lane adventure determine? Not whether the Knights Templars were guilty, nor who wrote Ossian, nor whether mankind have more than one origin. It did determine this to the mind of Richard, and others, — that by resolutely undertaking to do good, something might be done.

These matters, connected indeed with Richard, are yet somewhat in anticipation of his story. They were two or three years in progress, and during these years Richard had other matters to attend to, and to these we must recur.

CHAPTER XXVIII.

NOTES BY THE WAY.

A Tale is like a web; like muslin, where the thread is regular, visible, and thin; like sheeting, where it is the same but stout; and in both cases the fabric is plain and monotonous. It may be like Brussels carpeting, where the thread disappears for a time, and is not easily traced,—one color being now in sight, and then another,—and yet, in all mutation, the design of the artist is preserved, and what is lost in clearness of detail is made up in beauty of composition. A Tale may be like a garden, one quarter of which shall be devoted to cereal grains, another to kitchen sauce, a third shall be reserved for fruits, while the fourth is gay with flowers, and the connection between the several parts consists of naked paths alone; yet it is a garden,—Horticulture enforces its principles and maintains its dignity throughout, and the innate garden-love is satisfied. So a Tale may have its various departments, the only apparent connection between which shall be the leaves of the book and enumeration of the chapters, and still please Historical taste. There is a real connection in both instances;—in the first, it is that of the brooding and immanent power of Nature, which is always a unity and a beauty; in the last, it is the heart of the Author, which is likewise a unity, and should be a beauty.

A Tale is like this June morning, when I am now writing. I hear from my open windows the singing of birds, the rumble of a stage-coach, and the blacksmith's anvil. The water glides prettily through elms, and willows, and the back-sides of houses. There are deep shadows in my landscape, and yonder hill-side, with its blossoming apple-trees, glows in the sunlight, as if it belonged to some other realm of being. On the right of my house is a deep gorge, wet, weedy, where are toads and snakes; and fringing this, and growing up in the midst of it, are all sorts of fresh, green shrubs, and the flickering, glossy leaves of white birches. Superb rock-maples overhang the roof of an iron foundery, down under the hill at my feet. The dew, early this morning, covered the world with topazes and rainbows, and my child got her feet wet in the midst of glory. Through gully and orchard, basement windows and oriels, shade and sheen, vibrates a delicious breeze. Over all, hangs the sun; down upon the village looks that eye of infinite blessedness, and into the scene that urn of exhaustless beauty pours beauty; the smoke from the foundery, and the darkness of the gorge, are beautiful; cows, feeding in my neighbor's paddock, are pleasant to look upon; Paddy, with pickaxe on his shoulder, is happy; Rusticus, in the cornfield, is a picture; and the granite, through the verdure of a distant mountain-side, gleams out like silver. This morning's sun idealizes everything. Nature is not shocked at toads. A Tale might be thus diversified; and if through it streamed love and gladness from the soul of the writer, like sunlight, the structure would still be harmonious, and the effect pleasing.

A Tale is like human life,—of which, indeed, it purports to be a transcript,—and human life exhibits some contrast. The feelings even of a good man, for a single day, undergo sundry transitions; the subjects of thought and occasions of emotion crowd a little upon each other. There will be great bunches of shadow in one corner of a man's heart, and right over against them, and looking down upon them, and gilding, it may be, their edges, will be great expanses of brightness. Through all the peace and delight of one's being will be heard the perpetual wail of some sad memory, even as I now hear, in this sunny, enlivening morning, the melancholy note of the peewee.

Richard had his varieties. During this Knuckle Lane business, other things went on. Memmy and Bebby lived, — lived in his heart, and in his arms, and in his fingers, and in his ears, and before his eyes. They ran all over the carpet of his days; they sprawled upon it; sometimes they blew soap-bubbles on it; sometimes they were like twin cherubs asleep in one corner of it. Who shall follow their thread, or describe their figure? Plumy Alicia Eyre was another thread; or rather she was like the colored pile that is wrought into the plain warp of Brussels carpeting aforesaid, and is reproduced at odd intervals. Miss Eyre indicated, for a while, an interest in Knuckle Lane; but, for reasons which will be hereafter discoursed upon, that attachment was not lasting. Clover, — what has become of him? He has been absent a long time, — not a thread in the carpet, so much as a moth under it, and silently eating into it; and when the carpet is taken up and shaken, there will be found unexpected holes in it, and many rotten places. The Knuckle Lane attempt did not demolish Clover, nor did the Griped Hand win his fellowship. He was like a disturbed ghost, strolling through the earth, — a sort of disconcerted fiend. He appeared at Green Mill occasionally, the basin of his lower lip, and the crooks in his upper lip, in no wise diminished. In the night, going home from his meetings Richard now and then saw, through the darkness before him the arms of Clover describing their favorite contortions, like the vanes of a windmill; and when he got home, there were giant streaks of shadow playing in his imagination, and these would sometimes hang over and threaten his dreams. Captain Creamer seemed to wilt and dry up, after his failure; though whether, like the poisonous rhus, there might not be some mischief in him after he was dry, remained to be seen.

But we must advert to one or two things that bear upon the fortune of our friend.

During his perambulations, — and perhaps we should say his *noctivagancy*, if nobody will be troubled at the word — Here a verbal quiddity plucks at the sleeve of narration, and obliges us to stop and answer, that it is hard to please everybody. Leo X. preserved with care, and what wholeness he might, the remains of ancient Rome in the modern city. Sixtus V. would "clear away the ugly antiquities," could not endure the Apollo Belvidere in the Vatican, and righted the Minerva by substituting a cross for her spear; and so he went on idealizing the whole city, — that is, reducing it by what he would call the rules of a Christian Idealism. As if there were not a higher ideal in suffering Minerva to remain as she was!

There are those who would clear our language of its ugly antiquities, as if pagan Latin had not got into the English, and become a part of it, and the best thing for us was to make due use of it. We might say *night-walking*, but that has a bad odor. A certain one was sorely shocked when he found his good King, in his own palace, playing with a basket of puppies about his neck; — that was low. He was equally shocked, on returning to the street, to see a cobbler promenading with side-sword and silk stockings; — that was too high. Can any one tell us what is the *aurea mediocritas* of our tongue? Besides, even as Richard addicted himself to observation in behalf of his absent teacher and friend, Mr. Willwell, so, as has been already premised, we are writing with a latent reference to our Usbek cousins; and might it not be well for us to give them some insight into the structure and sources of our language, as well as into our manners and customs? May it not be conjectured withal that, in their incursions into the East, the ancient Romans dropped some portions of their language in that distant country, and that even ramifications or dialects of the Tarter tongue shall at this day be found cognate with our own?—

During his noctivagancy, we say, in the cause of Knuckle Lane, Richard made many discoveries, and some which disturbed him. He encountered the young men, Chassford and Glendar, at gaming saloons, in tippling houses, and sundry places where he thought they ought not to be, and where it reflected no credit on the simplicity of their characters or purity of their principles in being. Already, the winter before, he saw them at the Grotto, and the sight afforded him any but pleasant recollections.

Meanwhile he called once or twice at the Governor's, and found these young men there. Their air was well-bred, their dress fashionable, their conversation sprightly, and their ease absolutely overwhelming. With a twirl of his cane, or a touch of his goatee, Glendar could set Richard's composure shaking like an earthquake. And Richard was powerless, — he could not avenge himself. He did not esteem the young men, but he had no desire to vent his disesteem there. He sometimes thought he would speak to Melicent or Barbara about them, but he did not. They complimented the Knuckle Lane movement; yet Richard felt they could not in heart be much concerned for it.

An event of greater interest to Richard was his election to the Common Council of the city. It was the second spring after his arrival in Woodylin, when, at a meeting of those who styled themselves "The Friends of Improvement," he was unanimously nominated. Richard was young, and a new-comer. Yet, it may be remarked, the Ward in which he lived, comprising, as it did, the Factories and Saw-mills, and all the Beauty of Woodylin, had many new-comers in it, and this class of people were inclined to sppport one of their own men. More than that, Richard, by this time, had become sole proprietor of the rent of two saws. How did this come about? Richard's father owned a saw-mill; lived upon a stream emptying into the River, and was able to cut more logs than he wanted and send them down stream. We have said that Bill Stonners' Point was the best booming privilege on the River. Well, Chuk, Bill's sole heir, was sole owner of this chance. And whom should Chuk want to assist. if not Richard? Whom would he strike the picaroon week in and week out for, if not Richard? So it was arranged that the elder Edney should furnish the logs, Chuk boom them, and Richard saw them. More than that, what Bill never would do, Chuk was glad to do; he went up to the stream on which Mr. Edney lived, and "drove" the logs. He rolled them into the water; he helped them over shoals, rafted them, and tended them as a flock of sheep, till he got them penned in the boom. He would be out days and nights on this business, never leaving it, rain or shine, and often waist-deep in water for twelve hours together. This boom of Chuk's, lying, as it did, contiguous to the Mills, and so safe in all ordinary freshets, he was considered a very fortunate man who could acquire the entire use of; and Richard was considered a fortunate man. This circumstance added to Richard's consequence in the eyes of his neighbors.

Then he had so excellent a friend in Mr. Cosgrove, the

princely contractor for buildings, and who purchased of him to large amounts.

It made a great stir at the Saw-mills when it was known Richard had obtained control of Chuk's boom, though perhaps not twenty people elsewhere had the least intelligence of the matter.

These circumstances aided Richard's municipal advancement.

Yet, his success was not without impediment. In the first place, the Catapulters had long ruled the New Town, and expected to do so now. Next, the Dogbanes, for the sake of putting a pretty trick on their hereditary enemies, "over the River," declared for Richard. To defeat this ruse, the Catapulters proclaimed Richard a Hydriatic, and brought up Richard's connection with a certain horse, whose carcass Munk & St. John had caused to be thrown upon the ice. The Dogbanes mortally feared water; and inasmuch as neither party could use Richard, they silently concerted to pounce upon him, like the animals whose names they bore, and devour him. In other words, they united upon a ticket which should destroy that of the Friends of Improvement, and in place of Richard substituted the name of Clover! This will hardly be credited by our near or distant readers, nor would it have been credited in Woodylin generally, or even among the large body of supporters of either ticket. It was the result of despair in the two parties, and of indefatigable management on the part of Clover. At the caucuses, Clover, whose real character could not have been commonly understood, represented that he was the only man who could be led against Richard with any prospect of success. In addition, Clover, as we say, electioneered for himself and against Richard.

The union ticket did not prevail, and Richard carried the polls by a handsome majority.

In the city councils, Richard found problems enough to last Euclid one year at least, and grave responsibilities that would make an impression on the shoulders of a small Atlas. It was a post where a good man could do some good, and a wise man be of some use. Mr. Langreen was Mayor, and Nefon was an Alderman, and Richard was not altogether without friends at the board. He was able to do something for the furtherance of his favorite idea, the Knuckle Lane project. While this, indeed, had been conducted chiefly by individuals, there were many points in which the city government could render it essential service. It was proposed to new-lay the street that ran through Knuckle Lane, and furnish that precinct with water at public expense. A large space of ground that had lain neglected, quite in the heart of the city, was purchased, fenced, and planted with trees, for a park.

A new cemetery was consecrated, called Rosemary Dell. To this some of the tenants of the old ground were conveyed; here, also, a new grave was made for Violet, one of the Orphans. Richard selected the spot, — his friends erected a handsome monument; with his own hands he planted shrubbery and flowers about it.

On the back side of Woodylin, and yet within ten minutes walk of Centre-street Church, was what in some places is called a valley, in others, a gully, through which the Pebbles brook meandered. At a distance, this spot looked like a vast redoubt of foliage, or a hollow imbedded in trees. Within it the trees, elms and oaks, rose to a great height above the observer. He saw at the bottom the thread-like rivulet, flowing on like a lover's joy, as strolling, too, as lover's walks by moonlight, crinkling its way along, and scolloping the ground on either side, singing and shining all alone down its deep bed, feeding the roots of trees, flinging its dew on the mosses, and creating innumerable little pleasure-grounds for the frogs. The banks were broken, deeply embayed, and boldly projected. In this valley grew saxifrage, and spring-beauty, and wild columbine, and here children came May-flowering. The banks, too, were elevated and terrace-like, and the ravine narrow; and, with the canopy of trees overhead, it was a cool and shady spot, most refreshing to the imagination and the feelings in a hot summer day, and just such a place as one would wish to go into out of the sun. Among the children, this spot had gone by the name of May-flower Glen. But it had lost what the critics would call its unity, and was parcelled off by rough fences into small lots, and abandoned to cows and swine, and appropriated by little moss-trooping children, who crept under the fences, and by birds, who seem to have a life-estate in all that God hath made. Richard, in his rambles with Memmy and Bebby, had seen it, and admired it.

Through the influence of the Friends of Improvement, May-flower Glen was conveyed to the city; by which it was cleared, its bog drained, gravel-walks laid, and seats constructed. It became a favorite resort of the citizens, and tributary likewise to the cause of Knuckle Lane and the Gripped Hand; since here the rich and poor met together in ways at once fraternal and respectful, joyous and refined. So many of the Knuckle Lane people frequented it, there was danger at one time of its losing caste, and becoming not fashionable. But Evelina Redfern declared, if nothing else, she would make a Christian duty of going there, not to speak of what Ada Broadwell and the Lady Caroline did.

Among the first to call at Willow Croft and congratulate Richard on his accession to office, was Miss Eyre; and this she did in a way touchingly graceful, and insinuatingly delicate. Richard's name, as one of the Common Councilmen for Ward 2, had appeared in all the papers; and he saw it in the evening, and again in the morning prints; and it seemed to him as if he saw it the next day in everybody's face. Munk read it, and Roxy must look into the paper, and even Memmy spelt it out; and he felt as if in all houses it had been read, and looked at, and spelt out. Mr. Gouch and Silver, who were still in his employ, and of course voted for him, were overjoyed that he had beaten Clover; and now that he was, as it were, a part of the city, and was backed by the whole city power, they realized that Clover could do him, or them, or anybody else, no more harm. They colored Richard's triumph and advantage so strongly to his mind, he must needs feel it was great indeed, and feel, too, as if he were the whole city, and Clover a very small spot in it; and they were so enthusiastic for Richard,—they hurraed him so, with the wink of their eyes, and the legerdemain of their crowbars and pick-poles,—Richard might be excused for believing everybody in the New Town and the Old Town was his friend and constituent. The first little honors a man receives are very thrilling, and seducing, and softening, and make one feel as if he was all champagne, and roses, and fiddle-strings.

These were new sensations to Richard. It may be doubted if Teacher Willwell or Pastor Harold had prepared him for the emergency. He could not now make observations on what he saw, but upon what he was; and this was public elevation, and private satisfaction,—it was, being a Councilman of Woodylin, and an object of so much congratulation. How would his motto, To BE GOOD AND DO GOOD, and the great purpose of his heart, to love and serve God and his fellow-men, apply here? He mailed three

papers, the next day, containing the report of his election,— to his Father, and particularly *for* his Mother, and to his Teacher and Minister. He did think they would all be glad; and when he reflected on what they would think and say, and especially on what his pious mother would feel, he silently prayed, "O, let me in this be good and do good!" When he went to drop the papers in the office, the lobby was full of people. Did these men know what a precious message was crowding through them? Could they imagine what strong delight those three wrappers enclosed? Did they dream of the parental fascination in a single line of small caps in those columns? One man, intent on a newspaper, drew in his elbows to let Richard pass; another, opening a letter containing a remittance, Richard had to go round; a third, discussing the last night's play at the Theatre, and chewing tobacco, turning suddenly, mistook Richard for the floor. The clerk in the office, jesting at the window with a Dry Fish Culler touching the removal of the latter from his post, for a minute did not see the papers that Richard handed up to him; and when he did, still laughing with the other, he asked Richard if they were pamphlets, and was seen to toss them, like peach-pits, into some hole or other. The printers' boys jostled him with their great baskets. Who cared for Richard's Mother?

So Richard had it all to himself; and there was enough of it, and it was just as good to him as if everybody else had it.

The clerk's indifferent look, a hundred people's preoccupied look, weighed not a feather against his own feelings; and, perhaps, if he thought anything about it, he took some satisfaction in seeing his pride go to the stake, and having his pleasant little emotions suffer a slight martyrdom. It is natural to do so. If people won't notice us, we retaliate upon them by calling them very stupid and dull; or by inflating our merit in our own eyes, till we fancy ourselves too great to be appreciated, and then going off like a hero to oblivion. Our neglect is the measure of our greatness. We have a certain bigness; and he who belittles us belittles himself, — he who enlarges us enlarges himself.

So Richard was not discomforted. Indeed, he experienced all reasonable attentions. Nefon took him warmly by the hand, and expressed great pleasure in the election. Several smiled upon him, as he passed them, in a manner which said, "We know what has happened." The "Friends of Improvement" were delighted.

About this time it was, we say, that Miss Eyre called at Willow Croft. She only added fuel to the flame of Richard's self-complaisance. The little ripples that had been stirring about in his bosom, she set all going again. She was the breeze on his surface, and covered him all over with most charming wavelets, and foam, and agitation. She brought the color to his cheeks, and made the blood warm in his veins. She talked to him about his mother, and how glad she would be; and Clover, and how annoyed he was; and the Common Council Chamber, and how honorable to sit there: and, like a magician, she raised a mist that rose from the floor, transparent and luminous; her form and face were emparadized in it, and, like a cloud of transfiguration, it expanded, and enfolded them both. Never was Miss Eyre's voice so musical, never was her eye so tender, never was her sympathy so entrancing; and Richard's self-love, his susceptibility of encomium, his deep pleasure in what had happened, — that weak and soft spot in his and everybody's nature, — that spot which is so instinct with self, and so alive to public handling, — that inbred regard to reputation and character, which she touched so softly, so deliciously, — these were all carried away by her; and we might say, Richard himself — for there was not much else left to him at that moment — Richard himself was carried away by Miss Eyre. Plumy Alicia's triumph was complete. No, it was no triumph; she would not have it so. If he seemed to surrender, she magnanimously restored his arms; if he was like to grow impassioned, she wisely counselled him; if his eye had any unnatural fervor, she deliberately hushed it "Do not say 'love;' — speech, words, breath, — what are they to the doing, being, feeling? Not if you said it, but if you were it; not what you can utter, but what you can keep." She said this with a kind of *memento mori* motion of her finger, and left the room.

What he could keep! Keep, keep, keep; — that word rang a good while in Richard's ear, and with different inflections; — now upward, the doubtful interrogative; now circumflective, the ironical; now downwards, the grave and solemn.

That night, when he retired to his chamber, into his thought of God and the Holy Spirit Miss Eyre could not enter; into his hope of the Redemption of the world by Christ she could not enter; into his calculations for the success of the Griped Hand she could not enter; into what he most loved of the spiritual, the humane, the beautiful, she could not enter; to the deeper life of his soul she was not kindred; of his heart of hearts she was not partaker. Her only place seemed then to be to him in some little foolish feelings of the hour. Between her and his principal existence was a great gulf. He felt remorseful at what he had done; he was mean and silly in his own sight. Yet he reasoned that in what he said or did he had not committed himself to her; and while he would regard her with all kindness and affection, he could not allow her to be the mistress of his being.

But of necessity Richard must see Miss Eyre frequently. She was intimate at Willow Croft. She caressed the children; she was always chirp, limber-hearted, and free, as Munk wished anybody to be; she could tell Roxy what was worn. Then she had ministered to Richard when he was sick; she had that hold on his consideration which a communication of sorrows creates; she sometimes attended the Knuckle Lane meetings; she loathed and despised Clover; she was, moreover, in a certain sense, poor and friendless, — a dependent, an operative; and she appealed to the sympathies of Richard by whatever lies in the case of those who are sometimes deemed as belonging to a proscribed class.

We call her poor. She was an intelligent and industrious weaver, and could clear three and four dollars a week.

The next time Richard saw her, his manner was cool, and a little sheepish; — she laughed at him. The second time, she amused herself in endeavoring to rally him. The third time, by following the creep-mouse-catch-'em precedent, she brought him more nearly *en rapport*, as the mesmerizers say, with herself.

CHAPTER XXIX.

ON CITIES.

In this connection and chapter, and moved by certain things recorded in the two previous chapters, the author is induced to break through the proprieties of historical narrative, and, after a hortatory sort, to submit a few observations on cities and large towns. Discoveries are being pushed, and revelations made, in the principal cities of the civilized world, that, like the old tragedies, awaken terror and pity; and while sensibility is shocked, philanthropy is puzzled. What shall be done with the intemperance, licentiousness, beggary, disease, theft, that abound? Police-courts, benevolent societies, houses of refuge, foundling hospitals, are instituted; the pulpit and the press unite in the work of reformation. But as it is said the Ocean drives back the waters of the Amazon, so this evil deluges and prostrates the attempt to remove it. What is the cause of the preponderating and disproportionate vice of our cities? Why is there nearly ten-fold more crime and misery, in a given city population, than in the same country population? The answer is contained in one word,— *Density* — that the people are too crowded. You create a city; you multiply its facilities, you open inlets to it from all the region round about; you boast of its growth, and all at once, like King Edward, before-mentioned, you see a thousand little devils jumping about your wealth and your increase. Then you begin to cry out for sorrow. This density originates the Wynds and Closes of Edinburgh; it gives to London its St. Giles; it develops itself in the Faubourgs of Paris; it turns to Ann-street and Half Moon-place, in Boston, and the Five Points and Park Row, in New York. Out of it come what are named dens of infamy, haunts of iniquity. Density, — high houses and narrow streets blocked together, inlaid most mosaically with each other, — we designate as the root of the difficulty. From this spring stem and branches, or secondary and tertiary calamities. First comes a want of ventilation, and bad air; — this generates every species of moral and physical distemperature. Next appears filth, and this turns into a hot-bed of sorrows. This density of the city, like night, which it too truly represents, is a covert for vice. In it the lewd and the rascally nestle; to it, from all parts of the country, the criminal and the vicious flee for shelter. To over-people a given spot has the same effect as to overload the stomach, — there must be pain and disorder. Why should God's children, and Christ's little children, live in garrets and cellars? It was one of the Divine promises to Jerusalem, that the streets of the city should be full of boys and girls *playing in the streets thereof!* How could this be fulfilled in any of our modern cities? Willis reproaches the New Yorkers, that they are not willing to live more than *one layer* deep. It was a dispute of the Schools, how many angels could dance on the point of a cambric needle, and not fall off. Will the Home Journal — Home? — designed to bless and beautify the homes of our people, — will it tell us how many stories, or bodies deep, our people can live, and be comfortable, virtuous and happy?

In the State of Maine, we have understood, some distance up the Kennebec river, near the lumbering region, is a place where it is commonly reported the Sabbath stops. So, in New York, if we are correctly informed, during the hot season, the Sabbath stops, and the people are obliged to go to Hoboken, or Staten Island, or Brooklyn Heights, to find it. If these layers go on increasing, how long before there will be no Sabbath at all? Prithee, Mr. Willis, let the people spread, that they may have a Sabbath, and worship, and enjoyment, and breath, in their own city, of a Sunday.

In Rome, says Beckman, "for want of room on the earth, the buildings were extended towards the heavens. In Hamburg, the greater part of our houses are little less than sixty feet high." He adds that it is difficult to extinguish fires in these high-housed regions. Are such things a model, even with Palladio to back them up?

Cities, according to Mr. Alison, may have been the cradles of ancient liberty; they may have contributed, according to M. Say, to the overthrow of Feudalism; let it be, in the language of a writer before me, that "the spirit of independence was awakened in the streets of Boston, while it slumbered on the banks of the Connecticut;" yet if under the guiding genius of convenience and parsimony, we suffer them to go on crowding, — if like Jeshurun they only wax fat and grow thick, — like him, they will behave very unseemly.

But of the past we can only speak remedially, while of the present and the future we can speak more radically and decisively. A certain tendency, not only to city charters but to city actuality, prevails in the nation. Villages are changing to towns, and towns swell to cities. What would we have done? As the cardinal error of cities is *Density*, we would redeem them by *Openness*. Exterior walls are gone out of use, for the reason perhaps that the walls are all on the inside; as is related of the Irish, there are no old rags or cast-off hats seen in the windows of their houses, because they are exhausted on the bodies of the people. We would make a clean breach through these walls; or, rather, as we are speaking prospectively, we would not suffer such walls to exist. No street should be less than four rods in width; no lane, or court, less than three. Dwelling-houses should be blocked together in not more than twos. — Why, alas! deem the "corner-lot" the most eligible, when every house might look two ways? Why should "twenty-seven feet front" mark the aristocracy? Why the middle one of each suite of rooms dark and dungeon-like? — Churches should be the most conspicuous buildings, and stand in lots of not less than ten rods square. Every school-house should have twenty-five square rods. Every dwelling-house should be removed two rods from the street, and not more than two families be permitted to reside under the same roof, and within the same walls. There should be central, or contiguous, reserves of land, of twenty or fifty acres each, for public parks and promenades. There should be trees in every street, without exception, — trees about the Markets, trees in front of the shops, and on the docks, and shading the manufactories. "A city," says St. Pierre, "were it even of marble, would appear dismal to me, if I saw in it no trees and verdure." The glory of Lebanon, the cedar, came unto God's ancient city, the fir-tree, the pine, and the box together, to beautify the place of his sanctuary. So much for Openness. And this is what God gave us when he lifted the sky so high above our heads, and extended the earth so broadly at our feet, and made such a breathing-place for his children to inhabit. This would "countrify" the city, and that is what we desire. Mr. Downing, in a recent *Horticulturist*, proposes a plan for the more specific distribution of houses and streets, which combines much taste, neatness, and utility.

What is requisite for this? Land, — and, primarily, this is all. Our cities need not be less populous, but only more dispersed. And have we not land enough? Look at our towns everywhere that are growing into cities, bunching together their houses, pinching their streets, stuffing skinny apartments with men, women and children, as Bologna-meat; mowing away, as in a hay-barn, family upon family; digging cellars where the poor must hutch and burrow; cutting down trees, stifling the green-sward, — and have they not land enough? The fault is not wholly or primarily with real estate owners. It lies in the people generally. Every man is over-anxious to be near his business; so, in advertisements of rents, "within five minutes' walk" of Wall-street, or State-street, or the rail-road station, has become a leading recommendation. Our merchants and mechanics will not reside more than "five minutes" from their business; and in this circle of "five minutes," as a Maelstrom, they draw their homes, their wives and children, their peace and purity, — and within it, or very near it, must live the Minister and the Doctor, the drayman and the porter, the baker and the washerwoman. This is Socialism with a witness.

Our wishes in this matter are not unreasonable or singular. "The numerous instances," says Dr. Emerson, of Philadelphia, "wherein the mercenary character of individuals has tempted them to put up nests of contracted tenements in courts and alleys, admitting but little air, and yet subject to the full influence of heat, has often induced us to wish there could be some public regulation whereby the evil could be checked." "Some provision of law should be made," say the Health Commissioners of Boston, "by which the number of tenants should be apportioned to the size and general arrangements of a house."

"The number of cellars," they add, "used as dwelling-houses, is 586, and each occupied by from five to fifteen souls." There should be statute law against such things.

Very forcibly do this Committee remind us that "the whole subject of streets, and ways, in respect to width, ventilation, grade, and drainage, is one of very great and increasing importance." [See Report of the Cholera in Boston, in 1849.]

To our towns and villages as they are, — pretty, thriving, hopeful, — let us say a word. Preserve, so far as possible, the old homesteads; do not abandon fruitful gardens, and venerable trees, and time-honored abodes, to shops and tenements. There is land enough. Keep the burial-places intact; embellish them, — beautify that sanctuary. Do not allow petty speculators in lands to lay out your ways and define your lots for you.* If strangers are coming to reside amongst you, encourage them to settle a little further back, where it will be for your interest to open new streets and offer convenient grounds. All around you are millions of forest trees, the most beautiful God has made; — the elm, unequalled for its majesty; the pine, so glorious in winter, so musical and balmy in summer; the maple, sweet, clean, thrifty; the white birch, that lady of the woods; the fir, whose dense foliage and spiral uniformity mingle so well with the luxuriant freedom of the others; the walnut, with its deep green and glossy umbrage. There are tupelos, hornbeams, beeches, larches, cedars, spruces, all waiting to be transplanted to your villages, yearning to expand in your streets, and throw their refreshment and their loveliness over your grounds and houses, over your old men and children, your young men and maidens.

We do not say that Openness or trees will save the city or the town; we do say that with such things, those ren-

* All the miserable localities in Boston "are mainly owing to the fact of their having been originally laid out by private speculators." — *Report of the Cholera in Boston*, 1849.

dezvous and nests of sin and shame, filth and wretchedness, — those pests of every sense, which torture sympathy and exhaust munificence, which tax our religion and morality, our learning and wisdom, to provide some mitigation of, — will be rendered impossible.

Says the author of that admirable book, The Studies of Nature, "I love Paris. Next to the country, and a country to my fancy, I prefer Paris to every place I have seen in the world. I love that city for its happy situation; I love it because all the conveniences of life are assembled there, — because it is the centre of all the powers of the kingdom, and for the other reasons which gained it the attachment of Michael Montaigne." In like manner, and for the same cause, as a New Englander, I say, I love Boston; and, as an American, I love New York. Yet I cannot go to the extent of the good man before me, who adds, "I should wish there were not another city in France, — that our provinces were covered only with hamlets and villages." I could wish there might be many cities in New England, and in America — each, in its way, beautiful for situation, and the glory of the earth around it.

CHAPTER XXX.

RICHARD AT THE GOVERNOR'S ONCE MORE.

MONTHS wore away, and Richard was not idle. Green Mill prospered; "Knuckle Lane" steadily advanced; the "Friends of Improvement" were able to effect some wholesome regulations; the majority of the workmen at the Saw-mills devoted spare hours to the Griped Hand, and a better tone of feeling and manner prevailed amongst them; the parlor at Willow Croft was open, and Richard had much delight in it with the children and his friends. His Father and Mother had been to see him, and he, with Roxy, and Memmy and Bebby, and Munk & St. John's best carriage, made a journey to the paternal home.

Richard was happy,—at least, as much so as is ordinarily the lot of mortals. He was invited to a party at the Mayor's, to another at Nefon's, and to one at Judge Burp's; and these were things of which his sister made account.

He called at the Governor's,—he was quite often there; and, in fact, Roxy, and Memmy, too, began to suspect he was specially attracted there. Memmy used to say, "I know Uncle Richard wants to see Miss Melicent." It was obvious, on the other side, that his presence in St. Agnes-street was allowed by the Family, and agreeable to Melicent. So marked was the cordiality of these two persons, it became rumored, in certain quarters, they were engaged. The Family authorized no such declaration,—neither did Richard. "If Melicent has her heart set on Mr. Edney, I think she had better have him," observed Mrs. Melbourne.

Madam never committed herself. She said, still intent cutting out her pieces, "Yes, indeed; but young folks change their minds." "I should never change my mind," added Cousin Rowena. "Are you young?" asked Madam, with a start. Cousin tried to laugh. "But how am I to regard him?" inquired Eunice, — "as a suitor of Melicent's, or only a friend of the family?" "You will not regard him at all," replied her mother. "You will only behave properly towards him." "I think," continued Mrs. Melbourne, "Melicent ought to know something." "She does know something, and will have to know more all her life," answered Madam. "Keep a learning, — go on to wisdom; she need not be in haste to do it up at once; we must summer and winter our knowledge before we really know anything."

This was about the sum of what a bystander could collect of the feelings of that domestic circle. Not but that Miss Rowena had her asides, and pleasant innuendoes; and Alice Weymouth would not only laugh outright, but even relapse into great soberness, when she thought of it all. The Governor in no wise interfered, leaving such matters to the sense and choice of his children.

I know not that Richard asked any questions, or received any answers. He was happy with Melicent; happy to work with her in "Knuckle Lane," — to walk with her in Mayflower Glen, — to sit with her under the vines of the piazza. Into the full circle of his being she seemed to flow, and melt, and be as one with him; into his adoration of the Supreme, into his studies of philanthropy, into his estimation of man, and all his conscience of duty, she came. St. Cuthbert built the windows of his hovel so high he could not see the earth therefrom, and could only look out upon the heavens, which became his sole object of contemplation. Such was not the love of Richard and Melicent; it did not look into the heavens, or the ideal and dreamy alone. It looked upon the world at their feet, at men and things about them, and life as it is.

But lowly as Richard's feelings were, plain and simple as were his delights, he was still a conspicuous mark for the shafts of adversity. However, in his love of Melicent, he may have had no other consciousness than that of the lily-of-the-valley, there lurked an envious blast that would reach and rend him. His relation to the Governor's Family must of necessity become a topic of remark, — not to say an occasion of surprise, — to many. Roxy, of course, as the matter began to come into shape before her eyes, was overjoyed; Mysie, who knew everybody, said, "I'm glad, — she is one of the best critturs in the world." Mangil said, "She 's never hard up." Miss Eyre must say something, and do something. All that she said and did we cannot relate.

But Richard ere long became sensible of her attempt at something; and first, quite negatively, quite silently. She did not bow as he passed her in the street. That was nothing, — it might have been an accident. Soon he met her face to face. She did not look at him; she averted her eye, and slighted his salutation. That was positive, and palpable. She came no more to Willow Croft; — that meant something. He encountered her again at a party at Tunny's. Her face was dark with apparent rage or contempt. She flung herself from the side of the room where he stood, as if he were the jaws of a crocodile. This was awful, — it was dagger-like, — to Richard.

Here was food for speculation. Richard reflected that he had been friendly, and even indulgent, towards her, — that she had been free and easy with him. She had even sometimes rallied him on going to the Governor's so much. There was an outer door, a little porch-way of his feelings, where he and Miss Eyre could entertain each other, sit and chat; but into the inner chamber of his nature she could not come, and he supposed she knew she could not. Alas! here he was greatly mistaken. He had got out of the mist she once raised about him, and could see things very clearly, and, as he thought, see her very clearly; — here, too, he was mistaken. He had always been glad to meet her. She was vivacious, witty, pungent; and she seemed glad to meet him. Now, this change, — what did it purport? So sudden, too, so unpremised, — what had happened? She was absent from the city when the rumor of his engagement with Melicent transpired. After her return, he noticed the alteration in her manner. It must have something to do with that.

But what with that? — what with anything? He would find out, — he would speak with her. No, — she would not be spoken with; — she avoided him, — she went by on the other side, — she was deaf when he addressed her.

Did he communicate this annoyance to Melicent? He did not. He thought he would; — he was on the verge of opening the subject one evening, when Chassford and Glendar entered the room. This put his purpose to flight. Why pursue it? Miss Eyre, and Miss Eyre's coolness, were no part of him and Melicent; it was a mere fleck in the sky that was full of brightness and repose to him; a fleck, too, at his back, in some other direction than that towards which he was looking. It *was* an irritation, and for that reason he would avoid it, where all was quietness and joy. He scraped it off as he entered the door of the pleasant mansion, as so much mud on the sole of his boot. Was he not confidential with Melicent? Exceedingly so. But this was a transient, temporary grievance, personal to himself, that he need not trouble her with, — that he would soon surmount or forget. When one is introduced to the great and the good, he instinctively leaves behind his meanness and his littleness; and in the movement of the affections, what is hopeful, interesting, fair, clusters together, as in winter we gather about a bright fire, and forget how many cold and dreary rooms there are in the house.

Chassford and Glendar were an embarrassment to Richard; they embarrassed him by their looks, but more by their conduct. In the same room with him, they disturbed what we might call his physical equilibrium; in other rooms, and other places, they disturbed his moral equanimity. Could he shake them off? Could he disarm their insolence? Could he expel the consciousness of their dissipation? They were kind of suitors general of the Governor's Family, and suitors particular of Melicent and Barbara. Glendar was a fourth nephew and protégé of Mrs. Melbourne. His parents resided in a distant city, and he came to Woodylin to expatiate. Mrs. Melbourne saw no faults in her favorites. There was a certain blind passionateness in this woman's affection. She was, as some thought, the wilful supporter and prejudiced advocate of those she liked. She saw no reason why Glendar should not marry into the Family. If Melicent was preöccupied, he might attach himself to Barbara. But Chassford monopolized Barbara. Certainly, then, Melicent ought to know, to make up her mind, and have the thing settled in the house, whether she would have Richard or not. However, these were points discussed rather in her own mind, and just exposed edgewise in the presence of the senior females, and not produced before the girls themselves.

Chassford had a fine education, and fine abilities. He led his class at College, — his professional promise was great. But he was ruining himself by profligacy. And it so happened, Richard knew more of this than anybody. The shining talents of the young man, his boyhood fairness, his visible industry, all the hopes and expectations that had been garnered in him by doting parents and partial friends, concealed the defects of his character. With Barbara, he could be, and really was, musical, poetical, ideal, romantic, profound, spiritual.

Richard found he had eggs to walk on, and a plenty of them, and some not very sound ones, in the matter of these young men. Nor was he sure that duty required, or expediency would justify, any suggestions whatever as to what he might know or think of them. The Governor's Family, withal, was, to some extent, *terra incognita* to him; it had its own customs, preferences, and reasons, — its own connections and law of life, — and Richard might naturally presume it would take care of itself, and must be indeed its own keeper. Then it was a juncture of that extreme and finished delicacy, for which he was not adequate, either in tact or experience.

Lovers are oblivious; and when Richard was alone with Melicent, Miss Eyre, Chassford and Glendar, were like a dream of the night, which we never think of in the daytime.

But he could not always be alone with Melicent. One day he found himself at the Governor's alone with Mrs. Melbourne. Melicent and Barbara had gone on a journey with their Father and Mother.

"If you like our Melicent, why do you not propose?" Mrs. Melbourne said this not reproachfully, — not with any dislike to Richard, but simply for his sake, and to fetch things to a focus.

"The Governor and Madam Dennington both sanction our intimacy, I believe," replied he.

"Glendar wants her, if you don't have her," added the lady.

Daggers again! What could the woman think? Was love like a berth in a steamboat, and were lovers to say quick which they would have? Had Mrs. Melbourne forgotten that she was once young, and had the tender passion? Not exactly this; she deemed either of the young men an eligible match for the young lady, — or, if her judgment consented to Richard, her affection supported Glendar. She did venture upon liberties with Richard, which she would not have taken with some others, accounting possibly the hardness of his early education and habits a sufficient foil for her own boldness. She was kind-hearted in what she said, and would have Richard know, if he did not take the prize, he was only standing in the way of one eager to grasp it.

Yet it was not so much Richard's sensibilities that were startled, as his recollections; — it was that Glendar should be named, — the Glendar whom he had seen in so many unfavorable lights, and withal in so deep shadows, — and his thought of whom was as wide from Melicent as the realm of outer darkness.

He was moved to speak, and vent his mind. So he told Mrs. Melbourne that, not a month before, he saw Glendar drunk in a rookery, — that it was not possible for Melicent to love him.

Mrs. Melbourne was horrified, — too much so to be calm, or reasonable. She even went so far as to be more indignant at the teller than the story; — she flouted the idea; she would not believe such a thing; and, turning upon Richard, she charged the story to his jealousy.

Richard left the house.

A few days afterwards, as he was sitting on the door-steps at Willow Croft, the Governor's servant appeared at the gate, and handed him a note, which ran as follows: —

"Mr. Edney is requested to discontinue his visits at the Governor's. Depravity of heart, foulness of intention, and viciousness of life, cannot always be concealed. If he wishes for information, he can inquire of Miss Plumy Alicia Eyre. In the absence of the Governor and his family, the undersigned, retaining sole charge of the house, deems it her duty to protect its purity and defend its honor; and she would leave Mr. Edney no possible room to doubt that an authority assumed by weak and feeble hands will be supported by others stronger than herself, and as strong as anybody. CLARISSA MELBOURNE."

If one of those forty-feet logs, that thrash about in such hair-brained fashion, at the foot of the Dam, in a freshet, had struck Richard across the breast, it could not have affected him more sensibly in that region than did this note.

CHAPTER XXXI.

THE UNDERTOW.

Miss Plumy Alicia Eyre came to Woodylin young, destitute, and unknown. Her first service was in the Governor's Family, where she was little maid of all work, and particular little maid of Mrs. Melbourne. This lady always had a pet, — if not an animate, an inanimate thing; sometimes it was the asparagus-bed in the garden; now the horses in the barn; at one moment it was a poor widow in the neighborhood; again it was somebody arrested for murder, a thousand miles off. In the present instance, it chanced to be Plumy Alicia. Neglect in any shape fired her compassion, and Plumy Alicia was neglected; her feet were neglected, and her head, — she had no shoes, no bonnet, and a scant wardrobe. Here was a fine theatre for Mrs. Melbourne's piety and benevolence, and she improved it. She taught the child to read and to sew, and gave her books and bright clothes. She put the little maid under great obligation; but the little maid did not like the load. She was froward, vain, ambitious, or what it may be, and wanted higher wages and a higher post; and she left the Governor's. She exchanged Mrs. Melbourne's fine chamber for Mrs. Tunny's dark kitchen; but she got better pay, a more independent way of life, and a nearer view of the world at large, — or a view of Mrs. Tunny's view. Whatever aristocratic aspirations the Green Grocer's lady may have cultivated, she was free with her domestics, — very free with such as had lived in good families; and Plumy Alicia had lived at the

Governor's; and Mrs. Tunny seemed to feel that her house, or rather her means of making a house, went up a number of degrees in the acquisition of such a servant. Miss Eyre left Mrs. Tunny for the Factories and Whichcomb's, where this Tale found her.

Cessation of intercourse was not the only method by which Miss Eyre chose to signify her sentiments towards Richard; she matured a story that vitally touched his reputation. With this she went to the Governor's, and sought an interview with her old mistress. These two had kept up the remembrance of each other, and Mrs. Melbourne ever offered to her former servant and pet the assurance of a perpetual consideration. Miss Eyre looked pensive and sad; — she was really distressed; she was apparently outraged. There was truth with a coloring of falsehood, and falsehood with a coloring of truth, in all she said. Richard had been attentive to her, confidential with her, and often alone with her. These were things not to be questioned. "He won my heart," said Miss Eyre; — that might be. "I had no other friend but him;" — of the same sort. "He knew that I sacrificed many others for him;" — that might admit of question. Mrs. Melbourne could see no question in it. "I surrendered at discretion;" — true. Here she shed tears; — mixed. "Is he so black-hearted?" flared Mrs. Melbourne. "Heartless!" sobbed Miss Eyre. "Black-hearted!" continued Mrs. Melbourne. "He unites the vulgarity of the lower classes with the insolence of the higher. He is reckless from instinct, and designing from position. He is; he must be. That is it! I understand him now. I see through him. How blinded I have been! What creatures we are, when God leaves us to ourselves! How can I thank you for opening my eyes, and all our eyes, before it was too late?"

The result of this interview appeared in the note, a copy of which has been furnished for the perusal of the reader. The original remained in Richard's hand, and brain, and agony.

CHAPTER XXXII.

THE "BOIL."

He went to his chamber, fell upon his bed, and buried his face in the pillow; as if his pillow could help him, or cared for him, or could soothe the sensations that racked his thought. "Inquire of Miss Plumy Alicia Eyre." Yes, Plumy Alicia, you had done it; you were at the bottom of this; you thrust that iron into his soul! Richard knew Miss Eyre was rash, fickle, schemy, and fond of adventure; he did not believe her so infamous, so utterly abominable, so abandoned. What should he think now? What *do?*

When he came down to breakfast, the next morning, he looked pale, and had small appetite. He drank half a cup of coffee, nibbled at a slice of bread, and refused a piece of Indian cake Roxy had baked on purpose for him. His sister took alarm. "Are you sick, Richard?" "Not much," he answered. "Have some cracker toast, and sage tea?" No. "A good cold-water bath, with hard rubbing, is the thing," said Munk, who was a real hydriatic in his way. "If Uncle Richard is sick," said Memmy, "Plumy will come, and Miss Melicent will come too; and we shall have such nice times, with quince sauce, and lots of candy!" "Tanny, tanny!" shouted Bebby. "Pumy bing tanny!" and she wriggled for joy in her high chair, and displaced her bib and pulled her dish of bread and milk into her lap. "Dear me!" cried Roxy; "what trouble is in candy! I have sometimes wished I could never see the sight of those ladies. Bebby is all the whole continual time in mischief!" Richard availed himself of the slight breeze to make his escape. Roxy called after him, as he left the room: "You never will have anything done for you; and you will come back dead, the next we know!"

Richard felt, at the moment, there was more truth in her words than she always put into them.

He went to the Mill, and assumed his customary duties. But it was hard to carry them through. There was slipperiness in his hold, and dizziness in his calculations. He was like a man who undertakes to raise a barrel of flour in a fit of laughter. "Sick," muttered Mr. Gouch, "sick; and sick is foolish to be here. Go to bed, — be sick."

That afternoon Richard went to bed, on a cup of sage tea, and slept soundly; he slept none the night before.

He made no blunders at tea, but drank two strong cups of oolong, disposed of a large biscuit, and honored some new cake, for which Roxy had obtained the receipt of Mrs. Mellow.

In the evening he went to Whichcomb's, to see Miss Eyre. "Plumy Alicia may be in to some folk," replied the landlady to his inquiry at the door. "Is she in to you?" "She is," replied Richard, emphatically, endeavoring to smooth the way through the difficulty of his feeling by pleasantry of speech. "Not as you knows of," answered Mrs. Whichcomb. "Plumy Alicia said, says she, I am not at home, says she." "Is she at home to me?" asked Richard. "Can I find her?" He began to push by the doorkeeper. "Ah! Charley Walter, said I;" so the woman went on. "'No such a thing,' said he. They made the awfulest piece of work of it that ever was. Velzora Ann had on her spick and span new silk."

"I must see Miss Eyre!" cried Richard.

"Would you impose on the Ladies' Parlor, which Cain

hasn't, and Miss Elbertina Lucetta, Miss Allura, Miss Elzena, that was an orphan, and always slept four in a bed, till she found Whichcomb's, and nothing relishing —" "Are they all there?" urged the agonized caller. He enforced his way to the room which on the door was labelled "Ladies' Parlor." Several girls fled as he entered, among whom was not Miss Eyre. He did not wait long, however, before the object of his quest came in sight. With right thumb and finger she raised a fold of her muslin dress, trimmed her face three points to the left, and crushed herself forward in the direction of the floor, like a ship pitching, and, rising, sailed away to a chair at some distance from her caller. "What is the meaning of this?" asked Richard, or rather a voice from within Richard, that came up, groping and trembling, all the way, through the thickness and huskiness of his feelings. "Mr. Edney, having precipitated himself through a reserve which has been so long maintained, and with such obvious propriety imposed, cannot be too much out of breath to relate the nature of his errand," replied Miss Eyre, hammering the arm of the chair with her fan.

"Why have you so long avoided me, and why, at last, have you approached me only to wound me, — approached my happiness only to destroy it forever?"

"I shall not sit here to be accused," replied Miss Eyre. "I shall claim the protection of the house."

"The house," rejoined Richard, "and all its walls, and all its inmates, may tumble down upon us; — you must hear what I have to say."

Miss Eyre paced the room loftily, as if she were in a pair of buskins.

She turned and said, "Is your happiness my happiness, Mr. Edney?"

Richard stammered in reply.

"The question embarrasses you, I see; you need not answer it."

"I am at a loss to know why your happiness should aim so fatally at my wretchedness."

"O, you are unhappy! I am sorry for you."

"Have done with this, and tell me what has instigated you to poison the ear of Mrs. Melbourne against me!"

"Dare you charge that meanness upon me?"

"You know what you have done!"

"I told Mrs. Melbourne you had shown an affection for me."

"Was that all?"

"All you did?"

"All you told her?"

"Will you say it is false?"

"That I had a love-affection for you, — that I was earnestly interested in you?"

"Eh! earnestly, earnestly! Superficially? Partly, fancifully? I see! I see!"

"Why, at this hour, and in this place, and under these circumstances, can you harrow me so? Read that!" He gave her Mrs. Melbourne's note.

She read it, and said, "Do not feel so bad about that. Aunt Melbourne is a little notional."

"If any other than a bad feeling is proper to the case, I would dismiss a bad feeling; but I cannot dislodge the conviction that you have acted very ungratefully."

"Do you love me, Richard?"

"You bade me never say that I loved you."

"But do you?"

"How can I answer you?"

"You can say that you do not. It will be some pleasure for me to hear the word 'love' on your lips, — to see it pass them; even if it went reluctantly and slowly, — as if it was a sweet spot to go through, — as if it loved to linger among the impediments of feeling, — as if it loved to hear its own sound. Say 'do not' love; say 'do' love; — naughty little 'love,' that hides behind the 'not;' — yet it is 'love,' — and 'love,' or 'not love,' is the same. 'Not love' is love with a handle."

"I detest you!" Richard said this in a passion, quite wrought up. Miss Eyre coolly replied, "We are even, — let us part."

"Not until I know how you have implicated me with Mrs. Melbourne!"

"You did not once kiss me? You cannot say that. You have not that to think of. How you blush! Color fades from your lips into your cheeks! — Well, well; nothing should inhabit those lips but kisses; — all the girls say so. You are biting your lips to bring the blood back!"

The wretch! Spurn her, — crush her! Insane wickedness, intolerable absurdity! the reader is ready to exclaim; and so, perhaps, was Richard. What business has she here? Yet is not all villany absurd, unnatural? Could we get at the springs of misconduct, in any case, should we not be surprised?

The truth is, Miss Eyre had formed a strong and despotic attachment for Richard. She had been resolved to possess him. Her long silence and reserve was a mode of ascertaining his inclinations. She heard of his engagement with Melicent, and knew how often he was at the Governor's. Her communication to Mrs. Melbourne had a first object, to discover the nature of his connection with Melicent; and, secondly, to dissolve it, and free him for herself; and finally, if foiled herein, to be avenged upon him. At this meeting at Whichcomb's, she maintained, with cardinal steadiness, a single point,—the development of the actual state and movement of his mind and heart.

To be avenged upon him, in the last resort, we say. How could that be, if she loved him? ask our gentle, true-hearted readers. We might refer them to sacred writ, and Potiphar's wife. Joseph could not be more astonished at the order for his arrest, than was Richard at the conduct of Miss Eyre. We run no parallel between these two ladies, further than to the point of love and vengeance. We have never said Miss Eyre was ill-intentioned;—she was ill-regulated. The wrong she did Richard was rather the wantonness of passion than the deliberation of insult. As is said, the rare and costly manuscripts used in forming the Complutensian Polyglott were used for rockets, so it seemed sometimes as if she tossed up the sacred and precious feelings of Richard's heart merely for the pleasure of seeing them explode; yet it is evident in this pastime her own deepest sentiments were involved also. She scattered firebrands without seeming to think how hot they were. She followed her ends with great clearness of heart, but with utter blindness of eye; or, rather, with a distinct aim, but confused method. She was more capricious in appearance than in purpose. But she would sport with her victim, before she put him to death. Richard seemed to feel that his death was foreshadowed, while, at the same moment, Miss Eyre was loth to administer the final stroke.

"Tell me what you have done!" Richard said this so sternly and coldly, with look so sullen and menacing, and tone so hard and inexorable, that Miss Eyre must have seen the folly of dalliance.

She replied, "I will not tell you what I have done;—I will tell you what I will do and be. I hate you; yet not vitally, but as death hates, — as a bruised and broken heart hates, — as a woman that can feel hates! — "

"Spare me this!" cried Richard, smiting his hand upon his brow. "Anything but such a thing! any torture you may inflict, but such a torture! Do not strew my path with the mutilated fragments of a heart! do not doom my vision to the sight of sensibility in ruins! Kill *me* in some other way! — "

Miss Eyre leaned her head upon the arm of her chair, and was heard to sob.

"Dear Plumy Alicia!" said Richard, approaching and attempting to take her hand. She waved him off. "Go," said she; "your work is done, and mine is done!"

Richard took himself heavily from the house.

CHAPTER XXXIII.

DRAWN UNDER.

Miss Eyre was an enigma; to Richard, certainly, and to many who may be inclined to bestow a thought upon her. She was of the somewhat numerous family of Eyres, — of an obscure branch, indeed. When she was quite young, she demonstrated the superiority of her sex by romping with the boys. As if she had early imbibed exalted notions of womanhood, she once undertook to break a colt. But she had no Family, no Church, no School. Her tendencies, whether good or evil, were unsoothed by affection, unmoulded by religion, unrefined by culture. Her manner in the present instance was contradictory, and her intention uncertain. She deigned no explanation herself, and we might be balked to attempt one for her.

In five minutes after Richard left, the girls dashed into the room; and she was jocose, talkative as ever, and rattled away with the merriest of them, — all traces of concern having vanished, and her look as bright as if she had just washed in a sunbeam.

Richard did not recover so easily, — indeed his power of elasticity seemed for the moment destroyed. To rise from the blow he had received, was an attainment in his own estimation impossible. He was naturally of heavier mould than Miss Eyre; — such, at least, would be a reasonable deduction from the facts of the case.

He did not mention what had befallen to his sister, or to any one. He bore the burden alone.

Alone? Richard was, or professed to be, a Christian; and, like his Master, he might still have the Father with him.

He disburthened his heart to God; — he poured the anguish of his spirit into the ear of Heaven. Like a captive, he lifted his galled hands, and implored Divine mercy and love to strike off the chains. He listened to the starry night, that some voice from dimmest ethereal space might speak to his troubled soul, saying, Peace, be still!

Had he sinned? This thought shot like a lightning gleam through his brain. His conduct, as in a mirage, rose in sudden, pictorial, prolonged prospective to his view. Many things wore a sinful aspect. An affrighted imagination would readily detect many sinful spots. He cried out, with tenderest contrition, "God be merciful to me a sinner!"

But the worst was yet to come, if there could be any worse, where the desolation was so entire.

He did not go near the Governor's again. He could have no further communications with Mrs. Melbourne. His heart failed him at the thought of seeing her. Melicent was absent. What on her return? He did not write her. A letter he had from her remained in his desk, unopened.

What would the Governor say, and Madam, and Barbara, or Chassford, or Glendar, or ——; but why go over the series of interested persons, or conjure among possible events the recollection of any one of which pierced him so vitally?

Not many days afterwards, Melicent returned. The Governor's consequence in town rendered his movements matter of public rumor, and in this way Richard ascertained what by direct inquiry he might not have put himself upon finding out. He realized what was before him, and waited the progress of events, and the course of the hours, silently and awfully, as Alcestis did the unfoldings of Fate.

It came, — came like a thunderbolt which one expects; bowed, tense, hot, and almost shrinking, in the suffocating silence, and dismal darkness, he hardly dare open his eyes, lest he should see himself struck. The house shook, and his sight reeled, and he knew it had come. It came in the shape of a note from Mrs. Melbourne, covering one from Melicent.

Mrs. Melbourne flashed thus. "I will not accuse you, since your own conscience must have done that office for you. I shall pray for you, that God would lead you to repentance, and that you may be saved at last. It is unnecessary to remind you of the distress you have occasioned us, as I fear you are incapable of feeling it. The purpose of this present is answered when I inform you that your visits here are interdicted. Melicent, poor child, whose happiness you have so rudely and vulgarly assailed, will give the dismissal under her own hand."

If Melicent flashed, she rained, too; and her flash showed rather a confused state of the elements above, — rapid condensation of vapors, meeting of adverse winds, — than an attempt to injure anything below.

Her note had evidently commenced with "Dear Richard," and "Dear Sir" was the cover of a blot. And this little incident characterized the entire manuscript. She was in doubt what to write; — whether to regard Richard in the light of conscious rascality, or of scandalized innocence. If she thought that a tender word would be exposed to barbarous insolence, she more deeply feared that severe words would pierce to the quick a virtuous sorrow. So Richard passed before her imagination like the changing Spectre of the Brocken, — assuming a new phase of terror, or of beauty, according to the fluctuating mood of her own mind. She did say, "I shall delay, — not my decision, for I have none, but my feelings, — as to which I know not what to have. In my present course, I must be governed by others, who have always led me wisely and well, and to whom I have loved to render obedience. It is well that it is so, for at this moment I am incapable of directing my own steps. I thank you for your information respecting Glendar, since I persuade myself it was truthfully spoken and generously intended. I need not say that my instincts had presaged what your observation announced. I pray God to have mercy upon you, and upon me; — if you have done wrong, that you may sincerely repent, — if you have done right, that you may be vindicated; — if I am in the way of truth, that I may have strength to support the heavy blow, — if I am in error, that my eyes may be speedily opened. The excitement of our family is at present too considerable for deliberation, and too exacting for candor. I have but one alternative, — to listen and be silent, or to discuss and despair."

After all, "our family" must be construed as a figure of speech, or a natural trope of feeling, and, primarily, denoting Mrs. Melbourne. The Governor said nothing, though he looked a good deal. Madam vented her surprise and sorrow in a brief ejaculation, which she capped with a passage of Scripture. Barbara knew not what to say. Cousin Rowena became very serious. Mrs. Melbourne, as she preöccupied the ground, likewise preöccupied all judgments. She had seen Miss Eyre, and she knew what was what. She had the power of raising a breeze in the family, and obliging its members either to scud under bare poles, or to haul to. Then Glendar was sorely, and as she thought, honestly thought, wickedly involved. Then it was a grave and a dark matter. What could be done but acquiesce in Mrs. Melbourne's foregone conclusion, that Richard be interdicted the house. "But," added Madam, "to everything there is a time and a judgment."

Richard might have gone to the Governor's, and applied tongue and person to dissipate the gloom and perplexity that rumor and speculation threw over the subject. He might have cast his own consciousness at the feet of Melicent, and said, "That is my vindication!"

But he was unused to extremities, — he had had but little taste heretofore of what are called the trials of life. He had fortitude for distress, and boldness in danger. He lacked that rashness — sometimes a virtue — which loves a fiery peril, and possessed no dexterity adapted to the subtile and nice points of a dilemma.

More than this, — between Richard and the Governor's Family was a Brocken Spectre too, dilating in portentous dimension, and guarding the passage with audacious and shadowy arms. That was Miss Eyre, and Miss Eyre's assumed wrongs, and her real distress, and his own unexplainable complicity therewith. He could not banish her image, or dispossess himself of her impression and power. She had got into his imagination, and like a vessel in distress, she seemed to be stranded in his heart.

Now, furthermore, he must prepare himself for the afterclap. What had befallen must become public. Roxy must know it, and it would kill her; Munk must know it, and it would be a damper to his pleasant feelings; and Memmy and Bebby must know it, and they would be sorry. The "World" must know it; and how rejoiced it would be at this addition to its Cabinet of Entertaining Knowledge, — how wise it would become all at once, — how exceedingly endowed, — how sparkling and brilliant! Richard's valued friends would hear of it, — Mr. Gouch and Silver, Mangil and Nefon, Mysie and Chuk. The Church would have to consicer of it, and "Knuckle Lane!" What *would* Mrs. Tunny say? There was Clover to be elated, Miss Fiddledeeana Redfern to sneer, and Mrs. Mellow to deduce a solemn improvement. Aunt Grint had already been foretold it.

And Aunt Grint was the first to break it to Willow Croft. "What has happened?" she exclaimed, panting and staring; "my wrists ached Saturday, in the afternoon, and there must be a storm. I met Mrs. Tunny, and she was in the greatest state of mind. Mrs. Quiddy, who is hauled up with rheumatis, came out to ask me. Do be quiet, children! — pity sakes! what a noise! one can't hear one's self speak!"

"What *has* happened?" cried Roxy, amazed.

"I worked as tight as I could spring to come down. I had n't no more idea of it than nothing at all, if it had n't been for running out to hear a woodpecker; then I knew there was a rotten tree somewhere, — I knew it before Mr. Gouch passed the house."

"What is it?" emphasized Roxy.

"Don't you know," replied Aunt Grint, "that that Miss Dennington —"

"She is n't dead!" screamed Roxy.

"No, indeed!"

"Nor taken the cholera?"

"Only think!" Aunt Grint's loud and masculine voice sank to an unnatural susurration. "She has turned off Richard; the engagement is broke up. I might have seen it. The spider, — 't was when I was sewing with my basket on the table, and Sally a-sweeping the floor, — the crittur never come nigh, but kept edging round. I told Sally we should n't have a wedding gown —"

Roxy, meanwhile, let fall the bellows that she had been trying for five minutes to hang up; she suffered the milk to boil over on the coals; she did not prevent Bebby going to the sugar-bucket in the closet, — three things that she had not done or forborne to do, before, all her life. She attempted to listen; but her ear was clearer than her mind; — or, as is said of the telegraph wires, the auditory nerve was down somewhere. Sundry exclamations, however, indicated that she was alarmed, while her rushing to seize Bebby showed that, if her feelings could find vent somewhere, she might be calm and self-possessed. She quietly washed the child's hands, and sat down with her in the little rocking-chair. She asked Aunt Grint but one question, the reply to which removed the necessity of all further communications touching the credibility of the information she had characteristically but crookedly conveyed, and was still. She was very still, and calm, and motionless; so much so, the child looked into her face, as if something was the matter. She stroked the child's sunny locks.

Presently Richard came in. He perceived the condition of things. He was composed, but a little flushed; his lip quivered, and his voice was tremulous; — yet a smile shot up through his face, — a sort of Zodiacal Light, through which might be seen the gray infinitude of his sorrow, beneath which the sun of his hope had set, while in the still vault around burned the stars of pure feeling, like vestal lamps, that burned on only because it was in their destiny never to go out.

Roxy said nothing; she looked at Richard, and instantly her gaze was stricken to the floor. She rose, set the child deliberately on its feet, went to her brother, threw her arms about his neck, and they both wept.

Aunt Grint trotted her heel on the floor, drummed the window-sill with her finger, took the boiling milk from the coals, and went away.

It was a great sorrow to Roxy, and a real one. There was body to it. The petty annoyances, and transient disagreements, that ruffled so many of her hours, were drowned out by this profound woe; — or, to change the metaphor, as a heavy rain arrests the agitation of waves, and smooths the surface of the sea, this pouring event restored the uniformity of her spirits, and filled her with serene thoughtfulness. She seemed to comprehend the extent of the calamity of her brother, and, as by some inspiration, to take a sense of the mischief secretly working at the centre of it, and she rose to the height of the evil that so suddenly unfolded before her.

In sympathizing with her brother, Roxy lost much of her petulancy and caprice, and ingenuous concern for real suffering supplanted a morbid nettlesomeness to fancied evils.

Richard could but confirm to his sister what Aunt Grint had stated as to his separation from Melicent. He did not, however, feel at liberty to discuss all the causes that may have led to it; nor did he allude to the probable agency of Miss Eyre in the affair.

But Roxy, whose keenness of penetration exceeded Richard's wise reserve, said, in a knowing way, "Has Plumy Alicia anything to do with it?" Richard assented, by trying to be silent. "I will not press an answer," said Roxy. Now Richard nodded and added, "I do not wish to speak of that; I *cannot*." His sister replied, "I understand it; I think I do. I recall many things at this moment that have a bearing upon it. I will be silent as long as you wish me to be."

"You are not dead?" said Richard.

"How you talk!"

"I thought it would kill you."

"You banter me," answered Roxy. "I have been so

often at the point of death upon little things, this great thing may restore me to life."

This remark of Roxy's, generalized into a trait of character, is not without distinguished precedent. Great Henry of France "was less than a woman in a coach, and cried out whenever it appeared likely to overturn, and betrayed the utmost timidity. But in the field he was brave even to intrepidity, and accustomed to regard death in the ranks of war with the highest composure."

CHAPTER XXXIV.

FLOOD CONTINUES TO RISE.

RICHARD had now commiseration from his friends, in place of the congratulations that were still green in his memory. To be pitied is sometimes more disagreeable than to be blamed. The latter inspires rejoinder, while the former leaves us nothing to say. One befogs us in an uncomfortable stupidity; the other is like a bomb-shell in the midst of our activity, and arouses the impulse of flight. We extenuate our faults; we tremble at our misfortunes. We can remonstrate with malediction; we must submit to compassion.

The Mill-men expressed their pity chiefly in silence. When they were filing their saws, or squinting at the mark, or even bending over a cant-dog, they seemed to have one eye on Richard, — not tauntingly, not even vulgarly curious, — but with a sort of sympathy — with some genuine fellow-feeling; — for Richard was respected and beloved in the Mill. If they had only spoken, — if they had asked him something, — it would have been a relief. No: he was mistaken there. It would do him no good. He could not continue the conversation.

In the grating, rumbling, screeching, of the building at large, there was not much kindness indicated, but rather a sullen mockery.

Silver sat on a pile of boards, and clumsily beckoned Richard to his side. But Silver could n't speak; his tongue was always thick, and now it filled his mouth, — filled it even to the exclusion of his pipe, which he was obliged to withdraw. Taking out the pipe, like unplugging a hogshead of liquor, sometimes gives vent to words. It did not help Silver; he was still thick and ropy. He struck his iron bar tremendously on a log before him, and got up.

Mr. Gouch, pointing quickly to the Dam, said, "There!" and then, as he knocked up the bail-dog, he said, "There!" and every time he struck, he repeated, "There!"

The Dam, Richard could render. But driving in the bail-dog, — did that mean how the iron had gone into his soul? Perhaps it did.

Mrs. Tunny entered Willow Croft with a mingled air of disdain, triumph, and pity, over the whole of which was spread a very thin layer of magnanimity. But neither Roxy nor Richard was deceived or plagued by her.

Hitherto, Richard's fortune only was involved, while his character remained untouched. But in a few days, the more depressing intelligence reached his ears, that he was under reproach, that baseness of conduct was assigned as the cause of his dismissal, and that such a statement came authentically from the Governor's Family itself.

Well, here was blame, if that suited him any better. I think it did not. For now he would be expected either to affirm or deny; and he could do neither.

Now, not only the iron entered his soul, but it seemed to be rusting in, and gangrening everything in its neighborhood. It was like a return stroke of the lightning. His spirits, that had been bending like willows, appeared to be fairly draggled in the mire. He had now the world to encounter in its most dismal form, — that of contumely, sarcasm, and neglect. Frederick, at the siege of Brescia, when he could carry his point in no other way, exposed his prisoners on his battering-rams to the stones of the besieged, their friends. If Richard had one poor virtue in common with the rest of mankind, he hardly dare present it to what he conceived would be a general attack upon him. He would prefer to retire from the contest. The river-logs, with which his early years were familiar, in a freshet, are sometimes carried high up the bank, or floated into a contiguous flat, where the receding waters suffer them to mildew, doze and perish. Recent events, that had borne him a good distance from his proper source, and precipitated him down sundry cataracts, had at length landed him in a low thicket, where he was willing to die.

He lessened his visits to the Old Town. There was nothing pleasant there. One day he met Melicent. She stiffly bowed; but this was owing as much to hesitancy of feeling, as to purpose of will. Immediately afterwards, a man inquired if he could direct him to Munk & St. John's stable. He did not hear him, and replied, "No. 16 Victoria Square." Mrs. Melbourne passed him without a token of recognition. By this time, his heart had got pretty well into his mouth, and, like Silver's tongue, there would seem to be hardly anything else there; and he found it not easy to swallow again. It would get into his eyes, too, as big as a beam, and into his ears. We have said that Miss Eyre had got into his heart; of course, she accompanied that organ occasionally in its visits to the several senses. He met Glendar, and Glendar looked as if he could eat him; and Richard felt he should not be sorry if he did.

But Richard was a Christian, and the impulse of his life had been, doing good and being good. Nor could he now forget this original obligation. His closet, and the family altar he had helped to rear at Willow Croft, and his Bible, every day reminded him of it; — it caught his eye in large street-bill type on the wall of his chamber, where Pastor

Harold recommended his young parishioners to post it; Sundays, and the "Knuckle Lane" evenings, brought it round to him.

What should he do? He read that if he had offended his brother, before he offered his gift to the Lord, he must go and be reconciled to his brother. He had offended Mrs. Melbourne, and Miss Eyre, and perhaps Melicent. But how to be reconciled! He would endeavor to be reconciled in his own heart and before God, if he could not in outward relation and before his fellows. If reviled, he would revile not again, and abuse he would return with benisons. But the wall of offence seemed to grow thicker and higher.

In naval engagements, the Athenians were wont to reserve huge masses of lead in the tops of their vessels; and when they could subdue the enemy in no other way, they let fall these rather cogent junks, and sank his ship. There were some things in reserve for Richard.

Now, Madam Dennington had a feeling in common rather with her daughter than with her cousin-in-law. To be sure, if Richard was what had been represented, there could be no doubt as to the propriety of the course the Family adopted respecting him. But had the case been sufficiently investigated? Mrs. Melbourne conceded that the examination might be extended, though she anticipated no favorable result; nay, more, as if a new trial had been granted, she was willing to act in the premises, and collect and revise the evidence. She had had Mrs. Eyre closeted with her; and when, in her black silk and green parasol, she started on her tour of inquiry, who should be her cicerone but Miss Eyre?

The forenoon's work resulted in a sort of council or inquest, to be holden at Whichcomb's in the afternoon. Mrs. Melbourne sent a candid and polite note to Richard, informing him of what was a-foot, and inviting him to be present. He chose rather to appear by attorney, and Roxy went in his stead.

There were assembled at the Boarding House, — Front Stairs Carpeted, and that was not Cain's, — in the "Ladies' Parlor," the head of the establishment, Mrs. Melbourne, Miss Rowena, Mrs. Tunny, Mrs. Mellow, Mrs. Xyphers, Miss Eyre, Mrs. Crossmore, Nurse, Miss Elbertina Lucetta, Factory Girl, and Roxy.

Mrs. Whichcomb introduced the testimony. "It was a Wednesday," she said; "a Monday we did n't wash, which sometimes is, and the next day the things froze on the line. It was one of the coldest days that ever was; it was a heavy wash, as Cain's folk know, for it is right in sight of their basement, where they scour their pewter."

"Won't you tell," said Miss Eyre, "what he did in the house!"

"It was a Wednesday, for I had been up late ironing, and tending on the sick, and getting jellies, and carrying up wood, which is to be found at Whichcomb's, and is a most an excellent place to board at, as all the girls say, and nigh upon twelve o'clock, when he came in and went right up to No. 3. O Charley Walter! where is he now? My bones were aching in bed when I heard it; and he staid with them all night; for Miss Junia, and Violet that 's dead and gone, would n't dare to deny it. If Velzora Ann had only a thought; for Miss Elbertina Lucetta was just as sure to tell of it as the world; and there was n't a grain of need of his going in there."

"What did he go there for?" asked Roxy.

"I won't say it was for the silver spoon; I scorn to make such a charge, if folks was sick, and he was mean enough to do it, for they have what they please at Whichcomb's, and the things are always on the table. He knows what he was there for, and what never happened here before, as Charley Walter said; and he owned the next morning, and our reputation was good, and if they wanted to see them, they could always do it in the Ladies' Parlor, Miss Elzena knows, and the new comers know it the first day."

"He must have been there with an evil intention," said Mrs. Melbourne. Mrs. Tunny winked; Mrs. Mellow sighed a response.

"Rowena, what do you say?" Mrs. Melbourne put this question.

"I do not know as I can say but it looks bad," Miss Rowena replied, with a most uncomfortable attempt at evasion.

"It does so!" ejaculated Mrs. Whichcomb.

"It is impossible!" exclaimed Roxy.

Now, Roxy was unfortunately situated. Ostensibly the advocate of the accused, she really, by imputation, occupied the dock in his place; or she appeared an interested and most partial witness, and her word was worth just as much as the prisoner's would be in room of it, and no more.

Where was the Old Man? He was an imbecile. Where was Junia? Miss Eyre was willing Junia should be called; and added, with an air of confidence that silenced all expectation from this quarter, she hoped they would send for her. She had heard, indeed, that she had gone to parts unknown; but they might write.

"Did not Captain Creamer order Richard to stay by the old man?" asked Roxy.

At this question and moment, a new champion of Richard appeared, in Miss Freeling, the Dressmaker. She was at work at Tunny's when Mrs. Melbourne called in the morning. At some sacrifice of wages, and greater of Mrs. Tunny's pleasure, she resolved to attend the examination, and came in just as Roxy propounded the aforesaid question. She declared Captain Creamer ought to be sent for, and his testimony heard. Mrs. Melbourne saw the reasonableness of this. Word was accordingly despatched to the old employer of the arraigned; but he replied he would have nothing to do with the fellow, and that nothing was too bad for him, or after that sort: and this answer, while it palsied Roxy, and horrified Miss Freeling, was what the rest expected, as it entirely satisfied Mrs. Melbourne.

Moreover, by well-directed cross-questioning, Miss Eyre drew from Roxy that Richard seemed very attentive to Junia; that he obtained board for her at Willow Croft, and, finally, that he went with her into the country.

So matters went on. Mrs. Tunny corroborated Miss Eyre as to Richard's being some time alone with her, on the back stairs, at a party at her house. What was herein insinuated brought Miss Freeling to her feet. She was at the same party, and had a long conversation with Richard; she knew him better; he was a noble, high-minded man. But Miss Freeling was like a stray grasshopper in a brood of turkeys, each ready to devour her.

There was more than one mass of lead. Mrs. Crossmore, disappointed Nurse, resident in Knuckle Lane, had seen Richard in unseemly places, at unseemly hours.

Mrs. Xyphers, unfortunate woman, divorced from her husband, fooled by Clover, now a crony, now an enemy of Miss Eyre, — broken in spirit, confused in judgment, distrustful of everybody, — was induced to say, what she believed to be true, that she had no doubt Richard was base and unprincipled.

Miss Elbertina Lucetta attempted no more than the confirmation of Mrs. Whichcomb's story, that Richard was at the house, suspiciously, one winter night. She occupied the next chamber, and was awake with the tooth-ache.

Mrs. Mellow, Tract-distributor, had been in all parts of the city; she had tried the public pulse on the Knuckle Lane movement, raked for opposition to it, and collected whatever gossiping items might work against it, or its originators; and she was able to recount some things that reflected, not positively, she said, but presumptively, on Richard. But, from a little personal acquaintance, she knew him to be self-willed, bold, froward, and an instructor of evil things; and she was ready to believe anything of him. Especially, she said, "that a common laborer should seek to intermarry in our best families; that one should stride from the Saw-mill to the Governor's house; that, after rolling logs and handling lumber all day, he should expect to dispose of his fatigue in the evening on damask lounges, and wear off his coarseness under silken curtains, — indicated an effrontery as dangerous as it was detestable."

Why pursue details, when the result announces itself? Miss Freeling, with all her eloquence and good sense, could not arrest judgment. Mrs. Melbourne, who had not only the summing up, but the decision, of the case, said she was satisfied; though the full extent of her satisfaction she kept for other and more private ears.

Miss Rowena remained a silent spectator of proceedings. She was not inclined to side with Mrs. Melbourne, but she saw no loop-hole of extrication for Richard. At the close of the meeting, she drew a long breath of mingled surprise and disappointment, anguish and sorrow, and went home.

This may seem a tempest in a tea-pot to some; but it was a very large tea-pot, and one that held water enough to scald a good deal of happiness. If considerable events sprung from small causes, the instance is not unparalleled.

A silver medal involved the Dutch in a long conflict with Louis XIV. The true motive of the affair under review may not have been apprehended by the majority of those concerned in it; so Mr. Alison says the real object of a war is never understood by the people, who are expected to fight its battles, and not trouble themselves as to its meaning.

Mrs. Melbourne looked only on one side of a subject, and when that happened to be a dark side, she looked a long while, — so long, in fact, she saw nothing else. Where, in all this matter, were Richard's obvious excellences? where his piety, his benevolence, his heroism? where his straightforward consistency, and his transparent probity of character? She saw nothing of these. This was her position: she attributed the virtues of Richard to ambition, and his vices to intention. A feeling lurked in her heart, withal, which Mrs. Mellow more broadly hinted, that one of Richard's birth, connections, and calling, was ill-adapted for an inmate in the Governor's Family. More than this, but in connection with it, the different classes of society in the city did not understand each other. Between what Miss Freeling called the Pickle-eaters and the Gum-chewers, there were strange mistakes. The Cashmere shawls mistrusted what might lie under a Scotch plaid. In plain terms, the Governor's Family did not perfectly understand Richard; certainly the Mrs. Melbournism of the Family did not.

It will be remembered, moreover, that the evidence elicited at Whichcomb's was not primary, but secondary; not essential, but tributary; and, coming as it did on the heel of Miss Eyre's more private communications, and in the way of incidental circumstance, which some are so profound as to tell us never lies, and confirming in all points what had been directly asserted, it led to an overwhelming verdict against Richard.

Roxy reported proceedings at Willow Croft; but Richard, as if he had foreseen the course of things, manifested no alarm. He had been so diligently racked, an additional turn of the screw could not aggravate his distress. If he had any lingering hopes of a favorable turn of affairs, or plausible scheme for recovering the ground he had lost, these were finally blasted. The little radicles of a tree adhere tenaciously to the bank in which they have been nourished, after the rising flood has mastered the branches and trunk, and even undermined the main body of the root itself; so the tenderness of nature cleaves to objects in which it has had delight, when all energy and resolution have given out; but this fond hold of sentiment and feeling in Richard broke at last.

There were some sad hours at Willow Croft. The house was shaded, at times, so effectually, the want of window-blinds and overhanging trees would not have been felt. While the matter was in some respects too deep for the penetration, or rather for the business, of Munk, it was too serious for him to trifle with; and at the same time, like the effect of telling pleasant stories to a sick child, and making it smile, he could not forbear those feathery sallies and sunny quips in which he so much abounded. The change in Roxy, so noble and so visible, gave her husband almost as much delight as the sorrow of Richard did pain; and especially as that change employed itself upon the sorrow, and was an alleviation of it, and a visit of queenliness unto it; and as it rejoiced Richard so, and made him sometimes almost forget his sorrow, and made his sorrow seem so like a dark night full of glow-worms, Munk could not but keep some of his old flow of spirits.

"I have just read, in the evening paper," said he, knocking his pipe on the palm of his left hand, "that 'Mr

Brunel acknowledged he had taken his first lessons for forming the great Thames Tunnel from the ship-worm, whose motions he observed as it perforated the wood, arching its way onwards, and varnishing the roof of the passage with its secretions.' The evil is big enough, — it is like a mountain; and we are worms, — but perhaps we shall get through it at some rate. Queen Victoria has some hard times, — how she is going to tunnel that great English nation, so things will run smooth and easy, I don't see; but let us be good and happy, and happy and good." He had refilled his pipe, and uttered these last words simultaneously with putting it in his mouth, and holding a Lucifer match over the bowl to light it.

Richard would try to be good, but he found it hard to be happy. That a sense of innocence will always insure repose of spirit, — that, if the conscience be clear, the heart will be light, — is rather a dogma of fancy than a conclusion of fact. Those nations that employed the rack understood human nature better than this; they knew that, as compression of the waist drives the blood into the face, innocence was susceptible of the strictures of pain to an extent that blushes with apparent guilt; and demonstrated that through exquisiteness of agony, the most virtuous man in the world would confess himself the most criminal and reprobate, — in a word, that our nature can be implicated in baseness, by tempting it with sorrow.

Sometimes Richard gasped from a certain internal hollow of pain; sometimes cold prickles ran over him from head to foot, as if one were leisurely sprinkling him with a water-pot full of fleas and frost; sometimes he played with the children, but languidly, as an invalid takes a ride, and not so much entering into the pleasure of the thing, as that the pleasure of the thing may enter into him; sometimes he fell heavily on his bed, — sometimes he paced energetically his chamber; now he would be all strung up, and clenched, and wiry, — again he was flaccid, limpsy, dissoluble as water. He did not shed many tears, but there was a sort of burning aridness, combined with a swollen tightness, back of his eyes; at one time, he read all the papers, — at another, he devoted his leisure to looking from the window.

Roxy was good to him, — very good. She made him the best cup of tea, boiled his potatoes in the mealiest way, lightened up the bread till it lay in slices on the plate like tiers of new honeycomb from the Patent boxes. But oh, she had to be so considerate! If she could have asked him how he did, instead of complimenting the morning to him; if she could have looked at his tongue, instead of half ignoring his presence; if she could have asked him what she should do for him, instead of having to try to do so much; if she could have just inquired if he would have some arrow-root, or green peas without butter, or a rasher of pork; if she could have had the privilege of keeping the children still, instead of feeling obliged to urge them to entertain their Uncle; if she could have driven off the man with the hand-organ and the monkey, instead of tempting him with a few cents to the gate, to grind his organ, and make his monkey dance; — then it would seem to be better.

But there was Richard's Motto; sometimes it seemed to fly out of the wall, like a wasp, and sting him in the face when he looked at it.

CHAPTER XXXV.

INTROSPECTIVE.

HE must adjust himself to what was about him. He must ascertain the extent of his obligations and deficits, and square accounts with existence. He had relations to mankind that involved a personal attention, — offices to fill or resign, — scenes to be visited or abandoned.

"What will God have me to do?" he asked. "My character is questioned, and my influence neutralized; my pretensions will be derided, and my efforts opposed."

He was teacher in the same Sunday-school with Melicent and Barbara, one of whom had a class in the vestry, directly fronting him. One Sabbath he was at his post; but he imagined he could not repeat the endeavor. It was not so much a cross which he would heroically bear, as an execution that it were wise to dispense with. He told his class, with some emotion, he should instruct them no more, but that he should be happy to see them at Willow Croft. The children opened their innocent eyes with quite a burst of wonderment, for they were attached to their teacher and ignorant of events; but he quietly sat down and turned his back to them.

He had passed some of his happiest and most useful hours in the cause of Knuckle Lane, and at the Griped Hand. This was an interest that he loved, and a privilege that he prized. Shall he attend these meetings no more? Shall he maintain the "Be Good," but the "Do Good" become no other than a lost dream of his youth, — a ruined attainment of his piety? But how persevere in duties that brought him into so scandalized a juxtaposition?—how, with such a load on his heart;—how, with so much shame in his apprehensions;—how, with a sort of aha! aha! pursuing him down the street?

The Hebrew Scribes used to write in the margin of the Bible words that were to be pronounced in room of offensive ones in the text, which they dared not alter. Richard seemed to have the feeling that he was an offensive word in the sacred text of those movements in which he had been engaged,—movements that he reverenced and loved,—and that he ought to betake himself to the margin.

Richard had friends,—friends for adversity,—who adhered to him whatever might befall. Some of his Knuckle Lane associates, believing in his integrity, not only loaned him a generous confidence, but would incite him to vindicate his position, and repossess himself of what Mrs. Melbournism had taken away. There were those who did not like Mrs. Eyre, and were impatient at the injustice she seemed guilty of. But nothing could dissuade Richard from letting those matters alone. "Come back to 'Knuckle Lane,'" said Mangil, the Broker. "Cornered, sharp, hard getting round? Poh! poh! never heard of such a thing. Banks refuse? Come into the street; call,—you know where,—21 Exchange. Never mind backers,—you have a back of your own;"—he struck him there;—"perhaps you have forgotten some old deposites; if you don't call for them, why, they must pass over to your heirs."

Now, Richard made some mistakes, and one very plain one. He exaggerated the consequence that attached to his person and action, and seemed to imagine there was a public excitement about his affairs. The city appeared to him one great eye; and that eye, like the sun, looking straight down upon him, and making his shadow the measure of its intensity. In fact, there were twenty thousand eyes in the Old Town and the New; and it would be a miracle, indeed, if these had all at once become so disinterested, so curious, or so crazed, as, neglecting their own business, to mind nothing else but a lessee of Green Mill. It was as if there were no other self, — no other disappointment, or anxiety, or sorrow, — but his; as if the people he passed in the street, — that looked at him, indeed, but only to take the right side of him, — were not full of bargains and speculations, of hurryings and fears, of burdens and woes, of light, love, and hope, without him; as if the houses, that seemed to stare on him from their windows, were not veiled in their sick chambers, embroiled in their kitchens, turned topsy-turvy in their clearings, asleep in their luxuriance or their solitude, and cared nothing for him.

This turn of Richard's mind was not an uncommon one. A chambermaid, — I have this out Jonathan Swift, D. D., — talking with one of her fellow-servants, said, "I hear it is all over London that I am going to leave my lady." The same Divine has other instances, which I need not be at pains to repeat. An Englishman, having written a three-penny pamphlet against France, hearing that a French privateer had been seen off the coast, fled to town, and told his friends "they need not wonder at his haste, for the French King had sent a privateer on purpose to catch him." In a book-stall, Mr. Swift says he took up a volume entitled "Poems, by the author of The Choice." "Poems" were unendurable; "But what," asked the Dean, "is The Choice, or who ever heard of its author?"

"This," concludes our moralist, "arises from the great importance which every man supposes himself to be of."

Whatever he undertook, Richard might feel it would be

entitled, "By the author of a Certain Disturbance!" Yet how many there were in Woodylin who had never seen the book, nor heard of the disturbance! How many who had only seen the cover of the book, or read its title in a newspaper advertisement!

Perhaps being deplumed has the same effect as wearing feathers, in the fancy that one is the observed of all observers; and a sense of disgrace excites the reäcting imagination like a love of applause.

We have said Richard's heart, among other vagaries, got into his eyes and ears. In that heart was a variety of things, — the "World," the Church, the street, — this and that man, this and that circle, — many vague and indefinable objects, and strange and wonderful impressions of things; and he could hardly look up without seeing or hearing what pertained to himself, — even as we should suppose, more literally, the sweet singer of Sweden, who has filled the earth with her melody, could hardly open her ears anywhere without hearing the echo of her voice, as she certainly cannot open her eyes without seeing her name in all places and on all things.

Yet herein he mistook, — I will not say his duty, — but the fact.

In the city at large, the Old Town especially, and among the citizens outside of the Family connection, his rejection by the Governor's daughter was a nine days' wonder, with an evening or two of commentary, and no more; and even in that connection, except in the detached and remote hours of unreserve and reverie, it gradually dropped from the tongue.

We say Richard made a mistake. Yet it might have been difficult for him to be correct.

His great sorrow held up the world to his view as in a

kaleidoscope, which by invisible hands it kept turning round; and, at each revolution, men and women,—his fellow-beings,—like the glass and beads in the toy aforesaid, tumbled into unexpected groups, and darted off with every conceivable expression.

It would be hard to determine his precise footing with such folks.

For the most part, he left the public walks, and attached himself to the Saw-mill and Willow Croft.

He had plenty of time for reflection; and among the things that self-examination brought to light, he thought he espied a lurking ambition. Had he been too ambitious?—sinfully so?—or only to the extent that was natural, laudable, and Christian? His desire to do good, he feared, had been a desire to do great good; his actual superiority, in feeling and comprehension, to many about him, seemed to have been tinctured with conceit; his endeavor to rise in the world, honorable and praiseworthy as were the means, indicated some narrowness of motive; his energy and perseverance, in every benevolent word and work, were vitiated by a regard to human approbation;—perhaps he had relied less on God, and too much on his own activity of nature. Why did he feel, at times, so wretchedly, and mourn sore like a dove over his disappointment? If he were truly a child of God, and sanctified in soul, and imbued with resignation, and raised to the tranquillity of life in Jesus, and heir presumptive of eternal blessedness, would he breathe so heavily? These questions he could not revolve without solicitude.

Was there not a certain swelling up and inflation of selfish regard in the whole scheme of his life, and filling a space that should be occupied solely by God and duty? Was he not more mortified at the discredit attached to his reputation, than distressed for detriment accruing to the cause of Christ? Would he be willing that the works of godliness and humanity should go on, and he himself have no agency, or award, or figure therein? Startling topics these, that made his conscience throb, as if its nerve had been touched by a dentist's needle. It is said that ants, in a Church of Brazil, having bored through the floor, brought up from the vaults beneath bits of coffins and shreds of grave-clothes, and displayed them to the shuddering eyes of the worshippers. A great sorrow, even in a sanctified mind, sinks to the depths of one's being, and perforating the vaults where follies and sins lie dead and buried, will sometimes surprise him with the sight of remnants of things abhorred and rejected, and which he supposed had perished forever.

"The importance which every man supposes himself to be of" assumed an unusual aspect, and dilated in extraordinary proportions, in Richard's mind, about this time. He never had such a realization of himself before. If he would ever be great, he never felt himself so large, never experienced such an exaggerated consciousness, as now. He seemed aforetime to have lost sight of his own existence and individuality; and now that existence and individuality, — whatever he had done or been, — all the plans he had engaged in, — all the intercourse he had enjoyed, — seemed to confront him, and inflesh before his eyes, and well up in his heart, and to be himself, and to double himself, and to shut out from his attention all things but his attention. He had no idea of what he had attained, until compelled to retreat, and contemplate his ground from a distance. One measures his height more by his fall than by his rise. The fall is material and perceptible; the rise is spiritual, gradual, dawn-like. One falls with a crash, — he goes up with a kind of buoyancy.

Sometimes he exclaimed, with Job, "O that I were as in months past, — as I was in the days of my youth!" He wished himself like the boy David, a keeper of sheep again in his father's pasture; — he sighed for the obscurity and silence of the old forests where he had cut timber and slept on boughs. He wished that he had never left the station of slip-tender, under Captain Creamer; — he envied his own boy, the shingle-sticker.

He called to mind Cromwell's lament in Shakspeare. He had read Shakspeare. It was the advice of Pastor Harold for young persons to possess the great dramatist, — agreeably, perhaps, to what tradition reports of old Dr. Strong, of Hartford, Ct., who said he wanted but two books in his library — the Bible and Shakspeare. He pathetically repeated Othello's words: —

> "Had it pleased Heaven
> To try me with affliction; had he rained
> All kind of sores, and shames, on my bare head;
> Steeped me in poverty to the very lips; —
> * * * But (alas!) to make me
> A fixed figure for the time of scorn
> To point his slow, unmoving finger at, —
> O! O!"

This "O! O!" came to be quite familiar to Richard. It was all that remained to him in the way of expression. It was as a letting off of steam. Eructation is useful in disburthening the heart. The whole course of his days seemed to have suddenly struck into a funeral procession, and the noise of the world to be a beat of the muffled drum, and he himself to be keeping slow and measured tread, as he moved downwards to obscurity and silence.

Yet Richard recollected duty, and strove to carry forward

the intention, if he was obliged to deviate from the method, of his former goodness.

He went occasionally to Elder Jabson's evening meetings, in the neighborhood of Willow Croft. The Elder was kind and attentive to Richard, and, waiving reproachful considerations, treated him as a friend and brother. At this time the doctrine of the Second Advent was being discussed in the Elder's parish, and it agitated the meetings. The good Minister himself was not free of doubt. Some of his flock were selling out, in anticipation of the great event. Richard spoke on the subject with some warmth, and not a little judgment. He explained that the anticipated Coming of our Lord, so far as concerned this world, was a spiritual phenomenon; — that it was to be realized in the heart and life, and to be fulfilled in the amelioration of society and progress of the race. The fire, said he, is that which consumes iniquity. The cloud-glory is the beauty of holiness. The light is the radiance of universal love. The new heavens are what we may have in our families, our towns, our nation. The idea of atmospheric convulsions and geological ruin, he said, originated in error and superstition; and he explained how, in every age and in various places, it had been productive of terrible evils and unspeakable wretchedness. He must have been indebted for some of his facts to Pastor Harold. Then he expatiated with fervor, and almost a Pythian boldness, on the power, solemnity and grandeur, of the real coming of Jesus.

The Elder was pleased, and most of the congregation acquiesced. "I have felt under trial," said the former, "like a cart pressed under sheaves. I have sometimes thought, in this matter, we had run, before we were sent; but I have peace in my soul to-night, — I might say a shouting peace. We shall have cause to thank God in the day of eternity for Brother Edney's word. I believe he spake as he was moved by the Holy Ghost. Let us rejoice that we are not in hell, but still on praying ground!"

Richard felt refreshed, that night, by the vision of Jesus that had been kindled in his imagination. He compared his feelings when he got home with the thought he had at the meeting. He was sensible of a harmony between the two, — that he had uttered not merely what he knew, or what the occasion momentarily suggested, but what was profound in his convictions, bedded in his nature, and what, after all, seemed an indestructible tendency and appetency of his spirit. He was glad to have those old and beloved sensations revive; — it was a coming up from the darkness that covered them of sentiments and principles that he believed were eternal within him. The image of the coming kingdom of his Lord had a brightness and majesty that contrasted his situation indeed, but not his purposes; and if it discouraged certain forms of overt action, it animated all the more the interior sphere of his piety.

In the parlor, with Roxy and Munk, before retiring, he sang the hymn that begins, "I love thy kingdom, Lord." At these words, —

"If e'er my heart forget
  Her welfare or her woe,
Let every joy this heart forsake,
  And every grief o'erflow," —

they were all touched. Richard was a good and sincere singer, and Roxy not only knew that the pathos of his voice truly interpreted the condition of his soul, but she felt how with a certain choking resoluteness of heart, and solemn, painful heroism of intent, he sang.

The next day, obedient to the feeling of the night before, he purchased a small golden cross, which he lodged carefully within his vest, and wore over his heart. Every night he hung it up directly under his Motto.

Richard would still do good; nor was he without opportunity. Outside of the large and tempting field where he had so long labored, and from which he imagined himself in a sense banished, in the "margin" of things where he lived, he found enclosures, or rather wastes, that demanded Christian attention, and appealed to Christian fidelity. At Bill Stonners' Point, collecting his pupils from the neighboring forest, from the docks, and Islands, including Chuk, and two or three mill-boys and river-drivers, he formed a sort of Ragged School; and Sunday evening he had a small congregation of what are sometimes denominated the Great Unwashed; and Miss Freeling would call the Bare Feet. These had to be instructed, not only in the first principles of the doctrine of Christ, but in rudiments of behavior and decency, and the proper use of their mother tongue; and some must be taught reading and spelling. I know not whether it is an honor to Chuk, or a reflection on the rest, to say he was at the head of the class.

In this, Richard did not forget the Griped Hand and the Church. He loved and would serve both; and hoped that he might make of these Wild Olives, as he called them, plants that would do to graft on the domestic and civilized stock, and such as might adorn and bless those higher spheres to which he hoped ultimately to commit them.

CHAPTER XXXVI.

A SMILE.

MR. AUGUSTUS MANGIL, the musical money-dealer, — why should not such a man be musical? — approached Richard, as he was "shutting down" the Mill, one day, in his lively way; his little eyes pleasantly snapping, his left finger playing about his ear, and his right knee crooking rather antic-like. "An investment," said he. "A little down, but a good deal up. In plain words," he continued, "I have embarked in hens. Not deep, but high, — high, I call it; so;" — he marked an altitude with his hand in the air. "Flour-barrel high; — full-blood Shanghae; — eight dollars a pair; — feathered to the heel; — an egg a day, and ask no questions. I want a place to put them. If you will furnish that, it shall be joint-stock. At Willow Croft is just the spot, and your folks, women and children, are just the men. We shall want a few boards and laths."

They walked on together towards Willow Croft. Encountering Munk, the Broker's scheme was opened to him. Richard was ready, and Munk consented. The children were delighted, and Roxy was to have plenty of fresh eggs.

They selected a place at the foot of the lot. Richard ordered up the lumber, and Mangil superintended the structure. In a few days they had a "house" well appointed, and three or four families of the most notable Asiatic fowls.

Every morning one of the "Wild Olive" boys brought a box of what was termed fresh meat for chickens, — beetles, spiders, worms; and there was such a time feeding the family, and Memmy and Bebby did busk and pudder so, we cannot tell it all. There were eggs, and there were chickens; — the marvel! Munk liked to eat eggs; Roxy liked to cook eggs; Memmy liked to bring them in in a basket; and Bebby liked to hold one in her hand, — just once, — just a little, — so softly, — so shrinkingly; and Richard and the Broker liked to count the profits. There were so many questions, withal, about lime, sand, water, oats, barley, and what not; and how to prevent a hen setting when she was a mind to, and how to make her set when she was not a mind to; and which was best, one large egg, or two small ones; and about the value of the different importations; and there were so many persons to see the hennery, and so many inquiries to be answered, and so many suggestions to be considered, and so many wipes to be parried; — it was altogether exciting business; and it was just the sort of excitement that Richard needed.

Did Mangil know this? Ah! there is a question. Roxy said he did; and that this was a trick of his. Mangil had his way, the same as Climper had, and the rest of mankind have.

CHAPTER XXXVII.

INCIDENTS.

We were about to commence this chapter with the word "Our readers." But while adjusting the nib of our pen on our thumb-nail; — the prongs having crossed their arms, — tired and sleepy, we suppose, — it was late at night; — that word, sleepy too, impatient and fretful, began to mutter. "Readers! what does he know about readers? *His* readers I should wonder!" it seemed to say. This made us curl a little, and while we were meditating some stifling rejoinder to this impertinence, the solar lamp suddenly gave out. There was no help for that, and we sank back resignedly in the rocking-chair, and fell into a doze. It may be added, that we had been engaged, the day before, reading a work entitled "THE TRUE HISTORY OF THE EARTH AND ITS INHABITANTS; *showing the analogy between man and brute, and deducing the human race from five varieties of the oyster, recently discovered in a fossil state under the French Academy;*" a suggestive volume, with plates of sections and atoms of shells as microscopically developed, in which, among other things, are seen human forms in embryo, lobes of the heart, brain-shaped configurations, finger-nails; the chit of an idea, and a very perfect approximation to a Gothic church.

While sleeping, we seemed to be standing on a plain, where were many animals, and a number of books; and in the distance stood anxious-looking umbræ of authors. First advanced the lion, and with a slight flourish of the tail, he devoured fifteen of the newest books; a dream-allusion, I suppose, to a habit this animal possesses of taking fifteen pounds of raw flesh at a meal. Then came a kangaroo, who, lifting the lid of a book, instantly leaped from the imprimatur to the colophon, and proceeded in this way from volume to volume, as it were playing leap-frog among them. A chamois goat would open a book, and if he found crags and chasms in it, he gambolled amongst them, and seemed to be uneasy at a level spot. A book was seen sinking in a pond of water; instantly, at the beck of an author, a Newfoundland dog swam for it, and bore it safe to the shore. Marmots appeared burrowing in books, and making a home for themselves in the middle of the pile. A squirrel sat on the cover of one, with a nut in its mouth. A flock of crows alighted on the spot. The authors trembled; they seized the forlorn shade of one of their number, and set it on a pole for a scare-crow. Chimney-swallows flitted among the books, in pursuit of dark and smirchy places, where they could build their nests. An anaconda glided through the grass, and having first smoothed and polished the volume of his choice with a sort of mucilage, proceeded to swallow it. Then he fell into a swollen torpor, with the corners of the book protruding from his mouth. A rhinoceros came up from a muddy creek, having a terrible horn on his nose, which he turned every way; — the timid umbræ fled. The creature, approaching the books, gored some and tossed others. Looking in the direction where we were standing, he seemed to be aiming his horn at our shadowy self; — in exceeding terror we awoke.

This dream, mixed and incongruous indeed, as all dreams are, and the History above mentioned, set us upon reflection. Is there not, we asked, an analogy between certain zoological species and the readers of books? The law of analogy would seem indeed to be imperfectly developed; and yet its accredited results are striking. For instance, Ulrici discovers in the plays of Shakspeare a compend of all the points of Calvinism. Gardiner classifies musical instruments after the colors of the prism. Even in the Bible, we find David comparing himself in trouble to a bottle in the smoke. Should we transcend the proprieties of the case, if, in a matter of mere speculation, we discriminated readers of books by the marks of certain faunæ? In fact, is not this agreeable to the whole method of analogical and derivative science?

There is, then, the leopard. It is related this animal may be taken in a trap with a mirror at the bottom. Let an author bait his book with a looking-glass; this reader, discerning in his own image what he supposes is a monster that he is in duty bound to devour, pitches in headlong, and may be easily taken. The Newfoundland dog, we should imagine, would be a favorite of all authors. The cat is the delight of most persons; yet, if you chance to tread on the tail of one that has been a pet for years, the creature will turn on you teeth and claws. The giraffe goes through the forest of an author's thoughts, and plucks off the sweet buds and tender leaves from the tops of the trees; at the same time, with dirty hoof, he tramples the pretty stars-of-Bethlehem, and useful checkerberries, that grow beneath. Rather to be avoided, we should suppose. The hippopotamus sinks into a book, like water, and can be seen walking at his ease on the bottom. He is obliged to rise to the surface to take breath. The musk-deer reader is graceful and engaging; has beautiful dark eyes, with a voice like a sigh; but is said to be indolent. Wild turkeys, before proceeding, assemble on an eminence, and remain in consultation one or two days. At length the leader gives the signal note, and taking a particular direction, is followed by the rest.— Common in America. It is justly observed, that the sagacity which enables the domestic cock with such precision to announce the hour of dawn, is matter of astonishment. One is sufficient.— The bob-o-link is remarkable for changing his name, note, and color, as he goes from the North to the South. How fortunate is that author whose friends are the mocking-birds! Would somebody present us a cage of canaries, to hang in the bay-window of our study, and sing betimes to our melancholy, and answer when we whistle, we should deem ourselves happy. At rare and angelic intervals, — a shuttle-like iridescence, a feathery pause in the stillness of things,—a little humming-bird has been seen gliding about our verandah, and tasting with nicest relish the honeysuckles whose nectared goblets hang out all day long on the pillars. If we were to name a reader to be chiefly recommended, we should find the type in those very common objects, cows. They begin at the bars, the title-page, and graze to the end of the pasture, and regraze; they drink at the murmuring brooks, the pleasant fancies of an author, — repose under the shade of the great trees, and ruminate; they afford to the public tasteful and useful results of their labor. The swan offers points of interest. To see this graceful creature, with arched neck and half-displayed pinions, sailing over the serene surface of a great idea, which reflects, as she passes, the snowy beauty of her dress, flatters an author's vanity. The most terrible of all American snakes is the copper-head. An author need not be afraid of toads. They are useful about one's grounds. They feed on insects, and are good against vermin. There is a vulgar notion concerning this creature, it being supposed, from the great numbers that appear after a rain, they descend with the shower. This may be true.

The great lantern-fly is remarkable for the light that emanates from its head,—a light by which it usually reads.

These are some of the kinds of readers distinguished in the manner above mentioned. They are such as an author will meet with;—many of them he will be happy to see; others he will do well to shun. At first blush there is something dismal in a writer's prospect. Quite large portions of his world seem to consist of jungle overrun with rapacious beasts and reptiles, or of swamps crowded by venomous insects. But these must all live, Dr. Good tells us. Moreover, we may remember that insects are useful in disintegrating the soil, and rendering it light, loamy, and fertile. There is, it may be added, in the East, a tribe of barbarians who handle the most venomous reptiles with impunity, and eat them alive, from head to tail. Celsus and Lucan make mention of them, and they were called by the ancients, Psylli. A club of authors might import a few. Besides, Dr. Bell contends that there is no real ferocity in the lion, for instance; that his glare is merely excited attention, and his grin or snarl the natural motion of uncasing his fangs before using them. How many of the feræ, withal, can be tamed! In fishes the sense of smell is so acute, that if an author will rub his hand with extract of rose, or even leaves of marjoram, and dip it into the water, he can draw any quantity of these creatures into it. Good Pierre, before quoted, declares, and supports his opinion by striking testimony, that wild beasts will fly a naked man; whence I infer that an author would do well to present his thoughts simply, directly, as it were naturally, and not rely upon conventional adaptation, or academical canons.

And we are reminded, in this connection, nor can we forbear to mention, what a fine race of readers used to exist,—the Lectores of scholastic days. "Candidus," "ingenuus," "benevolens," "vigilans," were universal traits. Has that race become extinct?

We digress. We were about to say, our readers would remember — something. — Yet, after all, does not this imply considerable? First, that we have readers; secondly, that they have read the book; and thirdly, that they have attended to what they read. Can one imply so much, without a latent reference to other things, — say, to this whole matter of the different sorts of readers, that we have so pleasantly discussed? Nor can it be a thing of small personal moment for any author to know what sort of readers he shall be surrounded by, — whether by swans or anacondas, nightingales or cougars. If the reader of these pages has any of the properties of the domestic cat, for example, we can rely upon him, and while he honors us with his confidence, and has a place by our fireside, we will be cautious how we tread; for this creature inspects every portion of a new house before she makes up her mind about it. So our reader will have gone over that passage, and a short one it is, in Chapter V., where allusion is made to certain business transactions between the elder Edney and Governor Dennington; and will remember — it is a trifle — that the former was under indentures to the latter as relating to his farm; and that one of Richard's objects in coming to Woodylin was to obtain means for cancelling this contract. Being so fortunate as to have amassed the requisite sum, now, while his sorrow was fresh upon him, he repaired to the Governor's office to apply it. That gentleman received our friend courteously and quietly, as was his custom; greeted him with a cordial "good-morning;" shook hands with him; shoved a chair towards him, and had him seated by his table; alluded to the pleasantness of the weather, and inquired after his father. He took from a large file the papers in question, computed the interest, counted the money, and gave Richard a receipt. The Governor loved to do business; he did it in the softest and easiest way imaginable, Perhaps this made him so good-natured at the present moment.

Richard arose to leave, when, as if a new thought had struck him, taking a gold piece from his pocket, he extended it towards the Governor, and, with suppressed emotion, said, "Sir, I received that, two or three years since, upon resigning a horse, whose fright in the street had arrested my attention. I do not wish to keep it." "I recollect," said the Governor. "My daughter Melicent was in the sleigh. It showed spirit and nerve." "I do not wish to keep it," reiterated Richard, growing paroxysmal inside. "Melicent said," continued the Governor, unmoved, but bland, "few acts of heroism were better carried through, or deserved more honorable remembrance." "Will you have the kindness, Sir," pursued Richard, "to receive back that which suggests nothing pleasant to my memory?" The Governor did not, or could not, or would not, enter into the spirit of Richard's tender; he merely replied, "It is not mine,—it is yours." He opened his day-book, and appeared to be making an entry. Richard would have thrown the gold into the fireplace, or out of the window; but the manner of the Governor would not allow this, and, finally, forced it back into his pocket.

Richard was a little piqued, and a little surprised; and on his way home he could but wonder, partly at himself, and partly at the Governor. It was as if the latter was wholly ignorant of all recent transactions, and the former was sensible of nothing else; and this sensibility, and this ignorance, had a queer encounter.

Richard went to the office with any quantity of misgivings and chokings, yet the Governor did not, in any way, appear to be cognizant of, or willing to revive, disagreeable recollections. Wherefore? This puzzled Richard. Did politeness conceal contempt? Was the Governor's aversion, like deep water, silent because it was deep? Did business keep in abeyance all paternal and moral sentiments? Yet he alluded unreservedly to his daughter, and pleasantly to the reminiscences of Richard, who, on the whole, felt better after the interview than before.

From this incident we are disposed to draw an inference for our readers Ruminantes. It is said men are governed by their interests, — that is, pecuniary interests. We oppose the example of Richard, point-blank, to that theory. He would gladly be rid of money. Nay, men are governed by their emotions; in other words, moral sentiments. Again, it is asserted that the golden eagle is one of the American gods; nay, furthermore, Richard held in his hand a veritable golden eagle, which he would cheerfully have flung to the depths of Tartarus, into the face of Pluto himself, if he could; — a fact worthy of consideration. Gold, heavy as it is, will not outweigh a passion, be it individual, — be it national. This we suggest to those of our readers who do not affect the golden eagle, or the fustian eagle, and yet are like the mountain eagle, in the grandeur of their flight, intensity of their gaze, terror of their swoop, and especially in the way they pounce upon another of their tribe, the fish-hawk, to disgorge him of his prey.

Another incident. As Richard was walking, towards dusk, turning the corner of St. Agnes-street, he saw Melicent slowly approaching the gate of her father's house. Here she stopped, and stood looking in a direction opposite from him. She was a dozen rods off. Above her were the branches of the great elms. Beyond was the sunset. She had on the same blue shirred bonnet, white cashmere shawl with dark spots, and blue muslin dress, — the same that Richard had seen before. Her hand reposed softly and gracefully on the latch of the gate; her parasol was dropped, carelessly upturned, on the flagging at her feet. Richard's heart went to throbbing, of course. It was as if the sight diffused a fragrance, in which all his senses swam. She disengaged the shawl from her neck, and hung it on her arm, still looking the other way. If Richard had been a German, he would have wept; if an Italian, torn his hair; if a Frenchman, leaped towards the beloved one. He was an American, and did not know what to do. He could not remain stationary; he dared not advance. As he was about to retreat, or, rather, make a detour across the street, on the opposite walk he beheld Miss Eyre. She was loitering, and had evidently been watching him and Melicent. Well, go back. But in this direction, his eye encountered the person of Clover, partially concealed by the twilight shadows of the trees, who had been reconnoitring all three. Fly, sink, burst; he would have rejoiced in any slight miracle, or, as he was sufficiently distended, why not, like a kernel of corn in the fire, permit him to pop out of his dilemma, and drop, say, into his little chamber at Willow Croft? There was the glimmer of an equivocal smile on Miss Eyre's face; Clover satanically gloated; Melicent had her back towards him, with her eyes on the clouds. Silent, calm, unconscious Melicent, in her blue dress; what a fever she created, — what a prairie-on-fire, with the flames approaching and fencing one in on all sides, she incontinently aroused! She went through the gate, and into the house, and made an escape at once for Richard's person and alarm.

A reader of the manuscript, — perhaps a lion inspecting a flock of kids in the distance, — perhaps a musk-deer, pretty, but languid, — says the writer questions, when he ought to narrate; hints at what should be developed, is redundant in unimportant brevities, sparing in what is rich and copious, and that, hastening through pleasant fields, he loiters in barrens. For instance, that in this last incident, while there is much said, there is an omission of what is essential to the right feeling of the scene, — to wit, that the dress of Melicent, the contour of her person, the verisimilitude of her motion, the way she rested her arm on the gate, had been endeared to Richard by the deepest of all associations — love. That the gate-post supplanted his arm, and he must needs be pained at the interference. That the contrast between the pleasant past and the dismal present was provoking; that his heart was inflamed with a sense of repulsed, disdained love, that still loved on. Our reply is, that we described the case in its phenomena, if not in its substance; that we stated the external facts, if not their spiritual connection; in a word, acting upon the suggestions of our respected College Rhetorical Professor, made many years ago, and living in our memory still, we "left something to the imagination of the reader."

That night, as sometimes happened, Bebby slept with Richard. The Moon, bright and full, shone into the chamber, and upon the bed, and on the child, restoring the beauty of the features, and illuminating the silvery hair of the slumberer. Richard raised himself on his elbow, and bent over the unconscious enchanter with mingled agony and ecstasy. It was as if a vision of beauty and repose had been lent to him from some far off heaven. It was as if his own innocency and early promise had been collected out of his life, and laid in breathing form at his side. Was it his Childhood come back to mock him? Was it put there to reïnspire him? He worked his fingers in his dark hair, till it hung in tangled locks over the pearly fairness before him, and his worried brow contrasted strongly with the calm face of the little one. It was Despair bending over Hope; it was Sorrow confronted with Blessedness; it was penitent Aspiration weeping at the feet of some long-lost Ideality. He kissed the child, inhaled its balsamic breath, and laid down by the side of it to sleep.

Fourth-of-July came, and the evening was to be celebrated with a new display,—the illumination of May-flower Glen, by lamps suspended in the trees, and heightened, withal, by a band of music. Everybody was abroad that day, and Richard, with Memmy and Bebby, followed in the wake.

Richard's enjoyment seemed rather to lie behind him, in the children, than before him, in the scenes of the occasion. He appeared to be hauling his pleasures along, instead of going in pursuit of them. He labored under the mistake we have commented upon. There were, at a moderate computation, 30,000 people in the city and in the streets thereof, that morning, and all recreating; and how few knew anything of Richard, and how fewer were intent on anything else than happiness, or were unwilling that everybody should be happy too! Richard found this out before the day was over, and that he had really nothing else to do but forget himself, and care and sorrow, and be as happy as the rest. He found out, too, that he was not of any consequence compared with a show-bill of the Theatre, which a jam of people on the side-walk were almost in a quarrel to see, and never thought of opening for him to pass. There were gay processions through the streets, and great crowds following them; there were crowds about Dr. Broadwell's Church, where an oration was to be delivered; there were multitudes of boys and girls, from the country, filling the candy-shops and ice-cream saloons. Memmy and Bebby saw so many strange sights, and fell into so many novel situations, their surprise, curiosity and glee, were gradually communicated to their Uncle.

But May-flower Glen, in the evening, was the greatest spectacle. Half a thousand lamps shed a palatial, alabastrian light through sylvan corridors, and on grassy terraces; they glimmered in the tinkling brook, and glowed again in thousands of bright countenances. There was the vacant strolling to and fro, the chattering of animated groups, the roistering of children, and the quiet looking on of elderly people. There were fair young ladies, in white dresses, and lavender-colored dresses, and changeable silk dresses; girdled, tuniced, caped; with flowers in their hands, and on their breasts, and in their hair; and great luxuriance of beautiful hair, and great glory of joyous feeling, and a whole Avoca-vale of sweetness, loveliness, and hope, in their eyes and on their lips. There were noble-looking young men, in white trowsers and vests, and some with red sashes. Hidden music filled the place with enchantment, as if Pan and his nymphs, and their pipes, were concealed in the grove.

We have not said that Richard had anything to do in getting this up; — he had, nevertheless. He was on the committee of arrangements; and, if less conspicuous, was as effective as any. This committee wore red sashes; — Richard omitted the badge.

Richard was so caught up, subdued, or *etherized*, or whatever it be, by the pleasantness of the hour, he saw Miss Eyre pass without a pang, and beheld Melicent in the distance without emotion, unless it be that of simple gladness.

As he stood, with the two children in front of him, on a seat, Mangil approached, with Melicent and Helen the Good on his arm. Mangil bowed, and Richard bowed, and they all bowed; and Mangil took Richard's hand, and so did Helen the Good, and Richard and Melicent exchanged the same compliment. "Beautiful!" said the Broker; "fine, inexpressible, — a high quotation! It carries the board." "It was a splendid idea," said Helen the Good. "I enjoy it exceedingly. Don't you?" said Melicent. Richard replied that he did. "The children," added Melicent, "are so happy!" "It is a great treat to them," rejoined Richard. The children showed a joyous excitement when they saw Melicent; but Richard had the advantage of them, and kept them still. Mangil, being one of the committee, wore a sash, and, alluding pleasantly to Richard's want of it, said, "You are not in authority to-night." "It goes off of itself," replied Richard. "Then it must have been admirably contrived," added Helen the Good. "I think so, too," said Melicent.

At this moment, a lamp fell in the rear of Richard, and there was a shriek in the crowd. "Will the ladies please to look after the children?" said Richard, starting for the scene of alarm. It was Miss Eyre, whom the accident frightened into a swoon. Richard helped bear her to a seat, where, with due application of fans, and water from the brook, she presently recovered. Richard returned to the children, whom he found alone with Melicent. "Helen the Good," said the latter, "is always foremost in scenes of distress, and withholds from no terrors; and she, with Mr. Mangil, followed you." "I was apprehensive," said Richard, "in the haste of preparation, that some of the lamps were not made sufficiently fast. I regret it exceedingly." "Did you know the person?" asked Melicent. "It was Miss Eyre," replied Richard. "It is but a trifle," continued Melicent, "and produces no sensible effect on the general festivity." "More scared than hurt," said Helen the Good, who returned, laughing. "She is a sensitive creature," rejoined Melicent. "We were discussing the propriety of repeating these illuminations," said the Broker. "I should like it," said Richard. "So should I," said Helen the Good. "And I," responded Melicent.

Promenading commenced, and Mangil, with the ladies, wheeling into the ranks, moved off to music.

As Richard had received and conversed with Melicent, so he saw her retire, without agitation. He did watch the rose-bud in her hair, till it was lost in a thicket of flowers and the glimmering distance.

Ere long the band struck up Home, Sweet Home, the signal of dispersion, and the people obeyed the hint.

The sentimentalist asks, how could Richard keep his countenance and heart, during such an interview with Melicent? The reply has already been indicated in what was said of the general exhilaration of the hour. There is an effect in festivity like music, at once exciting and tranquillizing; it clears the atmosphere of the mind, and leaves one in a state of azure quietude.

But, interposes the lady judge, that may answer for Richard; — it does not explain Melicent. No woman, who had ever so loved, or was so separated, could be so insensible and emotionless in a subsequent encounter. We would not be wise above what is written, nor above what a lady knows. But we are at liberty to conjecture, — first, that the laws of emotion in the two sexes are not radically different; and, therefore, secondly, that a woman, under these circumstances, might be calm. We believe, furthermore, if the phrase does not offend, that a woman will swallow down more emotion than a man, and preserve a face of stone when the latter is flaming to the roots of his hair. Besides, it may be stated that the love both of Richard and Melicent was founded, as Miss Edgeworth would say, on esteem, and not on impulse; and this will afford some key to their subsequent conduct, throughout. Finally, Melicent was not the aggressor, — she was purely a sufferer; and Christian principle, to speak of nothing else, would save her from rudeness, — check the ferment of feeling, and help maintain the equilibrium of her mind.

What may be called the Philosophy of Blushes, in other words, the law of the expression of emotion, has not been written; or if so, we have not seen it. The subject is a curious and a serious one. Life and death hang upon it.

How had Melicent borne herself in trials so painful to the female heart, and to all hearts, through which she had passed? If we should say she sometimes lamented and wept, — that she had her hours of terror and anguish, — should we hazard any truth? Richard had arisen to her eye a splendid model of a human being; and to see this shattered by one blow, must needs distress her. But she had supports that Richard wanted; — one, in the unequivocalness of her position; another, in the multitude of her friends; a third, in the abundant and elegant ministries of her daily life.

In a letter to a friend, she says, "You will expect me to be dejected. I am saddened by Richard, and for him. He was so purely princely to my imagination, I am slow to comprehend his vulgarity. Could the great Enemy of souls dissemble so? My attention was first called to the heroism, simplicity, and modesty, of his outward life. My interest was awakened by contact with his sentiments. I first knew his heart, — was introduced to his reflections, and, so to say, made the journey of his principles and purposes; and found myself a lover. I loved him as soul can love soul, as sympathy yearns for sympathy, as weakness is won by strength, as aspiration adores grandeur. Was he great enough to deceive me? — simply, coldly, infernally vast enough? Harrowing suggestion! cruel imputation! My chamber, which has been enlivened by the flow of every pleasant feeling, is sacred to silence and to sorrow. A Sleeping Christ hangs on my walls; — let me repose on my God. Above sin and woe, doubt and questioning, is the All Love; — let me be the child of its bosom. Sparrows sing in the trees at my window. Sunshine, and the blue heavens above, and the green earth beneath, encompass them. In the midst of the beauty of Virtue and Hope that still surrounds my darkened life, let me sing too."

CHAPTER XXXVIII.

CLOVER DISTINCT.

CLOVER had been at Green Mill frequently of late, loafer-wise. The natural insolence of his look was deepened by a mock complacency. Richard gave little heed to him, until, at length, he would be heeded. He sat with his feet tossing on the mill-chain, — an endless chain, revolving on a toothed shaft, and running through the entire width of the building, employed to haul logs from the basin up the slip to the bed. He blew out the contents of his mouth in studied and very dramatic directions. With his fists he seemed to be kneading the air into strange shapes, which he wished Richard to look at.

"'*Good* morning,' did you say, Mr. Edney? Yes, very good; perhaps what some meekly call *morally* good. Certain*lee*. How was the night? That good, too? Night, — shadows, misery; is there such a thing? Misery is heaves in horses, — what is it in man? In cows, it is the horn-distemper. La la la, rol la!"

"I will be obliged to you to regard my feet, in disposing of your humor," said Richard, punning and reproachful.

"I do," replied Clover; "it is no put-out to me at all. I was fearful of losing your attention, — I did not know but you would get abstracted. That cutting-off saw, I should say, wanted filing; it has seen some hard stuff. Goose-oil and yellow snuff are good for croup, and all cases of strangulation, and when a man's heart gets into his throat, and for a wheezy old mill like this."

"I shall trouble you to remove your feet from that chain," said Richard.

"Certain*lee;* you want to start it,—you want to see it go round and round,—you want to see it haul up the great black trunks of old life and hope; and I could stop it,—I could prevent it."

"I only meant," replied Richard, "if you did not stand back, you might get hurt."

"I only mean," rejoined Clover, "that while my feet are on the chain, you would not wish to or dare to start it. Off? yes, I take them off; if you want to hear the clank, clank, and see, coming up the slip, the shivered butts of things, and the hearts all eaten out, and hollow and dead. That is the English of it."

"Of what?"

"What you have been thinking about, this morning."

"I dislike your presence."

"I know you do."

"I shall take some pains to rid myself of it."

"It cannot be got rid of. You must keep it by you. Your pains-taking makes it stick closer. It hugs,—absolutely hugs."

Richard had become considerably aroused, to say the least, by these words of Clover; and could not help but suspect him.

"Speak plain," he said.

"I do," replied Clover, with an unutterable sneer; "so plain you perfectly comprehend what I say. Shall I speak plainer?"

"Come this way," said Richard, and called the fellow to the rear of the building.

"You are acquainted with Miss Eyre?" said Clover.

"I know her," replied Richard.

"Too well!"

"None of your innuendoes, or I shall be tempted to pitch you into the water!"

"Where you have been, for some time. I doubt if you can be anxious for my company."

"Why do you assail me in this way?"

"I am acting out my unspeakable DESTINY!!"

"How long have you been at it?"

"Some months."

"Have you had any particular understanding with Miss Eyre? Answer me that."

"I have seen Miss Eyre."

"Have you conspired with her as against me?"

"A singular question, — a cowardly question; I don't wonder you look pale in asking it. But why set the chain a-going?"

"What do you mean by your feet being on it?"

"O, I like to rest them there. I skip and play on it; I DANCE ON IT!"

"You are a devil!"

"Nay, you mistake; my name is Clover, — John Clover, — son of Col. Clover, of Clover Hill. Moreover, the world is clover, and you are clover, and I am — you know what, — in it; a little one, a fat one, a bright-eyed one. Tweedle dum, tweedle dee, dum de dee dum!"

"You have instigated Miss Eyre."

"I have exercised my rights. Have you forgotten? I was afraid you would forget. Now, say your catechism. — Who was the first man?"

"Adam," replied Richard; waiting to see what would come

"Who was the second man?"

"In his own estimation, Clover."

"Well done! a bright lad. You slightly transposed;

Clover is the first man, and Adam the second. A mere slip of memory. Try again. By what did the French take Algiers?"

"Might."

"Good! Frame that, and hang it up to look at. By what right do they hold it?"

"Might."

"Bravissimo! Go to the head of your class. By what right are English laws in force in Calcutta?"

"Might."

"Make that a postulate of your whole life! By what right are men held in slavery?"

"Might."

"That is the story! You are now indoctrinated. MIGHT IS RIGHT!! Might creates right, — sustains right, — is the sober little thing itself. This is the first principle of human affairs. It is the universal law. It is the method of the world; and I am the world. I am an embodiment of it. Its principles are seated in my breast;" he thumped his ribbed hollowness. "Its laws are codified, if I may use the expression, in my fist;" he displayed that member.

"And you have interfered with my happiness?"

"You have insulted my banner! You have fished in my waters; you have interrupted my business; you have usurped authority in my domain; and I have crushed you! I could do it, and I did do it; that is all! Whooeehoo! whooeehoo!"

It flashed upon Richard, — nay, it blazed and burnt upon him, as if the sun had fallen at his feet, — that Clover was back of the difficulty with Miss Eyre, and beneath it; remedilessly, diabolically, and everlastingly, there; and, staggering at the thought, "Good God!" he cried, quite unable to contain his emotion.

"Perhaps you have not read," continued Clover, "what a great historian says, that the sufferings of war purge human nature. I mean that your human nature shall be purged. And as you begin to pray, I doubt not you already feel humble and penitent, and are ready to sue for peace, — for peace with me."

"No more!" said Richard; "no more! You have succeeded. You have crushed me. Heaven shall avenge itself, — I will not. Could I pray, 'Father, forgive thee!' I gather myself unto myself and my God. I submit to an inexplicable Providence. I cease from life in the flesh, that I may live the life of the spirit. Go, Clover! I will not say, go and be damned; but go and sin no more."

Richard clasped his hands bitterly, and exclaimed, "O my Father! had it pleased thee that this cup should pass from me! Nevertheless, not my will, but thine, be done!"

The Mill-men, as if a serious disturbance had arisen, with axes and poles, ran forward; and, at a word from Richard, it seemed as if they would have struck Clover dead. Richard waved them into silence, and Clover strode from the spot.

CHAPTER XXXIX.

IN WHICH THE AUTHOR BRIEFLY PHILOSOPHIZES ON MAN.

On a previous page, we undertook to say what a Tale, with Richard and sundry things in it, was like. We did not state what Richard, with sundry things in him, was like. How, with emotion succeeding emotion, excitement spooming across excitement, and the suppression of all elementary hope and life, could he exist at all? We found him joyous and glad in "Knuckle Lane" and Melicent, upset by Miss Eyre, trembling before Melicent at the gate, calm in Mayflower Glen, lively in the Hennery, and now "crushed" by Clover. Wave follows wave in the human breast, tumult vies with tumult. But what is the human breast? What is left of Richard now? Let him have a good night's sleep, some one says, and he will wake up feeling better. Nay, and let it be all solemnly said, there is an Underworking, as well as All-Encompassing God, who knits together the shattered fibres of existence, and repairs the breaches in the foundations of the soul. The great reaper, Sorrow, did seem to have clipped Richard close and clean, and stooked him out for aye; but there remained charity, truth, duty, and absolute submission to God. And Richard had the spirit of Christ; — or, at least, we shall for the present beg so much out of the main question at issue. He was so thoroughly in the feeling of his Master, that, in this his last trial, as it were instinctively and unconsciously, he expressed himself in those words which have become a formula of agony and piety in all ages. His moral existence, his self-counterpoise his capability of sustained exertion, would seem to be annihilated by the unremitting stroke of misfortune; yet he lived and worked on. How could this be, except through the power of God, in which he trusted, and unto which he clave? There is the Gulf Stream, which moves on betimes and proportionately, straight forwards, forevermore. The winds would head it off; — they only fret its surface. The tides invade it; — it lifts them up, and bears them in its arms. There may be a Gulf Stream of piety, conscientiousness, rectitude, and faith in man. We hope there was one in Richard.

CHAPTER XL.

RICHARD PERSISTS IN TRYING TO DO GOOD.

He kept up his Ragged School, and did his best to tame the Wild Olives. And in this charity he chanced upon two singular and very unexpected co-laborers. These were none other than Captain Creamer and Tunny. The Captain had become reduced in estate and in feeling, — so much so, as to beg small favors in money from Richard, whom he had both patronized and abused. This tested Richard's Christian principle. Would he assist a man who had so annoyed him? He did, — he was kind to the Captain when others abandoned him. The Captain became peevish and dejected, as he was deserted and despised. Under these circumstances, Richard not only helped him, but was able to secure his help. He told him there was work to be done in the Ragged School, and prevailed with him to unite in that enterprise. But how should Tunny be there? The Green Grocer, had fallen, too, — failed, and, like Richard, was crushed. Worse than the mice, whose inroads he so pathetically described, the vanity and folly of his wife had undermined him. He was reduced to what "the law allowed," — less then than now; everything else, even to his credit and good name, fled. It was rumored that he gambled; — and this hurt him.

Richard visited him in his bereavement, and his wife in her despair, and was a comforter unto both. It was a sight to melt one's heart, to see Mrs. Tunny in her faded kitchen dress, without a curl in her hair, or a bow on her bosom. Richard found employment in the Mill for Theodoric, their son. The Sailmaker, who had married their daughter Faustina, and between whom and Mrs. Tunny alienation never slumbered, Richard reconciled, and persuaded him to commiserate his mother-in-law, and take her to live with him. The husband he summoned in his train of beneficence.

These three men, sufficiently miserable themselves, yet found a lower misery to which they could minister. It made Roxy smile to see Richard start off for the Point, of a Sunday afternoon, with his two fellow-missionaries, on their work of mercy. Mysie was the sexton of this Church, — she opened the house, swept the floor, and lighted the candles.

There was a little pleasant reäction in Richard's favor. Captain Creamer repented him of the wrong he did to Richard, in refusing to testify before the court of females at Whitcomb's. He knew it was his authoritative injunction that caused Richard to stay in the chamber with the Old Man and orphan girls. He would make reparation. Unknown to Richard, who would not have suffered it, he went to Miss Freeling, — a sort of flame of the Captain's earlier and better days, — and reported the facts. This lady repaired immediately to Miss Rowena, whom she knew particularly well, and repeated what she had heard.

CHAPTER XLI.

RICHARD GOES INTO THE COUNTRY.

Miss Rowena, while she could not doubt Richard's wrong-doing, still felt that he had been harshly disposed of by Mrs. Melbourne. In discussing the matter with the latter, she even went so far as to seem to clear him altogether. She was not sorry for any fissure of brightness in the case. She thoroughly disliked Glendar. Keeping her own counsels, however, she had the boldness, in company with Miss Freeling, to come directly to Willow Croft. Could the testimony of Junia be had ? Would Richard be willing to go and see her ? "I ask this," said she, "not in relation to any other thing, or other person, than myself. I should really like to know if Mrs. Whichcomb misrepresented. For my private satisfaction, will you go ?" Miss Freeling and Roxy united in urging the measure. "It can alter nothing," replied Richard. But go he must.

It was midsummer, and Green Mill was active. — Captain Creamer, to say nothing of Mr. Gouch and Silver, would take care of that.

It was midsummer, and Richard had had his Night's Dream ; and he would be glad of daylight, — he would be glad of rest and recreation.

So he set off with Winkle on the road he had formerly traversed. Winkle was kind to Richard, as he was to everybody, and did all in his power to cheer the journey. What on his former ride had really interested and delighted Richard, in Winkle and in the way, now had a melo-dramatic effect, that served to divert him.

"That man," Winkle would say, as he passed along, "is n't dead yet. He has been dying this two year. — That girl lost her lover. I did all I could to save him. — The right eye of that goose has n't winked for twenty years. — That boy has swung on that gate so long the hinges have rusted off. — I wonder when Tim Doze finds time to eat! He began picking his teeth in the door-way under the old driver, and has kept at it ever since."

Richard at length reached the house whither he had originally conveyed Junia.

Junia was there, notwithstanding rumors of another sort. The Old Man, her grandfather, was still alive, but weak and infirm; and he remembered the kindness Richard had done unto him. Their abode was a pleasant one, in a region, on a moderate scale, of considerable diversity. Elms towered in shallow coombs. Corn-lots swept from the sky on one side to a gully on the other. Wheat eddied across sunny slopes. The light-green mowing was terminated by a belt of dark forest. In the rear of the house was a flourishing orchard. Cattle and sheep could be seen lying in clumps of trees in the pastures. The highway, passing a neighboring farm-house, disappeared in wooded hills. Venerable oaks were scattered about the premises. A white school-house, and its "bordering" of maples, crowned a swell in the landscape. There were many things that operated to remind Richard of his own home and childhood, and recall the days of his innocent and unfettered existence. The woodbine, that veiled the front of the house, rolled its tide of verdure over the roof, and shaded the snug parlor, was like one he himself set out, and had recently seen, in Green Meadow. The back porch, with its posts all alive with hop-vines, was so like his mother's. The dairy-room had the same white shelves and savory neatness as the one he had passed a thousand times. The gourd-dipper, — how often had he dipped water with it, and held it by both hands to drink! In the garden, too, was the old sage-bed and its border of marigolds and chrysanthemums. Farmer Cresswell was an intelligent and industrious, and of course a thriving man. His wife, the aunt-in-law of Junia, supported her side of the house. They had a son, who helped his father, — a daughter, the right hand of her mother, and little children at school. They bought books, and took a newspaper. It was a magnanimous and kind-hearted family. They welcomed Richard with rural hospitality to rural joys.

Here Junia had spent the years since she left Woodylin. The father of Junia, an artist, having gone to Rome to complete his education, on the return voyage was drowned. Her mother died while the children were young, leaving to them the legacy of a tender memory and unavailing regrets, — of a spirit attuned to purest impulses, and a malady that ere long appeared in Violet. They remained with their grandparents until one died, and adversity and weakness prostrated the other. The change in their grandfather, united with alarming symptoms in Violet, induced the girls to resort to the Factories.

Their aunt, the wife of Farmer Cresswell, and only surviving child of the Old Man, meanwhile had died. Junia was ignorant of her successor. If she had known what a woman she was, and what a home the farm might be to her, she would have been spared, if not her residence, at least some of her sorrows, at Woodylin.

In her new home, she assumed charge of the school in the neighborhood; but tendencies similar to those that prostrated her sister disclosing themselves in her constitution, at length forbade this species of exertion.

instant afflicted his imagination as a cloud on the joyousness of her greeting, and a solemnity pervading the cheerful courtesies of the house.

But sickness and sorrow are so much alike, this impression gradually assimilated with the prevailing mood of Richard's mind; his sensations became toned down to the color of Junia, and he seemed in spirit to be brought very near unto her.

The neighbors said she was threatened with a decline. She appeared, indeed, to have been summoned by the voice of Violet, and to be slowly following to the realm of spirits. The Old Man presaged the result, and, with decrepit hilarity, instructed Richard in the fatal signs, and demonstrated the veritableness of his predictions.

Yet Junia retained all her equanimity, and a good portion of her strength. She went with Richard into the fields, and took a long walk with him to a spring in the mountains; he helped her trim and relay the flowers in the garden.

Several days passed in delicious abandonment.

Richard imparted his distress to Junia, and she was prompt to reply to it. But these communications and this intercourse were not without a certain perplexity, the nature of which we will endeavor to unfold.

This brings us to a sacred precinct of the human heart, and one that we should shrink from traversing, did not the proper development of this Tale seem imperatively to demand it; and more especially were we not confident that no handling of ours could detract from the essential interest and value that invested the subject to the parties immediately concerned.

Let us briefly state the facts, leaving the mystical and unknown spirit of things to that interpretation which they may justly bear. Junia loved Richard, — not with an impatient, or imperious, or forestalling love, — but with a deep, strong love; — a love constant, if not adhesive, — a love that remembered, even if it was deficient in attention.

Richard's piety and charity, his delicate and constant assiduity, his devotion to her sister Violet, and subsequent care of herself, at that early period when this Tale opens, won upon the heart of Junia, raised her mere enjoyment of goodness to some desire of its possession, carried her from the common ground of friendship and esteem to that sometimes called hazardous verge, where such feelings slide into love, — slide unwittingly and unpurposely into it; — into a love that does not announce itself, but lives in the shadow of things about it, — lives, nun-like, in its own mystery, and novelty, and blessedness; — and, perhaps, like the nightingale, sings all the more sweetly for its confinement and seclusion. In all this, as we conceive, no trace of blame attaches to Junia. Richard, at the time, had some dim and unheeding impression of the fact. But, as an honorable man, he encouraged nothing; as a modest man, he was flattered by nothing; as a young man, preöccupied with business and apprenticed to a trade, he remembered nothing.

But when it was proposed that he should see Junia, dim impressions of the past revived, — passively and spontaneously revived, — and perhaps worked to confuse his decision. And really the matter troubled his approach to her. His errand related to his engagement with another, — related to what must indicate to Junia how hopelessly she was separated from him; — related, in a word, to topics that must give her pain.

Moreover, Miss Eyre knew of the state of Junia's heart. Having early consecrated herself to Richard, Plumy Alicia was jealous of any intervention or rivalry. She was witness of Richard's fidelity in the sick chamber; she followed Junia when she went to Willow Croft, and, by methods peculiar to herself, learned the secret that otherwise might have slumbered forever in the Orphan's breast.

Mrs. Eyre relied upon what she knew for the accomplishment of her subsequent purposes, or rather to prevent Richard accomplish his. She believed that Junia, deeply attached to Richard, would not lend an influence to facilitate his inclinations for another, and would prefer, of the two, rather to widen, than close, the breach between him and Melicent. She felt perfectly safe with Junia, and hence the freedom with which she alluded to her at the council at Whichcomb's. Miss Eyre mistook her own sex. Richard trusted the magnanimity of a virtuous heart!

The short and decisive inquiry he had to make of Junia, whether his conduct towards her was open to question, she answered with a prompt No! "But why do you ask?" said she.

"For the gratification of my friends."

"You say you are separated from Miss Dennington?"

"Forever!" he added, with energy.

They were silent. Junia plucked the grass on which she was sitting. Richard looked at the flickering branches of the tree overhead.

"You did love her?"

"I did."

"And do?"

"It is the mystery of my existence," replied Richard, "that I do when I may not, and the discipline which my heavenly Father imposes, that I must when I cannot."

"Do and may not, must and cannot," rejoined Junia, smiling; "ever and never; now and now, and no to-morrow; — how strange a world this is! There are others like you."

This declaration startled Richard. He thought he knew what it meant, and feared there was more meaning than he would be able to manage.

"May not a desolate heart," she said, "embrace a desolate heart? Embrace mine! Hope," she continued, "distributes flowers in her vases, and keeps them to look at till their brief day is over, when, like a careful housewife, she flings them into a heap to die together!"

She laid her hand upon his shoulder; then, taking his arm, they walked into the house.

It was a delightful home she had, and Richard was made very happy there, and the family kept him many days. He would hardly be sorry if it were decreed they should keep him always there. Rarely had he seen the sun shine on so pleasant a spot, — rarely had he seen so pleasant a spot, when there was no sun.

"I love you," said Junia, "therefore do not be afraid of me; — I love you, therefore I will be your best friend; — I love you, and I love those that love you. I have no selfishness, no vanity, and will do what I can to make you happy. I find my little all of bliss in telling you that I love you. They say I shall die soon, — I will die for you. You do not know a woman's heart, — you never can; — nor a young girl's heart, such as mine was, and has been, and must ever be; — nor how, as a wound in a tender sapling, even when it heals up, remains in the tree, and becomes a part of its heart, and gives its own shape to the fibres, and has veins through which the life of the whole flows, — you have been to me. And now, when you are lowest and most degraded, and, if it must be so, most hopeless to my wish, this love loves you the most."

If Richard ever felt drawn towards any human being,—if he ever felt repaid a thousand times over for all he had done for any one,—if he ever felt thankfulness at relief, like a sudden recoil in the jaws of a vice that held him,—he felt this now in respect of Junia.

To a paper, like a deposition, or affidavit, vindicating Richard from the calumny promulgated by Mrs. Whichcomb, and behind which Miss Eyre intrenched herself, comprising, likewise, the warmest and most forcible allusions to his probity and sincerity, Junia affixed her signature, as did likewise her Grandfather.

With this, Richard returned to Woodylin.

The document was conveyed to Miss Rowena, who, as to her personal rencontre with Mrs. Melbourne, rejoiced in the support it furnished. But more: she showed it privately to Melicent, who derived what consolation she could from its contents. Mrs. Melbourne, to whom it was communicated, admitted its truthfulness, and allowed its entire weight. But, said she, "Rowena, you must see that is not all,—it is not a beginning. If that was all, the case were quickly determined. I rejoice as much as you do in this. But the greater, the stubborn, the wicked facts remain. Our evidence is not like a chain that can be spoilt in its links;—it is like a stone-wall; and though you remove a single rock, the strength of the whole is not shaken." There was force in the remark, however it stood with the evidence;—and Melicent felt it, and was silent. Cousin Rowena, not quite abashed, said, "Perhaps we can make a breach through the wall."

CHAPTER XLII.

QUIET RESUMPTION OF LIFE.

Miss Freeling, who became a sort of messenger between Richard and the Governor's Family, told him how Miss Rowena was pleased with the paper; — beyond this, she could say nothing, and Richard expected nothing. In this, still, he was repaid for his journey; and added to this, his spirits seemed to revive in the remembrance of Junia. He wrote to her, and she to him; and her letters were as music in the night of his sorrows.

Clover clenched the nail of Richard's calamity, which Miss Eyre had already driven to the head; and despair becoming a habit and law of his mind, and getting himself used to it, it offered less and less obstruction to the routine of his days, and uniformity of his feelings.

He bowed to the will of Heaven, and addressed himself with firmness and sobriety to the days of the years of his pilgrimage. He read his Bible more diligently, — not to repine with Job, but to invigorate himself on Paul, and especially to imitate his Master, who went about doing good.

There were moments when he would abandon the city, and retire to the country, returning to the house of his father, or wedding the shadows of his heart to the evening of the days of Junia. But his business was extensive, and its concerns complicated, and it involved the interest of parties very dear to him.

While he would utterly banish Melicent from his thoughts,

we may suppose he did it somewhat like the poet in Gil Blas, who, having resolved to abandon his art, bade an eternal adieu to the Muses, in verse!

Did he never complain? Did no discontent overhang his brow? Did no imprecation attempt the purity of his lip?

There is no trial so severe as that of the heart. There is no furnace of affliction so hot as that enkindled in the sensibilities. There is no temptation from which a man had better pray for quick deliverance than that addressed to the affections and sentiments.

The fowls were a fortunate affair. They supplied his purse with cash, and his leisure with amusement. The crowing of the cocks set Memmy and Bebby to cackling, and Uncle must of course pipe up a little, too.

The ancient Church used to clothe its penitents in white sheets. Richard seemed to belong to this class, for Roxy declared his face was white as a sheet; but Aunt Grint, more lenient than those priests who ordered hair-shirts in addition, recommended the extract of valerian, under which he visibly amended.

And if still in any sense outside of the Church, he was willing to serve it in the humble capacity of verger; and he sought to get his Ragged children into some of the meetings. At least, he raised them to the Griped Hand, which was a stepping-stone to the Church. Chuk improved in manners and speech, and suffered Mysie to comb his hair and wash his clothes.

The golden apples which Hercules took from the garden of the Hesperides could not be kept anywhere else, and had to be conveyed back where they grew. Men may say what they will about the cultivation of virtue outside the Church, there will always be a sighing and pining of these virtues for the Church — the *true* Church. Richard especially, as he seemed to have derived the seeds of the good he was able to effect from the Church, was most happy in being permitted to return thither some of the fruit. In truth, are not all ragamuffins, gamins, sneaks, trulls, topers, Golden Apples, that at some period or other have been stolen from the Church?

Richard's old pupils of the Sabbath-school visited him, and he took them to see his "Olive-garden," and they assisted him in cultivating it. They brought their little library-books, full of pictures and pretty ideas, and gave them to these outcasts. They invited them to their picnics and rural celebrations, and their mothers and aunts made decent clothes for them. These Sabbath-school boys led Chuk to the Griped Hand! This was considered a great exploit, — a crowning triumph.

Dr. Broadwell and Parson Smith honored Richard with a visit. These gentlemen, while they supposed Richard essentially culpable, relied on his judgment and discretion, and could not question his good intentions. Parson Smith, indeed, had frequently seen Richard, and believing in the soundness of his piety and purity of his aims, notwithstanding the darkness that shrouded portions of his history, and seeing, as he thought, every token of contrition, was unwilling that his relations to the Church and Christian people should materially change. If he were a sinner before God, the Parson argued, he had better keep within reach of the appointed means of grace.

They called to converse with Richard on the Theatre, circuses, and similar things, that were the pests of recreation, and corrupted the proper pastime of the people. The discussion was harmonious and interesting. To concentrate on the Griped Hand, and make that attractive to Leisure and Weariness, to Ignorance and Grossness, and the varied desultory thirsts and instincts of men, was a foregone conclusion. But could it have a kind of municipal prerogative, — would the city confer upon the Rectors of that institution a licensing power, and compel the wandering disciples of Thespis, and rude children of the Centaurs, to submit to their arbitration, — a point would be gained. So these Churchmen thought, and Richard with them.

Both these divines, in conversation with Richard, wholly forgot that Richard was a bad man. The exercise of the mind on any good object is wont to give a turn of goodness to the mind. Moreover, Parson Smith theorized that bad men might have some good qualities, and Dr. Broadwell practised on the Parson's theory; — thus the working methods of these two men were identical. It was a favorite notion with the Parson, that you had better shake hands with a man's virtues, than kick at his vices. He was known once to have said he would sooner take virtue from the devil's back, than see it sprawling under his belly.

Some called this smooth preaching. "There are different kinds of smoothness," he replied. "There is the smoothing quality of the laundress' iron, the carpenter's plane, and the farmer's roller; there is a smooth road, and a smooth skin; there is the smoothness of silk and of liquor. If we can iron down some of the wrinkles in human society, — it is already well starched, — or joint religion and life, or roll the fields we sow, that they may stand a drought, and the Church be saved from dulling her scythe on stones, when she mows, — it were smooth preaching something worth."

Richard was an atom distressed by a letter from Junia, in which, after announcing the death of her grandfather, she says, "I am going to Woodylin. I long to be where Violet is buried and Richard suffers. My father's earnest, beautiful soul urges me. My mother's image, as an enmarbled pale reminiscence, in the shadows of the past, smiles upon me. Grandfather heard in the trees the same bird that foreshadowed the death of Violet, and looking at me, he said its note was Wood-y-lin! I tremble for thy misery, good, kind one! Have I not caused it all? Let me, if I cannot remove it, be where it is. Be not troubled for my coming. My excellent uncle consents to the journey. My cousin will convey me to the stage road. Winkle will take care of me then."

Richard replied, begging her not to come. Her presence, while it would rejoice him, would do his cause no good; — that was past attempt, or hope. Her health, he said, would be endangered. She would be among strangers, without a home, or comforts, or friends, like her uncle's.

She rejoined, "Leave me to my resolution and my love. Give me the ministry of your smile and gladness, for one day. Conduct me to the spot where Violet lies, and, with thy arm to lean upon, and the beauty of Rosemary Dell about me, I shall go cheerfully to my final rest."

Richard gave instructions to Winkle, — who was on the alert for whatever was pathetic, as well as prompt in what was purely commercial, on his route, — to be mindful of Junia, and bring her safely.

But Winkle could manage better than Richard. "Let her wait another week, and that will be, he said, a full week; and Mr. St. John will have to fit out an extra, and it shall be the pleasant little invalid hack, and Simon, the pleasant little invalid hack-driver, shall drive it; for Mr. St. John owes it to the route, ever since he lost his bet on Tunny's head; and Munk will not object. I always told them, if we only had a sick people's carriage, and a carriage with blinds for lovers, and Simon, with his pleasant way of singing, to drive it, we should do a swimming business. Did you ever drive lovers? It 's rich, driving them for nothing!"

CHAPTER XLIII.

AN UNEXPECTED VISITER ACTUALLY COMES.

A VIOLENT thumping was heard at the door of Willow Croft, which, before it could be properly noticed, answered itself, and burst into the house in the obese and burly shape of Climper, of Climper's, or rather of Merrywater. He had on a farmer's frock, and brandished a large whip in his hand. "I am an odd fish," he said; "I know I am. People abuse me, and I let them alone; — that is odd. They are kind to me, and I am kind to them; — that is odd. They won't be happy, and I make them happy; — that, again, is odd. Out of this," — he touched Richard with his whip, — "no more sulking! You would n't dance with Mrs. Melbourne, and I made you; and she likes it, and has had some more of it, and I mean she shall have more yet. I love to please people. Forward!"

This was concise and forcible, — rather too much so for Richard, in his present weak state. He would fain have an explanation. The commentary was as obscure as the text. But Richard learned as much as this, — that Climper liked Richard and the Governor's Family; — there may have been cause from the fact that the Governor and his Family, and the coaches belonging to Munk, Richard's brother-in-law, often visited Merrywater, and were profitable customers of Climper; — that he had heard of the rupture between them, and possessed, as he imagined, a clue to the origin of it in Clover. This fellow had been at Merrywater with Miss Eyre. Once, being out with them on the pond, and drowsily tending the tiller, and, as they thought, sleeping, he overheard Clover urging Miss Eyre to the assault of Richard, and particularly suggesting the method of approach, through Mrs. Melbourne. He thought little of it at the time, — believed Richard could take care of himself. But a party, comprising Captain Creamer, Mangil, Helen the Good, and Miss Freeling, being at his house, told him of the disastrous and irretrievable result. This man cherished, moreover, a particular disrelish for Clover, who ran up bills at Merrywater which he never paid, and plagued Climper by a little yelping terrier that he took with him. Coming to Woodylin with a load of vegetables for the Market, he went to Willow Croft with purposes that he whimsically and characteristically unfolded.

He would lead Richard to the Governor's. Richard drew back. "That 's pleasant," said he. "I like opposition. It stimulates me. Forward! I 'll cry fire, if you wish it, and raise the neighbors. Shall I run off with one of the children? Shall I go and let your hens out of the coop? Shall I get the city crier to ring your dumpishness through the streets, — or you will not start? He laid his hand on Richard's collar. The children clung to their mother, who was herself alarmed. "I am not much used to women and children," he said. "They are flesh, I suppose; and all flesh is vanity. If Richard knew this, he would be wiser than he is now. We must teach him."

At this instant, Aunt Grint entered the room, in one of her panics, though of a pleasanter sort than usual. "What is it?" she exclaimed. "We heard crickets as lively as could be! I could n't stop. I told Sally to mind the pot, and I 'd run out, and see."

"We want this fellow to go to the Governor's," replied Climper, "and he is n't willing. It 's a dreadful cross, but he must bear it."

"That 's it!" echoed the old woman. "I knew it was something pleasant. I could n't stay to put up the dishes, but come right out in the suds as I was. He shall go."

If Climper pulled at Richard's collar, Aunt Grint seemed to drub his shoulders.

Resistance was unavailing against this novel pertinacity. Richard took his hat, and went with Climper. Reluctantly, and with a shudder of trepidation, he allowed himself to be taken to and through the Governor's gate, and across the yard, and up the piazza, and face to face with the great front-door. He must endure the heavy tramp of his companion where he wished himself all cat's-paws, and his violent ringing of the bell when there was not strength enough in his own arm to shake a cob-web. Climper asked for Mrs. Melbourne, and they were taken to the drawing-room. Mrs. Melbourne appeared. She was formal and reserved. She did not know to what she owed the honor of the visit or the company. "To the pleasure I have in coming to see you," replied Climper, — "the same as people come to see me." "People often behave very rudely at your house," replied Mrs. Melbourne. "I know they do," rejoined Climper, "and that is what has brought me here. This young man —"

"I thought you would refer to his conduct," interrupted the lady; "but you need not. We are too well informed. We do not wish the subject broached in this way, Mr. Climper."

"There are some things you would be glad to know."

"Nothing, — nothing."

"There are some things I should like to tell you. I am an odd man, — very odd; I love to tell the truth."

"If anything more is to be said, I must call witnesses. I am disinclined to personal communications relating to Mr. Edney."

She left the room firmly, and returned with Miss Rowena, Barbara, and Glendar, — a formidable troop, that would have abashed anybody but Climper. Cousin took a seat on the sofa by Richard. Barbara posted herself behind the centre-table, where she thrust one hand into a book, as if she would let agitation discharge at the ends of her fingers into its leaves. Glendar sat very stiffly in a chair, with his hand in his vest. It fell to Mrs. Melbourne to face the occasion, and support its dignity.

Climper, in his way, related the plot Clover had concerted against the peace of Richard and the Family.

"I know nothing of Clover, — neither do I desire to," interposed Mrs. Melbourne.

"Perhaps you do not," rejoined Climper. "I always go against people's feelings, you say. I cannot stop that now; — you must know about him."

"You will not insult my Aunt," said Glendar.

"Nor you either, so long as you run up bills at Merrywater, which I suppose your Aunt is to pay."

Glendar grew more stiff in his chair, and seemed with the hand in his vest to be clutching at his heart. Mrs. Melbourne looked angrily at Climper, and worriedly at her nephew. Cousin bit her lip very hard.

"There is nothing frightful in Clover." Mrs. Melbourne tried to laugh the matter off. Climper laughed harder, and added, "You are right. I have got my heel upon him."

"He is not a brute." This was a fling at Climper himself.

"He loves dogs, and is a dog!"

"He is n't Miss Eyre; — you must know he is n't, Mr. Climper; and *that* is where wickedness lies."

Barbara trembled, and Richard, too.

"I have told you the truth about *him*," continued Climper; "and whether he is Miss Eyre or not, you can see. I rather guess Miss Eyre is n't him, and is somebody else, and you would do well to think so. He is a villain; and if she is n't him, perhaps she is n't a villain. Think of that. It may do you all good to think of that. And I mean somebody shall think of that. If you do not, and Miss Melicent would come in, I would make her think of it."

This allusion to Melicent brought Glendar to his feet, but it did not anybody else. Spending himself in an effort to stand, tired, the young man left the room, and was speedily followed by his indignant Aunt.

Cimper said, "My business was with Mrs. Melbourne, and I will go,"—and took his leave.

No sooner was he out of the house than Mrs. Melbourne returned, in haste, and flushed.

"We have been abused by that man. He was always a brute!" she said.

"You are very kind to the brute creation, Mrs. Melbourne," said Cousin, softly.

This was better said than received. It raised a storm, in which Richard would fain have got away.

"All this is nothing to the point," said Mrs. Melbourne. "You must see that it is n't, Rowena." She did not deign to address Richard.

"If it 's Clover's doings—" Cousin Rowena began to say.

"'T is somebody's else doings!" Mrs. Melbourne said this with a tone so terrible, and a look so scathing, Richard could not contain himself, and quite abruptly left the house.

He did, however, hear other words which Mrs. Melbourne uttered, with a loud and almost tragic emphasis—

"You must see, Barbara, that Clover's agency don't alter Miss Eyre's wrongs, nor that fellow's baseness!"

These words, and the ring of the voice, adhered to Richard all the way home.

CHAPTER XLIV.

JUNIA FULFILS HER INTENTION.

She came to the relief of Richard's spirits, and, as it were, to the care of his hands; and in the last, perhaps, carried out the idea of the first, since a little outward oversight of this sort, and secular responsibility, could do him no harm.

Simon brought her in the best manner Winkle could devise. She entered softly and quietly, with an air of lofty purpose, united to a sense of delicate position; her face was not so much sickly pale, as subdued by spiritual concern; her voice was sweet, but evening-like; her eye was mellow with love and enthusiasm. She kissed Roxy and the children.

After tea, she sat in the rocking-chair in the parlor. Junia had a more southern cast than Violet; she was born, her Grandfather used to say, in a warmer month. She had dark eyes, and small and firm lips. The twilight, — that blush with which Night introduces her starry train to the world, — from over dun hills, crossing silent hollows and entering the room through the cool trees Richard had planted in the yard, — was reflected in the pure and exalted fervor of her countenance. Was she, as one of the clouds that floated in that burning expanse, turned for a brief moment to flesh? Was she a Daughter of God, ready to be offered on some altar of human sorrow? Her thin fingers, the delicacy of her frame, and even the sculptured precision of her features, indicated, that if of mortal essence, purged of mortal defilement, she was even then undergoing translation.

"I have but one duty in life, Richard," she said, "and that is to thee; my next is to join the Immortals. The recompense and fulfilment of my love, that has been growing in the lonely places of thought, like the pitcher-plant, and filling its cup with the dew and rain of an ideal good, is to pour its contents on your parched life, and to see thee blessed, thou greatly noble, and greatly wronged one!"

Almost as if she were divinely inspired, Richard was subdued before Junia, and ventured no remonstrance to the course of her inclinations.

She had changed since he saw her; she was feebler, but more resolved, — less unreserved in her love, but more self-forgetful in its intents, — very cheerful and very serious.

In two or three days, having worn off the fatigue of her journey, she expressed a desire to visit the grave of Violet.

Simon, who had risen from stable-boy to hack-driver, who loved to serve Richard, and continued to sing, with new pathos to Richard's ear, that melancholy refrain, like a fragment from the ruin of some old dirge which he carried about with him, was ordered to bring up the invalid coach.

Junia entered the parlor from her chamber, clad in white; her dress and gloves were white, and a white rose-bud adorned her hair. There was a singularly clear and luminous effect in her person and attire; throughout, an unusual carefulness showed, and her appearance was suggestive almost of a bridal occasion, — an illusion which the pallid ardor of her look rather heightened than destroyed. Fair to the senses, her aspect was still more affecting to the imagination; and Richard, sacredly moved, drew from under his vest, where he had so sadly worn it, the small golden cross, which he reverently hung on her neck.

Simon's song was heard at the gate, and Junia, throwing on her bonnet and shawl, left the house. Richard would have done more than hand her into the carriage, — he would go with her; but she said, "Not now." He could do little else than listen to the wailing cavatina of the boy, as he drove off with the precious minister to his peace.

She was driven to Rosemary Dell. Under the shadows of pines, and along circling walks, she wended her way to the spot where Violet lay. A willow hung over the enclosure; and those flowers that gave the sleeper her name, in lowly beauty — little Vestal-fires of Nature — cherished the sanctity of her grave. Junia leaned upon the willow, and wept; in weeping she vented her sisterly sorrow, and at the same time, as it were, moistened and bedewed the springs of her own feeling. What went forth in sadness, like the exhalation of troubled water, returned in gentle showers of consolation and gladness to the wasting verdure of her soul. "Soon, soon," she said, "I shall be with you, thou blessed one! I thank thee that I can weep for thee, — I feel how nearly I am at one with thee! A mission which thou wouldst bless, for the friend of us both, and for one whom, oh my sister, thou couldst have loved, — an injured one of earth, — is the brief distance I must travel, before I come to thee, — and to you, Father, Mother, — and to Thee, oh Saviour of men!"

Having finished her prayer, she returned to the carriage.

Did she perceive that Miss Eyre was in the cemetery, alone, and apparently thoughtful and pensive, — like some penitent Spirit of Evil, meditating among those vestiges of decay? She was there; and with steadfast eye, — nor could it be otherwise than with deep sensitiveness of heart, —

behind contiguous shrubbery, she beheld the emotion of Junia. She followed her as she left the place, and overheard her direction to Simon, to Governor Dennington's.

We shall take the liberty to enter with Junia at the Governor's, and while she waits reception, look at the state of feeling the Family is in.

Miss Eyre had been summoned as a rejoinder to Climper. She denied Clover's complicity with her affairs; — this to Mrs. Melbourne. But to Miss Rowena, who questioned her more at length, she admitted, not that her wrongs were less, but that, her delicacy being greater, Clover appeared, and not only recommended, but potentially and portentously urged her to the course she had taken. Herein she spoke absolute truth.

The Family, then, we cannot say were in a state of doubt, but in a state of certainty, with its surface somewhat ruffled. Mrs. Melbourne, however, was ruffled painfully, — Cousin Rowena pleasantly. The latter rejoiced in the agitation Climper had given the Family, and was glad to feel anything like a disturbance in the career of those terrible convictions down which she was rapidly tending. Melicent, about whom all the interest and all the moods of the Family gravitated, must listen to varied accounts, and be torn by contending emotions.

Miss Eyre having become domiciled equally in Mrs. Melbourne's heart and rooms, by a side door, entered the house soon after Junia, and went to the chamber of her friend.

Junia inquired for Melicent, whom she had seen in Violet's sickness. Melicent did not recollect Junia. She extended her hand to the pale figure before her, whose mingled look of anxiety and earnestness, as well as the shadowy features and pure attire, arrested her attention and kindled her fancy. "I am Junia," said the latter. "When Violet was sick, you were with us; you laid flowers on her bier."

Melicent, moved by this recall of the past, and the vision of the present, affectionately saluted her.

"I wish to speak of Richard." Junia said this with an emphasis that quite thrilled Melicent, who, at once surprised and awed, echoed, "Richard!" In a moment, collecting herself, she said, "If of that, come to my chamber," — whither they went.

"I came," said Junia, when they were seated, "to intercede for Richard. I know him to be pure and good. I have long known him so. And you, Melicent, — you have known him so. Your heart, your memory, your reason, remind you of nothing else."

Melicent became pale, — paler, even, than the speaker before her.

"Do not think of *that*, — do not confuse yourself with it at all," continued Junia. "He has erred, — he may have sinned; but his sin is not beyond forgiveness or removal. It is lost in the depth of his piėty, — it is swept away by his virtues, as a leaf on the river."

"I do not think of that," answered Melicent, strongly agitated; "I think beyond that, of him."

"And he loves you!"

"Loves me?" cried Melicent.

"Loves you," replied Junia, "with unmixed, unchanging love, — loves as purely as an angel in heaven might love."

"How can you know that? — alas! alas!"

"I know him," replied Junia; "how, I cannot tell, — I dare not tell. I know him, as your own heart knows him; — and tell me, do you love him?"

"Ah!" cried Melicent; "where is that in my deepest

heart which I once was, and worshipped, and lost, and missed?"

"I recall it," said Junia; "I bring it back."

"To have once doubted," said Melicent, "not *that*, for that might be; but to doubt *him*, to fear him; to feel the approach of vague, invisible possibilities, which smite and stagger you, when you can do nothing; to have the venomous, bitter uncertainties of things, like reptiles from the Dark Mountains, get into your heart, and be shut in there, — there, where a woman's longing, and hope, and ideal, are all kept; to be once so disturbed and so sickened; — oh, what is woman? What are you? What am I?"

"Hear me," said Junia; "listen to me. I speak as a woman."

"A Great Evil," rejoined Melicent, "has befallen me; the Good Father knows why. Its terror chills my frame; its darkness obscures my thought. O, Parent of the Universe, teach thy child submission, — guide her heart!" She started from her chair, and with mingled despair, mournfulness, and hope, walked the room, wringing her hands wildly. She flung herself on a seat in the embrasure of the window, where the heavy tapestry concealed her face, but could not hide the voice of her anguish.

Junia rose, and deliberately laid off her bonnet and shawl. She approached Melicent, and solemnly knelt at her feet. As if a flash of pathos, inspired by piety, had knelt before her, the white array, ghostly complexion, and golden cross of Junia, mystically aroused Melicent.

"What is this I see?" she exclaimed.

"The lover and the bride of Richard," calmly replied Junia. "Such I plead with thee for him — "

"What do I hear?" Melicent cried, still more excited.

"Listen, oh best beloved of the best beloved! I love

Richard; — I loved him for his greatness and his purity; I loved him with the instinct of girlhood, — I have loved him with the meditativeness of womanhood. I love you, oh precious sister of my soul! because you love him. I know what you feel; I share your sufferings. He, too, suffers. I have been near his heart; I have heard its lonely anguish; I have felt its tortured throbs. I love his happiness; and his happiness is your love; and the happiness of you both is your mutual reünion. I am his bride, but through you. My love for him I give to you. Take it into your heart, — let it be your love! Let it survive in the depth of your affection! Let it shed its light upon the darkness that surrounds you! And when, in the rapture of being, you can call him your own, remember, oh remember, that one, young and inexperienced, — too susceptible, perhaps too constant, — that Junia loved him too!"

"How can I support this?" exclaimed Melicent. "In what heavenly transition do I awake? Art thou a mortal?"

"I am simple Junia," replied the other; "but hear me; — I am brided to Richard's and your felicity. I put on this little array, such as a fond girl's heart might choose; clothing not my body, but an irrepressible promise of things in my soul; clothing, it may be, some old, pleasant feelings, that once wished to be the bride of Richard; clothing, too, the brief remaining hour of my life for marriage with the ideal vision which your union with him is to my mind, — the union of Wealth and Worth, — of Refinement and Nobleness, — of Richard and Melicent!"

"Dearest Junia!" cried Melicent; "purest of beings! Let me embrace you, — let me fold to my heart its long-lost tranquillity!"

"I perish, — I die!" answered Junia. "The voice of the oriole has been heard. My happiness is complete when yours begins. I am called to the spirit land, — let me bless you and Richard ere I go — "

Her voice faltered; blood on her lips betrayed the violent hemorrhage that succeeded. She fainted; and while Melicent was attempting to support her, an outbursting sob, as of some one in the chamber, was heard. It was Miss Eyre, who instantly, but trembling with emotion, advanced, and assisted in carrying the languid frame to the bed.

Miss Eyre had followed Junia, — followed her with more than usual concern, and even approached the chamber of Melicent, where, moved by the impassioned language within, she opened the door, and beheld Junia at Melicent's feet, and heard her words.

She was at least awed. Solemn, tender, delicate, she exerted herself to bring back the spirit that seemed so suddenly and so affectingly to have vanished.

Opening her eyes, Junia said, "Ah, Plumy Alicia! and you too — you to bless the hour, — you to make us all happy?"

The house was aroused. Madam Dennington, confined to her room by some illness of the season, could no more than give directions for the sick one. Miss Eyre summoned Mrs. Melbourne, who was always kind to the unfortunate, and who forgot everything else in an occasion like the present.

Dr. Chassford, the family physician, was called, who, with other specifics, ordered quietness and rest. His manner showed, what all felt, that Junia could not live long.

"I am quiet," she said, a little while afterwards. "I have unburdened my heart, and I rest."

But she grew weaker, and could not be moved. "Send word," she said, "to Willow Croft, that I cannot return to-day, but not to be alarmed for me."

CHAPTER XLV.

THE HEART OF MISS EYRE.

THE immediate excitement of this casualty having subsided, the Family were left to ponder more serious matters connected with the visit of Junia. Mrs. Whichcomb and the council were disposed of, — Clover's villany stood revealed. What remained, that Richard should not be immediately summoned, and the reconciliation celebrated? Miss Eyre remained, broodingly, silently, awfully. She remained literally with Mrs. Melbourne, who would not suffer her to leave the house; — she remained mystically in all hearts and apprehensions. Why should not the Family throw itself upon its intuitions, and act at once in obedience thereto? It was *not* a way it had, — if we except Barbara, who had such a way, and put on her hat to execute it. But Roscoe, who was pruning trees in the front yard, prevented her; — Roscoe, the silent and unsocial one, reputed so queer and strange. "Plumy Alicia," said he, "has not spoken. If Richard is recalled, she must be banished; his exoneration is her perdition. We must wait a little. There are things to be explained yet. Who of us can pretend to fathom all this mystery?" Barbara loved Roscoe and yielded to him.

Melicent and Junia both felt, and they all felt, what Roscoe expressed. "God will help us," said Junia. "Let us wait on him." "I can wait, if you can," responded Melicent.

What would Miss Eyre do? We have said she betrayed extreme emotion at the sight of Junia and Melicent. What did she see at that moment? She saw an old, fond love, intent, not upon the possession but the welfare of the beloved; she saw hopelessness pleading with aversion in behalf of neglect; she saw virtue seeking to acquit turpitude to conscience; disinterestedness launched on destruction to render deliverance. She saw Junia supplicating Melicent for Richard; she saw woman's heart yielding heroically to rival supremacy; she saw a young girl's gushing, undying affection, sacrificing itself on the altar of another's love. She beheld cheerfulness where she anticipated moodiness, constancy where she had prophesied hatred; and was the witness of a defence from a quarter which to her own mind boded nothing but scorn and vengeance.

The sight overcame her; its novelty, mystery, pathos, amazed her; its incantation spun through all her frame. But while it swept like a wind across the forest of her sensibilities, we are not prepared to say it upturned a single root of her purpose.

The next day, being alone with Mrs. Melbourne, she burst into tears.

"I do not wonder you feel bad," said her old mistress. "If I were not more than usually sustained, I should cry too. What a height of impudence and vulgarity!"

Miss Eyre made no answer.

"Try the camphor-bottle; — oh dear, how wicked is man! how unfeeling are the lower orders! That Richard would kill you, if he were left to himself one moment! I have seen him strike a horse that was all in a foam of sweat. — Open the window, where you can breathe." This did not abate Miss Eyre's distress.

"I do not blame you, Plumy Alicia," continued her comforter. "I cannot; I have it not in my heart to see the least of God's creatures suffer, except some who deserve it.—Well, I will not,—I know you are tender on that point. Don't cry so, dear girl! you shall marry Richard. Lie on my bed,—smell of this chamomile. If Richard has wronged you, and you still love him, you shall have him. I know we cannot help our feelings. When I was young—oh God forgive me!—There, there; I will never speak against Richard again."

Miss Eyre wept herself to sleep, and sank from convulsions to repose.

Mrs. Melbourne smoothed her hair and dress, and sat tenderly by her side. "I did not know," she said within herself, "she could feel so much. But she shall not *be* disappointed. What could have induced that country girl to undertake such a thing? Why is she sick? Do we not see God's finger in it?—That Glendar should be rejected, and that bad man promoted, is impossible."

When Miss Eyre awoke, it was with a manner apparently averted from Mrs. Melbourne; so much so that this lady regarded her with surprise.

"Why don't you speak?" she said.

"I can't to you," replied Miss Eyre.

"Why not to me? I am your friend. What are you going to do?" She asked this with consternation, as Miss Eyre, with hidden determination in her eye, left the bed.

"To see Junia," answered Miss Eyre.

"She has told her story," murmured Mrs. Melbourne.

"What if there were some truth in it?" rejoined the other.

Mrs. Melbourne would have screamed; but she hushed herself, and said, "Plumy Alicia, how rash! Will you ruin yourself, and disgrace us all? May she not have deceived? There is nothing too bad for some people to do! Who sent her here, — who? I wish the truth might be told, — all the truth, — and I am glad there are a few honest ears to hear it!"

Miss Eyre disappeared. She went to the bed-side of Junia.

Junia looked up, with a serene, rill-like smile, and laid her thin, transparent hand outside the bed, as it were inviting Miss Eyre's into it.

"Did you love Richard?" said Miss Eyre.

"You know I loved him," replied Junia.

"And you gave him up?"

"God took him, and gave him to another."

"I am not religious. Tell Mrs. Melbourne of that. Had you no hatred to him for leaving you?"

"He never left me; — I only clung to him."

"In that clinging, Junia, was there not joy, rapture, life?"

"Alas, dear Plumy Alicia, yes!"

"But you gave it all up, and have helped another one to cling where you were clinging, and to exult in what was your bliss?"

"She had a better right than I. Besides, his happiness was concerned, and her happiness, and the happiness of so many. And, dear Plumy Alicia, I have never been so happy as I am now; — I have done no more than my duty, and what God would have me do. You will not make Richard unhappy, will you? You will not do anything to distress his noble spirit, will you? You have been weeping; you will never weep again when Richard is happy; — you will be happy too."

Miss Eyre could not answer; she meditated.

Junia resumed. "I could not go into the next world, —

and we must all go there, — with the sin of unkindness to Richard, and Melicent, and all these excellent ones, on my soul."

Miss Eyre withdrew to the window, and sat where Melicent sat and Junia kneeled.

The same day, Miss Rowena did slip away to Willow Croft, but simply to tell them how Junia was, and to tell Richard how nobly she had vindicated him. She dared only allude to Miss Eyre; and Richard, perhaps, wished her to do no more than that. He had himself a feeling about Miss Eyre which Miss Rowena could not fathom.

Another night passed in the Family, — a night of thick, silent darkness, when the clouds seem to be in the streets, and walking about the houses, — when the windows all become black mirrors of things in the room, and if the heart is sad, these images look very gloomy. The whisking of wind in the trees, or the pattering of rain on the piazza, would have been a relief. Mrs. Melbourne was very melancholy, and Miss Eyre very pale.

Junia was a little day-time in her own heart and chamber, — a pleasant taper of resignation and patience; and she made Melicent and Barbara, who sat with her, feel hopeful and cheerful.

The next morning, Miss Eyre sought a private moment with Melicent. She said, "Neither you nor I can abide this much longer. I do not speak. Do you wish me to? Do you wish me to open my mouth? Do you wish to look through fair lips and beautiful teeth — they say I have them, — and beyond the smoothness of my tongue, into the depths of what I am, — into here, — into this, — which they call a heart?"

"Let me see everything it is in your power to show, that will be of any use to see," replied Melicent.

"Under this roof," continued Miss Eyre, "that now accuses me, derived I the elements of my crime. Some of them, — not all. Here were sown the seeds of the bitter night-shade you now taste in me. Not you, gentle, great one; — not Barbara; — not the Governor. Mrs. Melbourne taught me the essential worthlessness of that large class of people among whom I was born, and with whom it might be my fortune to spend my days. Mrs. Melbourne is generous, humane, tender-hearted. I am under a thousand obligations to her kindness; but she despises the lower orders, and she would have me despise, betray, disinherit my own kith and kin. I was ambitious, — proud, they call it. What is that? You know not. You were born great. You cannot step out without stepping into littleness. Then how easy, how pleasant, to take a few steps in that direction, — merely passing from Wilton carpets to dusty streets, — and go home to your own greatness! But for me, born little, to step into greatness, — how hard, how hazardous! Then to go home to littleness, — to creep back, after a pleasant exaltation, into one's mean hovel, — you know not what that is!

"Then there is love. O burden, unreäcting fatality, organic sigh, of woman! But whom love? Where my hearth-stone? Who lie in these arms? You cannot understand this. You are in a gallery of fine portraits, and can take any one. I am surrounded by daubs, and must hunt for what is tolerable. Have I no desire for what is excellent? Pulsates not every fibre of this woman's frame for the embrace of purity, elevation, nobleness? I saw Richard, — I liked him; — I tell you I liked him! He united the loftiness of the higher classes with the solid virtues of his own. I sprang towards him, in my heart, wantonly wildly His reserve and moderation the rather inflamed me. I intrigued, — yes, I was trained to that. What selfishness of voluptuousness, what shallowness of mediocrity, what cravings of the hod-clopperhood, have importuned for me, and sighed at my feet, and cajoled my vanity! I tortured him. The Redferns tortured me, more than you know of, — more than I can relate. Virtue, — I am not virtuous! Is Mrs. Melbourne, who has so perverted my existence, virtuous? Is Fiddledeeana Redfern, who has so wounded every womanly sensibility within me, virtuous? Do not look so upbraidingly at me!"

"I do not upbraid you. I am only deeply concerned in what you say."

"Give me your smelling-bottle. I am not going to faint. I want to carry off my excitement with spirit. You cannot think of my faults worse than I suffer from them. I abhor Clover; but he menaced me, — menaced not only my happiness, but even my life. I should support his cause, he said, or he would overrun me, — he would destroy me. He would have plunged me into the depths of Merrywater. Well if he had! I could not endure Richard's union with you. Hear the whole, and then do with me as you will. It rankled here. I could not help it."

"You mean," said Melicent, "you did not help it. You never practised self-control; you had no religious humility."

"Practised nothing, — had nothing, that you call good. No, no! Little of that has addressed itself to me. Good men, — your good men, — do not speak to me; — bad men are false and selfish with me. My regard for Richard *was the only good thing of my life!* I believed he loved me; at least, I believed I could make him love me, — that I had made him love me. Others managed for my approbation, — why should I not for his? Glendar has adored my smile, — why should I not fawn on Richard's heart? You are interested, — you may well be. I come to the quick of the thing. *I have told no untruths about Richard!* — Do not destroy your fan; you may be glad to use it before I have done. — Have you not learned that nobody tells lies? They tell truths so that they shall seem a lie, — that is all. I let untruths be told; — or rather, surrounded by stupidity and fanaticism, I had only to let the false impressions of people take their own course. I gave to truth a little of the rouge, the twinkle, the fine airs, of falsehood, and I had no further trouble. I knew not precisely the nature of his visits at the sick chamber of Violet; nor did I care to know, — it was little to me, any way. Mrs. Whichcomb believed, or made herself believe, he had other objects than charity; and she made more than one believe it, too. The lower orders have their faults and vices. They do not understand nobleness, or intellectuality, or cultured simplicity and freedom. They misappreciate you, Melicent, and your father, and your church, and your minister, and your whole social circle and position. It is not a month since, down on the Islands, I heard a man say he hoped the Governor would come to his last crust, — he did not care how soon! How easy, then, to pervert a visit to a sick chamber! I knew Junia loved Richard; and that I did care to know. I first dreaded, then hated her. And afterwards, so far as his connection with you was concerned, I thought she would hate him. Here I was mistaken. Of that, presently."

"You acquit Richard of the aspersions that have been thrown upon him?" said Melicent, with some earnestness.

"Do not be impassioned; — that is reserved for me. Junia disappointed me; she appalled me; she has wrung my heart, — wrung its animosity, its fire, its intention, all out of it. She is the first gleam of light in this dark world of affections and passions that surrounds me. As Clover says, she has crushed me! Sorrow, remorse, hurtle pitilessly through this ruin of my being. Richard is too innocent, — too harmless. If he had only been guilty, — not that, — if he had been selfish or forward, — I should have loved him more: — nay, I should have scorned him! He has his weak points; and his weak ones are my strong ones, and there I should have mastered him, but for a something beyond. — What is that something?"

"Religion, — Conscience, — God."

"I did not ask to be told of that. I only asked in a reverie sort of way. Richard relies on the simplicity of things, and what he supposes to be the goodness of men. He deceives himself."

"Are you never deceived?"

"Richard is sorry for me. He knows I am not exempt from pangs. He feels committed, not to me, but to my misery. You can break a man's heart, sometimes, by breaking your own."

"Angelic Richard! Wicked, wicked Plumy Alicia!"

"Not on purpose, — not altogether with guile. — I was broken. He has even now to step over my desolation to reach you."

Melicent raised her handkerchief to her face.

"You can weep, Melicent. I have wept. I have drained myself dry, as the stubble after reaping.

"Did Richard have no intention and respect of love towards me? Could I raise none such? Ah! he said he detested me! I have been deceived, — I deceived myself. Junia! Junia! thou wert a woman; I was a —

"Where am I? Whither shall I turn? The world, that clutched at my story, and, bartering its respect for its envy, patronized my cause, and poured its venom on Richard, will whirl upon me."

"Is there not such a thing as duty?"

"Junia said so, and you say so; and I suppose it is so."

"You speak," said Melicent, "as if there were no goodness. Is there none in the Church, — none in the Griped Hand, — none in the little children, — none in every street of the city, or in a thousand families, and in innumerable individuals?"

"Yes, there are good, honest men and women among what are called the lower orders, — young men and young women, whom I have associated with, and worked with, — who would not do a wrong thing for the world, — who are goodness itself, more than you know of. But I must, forsooth, look down upon them! I must see among them a lower order of taste and feeling! And, in fact, I must find amongst many of them an ignorant, indeed, but systematic depreciation of what is ever and deeply to my eye socially bright and glorious, the Governor's Family. Who of them could afford me that sympathy which my heart craved, or my judgment would select? I must either marry a man whom I despised, or be the mistress of a man who despised me. I would do and be neither. A man like Richard, Lumberer though he be, can marry the Governor's daughter!"

"What if you should marry the Governor's son?" said Melicent, playfully. "There is Brother Roscoe, the odd one. He used to like you; he left his books to be with you; he used to swing you under the elms, and run of your errands. He is not fond of our society; he attaches himself to none of the young ladies that visit us. In all this dreadful affair, I have noticed that he abstained from reproaching you. I am not certain but you carried away a portion of his heart."

"Are you willing that I should marry him?" asked Miss Eyre.

"Indeed, I am."

"Pure, good, magnanimous Melicent, how I thank you, — how I love you — how I am all vanquished again, — killed by goodness! Not that I will marry him; I will not, — never, never! — but that you reveal yourself so, — you look out so prettily, and so Junia-like!"

"Then you give me Richard, if I give you Roscoe?" This, also, playfully.

"Richard is all yours, — was ever yours; his fair, large being, hidden to me, broods over you. I am healed, not by your promises, but by your goodness. Richard will see no bruises in me. But to the world I am dead, — I must be as dead. How can I be obscure enough? How shall I escape Mrs. Melbourne? Cousin Rowena, and Barbara, and all of you, must loathe me. I do not ask you to save me. Junia yielded up all her love for you; — you yield all the sentiments of your rank for me. What is left for me but to yield myself to — fate?

"God — "

"I am humbled; — teach me to be pious."

"And to my discretion."

"I am a child; — lead me where you will."

"I can take care of Mrs. Melbourne, and our family can take care of itself, and Providence will take care of the world."

CHAPTER XLVI.

THE SUN BREAKS OUT.

RICHARD walked down St. Agnes-street, with a tranquil, lydian step. At the gate of the Governor's, he saw Melicent standing in the vine-wreathed piazza, where she had come out to wait for him. She was dressed in her peculiar blue, which she remembered Richard liked; and she was a pure blue thought already, in Richard's imagination, and looked as if her Guardian Angel had bathed her in the azure of the sky, and the azure of Richard's feelings, and placed her there on purpose to meet her old and good beloved.

She received him with an affectionate smile, — a smile that bared her teeth beautifully, but pensively, as if joy still swam in the remembrance of a long sorrow; — a smile that, descending, clove asunder her arms, and parted the Doubt and the Fear that had hung over her being, and turned them into silvery clouds, on the right hand and the left, through which Richard passed to the brightness of her spirit.

CHAPTER XLVII.

ORANGE-BLOSSOMS.

THE Wedding Eve of Richard and Melicent was a splendid one, — splendid in its feelings, in its guests, in its appointments. All the friends of Richard and all the friends of Melicent were there, and this was a multitude. The Father and Mother of Richard were there, and his early spiritual and intellectual guides, Pastor Harold and Teacher Willwell. Through an illuminated archway of trees, and an illuminated portal, the guests swept to bright chambers, — bright as the day-spring of joy that had arisen on the house. The brightness flowed down and culminated in the ample drawing-room, — raying from astrals and wax-lights, from minstrel hearts and evening-star eyes, from fragrant flowers and glorified dresses, and, more than all, from the deep, central fires of holy, fervent felicitation.

Beneath one of the antique arches that garnished the space on either side of the chimney stood Miss Eyre and Chassford. Parson Smith was not sorry to be called to marry Richard and Melicent, and it is said clergymen generally are happy at weddings, and fond of wedding-cake. If there was one person in the room not fully penetrated with the spirit of the occasion, it was Mrs. Melbourne. She had the habit of saying a wedding was like a funeral; and, as if to actualize the sentiment, she came out in black.

There entered, to make the vow and receive the covenant which the State ordains and the Church supports, — which in all ages has been agreeable to the reason and religion of mankind, — Richard and Melicent, with their train of attendants.

The service was simple and affecting, brief and full, edifying and hopeful. Before the benediction, an appropriate hymn was sung, led by Mangil, chorister in the Church of the Redemption. There was a movement as of a flocking to kiss the bride, when Junia entered the room. The crowd held back; all eyes were suspended on her, while as a vision she passed through. She approached the altar-place, and kissed Melicent. Taking from her breast the golden cross of Richard, she hung it on Melicent's neck. She tenderly kissed Richard; it was her first and her last kiss. She was supported out of the room, and was seen no more alive on the earth.

The returning and irresistible wave of joy brought the whole room about the Bride and Groom, and kisses and congratulations fell upon them, like bouquets at the feet of Jenny Lind; — we cannot keep that woman out of our mind, though we have never seen or heard her, and never expect to do so; — not as if the spot Junia's lips had touched was holy ground, where no one might tread, but as if her coming in had been a ray of the sunshine of God on pleasant fields, where old men and children, young men and maidens, might freely disport. Cake and wine; — and, lest some feral reader shall find here a bone to pick with us, we will tell the whole truth, — it was Cousin Rowena's raspberry wine; — cake and wine were brought in, and quickly and pleasantly disposed of. Then followed the Bride Cake; the May Queen, in this procession of good things, mounted on a silver basket, and daintily adorned with flowers and shrubbery. This, appropriated to the unmarried, contained a diamond ring, with the significance that whoever got the ring would be married first. Bachelors and maidens were instantly as wounded birds. Cousin Rowena bit her lip. She made the cake, and knew where the ring lay, and superintended the distribution. Barbara got the ring.

This was hardly fair, as she belonged to the house; but there remained only one piece, and there could be no collusion about that; and it was to Cousin's mind as if Providence directed the matter, and she said, slyly, "Take it, take it;" so the talismanic bauble fell into the hands of Barbara.

CHAPTER XLVIII.

ATHANATOPSIS.

Toll heavily, — toll sadly! Ring out, oh Funeral Bell! Thou hast a place in this our world. Thy knell is needed as well as thy chime, and will find as many hearts prepared for it. There is a peal, not of exultation as of success, — not of terror as of the grave; but between these, and yet louder and deeper, more thrilling, more ecstasizing; prolonged in all the exercises of profoundest sentiment, — awakening dim and heavenly responses in the furthest-reaching glimpses of the imagination, — drowning the voices of the world, — attempering every vain, every selfish impulse, — coming upon the hours of meditation and feeling, like the pensive rhythm of the sea on the beach at midnight; breaking in upon the abodes of sordidness, lust, and all unrighteousness, with the hoarse clangor of gathering doom; a peal that kindles a thousand chords in every heart — new and strange chords — and shakes with a master hand old chords, — chords that strike through, eliminate from, and push beyond, all ordinary pulses of existence, — chords that, starting in the slumbering ages that have gone by, vibrating amid the turmoil and din of the present hour, carry forward the feelings to the regions of Light, Hope, Prophecy: — it is the peal of IMMORTALITY!

Toll on, — toll out, thou Passing Bell! At thy voice, the solemn owl awakes, and the cry of the whippoorwill is heard; amaranths and myrtles grow, and daisies and violets start in their humble beds; willows and cypresses, green fountains of sorrow, break out on the hill-side and in the valley; the rock sprouts in obelisks, and sterile marble yields fair cherubic forms; slips of roses are planted, to be tended in the long coming years of sorrow; and slips of old, departed feelings are gathered up, and reänimated in the bosom of loneliness.

Toll on, — toll out! At thy wail, softness comes over the sky, and piety into the heart; friendship and love throng to the cemetery, and tears distil as the dew on the green leaves that grow about the tomb, and climb as the ivy over ancient and beloved reminiscences; taste and art go forth on feet of affection, and, with an eye of tender inspiration, from all God's earth select the fairest spots for the dead to lie in.

Toll, toll! Envy departs, animosities subside, alienations are reconciled; the fretful insect that weaves in the loom of discord and strife intermits its labor; the corroding worm at the root of faction and party stops its gnawing.

Toll, toll! Thy plaintive reverberations spread everywhere, and melt humanity into one; the rich man speaks gently to the poor, and the poor man pities the rich; the bereaved Pagan mother folds to her bosom the weeping Christian mother; the ferocity of revolution pauses, muffles its grimness and its arms on the threshold of the chamber of the dying prince. Thy pathos sways the earth, and as the wind, in eddies of light and shadow, with lulling murmur, flows across a field of supple wheat, so mournfulness, in endless, soothing measures, rolls over the hearts of the people of the world; and from the line to either pole, all tribes and tongues undulate in one long, ever-recurring, harmonious tremor of sad sensibility.

Toll long, — toll loud, oh Soul-Bell! the requiem of time, — the matin of eternity; the dirge of earth, — the anthem of heaven; the bell that Faith rings at the door of Futurity, — the bell that summons the guests to the marriage supper of the Lamb! "Foolish man! that which thou sowest is not quickened except it die; this corruption shall put on incorruption, and this mortal immortality." The bell which ye hear is the signal-note of the great transition; it announces the final Germination, — it heralds the released soul to the paradise above. It rings out over the successive ages and generations, proclaiming the Quickening era of human existence, and conducting the grand emergence through Death to Life.

Strike once more, Christened Bell! Thou art not unwelcome. Thy solemnity jars not our festivity. As evening opens a higher, more studded immensity than the day, thy shadowiness reveals the dim, unspeakable glory which the sunshine of joy hides to our eye. The twilight of the mortal is the dawn of the immortal. A burial may succeed a wedding; — the burial-day of Junia comes not harshly on the wedding-day of Richard and Melicent.

Slowly, — tenderly! The city is hushed, and the people thereof listen reverently. Young maidens bring flowers to her bier, and young men bear her on their shoulders. Diligent girls from the Factories, and strong men from the Mills, come out; for Junia had worked in the first, and Richard belonged to the last. Many knew how Junia had contributed to the nuptials that had been so universally celebrated; and she died at the Governor's, and was buried from his house; and there were united in her death and burial not only the popular sympathies, but the prestige of the Family, and there fell into the procession a long concourse of citizens.

Slowly and tenderly! for Richard and Melicent follow as chief mourners; and there glide into the procession the fondness and true-heartedness of maidenhood, and the kindling and respectful admiration of young men; and much pursed and austere meanness of manhood relaxes, and walks after. Old and warm recollections of what once was, and the cherished but fading idealism of what may be, moved by the sound of the bell, lengthen out the throng. Aspiration comes up from the lowly hovel, humility leaves the lordly chamber, and pity breaks from many a hard and coarse environment, to wait on the burial.

Toll cheerfully! cheerfully! Memmy and Bebby are there, and other little children, walking two and two. There was a tear in Memmy's eye, for she had thought that she might become an angel too. In that morning of her days, and early dawn of thought, the dews of immortal feeling fell on her eye-lids. The "reminiscence of heaven" within her got glimpses of its bright home, and it seemed not a great way to Jesus, who she knew took little children into his arms and blessed them.

Toll mercifully, oh mercifully! for the traducer is there. In deep black, folded in a deeper night of sorrow and contrition, slowly follows Miss Eyre, — "the woman which was a sinner," weeping at the feet of that great Blessedness, so lately revealed, so suddenly snatched away, but from which to her soul descended the words of peace and forgiveness, which may yet dry her tears, and animate her for the duties of life.

On, on, to Rosemary Dell, through solemn shades and soft circuits, to the grave by the side of Violet!

The Minister sprinkled dust on the coffin, and said, "Dust to dust,—earth to earth;" and, looking aloft, he added, "Spirit to spirit, — the soul to its God! Behold," he continued, "where they have laid her! Sweet is the sleep of death, — beautiful the repose of the grave! No more shall storm disturb her peace; no more shall calamity afflict her days! But," he added "she is not here, — she is risen. The grave cannot contain the immortal essence. She has ascended to her Father and our Father, to her God and our God. A flower of the Spiritual life, she was permitted to blossom beneath our skies, on this our soil. We beheld her beauty, — we inhaled her fragrance. But that Spiritual life has not its eternal home here. She died, and is quickened; — she was quickened even to our sight. Dropping the perishable tabernacle of the flesh, her soul rises to the beatitude of the life beyond our life. The memory and power of her virtues remain for our comfort and edification."

CHAPTER XLIX.

EPITHALAMY.

Not incongruous, we trust, with any one's presentiments, or with the spirit of these pages, or with the solemnities of a preceding day, as we have reason to think it was not with the feelings of Richard Edney and the Governor's Family, was a festivity that came off a short time afterward, — a sort of bridal party thrown open to the public. It was a gift of the Governor to the city, or that portion of the city immediately concerned. No house had room enough, and Mayflower Glen offered its commodiousness and beauty. The invitation was to the Griped Hand and all interested therein ; and of course included a multitude of the Church, many of the first and last families in Woodylin, the Friends of Improvement, Knuckle Lane, the Wild Olives, and the Islands. The Glen was lighted ; music enlivened the scene ; refreshments abounded. None were excluded save such as banished themselves by indifference to the Griped Hand, of which Richard was co-founder, and those who could have no interest in the Glen, — a part of the system of urban regeneration that had been undertaken. Bronze-faced and tow-headed Wild Olive boys, in whole jackets, were there ; River Drivers and Islanders, in clean shirts, were there ; Chuk, looking like a tame, Christianized, happy young Orson, was there ; Mysie, in a new blanket shawl, — a benison she prized above all things, folded about her huge figure with a kind of Indian stateliness, — was there ; the clergy and their deacons, representatives from Victoria

Square and La Fayette-street, parents and children, enthusiastic young men, and a flowery troop of young girls, were there.

Richard and Melicent came, with their grooms-men and bride-maids, and other friends. They entered the Glen under a sylvan arch. Young children threw roses, white lilies, pansies, and sweet herbs, on the walks before them. Joyous music saluted them. As they approached the centre of the spot, an illuminated device sprang up as by magic over their heads, consisting of a True Love Knot, woven of laurel, and enclosing the two words, Virtue and Honor, and supported on one side by Wild Olive boys, and on the other by Clarence Redfern and Herder Langreen. At a turn in the promenade, in a mossy nook under the trees, and so lighted as to have the effect of a distant mountain side, they saw two figures in white, representing Junia bestowing a chaplet on Melicent. The procession broke up, and the multitude mingled together, and did what free and joyous folk are wont to do on free and joyous occasions, in the midst of so many pleasant surroundings, and moved by so many pleasant impulses.

This festivity, originating, indeed, with the Governor, had been prosecuted in detail by the benevolent and ingenious friends of Richard and Melicent.

CHAPTER L.

THE END OF CLOVER.

WITHOUT book, bell or prayer, unshriven, unhousled, with no procession and no sorrow, Clover died, and was buried.

There are bad men in our world, and bad things. That the substance of the first, or the type of the last, should perish, can excite no regret.

Clover, if we may rely on his own account of himself, however he possessed the first, certainly instanced the last; — he was an embodiment of all horridness.

Not merely poetic, but historic, or, we might say, prophetic justice, requires that he should die.

Nor, powerful as has hitherto been his influence, and great his terror, shall we be troubled to dispose of him, — for God took him away.

In the suburbs of the city was a tavern known as the Bay Horse, — almost the only spot within the municipality that had not been purged of alcoholic infection. It was kept by Helskill, — hacking, timid Helskill, — formerly of Quiet Arbor, who had fled thither with the relics of his property, his disinterestedness, and his customers. It was a stopping-place of teamsters, and the lounge of Belialism. In the bar-room, or " office," of this place, one night, Clover and his confreres were met. The " office," like many others of its kind, was a dingy, sultry, mephitic room, and its walls were plastered many layers deep with show-bills, circus pictures, and lithographic battle-pieces and heads of the Presidents. A large box of sand supported a Franklin stove, serving to insure the house against fire, and the delicacy of its inmates against alarm at not having a place to dispose of tobacco-quids, and other matters that distinguish man from the brute. Lamps burned as in a fog, the smoke of the room and dust of the ceiling absorbing most of the rays, and leaving the less volatile accumulations on the floor quite in the lurch.

It was a night of pitchy darkness, and cavernous winds, interspersed with thunder and lightning.

The fellows there assembled had been drinking, and some of them were quite "balmy."

There was Philemon Sweetly, whom we have before seen at the Green Mill, so lively and reckless. Clover had seduced him, and he was now out at his elbows, out at his purse, out at his cheeks, out everywhere save in his invisible tambourine. There was Weasand, an old attaché of Quiet Arbor, who had adhered to Helskill through all mutations of place and fortune. Mr. Serme, a broken-down Theatre-manager, Mr. Craver, an inhabitant of the hamlet of which the Bay Horse was the principal house, and one or two teamsters, made up the group.

Gusts of rain smote the house; flashes of lightning, — what perhaps nothing else would do, — revealed these men to themselves; thunder rolled and exploded over their heads; the windows became alternate mirrors of dismalness within, and breaks into yawning, blazing gulfs without.

"I suppose I am Jove's bird," said Clover, pacing the floor. "They reckon me in the family, I think."

"Your upper lip," replied Philemon, "favors the idea; — it is hooked, and dragonish."

"That is nothing to my talons, Phil." He clutched at Helskill; and Helskill, being a pliant man, suffered himself to be pulled to the floor. "But," continued Clover, "I am gorged. I have REPASTED on Richard."

"And feel qualmish?"

"I shall *revive*," replied Clover. "I worsted Richard, and he capitulated. But the smothered fire of rebellion breaks out, and that must be smothered by the fires of this red right arm!"

"Let us be easy where we are," said Weasand, scraping his thumb-nail with a jack-knife; "Helskill is accommodating, the old 'Horse' is in tolerable flesh, and we can have a few more pleasant rides before the Black Car comes along."

"I would n't speak of it," said Mr. Serme, who, stretched on a table, was trying to cover his eyes from the storm. "I feel as if it was here now, — as if it was all around us, and we were in it."

"REPEAT it!" said Clover.

"Let us not be too free," said Mr. Craver, a red-visaged but white-livered man, who preferred the Bay Horse to his own parlor and wife and children. He occupied a corner of the settee, and was trying very hard to locate his chin on the knob of his cane. "I see a coffin in the lamp, and a dead woman's eyes are looking in at the window. Let us be as easy as we can. I never wished to wrong anybody."

"O mighty thunderbolt!" — thus apostrophized Clover, — "I AM THY FELLOW!"

A blinding flash, that made Helskill shriek, and cry, "Don't! Clover, don't!"

"Say, Do!" rejoined Clover.

"O dear! yes, — do, then, do!" answered the peaceful, willowy host.

"I smite, like thee!" continued Clover.

"I wonder if it ever gets *its* knuckles hurt, and bunged in the eye?" asked Philemon.

"It is not afraid to try them," replied Clover, aiming a blow at Philemon, which the latter avoided by a little tambourining of the head.

"'T is horrible to die so, Mr. Craver," said Mr. Serme. "You can't even turn on your side to get rid of it, or take it easier."

"There will be one less to eat corn," observed a teamster, who sat in a broken-bottomed chair, with his cheeks reposing in the palms of his hands.

"I don't see why my wife takes it so hard," marvelled Mr. Craver. "What is she out such a night as this for? I always said to her, says I, 'Mrs. Craver, you have enough to eat.' Need she shriek so, and my daughters hang shrouds on the trees for me to look at?"

"I DEFY it!" said Clover.

"Please," said Weasand, "stand out of my light, the next time it comes; I want to get a look at Helskill's face."

"I am awful," continued Clover, "but useful; and, *if* severe, *yet* just."

"Just so, exactly," remarked the teamster.

"Look at Clover, Helskill," said Philemon; "I command you to look at him!"

"I will, I will," replied the obliging man. "Only this;" — he shook his head as if the lightnings annoyed him.

"History," Clover went on, "makes more mention of me than of any other living man. Art adores me, — lo!" He pointed to the pictures on the walls. There was a battle of the Florida War, supported by a figure of Liberty on one side of the piece, and Justice on the other. "O, reverend gods!" he exclaimed; "ye know, ye appreciate my worth!

O Divine Providence, how couldst thou get on without me?"

"Devils and damned spirits!" groaned Mr. Serme; "I am not ready. Hell opens to receive me! Mr. Craver, take my conscience, — cut it out, — hide it, — burn it! Quick! — *they* are after it."

"A man has a right to drink," replied Mr. Craver; "I always told Mrs. Craver so."

"What hands the flies are to get into things!" remarked the teamster; "here is one crawling under my shirt sleeve."

"Good Helskill, — kind, hospitable Helskill, — would you let a dry, a very dry man, have something to moisten himself?" asked Weasand.

A vivid and deafening bolt, that silenced them all.

"Appalling!" said Clover; "but sweet, and refreshing, like glory."

"Clover is a knowing 'un," said Philemon. "I wonder if he would n't like to go up among the lightnings, about this time, and touch them off, — perhaps ram cartridges for some of the big guns."

"Would they dare to touch me off!! Compeer of the Almighty, I, Clover, am; — the first and last resort of kings! I am lightnings! I wish I could fall to-night on two devoted heads. It is with difficulty, with self-denial, my friends, that I restrain myself."

"Folderol!" answered Philemon; "let them sleep. They are just married. You have done mischief enough."

"Mischief! If it was not you, Phil, — if you was anybody else, I would kill you, Phil. Thr'pence a pound on tea is nothing to what I feel. I can feel, — I can feel an insult. I can feel an invasion of my rights, — the rights of all governments, — the rights of the stronger. Mischief!

You have not heard of Trajan's column, or Nelson's monument, or the Temple of Fame? Lie still, puppy! I dare Almighty God!"

"Not that; — don't say that; — we are not quite up to that," said Philemon.

"God says," continued Clover, "Thou shalt not kill; — I kill. He says, Keep the Sabbath; — I never yet kept one. He says, Love your enemy; — now it strikes one it is rather presumptuous to say that to ME! Why, I suppose I am the only regular, Old Line, opposition left. If I were out of the way, these numbskulls of humanity would have a great time. My ancestors lived to a good old age, and I shall do the same. Consult the Clover genealogy!"

"Drink, Clover, and sit down."

"Not while you try to cow me, Phil. Not till my power is acknowledged."

Another flash.

"Ha! ha! that 's some. They smell me! They know I am up and dressed! I defy the storm! I challenge all the fires of heaven! MEET ME, YE DREAD MINISTERS, WHERE YE WILL, — I AM READY!!"

"Don't!" cried Helskill.

"Mercy! Clover, God, Devil!" agonized Mr. Serme.

"It is n't best," said Mr. Craver. "If the children would go to bed, and not be rummaging gullies so. It is n't best, Mr. Clover. I hold to moderation. If Mrs. Craver—[a flash]—wife, don't sweep that rock; — put up your broom! Take in more sewing."

"I 'll stump him to do it!" exclaimed the teamster.

"Yes," said Philemon, "let him do it, — he wants to so much."

"Do is the word!" responded Clover. "I will meet them at the Old Oak in the Stone Pasture! I will meet their Goliath, the lightnings, there! I will tweak the nose of Vengeance! Come, boys, — FOLLOW ME!"

He seized his hat, and rushed out of doors, followed by the rest. Neither Mr. Serme nor Mr. Craver dared be left alone; and they went too. Helskill, whom no emergency could deter from the systematic pursuit of his business, ran after, with a bottle in each hand.

It was a fearful hour; — gutters running in torrents, winds whisking the helpless trees, the wizard glare of the lightnings, the thunder bellowing a call to some unheard-of catastrophe, filled them with excitement and forebodings. On they went, across brook and bog, over fences and rock, dripping, blaspheming, headed by the satanic Clover.

They reached the Old Oak, a large, skeleton-like, wiry tree, whose stubborn branches unbent to the storm, and only the leaves were shaken, even as moss on a rock twinkles in the wind.

Clover smote his fist on the tree, and, looking up, said, "Ye powers of heaven, or hell, I HAVE COME!!!"

A flash of lightning struck him dead! It stunned his comrades, who recovered to find their old leader, whose last impious attitude the blaze at the same instant revealed and extinguished, prostrate and dishevelled at the foot of the tree.

That steel-nerved arm was wilted; — those scorn-glancing eyes were upturned in glassy impotence; — that redoubtable chest should heave no more. His long red locks seemed to sweal in the pouring rain; — his trunk and limbs dammed a brief rivulet that hasted to bury him.

Alarm of conscience crowding upon the shock of incident, these infatuated men knew not what to do. They consulted hurriedly and wildly, and proceeded to bury the carcass where it lay.

Turf, swale grass, stones, stumps, were brought together, and piled upon it. Philemon, snatching the bottles of Helskill, threw them upon the body of this wickedness, and they were buried, too.

Through long hours these men worked.

The rain chilled and impeded exertion; the lightning displayed a ghastly object to their eyes, and quickened more ghastly apprehensions in their bosoms; unrelenting thunders rung out a judgment-day alarum; Terror seemed to winnow with its wings the air they breathed.

Their task done, they returned to the tavern soberer, and we will hope, better men.

CHAPTER LI.

GATHERED FRAGMENTS.

We might say more things of Richard, and of what pertains to him; we might relate how, through the Governor, who was one of the corporators of the Dam and Mills, he became Agent of that extensive interest; how he built a fine house on land near Bill Stonners' Point, deemed one of the most picturesque spots in the Beauty of Woodylin; and how he got the land, with its fine park of forest trees, of Mysie and Chuk, who would part with it to nobody else; how he was respected and beloved by his fellow-citizens, and became Mayor of the city; and how the Griped Hand continued to flourish, recruiting the Church on the one hand, and replenishing the purity and beauty, the law and order, of the city, on the other. But, leaving these things, as, perhaps, we are bound in justice to do, "to the imagination of the reader," we shall briefly advert to one or two other topics.

Barbara, as Cousin Rowena forethought, and the ring seemed to announce, married Chassford. Their nuptials were celebrated with becoming dignity and lustre. Richard facilitated this consummation, — first, by his faithful dealing with Chassford's vices; secondly, by the support he afforded to his virtues. We have so far outlined the character both of Barbara and Chassford as possibly to afford ground for the opinion that they were eminently fit for each other, as regards native and genuine qualities of mind and heart, and in matter of taste and education.

There interfered a melancholy barrier to their mutual wishes, in the incipient profligacy of Chassford. If Richard had his sorrows, Barbara was not without hers. And it is worthy of remark, that while Richard was secretly laboring to reform Chassford, Barbara was equally active, in a silent way, for the restoration of Richard. Cousin Rowena was not a little inspired by Barbara. In fact, Richard understood Chassford better than Barbara did, and Barbara understood Richard better than Melicent did; and not unnaturally. A great sorrow often disturbs the judgment in the direction in which it moves, leaving it clear in other quarters. So Barbara, darkened in regard to Chassford, thought she could distinctly translate Richard to Melicent, as Richard presumed he had the key to Chassford. After his return to Melicent, Richard had freer opportunity to work for the hearts and happiness of these unfortunate ones. If the repentance of the sinner communicates joy to the heavenly world, there must be pleasure in the sight of Fidelity fondly sweeping among the waste of things for the lost piece of virtue, — Hope sitting on the shore of evil, trying to discern the form of the beloved one in the distant wreck, — Affection welcoming the weather-worn memories of other days, opening its doors to the promise and aspiration of a new life, and healing the wounds which sin has made. If Love cannot forgive, how shall Justice ever?

Glendar bowed himself politely from the Governor's Family and from the city, as he does from this Tale.

Mrs. Melbourne bore no malice, and would allow that she was actuated by no meanness, toward Richard. She believed Miss Eyre, — her prejudices reïnforced her belief; her energy, having so strong a team in hand, would easily haul Richard to perdition. His elevation, compassed in spite of herself, she had at length the good sense to see was deserved, and the candor to applaud.

We take our leave of Miss Eyre with an unaffected interest and the tenderest compassion. Forgiven by others, she could not forgive herself. She would lay a daily offering of loneliness and woe on the altar of the Great Good she had impeded. Roscoe would really have married her; there was an oddity in the thing that suited the oddity of his temper; — or, rather, there was romance in her history which kindled his imagination; and more, there was a deep, underlying vividness, freedom, struggle, in all her life, which comported with the sensibilities of his own nature, — sensibilities hidden by the roughness and reserve of his ordinary manner. She replied, "There is a spot sacred to the memory and peace of Junia, where she practised submission and obtained serenity; and, what I have never done, by schooling the importunities of her heart, and frowardness of her will, she became strong in faith, and heroic in action. Thither I would go. I have lived, I know not to what end, or with what motive. I must ripen in seclusion those virtues which can alone make life tolerable, or endeavor useful. If you can love me, remember me; and if you remember me, it will help me." She went to the farm-cottage where Junia spent so many agreeable months.

Miss Freeling married Mr. Cosgrove, and Cousin Rowena Teacher Willwell. This was Richard's doings, — nay, Teacher Willwell did it himself. Practising the rule he taught, — to see what things are made for, — at the nuptials of Richard and Melicent, he decided that Cousin was made for himself. She marvelled that so simple a rule could be so accurate.

Simon rose to the post of Richard's hack-driver.

Captain Creamer so far prospered as to be able to take of

Richard the rent of the identical saw at which he had originally offered Richard the chance of the slip.

Memmy and Bebby, — God bless their little hearts! words fail to describe their joy in seeing Uncle Richard happy again, and particularly at the sight of his new house; and all the fleeting, bird-like ways they took to show it, — and how they ran of errands between Mamma and Aunt Melicent, — and in a little basket, under a little cover, carried dishes of strawberries, and rounds of warm, light cake, and an occasional potted pigeon.

CHAPTER LII.

PARTING WORDS.

1. To the inquiry, "What business has Clover in these pages?" The same that what he represents has in the world at large.

There is a Something both principle and practice, organized, constitutional, customary, bepraised, canonized, consecrated in the Prayer Book, and in many pulpits, — in the public relations of the human kind, precisely like Clover in the urban and domestic connections of this Tale. Clover acts from the same impulse that that acts. That Something is a gigantic, international Clover. Clover is the same epitomized. It was agreeable to the original cast, as well as ulterior purpose, of this volume, that that Something, historically so conspicuous, should take a biographical form. Let it be incarnated, and in personal unity inhabit a town, and reside in our houses, and see how it looks!

2. To those authors from whom, in the composition of this Tale, we have borrowed, we return sincere thanks. If our publishers, who are obliging gentlemen, consent, we would like to forward a copy of the book to each of them. If they dislike anything of theirs in this connection, they will of course withdraw it; — should they chance to like anything of ours, they have full permission to use it. This would seem to be fair.

Pope Gregory VII. burned the works of Varro, from whom Augustine had largely drawn, that the Saint might not be accused of plagiarism. We have no such extreme intention.

First, it would be an endless task. What consternation in the literary world, should even the humblest author undertake such a thing! And such authors are the ones who would be most inclined to cancel their obligations in this way. We might fire the Cambridge library; but, alas! the assistant librarian, whose pleasant face has beguiled for us so much weary research in those alcoves, and, as it were, illuminated the black letter of so many recondite volumes, — to see him shedding tears over their ashes, would undo us! We are weak there. Secondly, it comports at once with manliness and humility to confess one's indebtedness. Thirdly, as a matter of expediency, it is better to avail one's self of a favorable wind and general convoy to fame, than run the risk of being becalmed, and perhaps devoured, on some private and unknown route. But, lastly, and chiefly, let it be recorded, there is a social feeling among authors, — they cherish convivial sentiments, — they are never envious of a fellow; there is not, probably, a great author living, but that, like a certain great king, would gladly throw a chicken, or a chicken's wing, from his feathered abundance, to any poor author, and enjoy its effect in lighting up the countenances of the poor author's wife and children. Wherefore it is that plagiarism, after all, is to be considered rather in the light of good cheer and kindly intercourse, than as evidence of meanness of disposition, or paucity of ideas.

3. To the tourist, who, with guide-book in hand, and curious pains-taking, seeks to recover scenes and places fleetingly commemorated in these pages, we are obliged to say, he will be disappointed. This Tale, in the language of art, is a composition, not a sketch. There is no such city as Woodylin; or, more truly, we might affirm, the materials of it exist throughout the country. Its population

and its pursuits are confined to no single locality, but are scattered everywhere. Its elements of good, hope, progress, may be developed everywhere; — would, too, that whatever it contains prejudicial to human weal might be depressed in all regions of the earth!

4. To the book itself.

"VADE LIBER."
GO, LITTLE BOOK.

"Qualis, non ausim dicere, felix."
What will be your fortune, I cannot tell.

"Vade tamen quocunque lubet, quascunque per oras,
I blandas inter Charites, mystamque saluta
Musarum quemvis, si tibi lector erit.
Rura colas, urbemque."

Yet go wherever you like, — go everywhere, — go among kind people; you may even venture to introduce yourself to the severer sort, if they will admit you. Visit the city and the country.

"Si criticus lector, tumidus censorque molestus,
Zoilus et Momus, si rabiosa cohors," — approach,
"Fac fugias," — fly.

"Læto omnes accipe vultu,
Quos, quas, vel quales, inde vel unde viros."
Look cheerfully upon all, men and women, and all of every condition.

Go into farm-houses and rustic work-shops; call at the homes of the opulent and the powerful; visit schools; say to the minister you have a word for the Church. I know you will love the family; — you may stay in the kitchen, and, as you are so neatly dressed, and behave so prettily, they will let you sit in the parlor. Let the hard hand of the laboring classes hold you, nor need you shrink from the soft hand of fair maiden. Speak pleasantly to the little children; — I need not fear on that score; — speak wisely and respectfully to parents. You may enter the haunts of iniquity, and preach repentance there; you may show your cheerful face in sordid abodes, and inspire a love for purity and blessedness. Go West, — go South; you need not fear to utter a true word anywhere. Especially — and these are your private instructions — speak to our Young Men, and tell them not to be so anxious to exchange the sure results of labor for the shifting promise of calculation, — tell them that the hoe is better than the yard-stick. Instruct them that the farmer's frock and the mechanic's apron are as honorable as the merchant's clerk's paletot or the student's cap. Show them how to rise *in* their calling, not out of it; and that intelligence, industry and virtue, are the only decent way to honor and emolument. Help them to bear sorrow, disappointment, and trial, which are wont to be the lot of humanity. And, more especially, demonstrate to them, and to all, how they may BE GOOD AND DO GOOD!

If it is thought worth while to take you to Tartary, be not afraid to go. Look up bright and strong. When those people come to understand your language, I think they will like you very much.

Should inquiries arise touching your parentage and connections, — a natural and laudable curiosity, which, as a stranger in the world, you will be expected to enlighten, — you may say that you are one of three, believed to be a worthy family, comprising two brothers and one sister. That a few years since, your author published the history of a young woman, entitled "Margaret: a Tale of the Real and the Ideal;" — and that at the same time, and as a sort of counterpart and sequel to this, he embraced the design of writing the history of a young man, and you are the result. The first shows what, in given circumstances, a woman can do; the last indicates what may be expected of a man; — the first is more antique; the last, modern. Both are local in action, but diffusive in spirit. In the mean time, he has written "Philo, an Evangeliad:" cosmopolitan, œcumenical, sempiternal, in its scope, embodying ideas rather than facts, and uniting times and places; and cast in the only form in which such subjects could be disposed of, the allegoric and symbolical, — or, as it is sometimes termed, the poetic. The two first are individual workers; the last is a representative life. "Philo" is as an angel of the everlasting Gospel; you and "Margaret," one in the shop, and the other on the farm, are practical Christians. However different your sphere or your manners, you may say you all originate on the part of your author in a single desire to glorify God and bless his fellow-men. "Philo" has been called prosy; "Margaret" was accounted tedious. You, "Richard," I know, will appear as well as you can, and be what you are, — honest certainly, pleasing if possible.

God bless thee, Little Book, and anoint thee for thy work, and m[illegible] thee a savor of good to many! We shall meet again, in other years or worlds. May we meet for good, and not for evil! If there is any evil in thy heart or thy ways, God purge it from thee!

THE END.

www.ingramcontent.com/pod-product-compliance
Lightning Source LLC
LaVergne TN
LVHW020938110826
845150LV00004B/892